ANITA de MONTE LAUGHS LAST

ALSO BY XOCHITL GONZALEZ

Olga Dies Dreaming

ANITA de MONTE LAUGHS LAST

Xochitl Gonzalez

FLATIRON
BOOKS
NEW YORK

This is a work of fiction. All of the characters, organizations, and events portrayed in this novel are either products of the author's imagination or are used fictitiously.

Printed in the United States of America. For information, address Flatiron Books, 120 Broadway, New York, NY 10271.

www.flatironbooks.com

Designed by Kelly S. Too

Library of Congress Cataloging-in-Publication Data

Names: Gonzalez, Xochitl, 1977– author.
Title: Anita de Monte laughs last : a novel / Xochitl Gonzalez.
Description: First U.S. edition. | New York : Flatiron Books, 2024.
Identifiers: LCCN 2023034782 | ISBN 9781250786210 (hardcover) | ISBN 9781250356307 (international, sold outside the U.S., subject to rights availability) | ISBN 9781250786227 (ebook)
Subjects: LCSH: Women art historians—Fiction. | Art students—Fiction. | Women artists—Fiction. | Interpersonal relations—Fiction. | Power (Social sciences)—Fiction. | Elite (Social sciences)—Fiction. | LCGFT: Novels.
Classification: LCC PS3607.O56264 A84 2024 | DDC 813/.62—dc23/eng/20230828
LC record available at https://lccn.loc.gov/2023034782

Our books may be purchased in bulk for promotional, educational, or business use. Please contact your local bookseller or the Macmillan Corporate and Premium Sales Department at 1-800-221-7945, extension 5442, or by email at MacmillanSpecialMarkets@macmillan.com.

First U.S. Edition: 2024
First International Edition: 2024

10 9 8 7 6 5 4 3 2 1

In memory of Ana
And all the women who endured solitude
never knowing the rest of us were out there

For my aunt Linda. And as always,
for my grandparents, without
whom I would not be here.

Why, indeed, should one not include artists who embody very different sensibilities from that of the European and the mainstream? There is, in principle, no reason to exclude them whatsoever. However, I have decided to limit this edition to Western art . . . I have taken a stand about what art I think is most significant that not all readers will agree with, since it favors universality over ethnocentricity.

—Anthony F. Janson
From the Preface to the Fifth Edition of
History of Art, Volume II
H. N. Abrams, 1994

I

FALLING

Anita

NEW YORK CITY • FALL 1985

If it weren't for what happened later, everyone would have forgotten that night entirely. It wasn't like the '70s, you know? Nights when you never knew what could happen; what to expect. No, by 1985, the parties in New York were all the same. One night, one party, bleeding into the next. Nothing specific or momentous enough to press itself into your memory. The guests, the conversations, the taste of the fucking wine on your lips, all more or less the same. *Especially* Tilly's parties. Formulaic; interchangeable. Some felt that's what made them work, but for me? It depressed me—that impossible distinction of the passage of time.

The drinks were always set in her claustrophobic galley kitchen. To force intimacy. The food—what little there was—WASPs hate feeding people—set atop the piano in the center of her massive loft. The poor young artists hovering while it lasted. The music just loud enough to soften silences, but too muted to inspire true revelry. Over the years, Philip Glass was replaced with Sun Ra. The "hot new" artists aging into establishment figures or disappearing altogether; replaced by other, younger faces. All the big museum people were always invited, naturally. Tilly enjoyed the thirst shared between those two groups in particular: the haves dangling their opportunities tantalizingly before the have-nots. It created a great "friction in the room," she'd remarked once. After years where I was the only brown speck in attendance, lately there'd been a noted effort to populate the guest list with more "Third World Artists." This sudden concern for diversity coinciding with the Met hiring their first Black senior curator. I'm not being cynical, just honest; it would be embarrassing to invite Rory to a party and have her see only white people there. But, outside of that, in all the years of these fetes, very little had changed.

Except, I suppose, for me.

If you were in New York and in the art world, you did not refuse an invitation from Tilly Barber. And, for whatever reason, that night was particularly crowded. Bodies and conversation packed close enough to create a hum. I remember feeling a restless excitement when I arrived. The kind you feel when you're giddy from holding a secret; one with wings that flap furiously against your palms. Knowing that, any moment now, it could fly up! Out into the world. Its motion changing fortunes and futures, oceans or even lifetimes away. And I, the only one containing it. Such a power! Giancarlo, raconteur that he was, was telling me a story. I was listening, but not. He always came back from Rome with the longest stories. I was distracted; knowing that at any moment, *he'd* arrive! Jack Martin. My husband.

And then, as if I willed it by simply glaring at the doorway, he did.

Jack likes to enter rooms slowly. To stand and hover before he makes his way, glacially, into a space. Some people think this is because of his size; he's become quite mammoth these last years. His physical form expanded, I think, intentionally to match his scale of import in the world of art. The more generous attributed Jack's heavy footedness to the rumored injuries sustained from years of lifting rods of iron and setting down plates of steel. "Each and every piece of art that's ever bore my name," he will tell you within breaths of meeting him, "was installed by me and me alone." That explanation is, for me, the most ripe—picked with callus-free hands from the vine of Jack's decades-old propaganda tree about working-class roots. But here is the truth, the kind of truth only a wife can really know: Jack enters the room slowly so that people will notice him. Plants himself like a lightning rod, drawing the kinetic energy of everything and everybody his way. Still and quiet so that, for a moment at least, the attention of the revelers is pulled from whatever conversation they were having or joint they were smoking or person they were trying to fuck and drawn instead toward him. The party, if not the world, spinning around Jack Martin.

So it was that night. From the corner of my eye, I watched him enter the loft and linger. Waiting. Around me, conversations, bright and raucous just seconds before, suddenly muted as people noticed his presence. All mentally calculating if and how and when they could talk to him. Even Giancarlo's voice trailed off. I stole a cigarette from him and pretended not to notice as Jack, finally feeling acknowledged, crossed the room toward the kitchen. I didn't need to look up to know that's where Tilly was.

Normally, this would have annoyed me: that he always sought her out before he ever even looked for me. That she was, in my opinion, the only one he genuinely respected, far more than for being one of the best art dealers in the world. For more than even making his career. Really, I think, just for being her. Steely. New England elegant. Any other day, this would have driven me up a wall. Drawn out my sharp cat claws. But on this night, I had the flapping wings of secrets, restless in my hands. I was excited—delighted, even—that he'd finally arrived. I was wearing my favorite dress, the one I'd bought in Iowa from a secondhand store. It was from the '60s, with big silver paillettes, each as large and round as the eye of a cow. Clustered so tight and voluminously, they tinkled, soft, like wind chimes when they rustled together. I had put on the only heels I wore anymore. Artists, when they are working, should have little need for heels. I wore the red lipstick from Guerlain I had gotten in Paris. Tonight was an occasion: the close of a special day and also the opening of . . . I did not know in that moment what. But it was going to be something new.

I was ready to start the adventure.

"Giancarlo," I said, as I grabbed his hand, "my husband is here. Let's go and tell him our good news!"

We wound our way through women in black dresses and seductions in progress and scrawny boys with paint-stained pants, arguing about nothing, until we finally reached the kitchen. I paused in the doorway for a second and watched them. Together. Tilly ruminating, cigarette in hand, lips parsed to say something thoughtful. Tactful. Jack, midway through opening a fresh bottle of champagne, the festive gesture in chiaroscuro to his dour expression. Both so wrapped in what they were talking about, in each other, neither of them noticed me.

"Perfect timing!" I finally said. Giancarlo, behind me, pushed his way into the tiny cookery. "We need a refill! To toast my wonderful news."

Jack looked me up and down, a closed smile curling up, tight against his teeth. He hated this dress. He thought it looked cheap. Like New Year's Eve in Times Square. Hated the racket it made. The way the paillettes shed like snake scales if I moved too quickly. Hated that I moved too quickly.

"Tilly was just telling me," Jack said, as he refilled our glasses, the grin still taut on his face. "A dozen prints sold to the Met. Not bad for my little orphan Anita."

"Anita!" Giancarlo exclaimed. "All night talking and you didn't even tell me! Well, that will definitely build buzz around your show."

I raised my glass and ignored the shock that seized Jack's countenance. Didn't even look at Tilly, lest she ruin my mood.

"Giancarlo is going to show me in Rome," I announced. "Solo."

"Congratulations, Anita!" Tilly said, genuinely impressed. The fact of which almost annoyed me more than if she'd treated it like garden variety information.

"What's the expression, Tilly?" Giancarlo offered. "A no-brainer! Have you seen her new sculptures?"

"Nobody has," Jack said, his voice strained and the smile, finally faded.

"I haven't," Tilly said, disregarding Jack. She averted my gaze. Her manners masked her cowardice.

"Tilly hasn't asked to see my work since 1979," I said to Giancarlo, "and even then, it was only as a favor to Jack. Isn't that right, darling?"

Jack pulled me tight to him, the sequins and my lungs crunching together as he did. He raised his glass.

"Well, cheers! Quite the lucky day for our shooting star," Jack said, saccharine dripping from his voice.

Human will is a particularly powerful magic. Alchemy happens when a person truly decides something; when a mind is changed. We'd shared exchanges like this hundreds of times before, my husband and I. Tiny acts of violence enacted with words. Exchanges that had cut and left me bleeding, with my best stuff—confidence, clarity—pooling down, away from me, onto the floor. But not that night. No. Because that day I had decided to reclaim my might; to cease to be shrunk. And in my decision, I'd grown a new version of myself. My new skin thick like coconut shells, impervious to his attempts to crack my joy. My triumph at my accomplishments, my exultation with my own art, euphoria at this new power I'd discovered in simply deciding to change my mind. All of it now in safekeeping, deep inside my new self. I pulled from his embrace and turned to him, with a smile so genuine on my face, and I said:

"Jack, the night is still young."

And it was.

Later, when I saw him across the room, practically entangled con esa cabrona gigante—Inga or Ingrid or whatever her name was—it wasn't that I didn't feel rage. No, it was that in my decision to strip him of his power, I was able to transmute that anger into joy. The specific type of joy one can only feel by really fucking with someone's head. Poking at exactly the right tender spots. The spots only a lover, and surely a wife, can really find. So, yes, I saw them—her, with her long blond hair hanging down like a sheet, leaning against the glass window; him, with his arms braced on either side of her, their faces practically touching—and my first feeling was anger. Resentment. Not just that we were in a room where everyone knew us—because I am someone too!—but because she wasn't even a good artist! She made derivative, exhausted, color-field shit that he would have pissed all over had it been done by someone with a cock. Instead, he bought three of them and hung them in his fucking living room. At least if he was going to carry on this way, he could do it with someone with real fucking talent! But, of course, talent scared Jack.

Then, like finding a five-dollar bill in an old coat pocket, I remembered my thick, coconut-shell skin and that I had changed my mind.

"Quimbara" trumpeted from the stereo, and I turned to my friend Jomar and suggested, loudly, that it seemed like a great time to dance.

"Someone turn the music up," I commanded. The boy Giancarlo was trying to seduce eagerly obliged.

Tilly's parties were not dancing affairs. They were more gatherings than celebrations. Openings without the art. While I knew this was not something she'd like, it was something she'd tolerate. Americans love to see Latins dance. Dance, fuck, fight. Anything, really, that's meant to be done with passion. And besides, the guests who remained by this point were the most drunk, the most high, the most bored. Thirsty for entertainment. Jomar was an amazing dancer, the kind who knows how to make his partner look better than she is. As we moved, I could feel the attention of the room now pull toward me. Not as a lightning rod, but as a wind, a wave. Something in perpetual motion that touched everyone gathered. Around me, I could feel their thoughts and assessments and presumptions. Anita de Monte, art star on the rise. Anita de Monte, winner of the Rome Prize, winner of the Guggenheim. Anita de Monte, a once-in-a-generation artistic voice. Anita de Monte, a one-trick pony. Anita de Monte, immigrant opportunist. Anita de Monte, wife of the legendary Jack Martin. Anita de Monte, lucky bitch. Anita de Monte, the most miserable bitch alive. No one realizing that I was all these things at once and more.

I remembered my task at hand.

"It's just that I miss dancing," I said to Jomar, with my best stage whisper. "My husband doesn't dance, you see. Not a salsa, not a waltz. He won't even do the twist."

I didn't direct any of this at Jack, of course. I didn't need to. I could feel his gaze on me, hot like fire. He hated a spectacle. Unless it was his. From the corner of my eye, I saw him swat la sueca gigante's hand away, sensed him heading toward me. To "save me" from embarrassing myself. My hero. I kept up my performance. That night, I should have won an Oscar.

"Did I ever tell you who taught me to dance?" I asked as Jomar guided me smoothly around him in a lasso. "Our servants. Jack hates that I was rich in Cuba. Detests it. It doesn't fit into his nice vision of us as a cute little Marxist couple. But I assure you, we had servants and they danced with me all the time."

Around us, those who could hear me were eating it up—these sycophants loved gossip as much as idolatry—but others began to clap to the beat of the music. They cheered us on through lunges and copas and dips. And then Jomar began—slow, and then faster, faster—to spin me. Around once: I saw Tilly stop Jack. Around again: glimpsed the giant Swede storming out. I laughed loudly. I had just ruined his night as he had ruined so many of mine. I felt radiant with delight, felt the flutter of my secrets, knowing soon they would be free! Jomar spun me around and around, again and again and again.

Later, when word got out that I had fallen (jumped? or, could it be, pushed?) out the window, this was what everyone would talk about. How they had just seen her! Anita de Monte. That very night! How she had been laughing. And how she had been dancing. And how, when she spun around and around, the silver sequins of her dress went flying. Up and into the air. Like the feathers of a molting bird.

Raquel

PROVIDENCE • SPRING 1998

Raquel Toro walked into Professor Temple's light-filled office and, for the first time, did not feel herself shrink. She'd woken up that morning and, admittedly, after a night of two-for-one cosmos with Mavette downtown, looked like shit. But she felt proud. Ready to meet the day, and John Temple, unintimidated. Neither by the mountains of books—catalogs, academic texts, tomes of criticism—that he not only owned but had, at least in part, authored. Nor by the exhibition posters lining the walls, featuring shows he had mounted or had a major hand in. Today, Raquel walked in feeling worthy, not just of the company of his brilliance but of her very place in this school.

Before arriving at Brown, Raquel hadn't spent much time pondering what an Ivy League college would be like. She'd been too grateful for the opportunity to have expectations. But during her sophomore year, when John Temple called Raquel to his office hours for the first time and she saw him behind his vast desk, she knew that this was it. This was what the "Ivy League" was all about: wool blazers and expensive, but understated, watches; salt-and-pepper beards stroked for effect while holding court for enraptured students. The Ivy League was John Temple, whose name held no meaning to the average or even above-average person, but whose work had the power to shape institutions, markets, and culture in its most erudite of forms. He was

A Man of Great Importance in the World. And in such proximity to that, despite the "brilliantly drawn constellations" he commended her on during his seminars, or the "incisive, yet accessible" papers that he praised her for, she had always felt deeply insignificant.

Until today.

"I got the fellowship," she said, noting the confidence in her own voice. "I'm going to be a curatorial fellow in the Contemporary Art Department this summer."

John Temple's handsome face broke into a smile, revealing his perfect teeth. He pushed the Eames chair away from his desk to fully face her.

"Brava, Raquel! Brava! Though I had no doubt."

She felt the flush coming up her neck and tried to contain her grin in a way that would seem less obviously delighted by his approval.

"Your recommendation put it over the top."

"Nonsense! It was a solid application across the board. It seems small, but the RISD Museum is a jewel box; their work has a lot of implications in the art world."

"Oh, I'm very aware. Three of the fellows are from Harvard and Yale."

Professor Temple looked impressed. He had, she then remembered, gone to Yale.

"Competitive field. Even better." He smiled again, leaning in toward Raquel. "A long way from selling sandwiches at the Met, huh?" he said, pleased.

She felt herself—her equalness—evaporate. Quick and sudden. A red flush of shame replaced it, the kind that morphed fast into anger. Raquel simpered, fought hard to suppress the *What the fuck does that mean?* that he would've gotten had he come at her with this bullshit back home. She reminded herself that he couldn't have meant it as an insult, even if it felt that way. This was not Brooklyn. This was Brown. Here was a place of measured tones and intellectual rivalries. Here was not a place where necks were rolled, nor teeth sucked, nor fucks flung around willy-nilly. Here was not, he just reminded her, a place for girls who worked concessions at the Met.

(Which wasn't even factually correct; he hadn't even remembered her story right.)

She had mentioned it during their first meeting, offhandedly. Before she'd learned to cautiously manicure her background. She'd been enrolled in his wildly popular course, American Art, 1940 to Today. The midterm was a paper examining art as social commentary using works they covered in class. Raquel wrote about Philip Guston and his paintings from the later '60s; the strange smoking Klansman stuff that, in the context of the era, was clearly meant to be a white man's tongue-in-cheek commentary on the absurdity of white supremacy. In passive protest of never getting to study artwork remotely connected to her life experience, she offhandedly lamented that, in respecting the assignments provision to confine her discussion to work from the syllabus, she was unable to *also* discuss Betye Saar or other minority artists directly affected by the civil rights movement. Raquel's TA was about to give her paper a B but thought it important to put her critique on Professor Temple's radar. (It was always unclear if their objective was supportive or an attempt to squelch dissent.) John Temple regraded it to an A– and left a note that Raquel should come to his next office hours.

His first question had been what drew her to art history, and she'd answered honestly: her mother worked in the Met cafeteria and Raquel had spent long hours there studying. Then, the summer after her freshman year, her mom hooked her up with a job at the gift shop. Armed with her staff ID and her mother's proud introductions to the curators and administrators she'd long been serving food to—"*This is my Ivy League baby!*"—Raquel saw before her a career path. One that could lead her to being the person responsible for what people saw on those walls. She never imagined that he'd remembered that story, her casual confession. No, it wasn't even a confession at the time, it was simply a fact of what had happened. A detail that, to her, was so innocuous. And yet, now, he'd weaponized it. Transformed it into a blunt reminder of just how irregular to this place, to this world, to this corner office, she was.

She composed herself.

"I'm grateful for the recommendation."

She stood to leave, picking up her knockoff Prada that she'd gotten on Canal Street during spring break. John Temple rose also, retrieved his pack of Dunhills from the desk, and inched closer to her.

"I'll walk out with you, have a smoke."

The only thing that made Raquel more uncomfortable than being with Professor Temple in his office was being with Professor Temple in any setting that was not the classroom. She knew there were students—like her freshman roommate, or the Art History Girls—who easily conversed with their professors. She remembered having that kind of ease with her teachers in high school, but that was just it. They were teachers, these were *faculty*. Doctors of Letters. She didn't admire her fellow students for being comfortable with their professors; she found it, frankly, disrespectful. But, in these random instances where someone like John Temple asked to engage with her in a basic human activity like walking to have a cigarette, wasn't it more discourteous to say no? Unsure of how to be, she feigned indifference, shrugging her shoulders, and headed out to the hall.

She pushed the button on the freight-sized elevator.

"So," he said, "who will you be working with?"

"Belinda Kim!" she said, her excitement a momentary distraction from her discomfort. "She's putting together an exhibition on the figurative in art."

The short elevator ride felt infinitely longer under the weight of Professor Temple's silent judgment.

"You don't like Dr. Kim?" she asked, more perplexed than anything.

He sighed and she noted a sense of apprehension. The elevator doors opened. For a second, he seemed the sheepish one, heading out of the elevator with his head down.

"Like? Don't like? These things don't mean much in academia, Raquel. Belinda and I just have diametrically opposite approaches to thinking about contemporary art. To me, biography is unimportant; for her, it's everything."

Raquel remembered his lecture on Cézanne and the inextricable link between Cézanne's work and his mental decline but decided not to wade into a debate she wasn't fully prepared for.

"Does she know that you're my pupil?" he asked as he lit his smoke. "She might not have wanted to work with you if she did."

Raquel felt heat rise in her again. Did advising come with a leash? "She didn't seem that familiar with you."

Professor Temple took a long drag and offered a cigarette to Raquel, who refused.

"Raquel," he said, some edge in his voice, "I'm going to level with you. The art world? Art history? It's all about relationships. In this world, we still operate under the apprenticeship system. And who you apprentice with says a lot. Not just about where you are right now, but where you are going. Do you follow?"

Raquel nodded. This wasn't that complicated. "It's why I was so excited that you agreed to be my thesis adviser."

He smiled. "And that's why I thought it was so important that I advise you. When I started grad school—it's hard to believe because this department is full of women now—but art history? Curatorial? Criticism? A boys' club."

"Clement Greenberg."

John Temple smirked.

"Among others. Point is, these places were all full of people like me. And let's be honest . . . if art is about the world, men like me are probably the least interesting subjects in it."

Raquel laughed genuinely, surprised at his self-awareness.

"It means a lot for a person like me to mentor a young woman like you, Raquel. And it means a lot for a Hispanic woman like you to have the endorsement of a person like me. A traditionalist. Not somebody who thinks you should be here just because you're Mexican."

"I'm Puerto Rican."

"Of course"—he grimaced—"but that's almost my point. Dumb guys like me don't know! And we don't care. Your excellence is what is going to distinguish you, not your heritage. I just worry that aligning yourself with someone like Belinda Kim, whose entire shtick is identity politics"—she could hear the disdain in his voice—"it leads with the wrong foot. Makes it seem like you aren't here for serious scholarship, only to point fingers."

"You agreed with me about the Black Arts Movement," she interjected. She was not trying to point fingers.

"I did. You made an intellectually sound point, which is why I amended my syllabus," he offered, kindly. "I just want to see you welcomed into the tent for the right reasons. You're so much more than a demographic."

"I know that."

She felt she couldn't leave before he finished, and it seemed the slowest burning cigarette in the history of time.

"So, what about the other girls? I wrote a few recommendations this year."

The fucking Art History Girls. Even in their absence, they somehow always claimed space. She was irritated that he thought her one of them. Frustrated that, despite being in nearly every art history class with them for the past two years, she most definitely was not. No matter how friendly she might be with Mavette.

"I don't know," she said, curtly. "They have other plans for the summer."

Other plans, Mavette had told her, that included traipsing around the South of France looking for Eurotrash boyfriends. Of course, Mavette had not put it that way. She'd gone on a rant about their futures and feminism's diminished emphasis on romantic partnership and how this summer could be formative beyond just professional development. It didn't matter. What it meant was that while Raquel was toiling away at the RISD Museum, Claire and Margot would be sunbathing on Mavette's parents' boat in Nice.

John Temple exhaled the last drag of his interminable smoke.

"Well, I'll see you soon, Raquel," he said as he threw the butt down to the ground.

A wave rose quick from Raquel's stomach to her chest as she watched him turn back toward the building. A rush of regret of how she'd handled this encounter. That she'd disappointed him in some way. Had not appropriately shown her allegiance and gratitude for all that he had done for her.

"Professor Temple?" she called out. "I almost forgot."

He stopped in the doorway to face her.

"I landed on a topic for my thesis: Jack Martin and his influence on architecture."

Even from a distance, she could feel the warmth of his smile. John Temple was the leading Martin scholar in North America. Perhaps, the world.

"Splendid. The catalog from his Berkeley Museum show is a great place to start. Hard to find, but I have it in my personal library."

As she watched him disappear inside the building, she felt, for a moment, satisfied. Her instincts hadn't been wrong: there had been a fracture in their bridge, and she'd mended it.

* * *

THE FUCKING CIGARETTE made her late, and now she'd have to hear Marcus bitch. She pulled her Discman from her bag, hoping music would cut through the pall the meeting had cast over her mood. Julian, a guy whom she'd met in her painting class last semester, had given her a couple of underground rap mixes. Though it physically pained her to admit it, this white kid from fucking Darien, Connecticut, really knew his hip-hop.

She'd taken the class at John Temple's suggestion. "*What better way to write about these mediums than to physically understand the practice of working in them?*" he'd implored. Raquel, in her quest for excellence, enrolled in a five-hour studio art class at Rhode Island School of Design that met once a week. For their first assignment, they had to paint from a photograph using only two colors. Raquel had made the unfortunate artistic choices of using what she thought were vibrant hues—yellow and cerulean blue—to capture an image of her mother's beloved (deceased) Lhasa Apso mix, Duran Duran. The results: tragic. During the critique, as the class went around the room, poor *Duran Duran* was picked further and further apart. By the time they got to Julian, he'd leaned forward, adjusted his baseball cap, and said with a smirk, "*It looks like a plate of broccoli*." Walking back up the steep hill to campus after class, tears scalding her eyes, she saw a dumpster behind the RISD cafeteria and hurled the two-by-two canvas with all the force her shame could muster. The next week in class, the painting, apparently rescued, was waiting at her station with a note: *I actually like broccoli*.

She killed herself in that class to avoid enduring that feeling again, the five hours in studio supplemented by weekends trying to wrangle some control of the impossible oil paints. She could immediately recall the anxiety before every crit anytime she caught a whiff of turpentine. But she did it. She finished with a respectable, hard-earned B, which lowered her grade-point average. All to prove to John Temple that she was serious.

It infuriated her that he couldn't see that she and the Art History Girls were not at all the same.

* * *

CLAIRE, MARGOT, AND Mavette had been a set since before they declared the major that would earn their sobriquet. Art history was, for them, a nearly preordained destination, as it had been for their mothers before them. Claire's mother was an interior designer in New York City; Margot's mom owned a gallery in Laguna Beach. Yes, Mavette's mother was a famous French novelist, but she'd met Mavette's father—a prominent dealer of Middle Eastern art—while enrolled in an Impressionists course at university. List Art Building was, in fact, littered with cliques of girls with similar biographies, but none of them as recognizable an entity on campus as the Art History Girls. While Claire was, from the outside, their obvious leader, it was Mavette's presence that made them stand out. Mavette would attribute this to her effortless European style, but Raquel knew that it was simply because Mavette wasn't white. She and Raquel were the only nonwhite students in the whole department.

They'd met during "Third World Week"—an orientation for every freshman who checked any box other than Caucasian on their application—but they bonded over their shared aversion to the program's unfortunate name. A name, they were told, rooted in activism and struggle. The program, according to the brochure, intended to be "an inclusive and empowering gathering of historically marginalized students in the school's long and illustrious history." But three days in, Mavette deemed it "too serious and too boring" and jumped ship for the International Orientation instead, one marked less by workshops in the "isms" and equity and more by wine tastings and EDM dance parties. Lebanese by way of Paris, Mavette had gone to a posh international school where they believed no one "saw color." America's "obsession with race" was, according to Mavette, "provincial."

For the next few years, the two women inhabited completely different social milieus. Raquel's life rooted in the Third World and Mavette's firmly ensconced in the First one, a name the two girls cheekily gave to the rest of the school. Outside of their class schedules, their lives on campus rarely collided. But a thread existed between them, each knowing that no matter where they chose to socialize, they were an Other in this place. Mavette, of course, refused to be defined by this, the otherness rendered irrelevant by the simple fact of them being there. Raquel, on the other hand, found this naïve. A rare blind spot in Mavette's preternaturally cosmopolitan worldview. Their differing perspectives on the matter a frequent topic of debate in their somewhat clandestine friendship. One that played out during coffee dates or meals off campus. Or, like last night, over drinks. Alone. Away from the eyes of their rigidly bordered universes.

Their time together—Mavette's strange fetishization of American whiteness aside—was utterly exhilarating to Raquel. Mavette affirmed so many thoughts she'd held in isolation: their shared frustrations with their all–white male curriculum, their mutual unease with John Temple's slightly dodgy demeanor. Their acquaintance provided a relief that none of Raquel's Third World friends did. So, she not only resented the Art History Girls for their performative intellectualism, she resented the space they occupied in Mavette's day-to-day life and the outrageous sway they seemed to have over her.

This summer situation was the most egregious example. Mavette had rather enviable plans that involved staying at her parents' New York pied-à-terre and working a highly coveted stint at Larry

Gagosian's gallery while her ne'er-do-well painter boyfriend Niles bummed around the city "looking for inspiration." Then Margot had the idea to go to Europe instead. It started in Feminism and Economic Agency, a course that posited that marriage was an antifeminist trap for women, one that weighed them down with gendered domestic roles and dampened their professional prospects. Margot chafed at this: her mother had been a wonderful mom who also excelled in her career, as had Mavette's, as had Claire's. But, when she attempted to argue this point, she had a revelation. "*Marriage isn't a trap, but marrying unstrategically might be*," Mavette had recounted to Raquel over drinks the evening before. Raquel was flummoxed. Future focused as she was, she had barely dated, let alone considered doing so "strategically." And then Mavette stated plainly what Margot so astutely observed—yes, their mothers were all professionally successful, but their fathers were also all rich. One could never have happened without the other.

"I mean, they're all brilliant, but let's face facts, they didn't get to where they are in life filing sales sheets at some gallery internship," Mavette had told Raquel, before adding in a quick, "No offense."

None was taken. Raquel thought it sounded like the craziest, most retrograde idea she'd ever heard and said as much. "You can't meet who you don't know," Mavette retorted, before explaining that when you laid it out, long-term, they'd be just as served by investing this summer in placing themselves in the right dating pool as they would by listing another accomplishment on their résumé. And so, despite being the only one attached to anyone, Mavette decided to break up with Niles. Truthfully, troubled rationale aside, Raquel did think it might be for the best. Niles was as famous for sleeping around as he was for being the only Black student in the painting department at RISD. Mavette could do better. But as Mavette kept talking, it became clear that the breakup had been more appealing in theory than in practice. Her sudden ambivalence over the decision illuminated tensions that had been brewing ever since Mavette found love with Niles in the first place. Something the other girls seemed to bristle at, "But not because he's Black," Mavette insisted. More than anything,

Mavette seemed upset about how her role within the clique was perceived from the outside.

"I never get credit for what I bring to the table."

"Which is?" Raquel had asked.

"I'm international. Do you know what that does for them? It makes them sophisticated."

* * *

ON THE STREET, the sun had broken through the clouds and the cool spring morning now turned muggy. Raquel stopped to take off her blazer and adjusted her headphones. After Julian rescued *Duran Duran*, a tenuous acquaintanceship was formed. When he eventually discovered that she did programming on Sundays for WBRU, he started passing her his mixtapes, which did—like it or not—inform some of her selections. This one, full of some kid named Slim Shady, was wild. A narrative rap where he dreams of murdering his girlfriend to the tune of "Just the Two of Us." Dark, funny, weird shit. Marcus would never play something like this. She raised the volume to quiet the noise of John Temple and those fucking girls.

She had been so lost in her own thoughts, she walked right past the station.

WBRU was located in a small, two-story brick building covered in ivy on the far end of campus near the Portuguese side of town. It was her place of joy. Raquel hurried into the station and waved hello to Jessica, the head of news, just as Derek, the lunchtime DJ, hit Play on "Father of Mine." The Everclear song filled the hallways.

She passed Deirdre, the senior who hosted the gospel show, in the narrow hallway.

"He's in the back," she said to Raquel, "and he's grumpy."

"He's always grumpy," Raquel said with a laugh as she made her way to the small backroom that housed the office for the 360° Black Experience.

The radio station at Brown was an anomaly. Other colleges, especially "liberal, creative" campuses like theirs, had experimental indie stations that prided themselves on weirdness. WBRU, however, was,

Monday through Saturday, the most listened to alternative-pop station in southern New England: a commercially viable entity that was completely student run. Advertising sales, news reporting, writing, musical programming, and on-air talent. Almost all from the First World. Except on Sundays when the Third World took over. For twenty-four glorious hours, the airwaves were given over to what the music marketplace called Black Music, with the tiniest of nods to Latin: gospel in the early mornings, soul and classics after that, jazz at brunch, new hip-hop and R&B in the afternoon, reggae and soca in the evenings. And, of course, the nights closed out with the best baby-making music north of New York's WBLS. Because the breadth and depth and diversity of the entirety of Black Music had to squeeze into a mere twenty-four hours, the day was named the 360° Black Experience in Sound. Marcus sat at the head of that. He also hosted, with Raquel's assistance, the hip-hop and R&B show. Both jobs he took immensely seriously.

"I brought you a falafel, because I promised to deal with lunch," he said as he opened a CD and popped it into the deck. "But you'd promised to be here fifteen minutes ago."

"Did you remember the hot sauce?"

"Where is the sorry? Or the thank you?"

"Crazy morning. Sorry and thank you." She cut her falafel in half, fingered the jewel case. "The new Big Pun. He's a beast."

New music came out on Tuesdays, but it came to the station the week before, on Thursdays, Raquel's favorite day of the week. She loved art history, but she was obsessed with music, hip-hop most of all. And while she was certain that John Temple and everyone in the art building would not understand, she could see the connection between the two so clearly. If she thought it would be academically acceptable, she'd ditch Jack Martin in a heartbeat and write her senior thesis on that. When Paris was changing, when Spain was in civil war, when Los Angeles was on fire, when drugs decimated her city—what did people do? They made art about it. Art unlike anything that had come before. Jay-Z, in her opinion, was no different than Picasso; Nas, on par with Manet. She studied, in class, the history of the world through the eyes of artists. She felt, in her soul, that what she was witnessing with hip-hop was some of the most inventive artists in history documenting the culture of her time. Plus, it reminded her of home.

She had taken them for granted, the sounds of Brooklyn. Wished them away, even. The ceaseless bachata and boleros of their upstairs neighbor, her own mother's blasting of La Mega 97.9 and 98.7 Kiss FM and the incessant singing when she was home. In her house, she was the quiet one, the one who shushed Toni and her mom. She had thought these were the sounds of poverty, of confinement. But as soon as she arrived on campus, she felt smothered by the blanket of silence that covered the place. She could have, she supposed, traded her hoops for CZ knockoffs of the studs Claire and Mavette wore; she could have gotten her hair blown out and pulled back. Could have really tried to fit into their world. But she couldn't stand the silence. Latino Night at The Gate blasting Selena, Unity Day at the Third World Center gossiping over the sounds of Tribe: these weren't just hangouts, they were releases. Opportunities to stop worrying about disturbing something, and simply be as noisy as you fucking wanted.

The Big Pun song featured an R&B hook by Joe. It was fire, destined to be a hit, and the kind of song both she and Marcus could agree on. She was drawn to the craft and art of the MC; Marcus, to the beats. So they always played more R&B or Bad Boy club music, which she tried to explain to him was going to be Top 40 before they even knew it. They were, in her opinion, squandering the chance to forward the art of rap. "*Just because you want to dance to it doesn't mean it's bad rap*," he would say, pissy.

"The rest of the album is too hard-core for us," Marcus offered up now, his head nodding, "but this is dope."

He looked at her for a second. "You look like shit."

"Thanks?" she said, mouth full of falafel. "I went out with International Mavette last night, the one I'm kind of friends with."

"The one who hangs out with the girls you don't like?"

She nodded and handed him a CD from the pile. Cam'ron's "Horse & Carriage."

"From last week. It's on a mix I got from home on break and it's a fucking earworm."

Marcus put it on and she could see from the first beat drop that he liked it.

"How the fuck did we miss this?"

She shrugged. "Do you know what she told me? These crazy bitches aren't working or doing internships or anything this summer. They're just going to travel around and look for rich boyfriends to marry after graduation."

Marcus laughed. "It sounds better than what career services is offering."

"Yeah, if this were 1950 and women couldn't have careers."

"Psssh. This is where you females get in your own way. If a rich woman came up to me today and said, 'Marcus, you handsome devil, let me take you away from all this. A man as fine and smart and wonderful and good in bed as you shouldn't have to work.' Well, I wouldn't say, 'But how will I prove myself as a man if I don't work?' I would say, 'Sign me up! Just let me keep doing my radio show, please.'"

"Fuck you with your 'females'!" She laughed.

She appreciated Marcus and his honesty; that they could be real with each other without it ever getting too heavy. He reminded her that everything didn't have to be so loaded. A Brooklynite like her, Marcus was the only effortless relationship she had found in college; she was a fan before she was a friend. In the First World, no one knew or cared who the DJs on WBRU were, but in the Third World, the people who gave Brown—no, the city—the 360° Black Experience? They were heroes. It would be effortless, she realized, for him to always have companions for meals or to study with or to go to Funk Night with. But he was almost always alone. She recognized herself in that. One day, she saw him eating at the student union, headphones on, reading the paper. She introduced herself, sat down across from him, and proceeded to make the case for him broadening the repertoire of his hip-hop to include the "hot shit coming out of Rawkus Records." Their first lively debate ensued, and he invited her to come by the station that Sunday while he did his show. The rest, as they say, was history.

"Hey, do you wanna come with me to this art opening tomorrow?" she asked.

"Whose show is it?" he asked, prompting Raquel to sigh.

"Does it matter? There's free food and drinks and it's on our way to open mic night."

Marcus was indifferent to Raquel's art world, largely because he was indifferent to any activity that wasn't unapologetically pro-Black. Or free. While Nick Fitzsimmons's senior show would certainly be one of the least Black things happening on campus, not just that weekend but that very century, it would surely have free food. And, from what she'd heard, free champagne as well.

Raquel knew *of* Nick Fitzsimmons more than she actually *knew* him. She was mainly going as a favor to his sister, Astrid. Someone she considered more colleague than friend, but whom, for reasons she couldn't quite place, she liked. Astrid was perhaps the only person in the Art History Department as obsessed with the subject as Raquel, and the only other person who secured a RISD fellowship too. Though she, like Claire, was wealthy and from the Upper East Side, outside of those demographic similarities, they had nothing in common. Astrid was a brilliant autodidact with a photographic memory who, despite a prodigious appetite for drugs, effortlessly maintained a 4.0 GPA. But she suffered the unfortunate circumstance of not only being odd but being the little sister of a campus legend, and as such never secured a place for herself in any of the university's worlds except for that in her brother's long shadow. Nick was a bona fide star of the First World and, if the buzz around the art building was to be believed, soon to be one in the real world as well. A double concentrator in fine art and semiotics who liked to work "at scale," he was the only person in the department with dedicated workspace in both the basement sculpture studios and the skylit painting studios. Though most art students only showed publicly once or twice while at Brown, Nick's senior show would be his fourth exhibition, to say nothing of his unsanctioned off-campus work. According to Astrid, the Guggenheim had already bought two of his pieces. "*My mom probably made a donation*," she'd said, "*but still.*" Raquel had found this bit of information staggering.

His work was remarkably derivative. And because she knew Astrid shared this opinion and because she felt sorry for her, when she asked Raquel to come to her brother's reception, she'd felt compelled to say yes. Compelled, but not confident enough to go alone.

"Marcus," she pleaded in response to his silence, "come on. Half an hour. An hour, tops. I'm trying to expand my social circle."

"What's wrong with your social circle now?" he asked, defensively.

"Nothing. But I'd like to spend my last year here with maybe one or two friends that can talk with me about something deeper than if D-Dot is a better producer than DJ Premier—"

"He absolutely fucking is," Marcus interjected, before moving on. "What R&B came in?"

"'Be Careful' by Sparkle, featuring one Mr. Robert Kelly."

"I've been waiting for this!" Marcus said with glee. "He does not disappoint."

"It's featuring him. It's *her* song."

"Let's see about that," he said, playing the track. "His magical fingerprints are on everything he touches."

The door opened and Delroy, the sophomore who hosted the reggae and soca show, walked in with his girlfriend, Betsaida, a Dominican junior from East Providence infamous for dropping off the Latina sorority pledge line in order to spend more time with Delroy. She kissed Raquel on both cheeks while Delroy gave Marcus the requisite dap.

"Bets, I hope you're not here to give me more shit," Marcus said when he saw her.

"First of all, I'm not giving you shit," she replied. "I'm just pointing out that it's exclusionary not to have a show dedicated to salsa and merengue—"

"And I keep trying to tell you that it's the 360° *Black* Experience."

Betsaida looked at him, her hip jutting out to the side. Silently, she put down her bag and pulled off her bright yellow spring jacket, revealing her bare arms. She leaned into Marcus, placed her smooth forearm next to his. Her skin, shiny with lotion and thick with the scent of Bath and Body Works, notably darker. Raquel and Delroy were already laughing before she said anything.

"Y punto!" Betsaida exclaimed. "Play my music or change the fockin' name of your little program, OK?"

"You can't argue facts," Raquel said, still cracking up.

"Anyway," Betsaida continued, "I'm not even here to school you—that was just a bonus lesson. I came to see to *you*."

"Me?" Raquel asked, puzzled. They were cool but Betsaida didn't kick it with anybody but Delroy, and outside of a club meeting here and there, they didn't know each other that well.

"I heard that you're staying here this summer?"

"News travels fast."

"Yeah, congratulations. Listen, I'm wondering if you need a roommate?"

"I'm her roommate," Marcus said.

Senior year was when you could finally move off campus and she and Marcus had gotten a cute spot on Ives Street.

"I heard you're gonna be in New York interning at MTV," Betsaida said.

"Damn, Bets," Delroy said, "you're all up in the business."

"What? You know I'm desperate, babe. I put in legwork." She turned to Raquel to plead her case. "I applied for a research grant with my professor mad late—studying the sociology of breakups, dope shit. Anyway, it came through, but now I'm scrambling for a place to stay. I can't be in my parents' house with all that chaos, trying to get work done and shit."

Raquel assessed her for a second. Marcus did have an internship in New York and there was a tiny third room, which would lower the rent. She admired that Betsaida was doing something cool. How comfortable she seemed in her skin. Plus, she'd brought mangú to the Latino History Month potluck that was bomb.

"It's three hundred dollars a month," she said. A smile of satisfaction broke out across Betsaida's face.

"What the fuck, Raquel? You don't even ask!" Marcus said.

"Your internship pays you in subway tokens and sandwiches. It's this or you can pay full rent for an apartment you're only visiting on weekends."

The pro of the show were the perks: freebies from advertisers, admission to the best clubs Providence had to offer, drink tickets. The con was that it was a fifty-two-week-a-year commitment and substitutes were frowned upon. Despite having landed his dream job for the summer, Marcus still had to schlep up to Providence every weekend if he wanted to keep his slot. She could see, without words, that he conceded her point.

"See," Betsaida said to Marcus, "I'm basically doing *you* a favor."

"Hold up," Raquel said, considering Delroy. "Some rules. Two of us live there, not three. You get my drift."

"Nobody wants to stay in your raggedy house!" Delroy laughed. "I've got an internship at Bank of America in Boston, OK?"

"Great. And you've gotta cook, like, one day a week."

"With pleasure!" Betsaida said. "I can throw down in the kitchen. You're gonna be so thick come fall, Flaca. Tendrás un culo que nadie olvidará."

* * *

List Art Building's defining feature was that the fifth floor, where the painting studios were located, extended several hundred feet beyond the four floors beneath it, the expanse supported by a half-dozen slender, concrete piers. The result of this architectural detail was a grand, several-stories-high, brutalist portico that started on College Street and went on for half a block to the building's entrance. This was where Nick Fitzsimmons chose to install the centerpiece of his senior show. A site-specific sculpture, Nick had created cone-shaped stacks of industrial tractor tires of massive scale: six feet wide at the base, narrowing at the top, and towering—Raquel estimated—at least thirteen feet high. He had arranged these stacks on the veranda like a funnel: broad at the mouth and then almost claustrophobically narrow where they flanked the building's entry. The tires themselves had been painted—no, lacquered, really, with a glossy finish—a pristine white. The smell of rubber and paint increasingly overwhelming as you walked through.

"Impressive," Marcus remarked. After promises of free drunchies, he'd finally agreed to accompany her.

"Impressive, or just large?" Raquel quipped. "It feels a bit like it's saying, 'Just so you know, I've got a big dick.'"

Marcus laughed. "Some people might be into that."

The reception was crowded: faculty and students she knew, anonymous faces she recognized from passing in the stairwells or crowding around the slide tables. Then, there were ones she'd not seen before: alumni from RISD, other well-heeled adults. She wondered if they were professors from other departments or—could it be, collectors? Gallerists?

"Raquel!" Her name came in a loud whisper from a concrete bench in the lobby; Raquel peered over shoulders and located Astrid. She waved, gestured to the bar—the quiet murmur in the lobby snipping her instinct to shout across the room—but Astrid vigorously shook her head no, sending her bleached blond dreadlocks flipping through the air, beckoning Raquel frantically with a wave of her hands.

"That's your expanded social circle?" Marcus asked. Astrid, with her face piercings and post-grunge meets post-goth sartorial aesthetic, cut a striking figure in the room, even tucked away in a corner as she was.

"Grab us some champagne?" Raquel made her way toward Astrid.

"I've been waiting for you," Astrid said, more frazzled than usual.

"Am I late?" Raquel glanced at her watch. She was not.

"I have to go," Astrid said, standing.

"What the fuck are you talking about? I came to meet you."

"I know. Trust me, I wouldn't have even shown up if I didn't know you were coming. You cannot imagine the day I've had with *her*."

Astrid cast a furtive glance across the room and Raquel followed her eye until it caught her brother, surrounded, as one would imagine the star of the hour to be, with admirers: a couple of fawning girls; John Temple, of course; and an older, well-dressed couple that she recognized almost immediately as his and Astrid's parents. Their mother was a buttoned-up, Titian-colored doppelgänger for her daughter.

"Nick got a commission from the city of Providence this summer, so even though they are buying him a fucking loft in New York—"

"Must be nice," Raquel interjected.

"I have to room with him this summer to 'save money,'" Astrid continued her lament. "Then, she insisted that she take me shopping for clothes for RISD—"

"Must be nice."

"Please. My gilded cage comes with barbed wire," Astrid said, pulling a flask from her tote bag and taking a sip. "Between her and Mavette giving me the death stare—"

Of course, they were here: the Art History Girls.

"Since when do you have a beef with Mavette?" Raquel asked, perplexed.

"Since she heard I'd fucked Niles," Astrid said. And at that moment, Raquel spotted them; saw Margot clock them and nudge Mavette.

"Oh God, they're coming over," Astrid said.

The Art History Girls were, indeed, crossing the room toward them. Or toward Astrid, really, who unapologetically made a quick escape. Raquel felt a moment of panic; she'd never spoken to them all together. Usually, she and Mavette would, at most, exchange a nod or a wave when they were in a group. Raquel plastered a smile on her face.

"Hi," she offered, giving Mavette the requisite double kiss. "I was so fucking hungover yesterday. Were you?"

"I survived," she replied, her eyes scanning the room, Raquel assumed, for Astrid.

"Raquel," Claire said, a little mischievous, "I didn't realize you went out with that hot Black guy. I always notice him in the Ratty."

Claire had never said her name aloud before despite having been in at least four classes together. Raquel forced her smile even wider.

"Marcus? We're just friends. We're gonna be roommates next year."

"Your parents are letting you live with a guy?" Margot asked, semi-impressed. "My dad almost didn't let me come here because we had coed dorms."

It hadn't occurred to Raquel to run this idea past her mother. She'd paid the deposit on the apartment with her work-study money and never even mentioned it. Besides, her mother loved Marcus, or at least she loved that he drove Raquel back home for long weekends and breaks.

"Raquel's mom is very progressive," Mavette offered. "She also works in the arts."

Raquel had told Mavette her mother worked at the museum; conclusions were drawn that Raquel never elaborated on but never corrected either. She'd felt weird about it at the time but was grateful for Mavette's unintended spin now. She gave a quick look around the room to see where Marcus was with her drink. Her only chance for escape.

"Mavette said you two had a blast the other night," Claire said, "and we realized we should all hang out! Have you over. It's weird we haven't done it yet, honestly."

Raquel had no real desire to give time to these women. But she was still holding out hope for her friendship with Mavette and wanted to prove herself "open-minded."

"Absolutely," she said, straining for enthusiasm, "that would be great. Maybe during reading period?"

Before anything could be affirmed, they heard the voice of John Temple.

"All of my brilliant pupils in one spot!" he said, seeming a bit drunk.

The Art History Girls greeted him coquettishly, laughter and thrown-back heads. Raquel smiled, relieved that Marcus finally reappeared with champagne in hand.

"Ladies," Professor Temple declared, "I am so curious about what you're getting up to this summer. Please tell me you're not just partying on a beach somewhere."

An amused smile broke on Marcus's face. Before Raquel could wonder how much of their philosophy they would share with John Temple, Mavette chimed in.

"Hardly, John," she offered, with her classic poise. "We're traveling with my parents to Europe while my father advises some of his clients on how to build their collections."

Professor Temple began going on about how wonderful this "field training" would be and Raquel felt her temper flare. When he finally noticed Marcus and introduced himself, she was focused on Mavette, looking for even a hint of deception on her face but finding none. The one who seemed noticeably uncomfortable, however, was Claire.

She kept shifting her weight and putting her gaze on anyone and anything other than John Temple.

"Claire," he eventually said, "I hope you know I did everything—"

"We need to go," she announced suddenly, cutting him off midsentence. Her gray eyes searched those of her companions, imploringly. "My aunt is in town and taking us to dinner."

Then, a chaotic flurry of rushed goodbyes. Claire looped her arm through Margot's and charged toward the door; Mavette followed, turning for a second to blow Raquel a kiss.

"I'll call you," she said from across the lobby.

"That was a bit abrupt," John Temple said, before taking another sip of his drink. He changed the subject. "Some show, isn't it? A tour de force for such a young talent, don't you think?"

"I dug it," Marcus said. "But, Raquel, I think—"

"I thought it was a big statement," she interjected, aware that she was as guilty of lying as Mavette, but finding solace in the diminutive scale of her falsehood. She looked around the gallery for something generous to say that might affirm the impression that she shared her professor's opinion. The interior portion of the show was a series of paintings of . . . stacks of white tractor tires. Monochromatic, white on white, caustic things. Derivative. "They have a Jasper Johns–like pop-art quality."

"Exactly what I was telling Nick!" John Temple said, voice full of excitement, before he finished the last of his wine and reached for his Dunhills. "Well, enjoy the rest of your evening."

"Have a great weekend, Professor Temple."

"Raquel, if you want me to be your thesis adviser, promise you'll start calling me John. 'Professor Temple' makes me feel about a hundred years old."

She could not seem to get it right, this calculus of respect and casualness. She forced out with a smile, "Of course, John."

Professor Temple extended his hand out to Marcus. "And great meeting you, Mark."

"Same here, John."

John Temple made his exit, cigarette in mouth before he reached the door, vanishing through Nick Fitzsimmons's white-washed rubber shaft. They made their way to the table of cheeses and finger foods, Marcus piling his plate high.

"So, why'd you do that?" Marcus asked.

"Do what?" She knew exactly what he was talking about.

"You know what. Why'd you pretend you like this stuff when you definitely don't?"

"Why'd you let him call you Mark?"

He shoved a cheese cube in his mouth.

"For the exact opposite reason you didn't tell him what you think."

"Which is?"

"He's so unimportant to me, son, I don't care what he calls me."

"Damn," Raquel said. She contemplated a pig in a blanket and decided to pass.

"He's not interested in me at all either. And that's cool. He was just being friendly because he wants to sleep with you."

"Ew." Raquel grimaced. "He's old."

Marcus shrugged. "He's handsome. For a white guy."

"Don't be gross."

Raquel did think he was handsome. For a white guy or otherwise. But she was weirded out by his vibe, which was not quite paternal, but not overtly sexual either?

"You know," she continued, "I used to feel so smart. Before I got here, you know? I would just blurt out opinions. I believed in what I was thinking. And now, I don't know. If I don't have fucking footnotes and firsthand sources and shit ready, I'm afraid to talk."

"Come on, Raquel." The absence of food in his hands or mouth hinted at his sincerity. "You're fucking smart. Not just because you're here. Being here is a bonus. Think of all the smart people you know that aren't here."

And she had to concede that he was right.

"I guess, I just worry that if I don't see things—art, especially—his way, he won't be as supportive of me. He offered to help me find a gallery job after we graduate. They're impossible to get without connections."

Marcus sucked his teeth. "They're teachers, not dictators. If you don't like this guy's art, you shouldn't pretend."

"Who doesn't like my art?" came a voice from behind them and Raquel's stomach dropped. Marcus giggled—high-pitched and fast.

"I think I need another drink," he said and hurriedly stepped away, Raquel looking up in total and complete mortification at the inevitable face of Nick Fitzsimmons.

The smile on his face was not the cocky smirk Raquel had been expecting. It was warm, the same warmth she liked about his sister's smile. He was a ubiquitous presence in the art building, of course, but Raquel never spoke to him. She both admired and had been revolted by his particularly Aryan good looks: slim build, muscular arms, white skin with a kiss of sun, the sandy blond hair, pale blue eyes, precise nose, his chin defined. His attire was an ever-simple ensemble of Diesel jeans and a T-shirt, and the lack of piercings stripped his familiar face of the distraction that Astrid had created for herself.

"I wouldn't say I don't like it, exactly," she said, trying to find a way to own what he'd heard, but not certain she could summon the mettle to give her unvarnished opinion right to his face. "I would say that I'm not convinced of what it's about."

"It's about the material. The only meaning is what the viewer brings when they see the materials," he offered, with that smile again.

"That sounds like some bullshit Jack Martin would say." She laughed.

Nick Fitzsimmons chuckled. "Oh, it one hundred percent is. I read that in *Artforum* and thought, I'm gonna save that one up for a rainy day."

They both laughed now.

"Don't get me wrong," she said with a grin. "I love Martin. I'm doing my thesis on Martin. But he sounds like a tool sometimes."

"A role model for bluster, really," Nick replied.

She was surprised at his charm. That he wasn't afraid of being a little challenged.

"So, do you want to try again?" she asked, daring him a little. "What's this show about?"

"Yeah, totally." He took a sip of his beer and exhaled, stood a little taller, put on what she could tell was his "presentation" voice. "It's about man and nature, about industrialization and claustrophobia, and the corporatization of the American Farm."

"The American Farm. . . . Aren't you from the Upper East Side?" she said with a suspicious giggle. He met her eyes and giggled too.

"You got me." He ran his hand through his hair, almost nervously, she thought. "If you want to know, I thought it would look fucking cool."

"Well, it does look fucking cool," she said, and raised her glass to him.

"You're friends with my sister, right?"

"Yeah," she said. "I mean, we're Art History Friends. I came to meet up with her, actually."

"Wow, really doubling down on how uninterested in my work you are!"

"God, that sounded terrible," she said, embarrassed. "I just . . . I don't come to these things, usually. Anyway, she slipped out a while ago."

"Unsurprising," he said, clearly contemplating something. "What does that mean, 'Art History Friends'?"

Marcus reappeared then, as much a goodbye as a hello. He looked them over, offered his hand out.

"Marcus, man. Congrats. This shit looks dope."

"Nick Fitzsimmons." He gave Marcus a firm handshake.

"Yo, Raquel, I'm gonna head downtown. You'll catch up?"

She contemplated doing what she would normally do—retreat to her comfort zone, her turf, her people. But, while hardly the most experienced person in this arena, she was feeling a connection. The way she felt when she'd run into Mavette. The way she felt when she met Marcus. But more electric. More urgent.

"Yeah, I'll catch up with you later," she said. Eager to stay in this strange bubble of just the two of them, she returned her focus to Nick.

"Art History Friends just means that we mainly socialize in class, but we're both fellows at the RISD Museum this summer. So, maybe we'll become real friends."

"Maybe," he said, and looked off. Raquel noticed the crowd was dwindling and his parents were gone. "So, friend of my sister. Marcus's friend. Your name is Raquel?"

"Toro," she said, offering her hand, "Raquel Toro."

Then he did something that she normally would've thought corny as hell: he bowed and kissed her hand.

"Nice to meet you, Raquel Toro, the tactful," he declared. "It's not every day I meet someone who can insult me without making me feel badly *and* knows her Jack Martin quotes."

"I didn't know it was a quote," she said, playfully. "It just sounded like him."

"Credit where credit is due," he said. "And honestly, I should thank you—"

"For what?" Raquel said, incredulous.

"You walk into these things knowing somebody—maybe lots of somebodies—think you're a fucking bullshit artist. And you're, like, terrified someone will say it out loud."

"You're welcome?"

"No, seriously," he said. "You had the balls to say it, and hearing it was easier than worrying about who was thinking it. Most people are phonies, you know?"

Before Raquel could decide if she agreed with this statement or not, Nick Fitzsimmons smiled at her and said, with a little mischief in his eyes, "Let's get another drink before they close this down."

Raquel felt a flush come over her as she nodded yes.

Anita

BERKELEY, CALIFORNIA • WINTER 1980

Endings, and even beginnings, are tricky things to pinpoint, aren't they? The conventional mind likes to make them nice and neat, a light switch that goes off and on. One night I didn't know Jack and the next day I did. And that was "the beginning of us." But really, maybe the beginning was the first time I saw his work? In my art history class as an undergraduate at Iowa. When the seed was planted in my mind that he was a person of importance—long buried and then suddenly sprouted up when he validated my existence with attention and time. Or maybe the beginning was when he accepted Leslie's invitation to be a part of my opening? Setting wheels of fate into motion. The Iowa River, for instance, starts when two streams join together in Hancock County. Is one of those streams more the beginning than the other? Endings are the same. Possibly even more nebulous, messy things.

We weren't yet married, but even so, I'd say that the night Jack's Berkeley show opened was the beginning of the end for us. This night where, at a large dinner on "*one of the most important nights*" of Jack's career—when I couldn't take another minute of being ignored—I made "*a spectacle of myself.*" But someone else could say no, the beginning of the end was when I agreed to go to Berkeley with him in the first place, instead of taking the artists' residency in Florida. By that reasoning, I would also have to consider that, actually, the beginning of the end was the very first time I ever chose Jack Martin over myself. But that line of thinking is depressing, isn't it? Because if I were to think of the first moment I prioritized Jack's desires over my own—if I were to truly pinpoint it? Well, I think I would find it uncomfortably close to the start of things. So close, I would have to say—in complete hindsight, of course—that perhaps we were always doomed.

Oh, but there was so much happiness there between us at one point!

In any case, endings are long and messy. And, honestly, I'm not even certain they exist. The Iowa River meets the English River just south of Iowa City; is that when it ends? They both get swallowed by the Mississippi a few hundred miles after that. Is that the end? Because it's still there, isn't it? The current that started in Hancock County. Flowing, even when spat out, fresh water licking salt, into the Gulf of Mexico.

* * *

IF JACK HAD architected the building himself, there could not have been a more perfect location for his *third* midcareer retrospective than the museum at Berkeley. The place was like his pieces: sterile, devoid of color, and devoid of life. But also like him: full of hot air. The kaleidoscope ceiling was made entirely of glass plates; all day long the sun baking the poured-concrete walls of the place. It was a big, brutalist mess. One that insisted, as Jack did of his sculptures, that it was about nothing but the materials that it was made from. Why, I still ask myself, is that something to be proud of? Whether they were about something or not, the building and the sculptures Jack showed there were certainly devoid of feeling. No, actually. The museum made me feel I was in a mausoleum and Jack's art made me feel dead inside. Or, maybe, if I were to be honest about it, it was Jack who made me feel that way.

The museum sent a car for us and Jack had us waiting in it outside for a good fifteen minutes until he'd seen enough other "important people" arrive and decided we too could join his celebration. He was so nervous and I wasn't really sure why. There were some new pieces:

stuff with ingots, a ball-bearing piece arranged on the floor. But he was also re-creating some very famous installations and there was enough old to please the crowd even if the new wasn't well received. Also, the truth is, if you liked what Jack was doing—and nobody shows up to this kind of opening if they didn't—well, how does the expression go? "Seen one, seen 'em all"? In any case, he was nervous, and he had my hand wrapped in his so tight, my fingers were going numb. I remembered finding it charming, his nerves as we made our way to the doors. I could feel them run through me, through our hands, like a current.

The reception was packed. The museum itself winds up and up via concrete ramps, until it's close to the skylights, with these sharp little balconies jutting out, here and there, all around. The moonlight through the glass ceiling, the hum of people and music and clinking glasses, lent the space a warmth it normally lacked. Jack stood at the entryway, as he does, my body just a bit behind him. Marlon Brando wouldn't have caused as much of a stir! Everyone stopped in their tracks when they noticed him; the people on the ramps, the people on the balconies. The chatter ceased. Everyone motioned to one another, directing their attention to us. All eyes fixed on us. Well, no. Fixed on him. Then the people near the entrance realized that the guest of honor had arrived and began clamoring to make their hellos, extend their congratulations, extol his genius. And his clasp on my hand that had been a death grip just moments before grew looser and looser until he dropped it altogether. Current broken.

Someone—maybe it was Rebecca, the curator, or Tilly, in from New York—grabbed his arm to lead him off. And I was left standing there as the rest of the party resumed, just as they had been before. Feeling empty. A waiter offered me a glass of wine and I began to fill myself up.

Some artists I knew were chatting together and I went to say hello. A dread rising up in me as I crossed the room, anticipating the inevitable question of "*What are you working on, Anita?*" And my answer would be . . . what? Supporting Jack emotionally? A feminist performance piece about retrograde relationships? Being bored out of my mind at interchangeable dinner parties and cocktail parties during the month we'd been in Berkeley? Drinking way too much and waking up hungover, unable to do much, let alone be creative and productive? When they *did* actually ask the question, I just pretended I was further along with something than I was. Talked up the Florida residency without mentioning how I turned it down—last minute at that—for a pair of fucking earrings and a first-class ticket to California.

There turned out to be little to fear; they were a good group, kind and generous. I had another glass of wine or two with them and we were in the midst of a lively debate about the new critic at the *New Yorker* when a young woman approached me.

"Are you Anita de Monte?" she asked. I got excited because I thought she had recognized me. Then I remembered. How? I had barely shown at all in the two years since I'd been with Jack.

"I am," I said to her. "Can I help you?"

"Mr. Martin asked me to come and find you; I work here at the museum."

I looked around, spotted Jack in his denim coveralls, holding court with Rebecca, Tilly, and a small cluster of others. The Proletariat in Chief, tended to like a king. Clearly not in need of anything.

"Tell him I'm catching up with some friends."

I felt badly for the girl. You could see on her face that having to go to Mr. Jack Martin and explain that, unlike the champagne or hors d'oeuvres or whatever other whims they'd tasked her with chasing down for him, I was not something you fetched. Not five minutes went by when Rebecca appeared by my side, politely asking me to come with her.

"I hate to pull you away, but there are some people I would love to introduce you to."

Of course, I agreed, and followed her off into the crowd, eager for the moment with her. In the month we'd been in Berkeley as Jack prepared the show, I'd been in her company a number of times. She was old friends with my Isaac—my former teacher and only lover before Jack—and had shown some interest in my work. You never knew what could lead to an acquisition of a print or a photograph.

"Great crowd, isn't it?" she asked. I was about to make the kind of polite, uncreative response that these situations require when she added, "Gorgeous earrings, by the way."

I smiled.

"Thank you. I sold my soul to Jack in exchange for them."

Admittedly, I can be melodramatic, but you see, in that moment, it was how I felt. They were beautiful, the earrings: circular gold things with large, smooth-cut round rubies in the center. The most magical, spectacular things that I'd ever had in my possession. They were from Bulgari and had come in a luxurious, oversized brown leather box with gold embossing on top and chocolate velvet on the inside that felt the way you're told bunnies feel like when you are a kid. Mainly, I'm a tomboy. I never wore so many dresses till Jack started taking me everywhere. I didn't even get my ears pierced until I was twenty! And only because when my mother finally escaped Cuba and joined us in Iowa, she absolutely insisted. But when Jack showed up with these earrings, I squealed like Marilyn Monroe in that movie, you know? The luxury of them; the extravagance of even just the box! I was packing; it was the night before I was meant to leave for the residency and suddenly, there he was: in the doorway with champagne and earrings. A first-class ticket to fly with him to Berkeley and promises that this would be a chance for us, both of us, to recommit to our art. Recommit to producing new things, to supporting each other. To supporting *my* ambitions. The way it had been in the beginning. Oh, and my heart nearly leapt out of my chest. "*Bulgari from the Bolshevik*," I had joked as I put the earrings on. And yes, I loved them, but more than that, they felt like a symbol. A symbol of his respect: respect that my creativity was as vital to me as his was to him. And we made love on my Murphy bed and in the morning I called the residency and told them that I was sorry it was so last minute, but I wasn't going to be able to come after all. A week later, we were sitting together, side by side, on the airplane. And a month after that, all those promises and dreams now proven false, all that was left were the earrings.

Rebecca was, in fact, just leading me to Jack. I guess I was fetchable, after all. Jack was still holding court with the same group of dapper guests, save one man, in jeans and a tweed jacket. There was always the one who tried to seem "creative" and ended up just being badly dressed. This particular slob likely thinking Jack would like this, his lack of pretense. Little did he know that regardless of the bullshit Jack spewed about being the working man's artist and about there being as much beauty in this museum as in a construction site, make no mistake, he loved bourgeois shit. This was an open secret: material things, status symbols, rarities. All of it delighted him.

"Here she is!" Rebecca exclaimed and Jack put his hand around my waist and pulled me close. Immediately, a waiter refilled my wine and I realized he must have been assigned to follow Jack around to ensure he never ran dry.

"Claude, Lee," he addressed the one with the jeans, "this is my girlfriend, Anita, who I was telling—"

I jabbed him in the ribs with my elbow—as sharply as his omission dug into my ego. His wine spilled a little. Tilly's eyes widened.

"This is Anita de Monte, the *artist*."

Oh, he laid it on very thick, he did. I held my hand out to both of the men.

"Pleasure."

It seemed like a little thing, but it wasn't. We'd discussed this before. This had been what sparked me applying for the residency in the first place. There'd been another dinner. This one in New York—a collector who'd acquired one of Jack's works. And when Jack introduced me, I was Anita de Monte, his girlfriend. Period. Now, whether it was the first time it happened, or simply the first time I noticed—because I had become so complacent about my own life and work—I don't know. But what I can tell you is that for the first year that we were together, he never took me anywhere without telling everyone that I was an artist. Not just an artist, but an artist of importance. And somehow, in the frog boil of this relationship, he stopped. Because somewhere, along the way, I lost my rigor. Stopped working. Stopped dreaming. This wasn't Jack's fault, but mine. I'd already lost my homeland and my family; I couldn't afford to lose my art. Working in the city challenged me; so very quietly, I applied for a three-month residency that the Mellon Foundation was offering. When Jack found out I was leaving, he was beside himself. Couldn't understand why I needed to leave him to work, said that I was an artist no matter where I was. And I explained to him that he was a liar. He, himself, stopped seeing me that way, stopped talking about me that way. And then, there were the earrings and the plane ticket and the rejected residency and his promise to never forget that I was an artist above all ever again.

Except that he already had.

"Oh!" Lee, in jeans, exclaimed. "You're an artist too. That's amazing!"

"Why is that amazing?" I asked. White men loved to use words that implied astonishment whenever women of color accomplished anything they deemed their "terrain."

"I just meant," Lee now attempted to correct, "that two artists in one home is remarkable. That must be challenging."

"Hardly at all," Jack chimed in, breezily. "Our work couldn't be more different."

I hated the way he said that, as though by different, he meant one of us was doing good work and the other doing crap. Guess who he thought was who? I wanted to defend myself, say that I was a conceptual artist. That I did body work. That my art, unlike Jack's cold, soulless pieces we were surrounded by, had blood and life in them. Literally. That my work was about the soul of civilizations we've long since paved over, about the universality of life. That my work was so innovative I had just won a residency from the Mellon Foundation so that I could get back to it, and that I turned it down to be Jack's handbag. But I hesitated, and in the moment of silence, I could feel their opinion of me and my work being solidified. The topic changed. Another man—Claude, the well-dressed one—chimed in.

"Anita, Jack was telling us that your father was a Castro revolutionary."

I grimaced. Why, on earth, were we talking about this again? Perhaps because in New York we saw the same couples, the same artists, the same friends of Jack's over and over, dinner conversations were about petty gossip regarding mutual acquaintances. But here, in Berkeley, where there was constantly someone new to talk to,

I noticed how often Jack was telling this story. Night after night about me arriving on Peter Pan, about my father being jailed in Cuba, about the revolution. Anita Tropicana, his little Communist Cuban girlfriend. It gave me an uneasy feeling. That I, like the coveralls and raw materials, had become part of a persona for Jack. Stripped of my profession, distilled to a few anecdotes that bathed him in a cascade of edginess. The working man's little woman. I didn't like being part of a shtick.

"My father worked in a government office in Havana," I said. I held my glass out for more wine.

"Where he was a white-collar plant for Castro until he fell on his wrong side," Jack corrected. "Darling, tell them how he ended up in jail for fifteen years."

My heart hurt, because I had cried to him many nights, worried for my father. My sister and I had written letter after letter to the Cuban and American governments, begging to get him out of jail. My mother, nearly suicidal for years, over guilt that she left the island with him sitting in a prison. Our family destroyed, all because of his belief in Jesus Christ; all because he'd pissed off the wrong person. But now, for Jack having a whole museum full of people talking about him and his work, that wasn't enough. He needed to turn my pain into cocktail conversation.

"Jack likes to say that I'm dramatic, but unfortunately, in this case, my sweet has watched too many movies. My father was anti-Batista, the way a lot of middle-class Cubans were. He wasn't in the mountains with rifles or anything like that. He was just pushing papers and telling a few people some useful information. Hardly a rebel. And it's true, he ended up in jail, but for staying a practicing Catholic. Like Jack's family. In truth, we were a boring family stuck in the middle of an extraordinary moment."

I could feel Jack's glare on me, his frustration. We'd performed this vaudeville routine countless times before—Jack setting up the story, then me coming over and coloring it in with details. About Castro coming for dinner, about hiding rifles in the house, about the rebels finding my parents' secret little chapel, my parents taking my sister and me to the airport for Pedro Pan before my father's arrest. Oh, I had learned to put on a good show. I just didn't feel like doing it that night.

"But you did come on Peter Pan, right?" Rebecca asked after a moment of awkward silence. "How wonderful that your parents were able to get you out when they did."

"Yes, truly wonderful. The U.S. convinced the parents of Cuba that the rebels were going to steal their children, just so they could take us all away and throw us into orphanages and delinquent homes. But, hey, at least we're Americans now, right?" I said and I felt that I could almost weep. "If you'll excuse me, I need to use the ladies' room."

In the powder room, I splashed water on my face, looked in the mirror, and felt a sense of profound disappointment. In myself. I had already realized, months ago, that Jack was a selfish man. I already knew how important it is for an artist to protect their time; time, that critical thing required to think and ponder and question and perfect. But I hadn't learned to assert myself. To assert the value of my own hours. To protect them, aggressively. Even from the man I loved. Because, it was not Jack's fault or Rebecca's fault or anyone else's at this opening's fault that I had not made anything worthwhile in months. What made the disappointment more sour, of course, was that I knew all of this. And still, here I was: in Berkeley instead of Florida.

If the people I met here tonight, if Jack himself, treated me like someone inconsequential, it was only because I hadn't done anything to prove otherwise.

The door to the restroom opened and it was Tilly, carrying a drink.

"Hi there," she said. "I thought you might need this."

"Thank you." I set it on the counter while I reapplied my lipstick.

"You look very fetching, Anita." She sounded sincere. I was about to thank her when she added, "That dress was made for you. Is that a Dior?"

"Halston," I said, flatly. My antennae went up, Tilly knows a Halston from a fucking Dior. "Jack has a woman at Bergdorf who helps him pick things."

"He's mentioned it."

Tilly was what I'd learned wealthy white people called a handsome woman. Tall and lanky, but dressed in a way that was elegant. She was brilliant; absolutely the greatest champion her artists could have behind them, but ruthless. Was never a fan of mine. Well, at least not my work. She told me, in her own polite way, to my face. But as far as I'm concerned, to dislike my work is to dislike me. Unlike my husband, I don't separate the two.

"This is a big night for Jack," Tilly said. "And he wanted you here by his side. Wanted to be sure you looked as gorgeous as possible, for you to be the one that he introduced people to."

"Tilly"—I picked up my purse and took a sip of my drink—"Jack has lots of big nights. I know because they take up a lot of mine."

"I'm trying to be a friend here, Anita."

"And what's your friendly advice? Just shut up and let him make my family history a prop in his one-man show?"

"My advice is this: choose. Lots of women come to New York to become things: actresses, artists, singers. And they don't all have the talent to make it, but they also don't all have your luck either."

"Excuse me?" I said.

"I heard that you saw my facialist at Helena Rubinstein," Tilly replied. And it was true, I had. She was excellent. "The personal shopper, those gorgeous earrings. Getting to travel around the world with someone who finds you gorgeous and fascinating and doesn't mind at all that you're a bit abrasive. Finds it challenging, even."

"And what the fuck are you trying to say, Tilly?"

"Lots of girls try to make it big doing something really hard and fail. There is no shame in that. But most of them don't meet and seduce the most successful artist of a generation."

"Seduce?" I said with a laugh, but I felt the vibrato in my voice. Not the quavering of tears but of anger. "I didn't move to New York to be a kept woman. I came to do my work."

I was much shorter than Tilly, and she looked down on me now with such a patronizing gaze. I wanted to slap her.

"Anita," she said, exasperated, "the only reason you can't sit back and enjoy it, the only reason why you bristle at how you're introduced, at how Jack talks about your family or your history, is because you're so intently caught up in being taken seriously as an artist. And I'm just telling you that you don't have to be. Jack doesn't care."

Her words, said with her clipped boarding school enunciation, clawed and scratched at me like a feral cat. Cloaked in the coo of gallery talk—the politeness of a museum powder room, but vicious. Made worse because I knew this wasn't conjecture; he had told her as much. He told her about the shopper and the facialist and that he didn't give a fuck if I was an artist or a housewife.

"But *I* care that I'm an artist."

A smile appeared on her face, one I remembered from when she looked at my portfolio; it was a smile doused in pity.

I bit my tongue. Resisted the urge, because the truth of the matter is she was just the messenger. An intervention based on what I could tell were many, many heartfelt conversations. I wanted to say, *You fucking puta! Wait till you see what I do with my career now. I will not stop until you can't walk into a museum anywhere in this world without seeing a fucking Anita de Monte. I won't stop until they refer to Jack as "Anita de Monte's boyfriend." Wait till I fucking show you.* But instead, I just said: "Well, thank you for that advice." And I walked out of the bathroom, slammed the rest of my drink, and got another.

After the opening, there was a dinner for donors and curators at a restaurant across town. Jack was drunk and I was on my way, but less so, as we made our way into the car.

"Did you have a chance to talk to Tilly?" he asked.

"I did."

"Good," he said. Cat grin on his face. He pulled me close to him and kissed me, as though this settled the matter. As if this meant that now that Tilly had spoken, I would cease to pursue my interests or request that I be introduced as having a profession or take issue with being exploited in order to make him more interesting. As if because Tilly had spoken, I obviously would just agree to get in line and stop making things awkward for the great Jack Martin. And when his lips were on mine—though there were many, many nights I had longed for Jack, lusted for him, actually—in that moment, my stomach churned in revulsion.

The private dining room of the French restaurant was gorgeous—one big, long table lined with candles. Someone, probably the earnest young woman who worked at the museum, had gone through the trouble of assigning seating—everyone's names elaborately calligraphed atop the menu cards—European style; spouses and partners separated to keep the conversation more lively. I found myself seated across from Jack, but next to Giancarlo, whom, at this point, I had not yet met—though, always one for a scandal, after this we became fast friends.

Everyone was drunk and high on coke except, maybe, Jack and me. The only two people I knew back then who didn't do coke. It was a funny thing that we bonded over, but it was also the reason that we could always tell, right away, when we were fucking with each other. Jack was, of course, in the center of it all. Always doing the absolute most anyone could in that situation. Ordering champagnes and caviar, insisting that he taste everything. It's funny how two years later, the same behavior that I once thought was the height of sophistication, I now registered as boorish and grotesque. And still, I married him! Romance is a bitch.

On one side of him was Rebecca, the curator, but on the other side, the young wife of a board member, and through the chatter I could hear him. She liked the Postimpressionists—loved van Gogh, Gauguin, all the heartbreak kids. And he kept, condescendingly, explaining to her how her opinions were at turns pedestrian, stupid, naïve, sentimental. All, of course, while placing his hand on her chairback and letting it graze her shoulder. At some point, he even brushed hair away from her face with his thumb. Then he went on to explain how only *his* art form—minimalism—would save us from racism and sexism and homophobia. How it was the removal of these things from the conversation of art that would allow us to see that we are all, in earnest, equal. You could see on her face that she wished she was next to anyone at all other than Jack. And in the meantime, Giancarlo—the only person who seemed remotely interested in me—started asking questions.

"Anita, are you still doing the works with blood that I had seen in *Art in America*?"

"Oh, no, darling, I'm not doing anything at all."

"But what do you mean?" Giancarlo replied. "You haven't stopped working, have you?"

"I think I am about to embark on a period of tremendous growth."

Rebecca, from the museum, gave a toast. They began serving the entrées. I had ordered the tartare; Giancarlo, the mussels. Everyone was settling into their meals when I decided that I wasn't going to fall in line. Not that night and, frankly, not ever.

I clinked my glass a few times, quieted the room.

"Escuuse me," I said, in my best Ricky Ricardo. "I would like to make a toast to de man of the night, Señor Yack Martín."

Everyone around the table now had their eyes on me, genuine expressions of curiosity on their faces. Jack, though, wasn't looking at me. His eyes bore into his tartare instead.

"Joo know what?" I said to the crowd. "I no think joo all can ear me so good. I am muy pequeñosita. Lemme make dis nice and easy."

I stood up on the chair, felt my stomach drop getting off the ground. But when I looked at Tilly's face of absolute horror from five place settings down, I decided it was worth it. Just for a minute or two.

"If joo don't know me, I'm Anita Tropicana and I'm Yack's novia Cubana. Jooo all know Yack is a briyiant arteest, but no many peeple know Yack es un oomanitarian muy grande. America save me from Castro y Yack save me from the life of a starving arteest."

"Get down from there, you fucking bitch." He gritted his teeth from across the table. It was more than a whisper, but not his full voice. I was too frightened to look down at him. I looked straight ahead and put a big smile on my face and kept going.

"Yack said, 'Joo no need to make art, Anita, I make art goo enough for both of us. Joo just sit and look pretty.'"

I could sense him moving, even though I couldn't look down. I could hear his footsteps, heavy and quick, close and then far and then close again, as he walked around the table. I just kept going.

"Y I yust say, thank joo! I no want to work so hard, anyway. Is so nice joo all celebray Yack tonight, y—"

I screamed despite myself, at the shock of being yanked off the chair. He threw me over his shoulder as he cursed me, quietly in my ears, calling me a bitch and a cunt and a fucking nightmare.

"Adios errrerybody! Adios!" I called out to the crowd, as he marched us out the door.

He walked us out to the car that the museum had sent, opened up the back door, threw me into the back seat, and told the driver to take me to the fucking house. I was on my way to the airport before he even got home; and I never, ever put Jack in front of myself again.

Jack

NEW YORK CITY • FALL 1985

By the time they came home—his home—from Tilly's party, they'd both quieted down, albeit for different reasons. He was drunk and hungry and utterly exhausted by the constant spectacle that being the husband of Anita de Monte had condemned him to. They screamed at each other the whole walk home. He tried to let up in the lobby—seriously, why give the doormen more to talk about? But she, of course, couldn't let it go. Not for a second. "*Oh, what? You don't want Doug to know that you're a jealous has-been?*" she taunted as he quickened his pace to the elevator bank. *Oh, you fucking bitch*, he'd thought to himself, *can't miss a chance to have an audience.*

Fighting was not new to them, of course. But lately, it had evolved. Early in their relationship, it was about her leaving. Always trying to pick up and head out for two, three, four months at a time. They were, he'd thought, building a life together and she simply gave no care about disrupting it. All because she claimed she couldn't work in the city. A real artist can work anywhere. "*My first sculptures I made with a typewriter because that's what I had access to*," he would tell her and she'd say, "*Those are poems, Jack, poems.*" And back in those days he would look at her, at her tiny, perfect face like a little doll, her round eyes perfectly deadpan when she said it, not even an edge of maliciousness behind her words. Just what she saw as a straightforward, honest correction. And he would melt; he would just fall back in love with her all over again. Scoop her up in his arms and carry her into the bed or the sofa or the nearest place he could lay her down and bury his face in her breast. Her belly button. Cherish her with a nuzzle of his rough beard in gratitude for being so immune to his pretense. They *were* just poems. They were just poems and people had let him go around for two decades calling them word sculptures and she was the first one to tell him to his face that they were just poems. Poems somebody hung up in a museum; framed. (Poems, he had to wonder to himself, that if they'd just been called poems, would they have gotten published anywhere? Jack Martin poems, of course. *Now.* But what if they didn't have his name on them? What about back then, all those years ago? Maybe. Maybe.) Anita would call them poems and then they would make love and then, a day, a week, sometimes a month later, she would leave. He hated it. Not just being away from her. He detested being leave-able. Of course, he wanted her to create new work. He had always wanted to help her. He just didn't like being left.

In the elevator, where normally she closed her eyes to mask her fear of the ascent, she was wide-eyed and vicious. "*You can't handle me rising, Jack. It just kills you inside.*" *The nerve*, he thought. Half the reason anyone knew her name at all was because she was his lover. His partner. His wife. He decided that he wasn't going to do this with her anymore tonight. Was no longer going to scream back. He thought this would deflate her, but it didn't. "*You can't handle that you're fading into extinction*," she taunted him and then she started muttering to herself in Spanish. She was performative. And not just in her art. Pacing the elevator in that ridiculous dress. Thousands of dollars' worth of dresses that he'd bought her hanging in his closet, some with tags on, and she was wearing this ridiculous thing that made her look like a guest star on *Laugh-In*.

By the time they got to the apartment door, though, she'd gotten the better of him. Again. "*What I can't handle is how delusional you are*," he'd hissed. "*When nobody even remembers the name Anita de Monte, they'll still be mounting exhibits of my work.*" And she'd laughed and patted his arm. "*Of course they will, Grandpa. In nostalgia shows about the big-dick swinging artists of the sixties. My steel rod is longer than your big fluorescent light.*" He put on the TV, loud, to drown her out as she padded around the apartment, ranting at him, pouring more fucking champagne for herself, taking out the leftover Chinese. He had forgotten about the Chinese. (Tilly never has enough food at these things.) He got up; headed to the kitchen as well. It was too small for the two of them but he didn't care; it was *his* house. She cursed him in Spanish and he didn't know the exact words, but knew she was calling him a fat pig. She's said it enough in English for him to know; to hear the disgust in her voice. He used to care, and he simply no longer did. He poured himself a scotch and took out the lo mein and scooped a big wad of noodles into his mouth with his fingers and just ate it in her face. Chewed it with his mouth open.

"It's a good thing for you that la sueca gigante wants to fuck you, Jack," she said.

He laughed out loud. This was more like it. This was their old fight. The imagined career rivalry shit, that was only the last year, maybe year and a half. But this—her jealousy, the anger about the other women—was classic. They'd been having *this* fight since at least 1980. He kept eating the lo mein. Ingrid loved him just as he was; didn't care that he'd gained some weight.

"It's only because you're famous that you can get away looking the way you do, you know," she hissed.

The MGM lion roared on the TV; the movie of the week was starting.

"Why don't you show me your work anymore?" he asked. He decided to just ask it. He'd been hinting and poking and passive-aggressively complaining about it. She used to show him everything. Asked his advice; sought his approval. Then, three years ago, she won the Rome Prize. She had a "breakthrough" and was barely in New York anymore. Always working and it was true, getting more notice, getting more high-profile attention. And suddenly she stopped showing him her work.

"This shit again?" She walked out of the kitchen, left the container of fried rice she'd been eating behind. "You don't like my work; never liked it. What am I showing it to you for?"

The phone started ringing.

"Get it," she yelled from the bathroom before he heard the toilet flush, "it's probably one of your other whores."

"Fuck you, Anita." He picked up the phone and immediately regretted it, because he could tell from the silence on the other line that it was her sister. She hadn't spoken to him since before their wedding nearly a year ago. "It's your sister."

He let the receiver drop to the floor, took his lo mein and his scotch and went to his easy chair in the living room; turned up the volume on the TV. It was *Without Love*, not his favorite, but any Tracy and Hepburn was better than listening to her complain about him in a language he couldn't understand. It was worse, somehow, than her going on and on at him in English. Rendered him powerless to defend himself.

When Anita criticized him, he'd wish himself a hermit crab; that he could shrink into himself and hide from her diminishments. Other times she filled him with rage. It drove him mad that she wouldn't show him what she was working on. It felt like deception. Like she was trying to hide something. When he'd accused her of that once she'd asked, "*Are your putas deceptions or omissions?*" He took this on the chin.

He blamed her for the other women. It was immature of him to do, of course, but he'd always been very up front about what he needed: companionship, emotional support. He was unaccustomed to a woman so intimate to his life not championing him. He didn't feel that his affairs were transgressions as much as logical outcomes to her absences. Yes, he had always slept around—from the very beginning. (If they were French, no one would have thought twice about it.) But it wasn't until she took the residency in Florida that he began the full-on affairs. To take the others out publicly. Was it meant to humiliate her? Not exactly. Was it meant to be punitive? Well, it was meant to show her that there were consequences to her actions. That yes, if she truly felt she could only work apart from him, fine. But he also had needs.

Of course, when she'd won the Rome Prize, he promised it would be different. *That* was not the kind of thing you could turn down; she had to go. He was opening a show in Germany that year and would fly back and forth to see her, but when Anita found out about the other woman in Berlin, she really lost it. He'd flown to Rome to reconcile and soon enough, they were planning a wedding. Marriage, he was certain, would change things. About her. About him. But a few months later he was showing in London and met Maeve. And shortly after that, Anita stopped showing him her work.

On the TV, Katharine's character and Spencer's character are trying hard not to fall in love with each other in order to save their marriage of convenience from jealousy and bickering. He wished them fucking luck.

He loved Anita ferally—raw, untamed, unapologetic. Oh, how she had needed him once! She needed him before she even knew him. His friend Arnold had called him, asking a favor for his wife who was trying so hard to break this new Cuban artist nobody had ever heard about. Would Jack be so kind as to sit on a panel with him at Leslie's new gallery? And he said yes, because he didn't believe in identity politics, but he knew there were politics of identity. That it was harder to make it in this world, let alone the art world, as a woman. And doubly hard if you were Black or Latin. Maybe even harder if you were Cuban; the faintest whiff of Communism floating in the air usually sent people running. He only got away with his beliefs because he was known for being countercultural. Anita had nothing but grit and a handful of numbers that her professor-slash-lover had handed her and, what he would admit, a very strong aesthetic sense. (Not his taste, this was true.) But she had no network; had no sense of refinement about how to discuss the work, how to defend it. And he was so eager to help her. He asked Tilly to look at her portfolio. (It was not his fault that it wasn't Tilly's taste either; she gave it an earnest look.)

Her portfolio! She'd met Rory from the Met that morning, had shown her the drawings she ended up buying. He lowered the volume of the television for a second. She was crying. Crying in Spanish to her sister. Very much in the midst. He went to the duffel bag she kept in the corner of the bedroom and saw the portfolio wedged against the wall. He opened it up on the bed, began to flip through. The empty sheets where the drawings Rory scooped up must have been; sketches for some of her body work: a figure whose arms and fingers were flowers, a buried silhouette on the shores of a beach. He kept flipping until he spotted the photographs, clearly taken recently in her studio in Rome. Beautiful clay sculptures in labyrinth shapes. Ancient, primitive things. He flipped another page and his heart stopped. His blood grew cold. Sick, sick, sick. Tall tree trunks, sliced in half, standing erect, all lined up together in a row. Just like his work! Just like his work! How many times had he set out 4 x 8's and 5 x 10's aligned in the shape of a pyramid or assembled like chess pieces ready for battle? That little witch! The fucking pirate! They were full trees, bark on, not like the lumber he used. And yes, she had carved out and burnished shapes and forms that reminded him of Kali or bodhisattvas on the inside of the trunks—crude illustrations. But the concept! The concept was his. The concept was *purely* his. And it became obvious why she had not been showing him her work. Because she was withholding. Hiding her theft. He was consumed with rage.

"Get off the fucking phone!" he bellowed.

"Make me!" she screamed over Katharine Hepburn's voice. He could hear her laughing at him to her sister.

He charged across the apartment, portfolio in hand. She was sitting on the floor, leaning against the wall under where the phone was mounted, and it took everything in him not to grab the receiver from her hand and beat her head in with it. He hurled the portfolio toward her and struck her in the face.

"What the fuck is this?" he screamed. "You're stealing from me now?"

She jumped to her feet, hung up the phone. Never taking her eyes off him, a smile came over her face.

"I'm stealing? Of course! Yes. *This* is why I didn't show you my work."

He picked the portfolio up, flipped to the tree trunk sculptures. "What is this then? What is this?"

She glanced at it and laughed. She laughed and laughed and he was stupefied. She had no shame. No shame at all.

"What did I steal? I stole wood, Jack? Jack Martin is such a god, he invented trees? Is that what's happening? I guess by that line of reasoning Picasso ripped off El Greco, huh? Because he also used paint?"

"You know what I mean, Anita. The exposed material. The formations."

"Do you know what Rory said when she saw these? She said that they were evolving the conversation around fine art. They were making it continually relevant. Do you know what Giancarlo said? That he'd never seen anything like them. That they would be instant classics."

"Classic because they remind him of my work."

"Jack, I know it's convenient for you to think that I'm a talentless nobody. It makes it easier for you to treat me like shit, but unfortunately for you, it's simply untrue."

She pulled the portfolio from his hand and retreated into the bedroom. He refilled his scotch and went back to his chair.

No one else could do this to him, strip him so raw. Like when she called his word sculptures poems, but now without the lust. He *didn't* own wood. He *didn't* own trees. What was he saying? No one could line up wood anymore? Should forests pay him homage?

She'd needed him when they first met, yes. But she was never afraid of him, ever. Never remotely fulsome. He had to give her that. She was a tough fucking cookie. It was so obvious she didn't want him at her opening; he remembered how annoyed Leslie was about it. Complaining to him and Arnold about how ungrateful she was; how fucking pushy. So Cuban. And then, he said something that he had, frankly, walked in knowing he would say. Something to the effect of *there shouldn't be feminist art*. It was the kind of thing he used to say back then, to provoke people. Knowing that people would hear it and flatten it into "*Jack Martin is a misogynist.*" Or "*Jack Martin is a racist because he said that we shouldn't have Black art.*" He liked to fuck with the public that way: obfuscating who he really was to push against this notion that the artist's psychology was the *real* art. So he said it and she popped up and told him to go fuck himself. Gave voice to the thought he suspected all the other women in the room probably held, but only she had the balls to articulate. And then.

And then, the thing happened that drew him to her with animalistic intensity—the very thing that *should* have made him run for the hills, to be completely fucking honest. The room was eerily still, when, as if given some sort of silent command by her, all of the pictures fell from the wall. Not one crash, not one nail jostled out of a piece of sheetrock. But one by one, each piece just popped off the wall, up, into the air before they fell and hit the ground. Like little paratroopers free-falling into combat. And they crashed, one after another, around the whole of the gallery, to the ground. At first everyone was quiet, trying to make sense of it all before a feeling came upon them; like a haunting. Then, it was like something out of a Buñuel film: everyone was screaming and jumping out of their seats. Surreal. And—he will never forget this for all his days—there in the center of it all was Anita. Sitting, calmly in her seat, not moving a muscle until the glass from the last frame fell to shards on the floor. And it was her work! *Her* show that was literally crumbling to the ground. He swore she had a tiny smile on her face, even, but wondered if he added that in his memory later. (Later, when he knew what a witch/bitch she really was.) As if she'd rather sit there and let it all burn than allow them to ignore her art. As if she was happy for all the fuss.

And in that moment, he just thought she was so fucking cool.

As a boy in Worcester, he'd saved a young little wren in his yard. His father thought it must have fallen from its nest. The first time he made love to Anita she reminded him of the little thing. Small and all alone in the world, undeterred by her weaknesses. Just determined to fly. And he wanted to be gentle with her even though she never requested or even required it. How he loved to cup her tiny, beautiful face between his hands and look down upon it. Just kiss those delicate eyelids and tell her everything would be OK. Not that she ever asked. How he loved it when she would cry, desperate to return to Cuba; still devastated that her parents had forced her to leave it. It wasn't that he loved her pain, he loved that she needed a home and he had wanted to give one to her.

He got up to refill his scotch. For a second, he lowered the volume and he could hear her riffling through the hangers in the closet, picking through her clothes. She was probably packing her stuff. Heading to her own apartment. Seven years of this. The marriage experiment less than one disastrous year old.

This time, he thought to himself, he should just let her go. He should really just let her go.

Raquel

PROVIDENCE • SPRING 1998

She couldn't help herself; she had to go through the medicine cabinet.

Raquel was well versed in the luxuries her classmates' parents availed for them: fancy video cameras, laptop computers, designer handbags and clothes. She envied little of it. These, she knew, were the signifiers of wealth that were easily simulated. Pedestrian markers that were, for the truly wealthy, merely window dressing. How many kids did she know who lived on her shitty block in Brooklyn that rocked head to toe Hilfiger or Ralph Lauren? How many girls were running around, like her, with a "Prada," even if some of them were real? Accumulating things that *seemed* to matter, but only because they were uninitiated to those that actually *did*: homes and stock portfolios and cars and watches and the furniture in those homes and art on those walls and second homes and boats and private planes. Things far from the grasp or even imagination of most of those who pretended. And, while Raquel aspired to one day have a base of wealth for herself, right now she coveted the less obvious signifiers. Things so private, so expendable, that no one of normal means would entertain spending money on such invisible extravagances. Raquel was obsessed with luxury toiletries.

Shampoos sold only in Paris. Cosmetics and perfumes you would never, ever find at Duane Reade (or even Macy's, for that matter).

From the first week on campus, when she took her shower caddy to the communal bathroom—filled as it was with Noxzema and Lemisol and Palmer's Cocoa Butter—she couldn't help but notice, as she looked around, how many girls were primping themselves with products she had never seen before. Beautiful packages that released even more magnificent scents. She'd note the look of the bottles, study the names on the tubes, zealously hunting them down in the fashion magazines she subscribed to, religiously, upon her arrival at Brown. And, on occasion, like a perfect grade on a paper, she splurged. Bobbi Brown, Lancôme, Aveda, Clarins, MAC. Each expendable item a secret way to remind herself of where she was headed. Of what she deserved.

Raquel suspected that the Art History Girls' shared medicine cabinet would be a treasure trove of products that she both envied and, perhaps, had not yet even heard of. It did not disappoint. There were French soaps that she suspected belonged to Mavette, Italian facial oils she'd never seen before, and not one but two different bottles of Benefit Benetint (retail $19.99 only in select department stores, none of which were near Providence). Hailed as a miracle product, it purported to give anyone of any complexion a natural flush on their cheeks and lips. Raquel, who planned on seeing Nick after this dinner, imagined herself ringing his bell with a perfectly lush berry lip like she'd seen in the advertisement. The girls, a little tipsy when she arrived, were now positively buzzed. If the results were as natural as they claimed them to be, no one would notice if she used a little dab, right? And if they did, it would be worth the risk to show the results off to Nick later. Outside the door there was a change in songs, and in the moment of silence she could hear them whispering about her. She shrugged it off and dabbed two dots on her cheeks. Let them talk. The product was even better than she'd read about. She tapped a dot on her lips, blended it with her fingertips, and then washed away the evidence.

At the small dining table, Claire was opening another bottle of wine, while Mavette served herself seconds of the elaborate salad Margot had made for them for dinner. The place was thick with incense.

Lou Reed played from the record player and Raquel wondered whose vinyl collection it was. The common area was just a vanilla painted cinder-block room with popcorn ceilings and a tiny kitchenette, but the Art History Girls had given it an atmosphere. Around the perimeter, they'd strung Christmas lights, but rather than litter the place with cheap art prints, as she would have suspected, they'd hung just one: a massive *Ciao! Manhattan* poster that went from the top of the ceiling down to the edge of an old velvet loveseat they had brought themselves. Edie Sedgwick's dark kohl-lined eyes looming large over the whole space. "*She's our patron saint*," Claire had explained when Raquel complimented the poster. The place was a veritable greenhouse and Raquel wondered if they shared the caretaking of these immobile children or if it fell to just one. Margot, she suspected, watered the plants.

"So," Claire said as she refilled Raquel's glass, "Nick Fitzsimmons."

"Is that what this dinner is about?" Raquel said, laughing. She'd anticipated them asking about him, but still found herself flushed under the Benetint at the thought of him. For two weeks there had been nothing but Nick. Indeed, this dinner was merely the cream in a delicious Oreo of him: they'd spent the afternoon in his studio together, him working on sketches and her studying for her art semiotics final. Barthes made so much more pleasant when broken up with the most savory of kisses. After dinner, Nick was taking her to a RISD party. A party, she realized with a bit of smugness, the Art History Girls had not been invited to.

"We suggested dinner *before* you got together," Margot said, pushing her plate aside and pulling out a lush green sprig of weed from a container on a side table. "I think."

"That's part of what we want to know," Claire offered, leaning in.

They had lit a number of candles on the dining table, all in elegant holders she suspected had been pilfered from their parents' houses. The light softened Claire's harshly chiseled features, lent her ordinariness a Dutch master luster.

"This was like a magic trick. One day you're wandering the campus alone and poof, the next week you're part of an inseparable couple. How did this happen?"

Raquel looked at Mavette, who shrugged her shoulders. "I'm Fort Knox," she said with a smile.

Raquel had run into Mavette on Thayer Street earlier that week and found herself gushing at the unexpected and seemingly miraculous turn of events not just in her heart but in her very life. Recounting to Mavette their meet-cute: how they lingered in the stone garden just behind the art building, finishing off a bottle of champagne. How she needed to go, though she didn't want to, but she and Marcus hosted an open mic thing downtown. And how, despite it being such a big night for Nick and his parents being here, he'd offered to walk her. It surprised her, but also, "Mavette, you just can't understand how easy it is to talk to him; it was like the greatest conversation of my life with someone I just met." And how they walked along the river and it was like "*Before Sunrise* but, you know, in Providence." ("Providence is no Vienna," Mavette interjected.) But he didn't kiss her goodbye and for the rest of the evening, she could barely focus on the music. The butterflies in her stomach that night almost stopped her from being able to sleep, and she woke the next day wondering when she might have a chance to run into him again. And then. "And then, the next morning my phone rang. And it was him. And he wondered if I wanted to get coffee. And I said, 'Sure, when?' And he said, 'I was thinking right now.'" And she told Mavette about how the coffee turned into a walk, which turned into lunch at Basha, which turned into a movie at his house, which turned into a kiss. "The kind of kiss that, I don't know, you can just viscerally remember it, you know?"

They didn't sleep together. They still hadn't slept together. Raquel didn't want to explicitly tell him that she was a virgin, but she felt OK letting him know that she didn't have a ton of experience and wanted to "take things slowly." She was sure that he would rebuff her at that point—head out into the night seeking more satisfying prospects for company. She was sure he could find a girl who didn't have their mother's voice in their ear tormenting them about the perils of penises derailing dreams. But he hadn't done that. Instead, he suggested another film for them to watch, made popcorn, and gave her sweats to wear. When it got late, he said she should just sleep over. She was skeptical, but he assured her that's all he meant. So they slept side by side on his futon, his arms around her waist, sometimes waking in the night and finding each other's lips, his hand fluttering under the T-shirt that he'd given her to sleep in, but not much more. In the morning, he took her to Louie's for breakfast and then walked her to the station, where she tried her best to hide the extent of the explosion happening within her chest, the sensations pulsing in her breasts and body. She tried her best, but everyone noticed something was up and clowned her for it, in the best-natured way. "*I think*," Marcus said, "*Raquel's been bitten by a white boy.*"

But, of course, she wasn't going to tell the Art History Girls all of this. Didn't tell them that she'd never longed for someone's company the way that she longed for his. Never had someone who confided in her about his ambitions and insecurities and pressure to live up to his parents' high hopes for his career. No, she did not share that; instead, she said:

"I mean, I don't know. We met at his opening, after you guys left, and he was just really different than what I'd imagined."

"You'd never talked to him before?" Margot asked skeptically. She finished packing the bowl and was about to light it. "You're friends with his sister."

Raquel decided not to add her typical caveat about Astrid being her Art History Friend. Astrid, she realized, was her actual friend. She knew this because Raquel hadn't quite been able to tell Astrid that she and Nick were—she felt a rush of excitement even thinking the term—"together" now. Fearing, she supposed, that it would seem like a betrayal. Or, maybe, that it wasn't yet quite real. In any case, if Astrid knew, she hadn't said anything either. Likely, Raquel imagined, hoping the whole affair would just quickly pass.

"They, um"—Raquel hesitated here, unsure of how to protect all parties involved—"they aren't very close and Astrid likes to have her own social circle."

"Interesting," Mavette said, a little edge in her voice. She took the bowl from Margot, but her focus stayed on Raquel. She wondered if Mavette knew that she knew about Astrid and Niles. She wondered if Mavette meant something more; what she might know about Nick. But she was too afraid, in front of the others, to expose her raw heart and ask. Too distrusting of them to let them see the way in which she had absolutely fallen.

"So," Claire said, as if she could read her mind, "is this true love? Like, the real deal?"

"We're just kind of hanging out, I guess."

Claire looked toward the door where Raquel had left her blazer, faux Prada, and a small tote bag full of clothes.

"Looks like a little more than hanging out," she said as she took the pipe from Mavette.

"Listen, Raquel, we're happy for you," Claire said, but it was hard to miss that she hardly seemed happy. "This is a big level up for you, socially speaking."

"Excuse me?" Raquel said and felt a knot cinch quick and tight in her belly. "What the fuck does that mean?"

"No one on this campus knows who you are and suddenly, right before your last year here, you've managed to enter into a very public . . . whatever it is with Nick Fitzsimmons? This super well-known, up-and-coming artist."

Raquel knew that Claire would never understand or comprehend that in *her* world, the Third one, it was Nick that nobody had heard of. That it was only her budding relationship with him that had served to differentiate him from the thousand other clean-cut white guys on campus.

"If this was a popularity ploy, Claire, why would I pick a fucking senior who won't even be here next year?"

"He's like, up-and-coming in the real world too," Claire retorted. "You think that won't carry some weight with the faculty when it comes time to apply for jobs?"

Raquel was proud of Nick's accomplishments, but she was also proud of her own. Of course, she felt the tiniest shimmer of excitement when and if she was spotted with Nick by one of the professors from the art building. That she was serious and smart and knowledgeable (and pretty) enough to excel in her studies *and* attract someone like him.

"*And*," Claire continued, "not like you don't know this, but he's super rich."

This last part surprised her when she heard it out loud. It was not like she didn't know. Of course, she was always aware—with her entitlement and disregard—that Astrid had money. Knew the schools they had gone to. All the family trips she would casually reference in conversations about art: China, France, Istanbul, South Africa (to meet Mandela). By the transitive property, that meant that Nick had money, but she had not actively thought of him as a "rich person." He just was.

"Did you guys know his parents own a custom Jack Martin?" Claire said to everyone and no one at once. "His mom went all over the East Side bragging about it a few years ago."

That information surprised her until she remembered that Astrid had mentioned it—and her mother's embarrassing level of pride in it—during their lecture on Martin and Stella. Raquel's brain now took inventory of all the signs. The champagne at the reception, the quality of towels in his bathroom. He always paid when they went anywhere, but *that* Raquel had not thought about at all. Her mother had repeatedly told her that a man should pay if he was interested in spending time with a woman, and nothing feminism had proffered seemed to convincingly counter that logic. But she had not actually labeled him, in her mind, a rich guy.

Claire had put the bowl back on the table. Didn't even offer it to Raquel.

"I mean," Raquel started to say, "even if he is, that's got nothing to do—"

"It's just kind of a riot, isn't it? Mavette told you our summer plan, told us how you shat all over it and now here you are—"

"I am not into Nick because of his money," Raquel retorted. "That's ridiculous. My summer plan is to stay here and work at the—"

"You're a racist, Raquel!" Margot suddenly shouted. She had been sitting in stoned silence all this time; Raquel had barely remembered she was there. Before she could even wrap her head around this accusation, Claire jumped in.

"She's kind of right, Raquel. All this time, you don't even talk to white people unless they're faculty, and suddenly Mavette tells you our idea and, next thing you know, you've got a white boyfriend who happens to come from not one but two New York trust fund families?"

"What? What are you talking about? I'm not a racist."

"Tell us the name of a white friend that you have," Margot asked flatly. "*Besides* your boyfriend's sister."

"I can't be a racist. Minorities can't be racist because we are the victims of racism."

"Everyone can be racist," Mavette added casually. She was flipping through a magazine. These girls were pulling her apart and Mavette was reading fucking *Seventeen* magazine.

"See," Claire said, the edge familiar to Raquel from classroom debates suddenly back in her voice, "Mavette agrees and Mavette is a minority. So that's that."

Raquel's heart was racing. How had this unraveled to this point? How had she arrived for a dinner and was now being called a racist gold digger by these women she barely knew? Her instincts said to leave, but she felt compelled to defend herself.

"Racism is about power," she said, icily to Mavette before turning to Margo and Claire. "I have no power here. I can't be racist because I don't have more power than white people. I don't have more power than you, here."

"Oh my God," Margot said, with some disgust in her voice. She leaned forward and picked up the pipe again. "This is exactly why my father didn't want me to come here."

"I thought it was the coed dorms," Raquel managed to quip.

"It is. It's all of it. All of it." Margot had a manic edge in her voice, despite the pot. "All of the fucking whining. You're here the same as me. That makes us the same. If I have power, you have power. If you feel like a victim, it's because you choose that role."

Raquel felt the wrongness of this in the gut of her stomach. The fundamental lie of it. They were both there, yes. In the same school, in the same class, in the same major, even in the same dorm room at that very moment, and yet she could not even begin to list the litany of ways in which they were not the same. Her throat was closing with anger, but also overwhelm.

"I never said I was a victim," she choked out through gritted teeth.

"Right," Claire sneered, "you only said you were powerless."

Before Raquel could think of what to say, Claire continued.

"Lucky for Raquel, Nick's family is very powerful. That should help. His mother is on the board of MoMA, did I tell you guys that?" She looked at Mavette. "Do you have a clove?"

Raquel did not know his mother was on the MoMA board. Or maybe she did and forgot that too? Honestly, she did not think of the names on those brass plaques as being real people.

"The fucking MoMA board!" Mavette replied as she gestured to the cloves on the bookcase. "Damn, Raquel. You really did it."

"I didn't *do* anything," Raquel said now. Mavette hadn't seemed cruel in her words but Raquel felt the room shrinking under the weight of the inquisition. "We're just hanging out."

"You know, Raquel," Claire said, "you're not stupid. That's the thing. And I don't mean in class. We all see how you work John Temple; how you manipulate the faculty. This poor, pitiful public school kid routine. Poor little minority, always so fucking earnest about how hard she works."

"Who," Margot interjected, "just happens to be this hot Latin girl who throws herself at her adviser."

Raquel wasn't going to take this anymore. She stood up and headed toward the door, but Claire stepped in her path.

"I want to leave now," Raquel whispered, her voice choked by the tears in her throat.

"You can only imagine what she did to get Temple to write that RISD recommendation," Margot continued, rising now to stand shoulder to shoulder with Claire. The pale skin on Margot's bare arm touched Claire's freckled one and, even through her wet eyes, Raquel noticed Claire's flesh goose pimple.

"For fuck's sake," Mavette said from the sofa, exasperation in her voice. "You're out of line, Margot."

Raquel glared at her. That was the best she could do? Mavette was watching an assault and all she could do was sideline referee?

"Let me go," Raquel said as she tried to push her way past the two girls, who moved in tandem, blocking her in each direction. She desperately wished to channel the Brooklyn in her; to scrape and tear at these bitches' faces, but Brown had washed the street away from her. Left her clawless in a different kind of wild.

"Not till you admit it," Margot said.

"Admit what?" Raquel said. She physically felt herself ill. Her breathing became more difficult, ensnared as it was by these twists of words and logic. "I didn't do anything."

"But you did."

Raquel thought about the Benetint. This couldn't be about the Benetint.

"Just tell me what to admit and I'll admit it. I just have to get the fuck out of here."

"You stole our spot!" Margot screamed, her pale pink skin red from anger.

"What the fuck are you talking about?" Mavette yelled, rising now.

"We all couldn't make it, fine. I get that. But Claire practically grew up in a gallery and there is no way that you were more qualified for that RISD fellowship—"

"What?" Raquel said, desperate to summon a rage and unable to find it. Her only attempt at defense were the words, "No! No!"

"What the fuck are you talking about, Margot?" Mavette said, but Margot ignored her.

"Just admit that you are a talentless nobody who rode affirmative action into that spot," Claire said sharply. "And then we'll let you go."

A sweat was coming on Raquel's temples and chest, the room claustrophobic with pot smoke and cigarette smoke and the fucking Lou Reed droning on in the background. And none of it was true.

Nothing that they said was true, but she wanted to get out of that room so badly she would have said anything that they wanted.

And so she did.

* * *

"YOU LOOK GREAT," Nick said when he'd first seen her, pulling her toward him for a kiss, his hand firm on the small of her back. Electricity down her spine. He'd said it with such sincerity that Raquel wondered if "tear-stained" could be an emergent beauty look. "Mitch's place is just up the street."

"Great," she said; happy to be with him but nervous to be on display meeting all these new people.

"You aren't cold?" he asked.

Her blazer! She'd grabbed her bag so fast that she forgot her jacket. And her bag of clothes! Fuck. She'd never see those things again, she decided. Would rather throw them away than talk to those putas again. There was a mist in the air that made the night damp, and yet she hadn't noticed until Nick said something. The adrenaline pumping through her generating such heat, she'd walked the dozen blocks from Young Orchard to Nick's place on Wickenden without once feeling the chill.

"I'm OK," she said, dismissively.

But Nick had already taken his jacket off and was draping it over her shoulders.

"Nordic blood," he said. "I don't notice the cold. It's a quick walk anyway."

"Thanks," she said, warmed in equal measure by the jacket as his much-needed kindness.

"Have fun at dinner?" he asked.

She actually laughed out loud. Hadn't intended to, but the dinner had been absolutely the opposite of fun. Distressing, disgusting, degrading. But definitely not fun.

"Wait," he said, with a little chuckle. "What did I miss? I just asked if you had fun with your girlfriends?"

She giggled even harder, at how clearly misaligned his vision of her evening was from her reality. Him imagining girlfriends, sipping wine and sharing *Cosmopolitan* articles, utterly clueless to her having been humiliated and made to beg her way out of their presence. Maybe it was because just moments before she'd been doubled over in sobs so guttural, they had frightened her—that such quantities of shame and sadness needed a release—but now she could not stop laughing. Her chortle so riotous—bubbling up from the belly—that Nick started laughing too.

"I have no idea why I'm even fucking laughing," he said now. "Why are you laughing? Tell me why we're laughing?"

And this just made her cackle more wildly. How insane the whole thing was, how fucking crazy those bitches were. They both had tears coming down their faces, the giggles so intense in Raquel, she had to stabilize herself against a parked car.

"I'm laughing because . . ."

But her laughing was too intense to continue.

"You can't even fucking talk," Nick said, in hysterics. "Get ahold of yourself, Toro!"

He put his hands on her shoulders, tried to get her to stand up straight, tried to keep his own serious face, which only caused them both to laugh more. A joy washed over her then, a relief. They might have tried, but those girls hadn't succeeded in tainting this: the one perfect thing she'd found in this place. She caught her breath.

"I'm laughing because I hate those cunts and it was one of the worst nights of my life."

Which only set them both off again, giggling so hard that Nick's face turned a full lobster red and Raquel started to cough; falling into each other's arms to try to make the laughter stop because they had lost control of it. Their stomachs and faces now in actual pain. And when they finally calmed down, and the laughter finally subsided, they stood, wrapped in an embrace, letting the endorphins wash over them, the hysteria replaced with a calm, soothing sense of being together.

"For what it's worth, those kinds of girls are always the worst," Nick stated after they made a quick stop in a liquor store. "I've been in schools with them my whole life. Scratch the surface and there's nothing but layer after layer of beige paint."

"Yeah, I sort of figured," she said. The Art History Girls suddenly felt so far away, pushed away by Nick's hand, now interlaced firmly with hers. "Tonight was just confirmation."

"If you knew you didn't like them," Nick asked, "why'd you say yes to the dinner?"

She squeezed his hand a little tighter.

"I don't know," she said. "You don't ever do things you don't really want to do?"

"I try hard not to. My own way of bucking the bourgeoisie, I guess. Just allergic to that whole upper-class phony thing, you know?"

She wasn't a phony. Didn't want him to think that of her. How could she tell him that she was lonely and her best friend only wanted to talk about which Bad Boy releases were coming out when and if the local tattoo parlor was going to renew their advertising package or not? How would she explain that she knew the Art History Girls were pieces of fucking basura, but thought it was a step toward a future friendship with Mavette? How could she tell him that she wanted a best girlfriend for her last year at this place without sounding like a loser?

"You always knew you were gonna come to a school like this, right?"

"I thought I'd be at Bennington, to be honest, but my dad went here—"

"Same difference. It's a place like this," she said, a little annoyed at his naïveté. "See, I didn't. Or, maybe I didn't know what it meant."

"What do you mean, what it meant?"

"I had a best friend in high school," Raquel said, "this girl Denise. She's Black. Our school was mad diverse, but not in the AP classes, and we were in *all* the honors classes together. We rolled deep: in class, after school, studying. She got into Notre Dame and I got in here, but when push came to shove, Denise decided on SUNY Buffalo."

"Over Notre Dame?" Nick said, with a note of skepticism that got Raquel's back up.

"Don't judge her; she'd gotten a full ride. But, I remember thinking she was taking the easy way out and not betting on herself like I was—"

"So, *you* were judging her, is what you are saying?"

Raquel rolled her eyes.

"Coño," she said, "lemme finish my story! That's part of my point. I figured, what were some loans to come out of a place like Notre Dame? And do you know what she told me? She told me when she went to visit she could count the other Black kids on her fingers and why would she pay good money to be tokenized. Anyway, three years later, she is having the time of her life. This summer, she's interning at *Vibe*—for no money, because she can, since school is free. And she just has a ton of friends because, well, everybody is like us."

"There's a lot to be said for self-improvement, Raquel."

She stopped in her tracks and looked at him. Something about the laughter made her feel she could be herself—her real self—with him.

"You think *you're* an improvement? Is that what you're saying?" she asked.

He had the same sheepish look as when she'd confronted him about his art.

"I just meant," he said, very tenderly, "that the entire world wouldn't think coming to a school like this wasn't a better opportunity than where Denise is if it wasn't."

She accepted that. The whole world couldn't be wrong, right?

"Besides," he continued, "you have this amazing internship this summer, that pays well—even if Astrid did tell our parents that it paid nothing so that she can keep getting her funny money from them."

"Your sister can scam with the best of them," Raquel said with a chuckle. "That internship pays hella good too."

They walked in silence for a minute and she thought about her visit to see Denise their freshman year. Nick was from New York, but not *her* New York. It would be impossible to explain to him—who had never been around kids like her and Denise and the people they grew up with—just how easy it was to *be* at SUNY Buffalo. How nobody had enough of anything and it wasn't a thing to be ashamed of. How you could go to and from the bathroom with your bonnet on in the morning and not have to field twenty questions from white girls about what that was and why you were wearing it. (It wasn't that there weren't tons of white girls or that Denise didn't know any. They just weren't ignorant or at least not spoiled enough to feel entitled to know.) More than anything, she felt that the whole campus belonged to Denise. Every facet of the experience. And it wasn't as nice as Brown, not at all, but it was all hers. They barely saw each other now, her and Denise. They were both too broke for the long-distance calls and Raquel was hardly ever in New York anymore. Just the occasional email to say hello, fill the other person in, see if they were OK.

"I guess," Raquel said now, "the real reason I went to the dinner is because I thought it might be good—since I only have one more year here—to try and expand my social circle."

Nick stopped walking, placed the bag from the liquor store on the hood of a parked car, and pulled her tight into him.

"Isn't that what we're doing?" he said before he kissed her, winding his fingers into the curls at the nape of her neck, and she felt her body tense and then relax.

* * *

THE PARTY ANNOUNCED itself as unusual for Raquel by the giant pile of shoes on the apartment landing.

"Mitch is a neat freak," Nick said, "absolutely zero-tolerance shoe policy. Fantastic host though."

Past the threshold, a shimmery space, the likes of which Raquel hadn't seen at a college party before. It had neither the sloppy, aggressively sexual air of the First World parties she had been to, nor the approximated nightclub vibe that Third World parties have: bass booming, lights off, anything anybody could do to make the space better to dance till you sweat. Mitch's living room glowed. From scarves draped over lamps, twinkle lights set on top of bookshelves, candles. The room heady with the scent of pot and, strangely, potpourri. The crowd had dressed to be seen: the fashion students at RISD clearly the standouts, but sartorial statement was clearly a point of the evening.

There were bowls of snack mix set around the room; a fancy, old-fashioned punch bowl set on a table with a few trays of deviled eggs. All around were clusters of people clutching their red cups—flirting, arguing, telling stories. It all felt very . . . adult. The music, older, indie stuff—Björk, the Pixies, Portishead—was just loud enough to allow conversation, but also claim this as a creative (white) space. And it *was* white. By this point it was reflexive instinct for Raquel to scan a room and try to find the people of color, the way someone might locate emergency exits on a plane. For a sense of security. She counted, at quick glance, two people who might be biracial, and three Asian or Asian-Americans in the room. Plus her. Six. Out of probably sixty guests. It didn't matter; this was about exploration.

Someone—she assumed Mitch—greeted Nick with a degree of excitement Raquel realized could only be reserved for someone bringing more alcohol and led them into the kitchen. Mitch had graduated from RISD two years before but still retained that ironic art school thing where he dressed like an off-duty mobster—wifebeater, suspenders, khakis—but with no sense of irony. He was from a wealthy family in Virginia who supposedly did something with the Clintons. He was, however, an incredibly attentive host, who immediately started putting the beer Nick brought into a lovely silver ice tub and offering to make them cocktails.

"Mitch," Nick said, putting his arm around Raquel, "this is my girlfriend Raquel."

Mitch grabbed a Costco-sized bag of Chex Mix from off the kitchen counter.

"Great meeting you," he said, giving her an air kiss. "I've gotta freshen up my snack bowls before somebody gets too hammered and makes a mess in my bathroom."

When he left, Raquel couldn't hold back her surprise.

"Really now? Girlfriend?" she said with a laugh.

Nick gave her a quick kiss. "I mean, I've let you sleep in my gym shorts. I don't do that for everybody. Ready to meet the masses?"

She grimaced a little bit. The Art History Girls had worn her out. She wished they'd stayed in and just watched a movie. But before she could say anything, he grabbed her by the hand and led her into the vast unknown.

The evening was, for Raquel, a revelation. She had grown familiar with the many nameless faces she encountered in the art building but had ceased, she realized, seeing them as people. As people she could come to know. She assumed that, because they resided in different campus universes, they must have nothing in common. And yet, here she was, Nick introducing her to everyone as "the brilliant Raquel," and finding herself floating easily between conversations about independent films, art, and the faculty, whom everyone loved to gossip about. She found that she more than held her own in a space where she had been certain she would drown. She felt herself a star. Yes, surely she was haloed in the glow of being there as Nick Fitzsimmons's date, but she also brought her own light. She could feel it.

They had been there for a while when Mitch came up and pulled Nick aside, a look of concern on his face. Nick excused himself with assurances of being right back and, for a second, Raquel—untethered to any particular group or tête-à-tête—felt a panic. She was willing the social strength up to insert herself into a conversation when she heard a voice behind her.

"Broccoli! What are you doing over here?"

It was Julian. A smile broke on her face—somebody she knew on her own.

"What are you talking about?" she said, even though she knew exactly what he meant. "I go to parties!"

"Not these kinds of parties," he said. Because he loved hip-hop nearly as much as Raquel did, she often emailed him about Third World parties happening off campus or might run into him at Funk Night at the campus bar. He was a crazy dancer, but the Third World gave him a lot of props for being so chill with being the only white dude in a room. She noticed how easily he blended into this world too. His oversized Knicks jersey and his paint-stained cargo shorts reading less "urban" in this setting and more blasé art student.

"It's different, huh?" She laughed.

"Lots of 'scintillating conversation,'" he joked. "But Mitch is mad cool; lets me deal a little weed. It's like minting money at these things."

"No shit?" she said. She'd always assumed he, like almost everybody at RISD, was rich.

"I'm trying to make my own beats; set up my own studio," he said.

"That's dope."

"You're here alone?"

"Oh no, I'm here with Nick. Fitzsimmons," she said, and found herself smiling before she added, "my boyfriend."

And though she'd had a few drinks, it would have been impossible to ignore the smile fall from his face. Before she could press him, she heard Nick yelling her name from across the living room with a passed-out Astrid in his arms.

"Raquel!" he yelled again. "We've gotta go."

She wove her way through the crowded living room, but Nick was already heading down the stairs by the time she got to the doorway. A very anxious Mitch hovered on the landing.

"What the fuck happened?" she asked as she rushed to find her Air Maxes.

"This fucking bitch went down a K-hole with Niles, had a freak-out, and locked herself in my fucking bathroom," Mitch said, exasperated. "Just sloppy, sloppy kid shit."

"People still do ketamine?" Raquel said, as she struggled with her laces.

"People still do everything," Mitch said. "Shut the front door on your way out."

Outside the mist had thickened to a fog, and she could barely make out Nick's figure, silhouetted by the streetlamps—Astrid's head and feet, dangling on either side of his arms, like a strange pietà.

"Nick!" She screamed out, but he didn't pause, just kept up his trodding. She jogged a bit to catch up with him.

"Hey!" she said. "Fuck, is she totally out of it?"

"Where were you?" he snapped.

"What?" she said, confused. "You said you'd be right back—"

"Right, and when I wasn't, you didn't notice?"

"I ran into a friend," she said.

He met her words with a strong silence. She felt as chilled by him as she was the damp air. She wasn't sure if he was embarrassed by his sister or what, but his reaction felt outsized for the situation.

"Look," she said, "I'm here now. I'm sorry this happened. I was having fun."

He finally stopped, draped his sister over his shoulder, shook out his arms, and let out a sigh before he started walking again.

"She loves to fucking ruin good nights, I'll say that about Astrid."

Raquel winced; she felt weird about this.

"She does it for attention," he continued. "I've always just been good at things: music, art. People pay attention to me. And, I don't know, the drug shit is like her way of trying to stand out."

Raquel went to touch his arm, to comfort him in this small way.

"I can hear you, cocksucker," Astrid mumbled.

Her voice startled Raquel. She let out a small yelp, which caused Astrid to open an eye, lift up her head.

"And you," she said to Raquel, "can do better than my brother."

She immediately closed her eye and her head fell like dead weight over Nick's shoulder again. As though all of her energy to come out of her K-hole had been expended on delivering those two messages and the hilarity of it—her intergalactic travel to curse out her brother and tell Raquel he wasn't good enough for her—gave them both the giggles again.

After Nick put Astrid down in the extra bedroom; after he pulled out a couple of beers from the fridge and they sat on the porch downloading the night; after he gave her a foot rub using, she noted, Kiehl's hand and foot cream, Raquel told him she was ready. He asked if she was sure. She had never felt more certain of anything except taking a chance and coming to Brown in the first place. She'd felt her life had already changed so much that night, why not change this one, last thing. And though he was very gentle, and though she pretended that it didn't when he asked her later, it most definitely hurt. Sharp and tearing and it lasted the next day and the day after that. But, by this point, Raquel already knew.

Everything worth doing hurts at least a little bit.

Anita

NEW YORK CITY • FALL 1978

So, the beginning of the beginning; that's probably important to know. It was a gimmick. A ploy. A desperate marketing move—like when they made Billie Jean King play tennis with that chauvinist buffoon—mounted by my gallerist to draw a crowd to my first solo show in New York. That is how Jack and I came to meet.

"*Men talking about women's art!*" Leslie had said. "*Isn't that just marvelous?*" But I didn't think that was marvelous and I told her as much. Men, I said, can talk about anything. Anywhere. Why must they opine about us in a gallery for women? And why must they do so at *my* opening?

Leslie ran the Venus Collective, a small gallery founded by a group of white feminist artists who were "beyond excited to show Latin art." Especially work as innovative as mine, Leslie had said. I believed that, actually. I still believe that. Leslie was a champion for me. It's just that she had no spine. Despite whatever potential she thought my career had when she offered me the show, ultimately she panicked. Gripped with concern that no one would come out, "*just to see an unknown 'Third World Artist.'*" Particularly since I didn't come out of New York. "*You say Iowa to people here and they just shut down,*" she said. I assured her that I would pack the place with people. Yes, I was new to the city, but I'd also made a lot of friends. Well, acquaintances, but who cares? Leslie was unswayed. And so, in addition to the traditional opening reception—the requisite wine and cheese and crackers and bossa nova—the gallery would also host a "talk."

"*I'm only trying to help you pull a crowd, Anita,*" Leslie had said, not even trying to hide her exasperation. It was obvious that I annoyed her. Not for calling out her hypocrisy but for seeming ungrateful. Little brown immigrant girl getting this big, shiny white chance in the city. Why couldn't I just take my opportunity and like it? And I didn't know why, actually. I only knew that I couldn't.

"*Besides, isn't just* any *men. It's my husband—who is very well regarded in the land art movement—and Jack Martin.*" As soon as I heard his name, the tiny little hairs on the back of my neck rose up. My skin prickled. Not with some sort of sense of romantic foreboding. Please. No, because who invites a supernova to the launch of a star? Leslie, that's who. In all the publicity—the press release, the advertisements in the *Village Voice* announcing the show—his name was up top. Big and in all caps.

JACK MARTIN
In conversation with
ARNOLD GOLUB
How feminist art practices impact male artists
Moderated by Leslie Golub
Presented by The Venus Collective
in celebration of the opening of
Anita de Monte
"Dirt, River, Blood"

The only thing smaller than my name was the time, date, and address for the event. And yes, Leslie was right. The night of the opening, the place was packed; full of people and smoke. I was talking with two of the members of the collective. They were congratulating me on the show, commenting on how Third World art was really having a "moment." "*Yes,*" I'd replied, "*but don't you think a permanent place would be better than a passing measure of time?*" The women laughed. Awkwardly. And then I heard it. The comment caught in my ears like a fly on a trap. "*Is it art? Or feminist stunts?*" A man's voice. Of course. I willed myself to stay focused on the women, one of whom replied with some bullshit about progress being incremental. But in my mind, I was turning around, hunting down the body attached to the voice and hissing, *Cabrón, let me see* your *art. What gallery is showing* you, *you prick?* What Leslie hadn't factored in, that frankly seemed obvious to me, is that yes, Jack Martin drew lots of people to my opening, just not many with interest in me. Instead, the room was full of men who came to hear Jack Martin—the messiah of minimalism, the evangelist for divorcing identity from art—reaffirm their worldview: feminist art was unnecessary. And, from what I was eavesdropping in the gallery that night, most of these men not only hated feminist art but, I suspected, hated women as well.

Sure, there were positive things being said. Let me not dismiss that. That night launched my career. Not just because of the gossip it generated. There were people who left and talked about the work. Really connected with it. I overheard the critic from the *Village Voice* say that he found the show sensual and real. The woman from *Ms.* magazine told me she found it "*organic and imperative.*" And, of course, my friends came and brought their friends. I'd only been in New York for three months, but someone made the introduction to Jomar Burgos, and I found a brother. He was a Boricua from New York. Brown like milk chocolate and tall as a streetlamp. Had never been to his island, had been thrust from his home at a young age. Maybe that's why we bonded, both of us strangers to our mothers and our motherlands. He was a phenomenal painter and knew all the Latin artists. The poets, the actors, the filmmakers. We'd stay up all night, rambling in Spanish about art and sex and film and books. And it was thrilling. In Iowa it was *always* English. And when my sister and I did speak Spanish, it was about sad things: my mother's depression, my father's imprisonment. So, it delighted me to have them there, buzzing about me in Spanish. Yes, there were positives that night, this is true. But the panel, and the people it called in? Well, it was a piece of shit.

I believe in energy, you know? Energy is a real thing. The energy an artist imbues into their work, the energy that transforms two strangers into lovers. People carry their energy with them when they enter a room. These spaces, these events: they are pockets of it. An art viewing less about one individual's objective reaction to the work they're seeing than about how they felt while they were viewing it. And the Jack Martin acolytes brought the energy of resistance that I worried would taint the way the work was received. That the conversation was happening *after* the reception only made it worse. The last impression people would have of the night was not going to be of the pieces—my pieces—that I had *literally* bled and sweat for, but of the careless opinions of Jack Martin and Leslie's husband. And that just pissed me off. Because the work was good. Better than good.

I had organized it by subject. Land was to the north: still images of my earth-flower-body works. The ones that grew from my dreams of being buried alive, swallowed whole by the soil of the American Midwest. Water was to the south. Photographs from my river series: my body, wedged between rocks and camouflaged with silt—eyes shut under it, my mouth a barely discernible slit. A short film from the same project: my figure—gradually unearthed, washed clean, by the flow of the Iowa River. Water running over my face and fingers and breasts and legs. The flow carrying my Cuban-ness—my language, my tan skin, my sense of self—out to the great Mississippi. I nearly drowned making that piece, the current filling my nostrils as I lay perfectly motionless. The western wall was windows, but on the east, the longest wall, I hung blood and fire. My favorite pieces. Close-ups: my eyes gory and face bloodied. Stills of my naked frame, covered in blood in an empty room surrounded by chickens, their feathers sticking to my thighs and arms and face. That series: an exorcism; a terrible recollection of one of our foster homes. You can't imagine the things that happen to children when adults see them as dispossessed. On either side of the blood work I'd hung stills from the fire series. My silhouette running, ablaze, through a cornfield in Iowa. It was the last happening I had staged before I moved to New York. The piece I'd finished with Isaac's help.

It was Isaac who named me. Called me an artist and in doing so introduced me to my true self. I didn't see myself that way then. What I'd been doing—drawings, paintings, playing around with a camera—was simply a matter of self-preservation. The only way I'd found to feel joy and happiness after our parents had sent us away. So, I decided to study it. Because why not? Isaac was my teacher before he became my lover. Head of my program in experimental art practices. He was blond and brilliant and from California and he believed in me. The first American man to see me. To want to help me. And I was eager—so eager—to have help. He taught me how to turn my pain into beauty and for that I was grateful. And after so many less handsome, less brilliant boys told me I was ugly or ignored me altogether, when Isaac told me I was beautiful, I believed him. He was far too old for me, and though my sister liked him, felt he was a product of "daddy issues." I didn't care. She read too much Freud.

Isaac was—unlike *some* people—a man with talent and integrity and a profound sense of care. He was a teacher, and it showed. It was Isaac who loaned me money and his time to finish the fire piece, the last piece I needed to secure my first solo show in New York. It was Isaac who designed the frames I used to hang everything: borderless plates of glass affixed to plywood with thin tension clips, which were then hung on the walls. Isaac helped me show them as more than just photographs. "*Let them know you are not trying to be the Latin Cindy Sherman*," he'd advised. And as soon as I hung them, as soon as I saw Leslie's reaction—a bit startled at the shock of them—I knew that he had been right. And Isaac did all of this even though he knew it meant me leaving Iowa. That any success I found in New York meant me leaving him, his house, his bed. He helped me because he had ambition for me and my work before I ever did. He helped me because he loved me. Wholly. I didn't really appreciate what it was that I had. Not then, anyway. God, I should have just stayed there.

But who am I kidding?

In the gallery Leslie clinked a glass and called for everyone to take a seat. They'd arranged some folding chairs in a semicircle, and I, having no poker face, buried myself in the third row. Cover for when I inevitably got annoyed. Director's chairs were set for her and the two speakers, who were huddled in the corner. Leslie's husband was a slight man with a soft, kind face. A mensch, was how Leslie had described him, and though I had no idea what that meant, as soon as I saw him, I understood. And then, there he was: Jack Martin. A different beast altogether. Tall and broad. Hunched at his shoulders. Clutching his glass of red wine. His face—what wasn't obstructed by his horn-rimmed glasses or scraggly, graying blond hair—was ruddy; his nose, red. But his eyes were a piercing blue, even from far away. He wore coveralls and a thermal shirt with work boots—an outfit I'd come to realize was as much costume as sartorial choice. His appearance, his body language, all alluded to a man who'd much prefer to be in a pub with some longshoremen than in a gallery talking about art. From across the room, you wouldn't think this man had any ego at all, let alone one earned by being the youngest artist to ever have a midcareer retrospective at the Guggenheim.

Leslie took her post in the front of the room.

"On behalf of the Venus Collective, welcome to the New York debut of the sensational Cuban artist, Anita de Monte. I cannot think of a better backdrop for what I know will be an important conversation: how women's art practices have affected male artists' social attitudes. So, without further ado, can I please invite up our two panelists: my husband, Arnold Golub, and the one and only Jack Martin."

The room burst into applause and I witnessed the most fascinating thing. Something that in the ensuing years I would reflect upon again and again and again. A transformation. The helium going into a Macy's Thanksgiving Day Parade balloon—chest puffed up, shoulders back, the hair suddenly pushed out of the face—all as he made his way across the room. The man I'd seen in the corner was no more! Jack Martin, The Artist, took his place, center stage of the room. Oh, how he played the part! Leaning back into the director's chair, taking his glasses off and putting them on and thumbing them between his fingers for effect. Lots of five-dollar words about Marx and capitalism and the workingman. My irritation began mounting as he and Arnold volleyed Leslie's unchallenging, simplistic questions. "*Do you feel intimidated by women taking up more space in the art world?*" *What fucking space?* I thought. We were given the corners men deemed too dark and dusty. "*How do you think the softness of women's work helps to reinforce the linearity of men's art practices?*" Who the fuck said women's art existed to do or say anything about male art practices?

"Leslie, this might be controversial to say here," Jack said with the air of a provocateur, and I could feel the room—the men, especially—lean in toward him, eager to lap up the crap he was about to serve. "Because I admire what you've done. But, should this gallery even exist?"

There was an audible reaction, gasps and clucked tongues and sniggers. I, for my part, had a big smile on my face. Because I realized in that moment that this guy's art form wasn't sculpture, it was bullshit. How many times would I remember realizing that? How many times would I come to kick myself for forgetting?

"Jack," Arnold said, his voice taut in his wife's defense. "We're Leslie's guests."

"What?" he said, puckishly. "I admire what you've done here, Leslie, but women's art? There should be no women's art or men's art. There should simply be art—genderless, makerless—left to stand on its own and be whatever the viewer thinks it is."

Behind me I heard a man whisper to his female companion that this was exactly the point he had been trying to make earlier. A heat started in my belly and began to spread, up and out, through my limbs. There Jack was, surrounded by *my* art—art that could only be birthed through the pain and life and history that *I've* lived—undermining the root and reason for it! Anybody could lay his fucking steel plates and gold bricks, but what I knew was that there was no Anita de Monte artwork without the life and mind and body and fucking pain of Anita de Monte!

"Excuse me?" I said, jumping up from my seat. "I have a question."

"Anita," Leslie scolded, "there will be time for Q&A in just a moment."

Really, like I said, Leslie has no fucking spine. Here he was shitting in her living room, and there she was cleaning it up. With a smile.

"Does nobody have an issue with the fact that our conversation about feminist art practices involves two white men? Does no one else find this ridiculous?"

I addressed this question not to Jack or Arnold or Leslie—because it was clear what they thought—but to the rest of the crowd. To the men who had thought my work indulgent, but also to the women who said they had found it urgent and necessary. Waited for someone to publicly defend me: one of the members of the collective, or the woman from *Ms.* magazine. I wondered if any of them really did care. Or if their feminism, like my artwork, was performance. I should have felt shame or embarrassment in the long silence that followed, but I didn't. The shame, I felt, should fall on the women who had gathered there to support me. The women who let me stand there alone.

Leslie cleared her throat, began speaking again; addressing her husband. I realized that they were all going to just ignore me. That they were going to treat me like a gnat. A passing nuisance. Eventually, I willed myself to sit back down. Jomar, who was sitting behind me, put his hand on my shoulder and I shoved it away. Pissed he had not defended me either, but also . . . I wasn't looking for comfort. I was looking for outrage! Why wasn't someone—anyone—as angry about what had just happened as I was! But no! Everyone was just focused on the panelists. As if lingering on them would erase the social unpleasantness I had inconvenienced them with. Oh, and that revelation only compounded my rage. I wanted to storm out, but I was fixed into place with my anger. I couldn't escape. So, I dove deep inside my body. Listened to the sound of my throbbing pulse. Went swimming in the depths of my boiling blood. Waiting for it all to be over.

Around me, though Leslie's perky voice continued and Jack and Arnold droned on, all I could hear was the sound of my breath. In and out; out and in. Chest up, chest down. Waiting for it—the sound of the first pop, which no one noticed but me. It was the crash of the glass that got everyone's attention. Stunned the room silent. In and out, out and in I breathed as one of the earth-flower-body works jumped off the wall, the glass frame shattering onto the wooden floor. Leslie and several other guests jumped up with surprise. Behind me, I waited for the sound of another tension clip surrendering to the flick of an invisible hand. The glass plummeted to the ground. This time the print itself—one of the blood works, a close-up of my bloodied face—caught a gust of air and flew toward the center of the room. I sat placid as the pace quickened.

Pop.

Shatter.

Pop.

Smash.

Pop.

Crash.

One by one, piece after piece, choosing to end its time here. Choosing destruction rather than sit there and be dismissed. The gasps and exclamations of *Fuck!* and startled screams eventually drowned out the pops, but the sound of the shattering plates crescendoed as piece after piece—fifteen in total—leapt off the wall. And I just breathed, calmly. In and out; out and in. Not moving a muscle or even an inch. It was only after the last piece of glass hit the ground, broke into a dozen shards, and the print it had protected slid down to the floor and Leslie shouted "*Anita! Anita!*" did I even stand. Only then that I moved. Everyone surrounded me, hysterical in the way people can only be when they need for everything that happens in life to be explainable. Everyone exclaiming how sorry they were. *A wasted apology*, I thought. *This isn't what you should be sorry for.*

Energy. I told you, it's a real thing. I lived in those fucking pieces and they didn't like being ignored any more than I did. What better way to pull the attention off Jack Martin and back to themselves. Sure, it was all a bit dramatic. But you know what? *I'm* a bit dramatic. This is their maternal inheritance. So, what?

* * *

THE RESTAURANT WAS Japanese, as was the mode at the time. When we arrived, the table had already been set in their anticipation, the bottles of Jack's preferred champagne, already chilled. Everything perfect. Minus one seat too few. Mine. I was a last-minute pity invite, the request coming from Leslie as I was picking my pieces up off the gallery floor. How could I say no? I was literally a starving artist. We hadn't sold a single piece that night and frankly, Leslie and Jack Martin owed me *at least* a nice meal. At Jack's insistence, the chair was fetched and placed at his right side at the center of the dais.

"Isn't this usually reserved for Peter?" I asked playfully when he pulled it out for me.

"Peter?" he said, gruffly. "It's for you. It's your night, right?"

"A little Jesus joke, get it?" I said with a smile. "Bad habit. Raised by nuns."

He laughed. My humor surprised him. Or maybe he just liked a good pun. I was in a good mood. The pictures coming off the wall had changed the energy. Catastrophe can be a course correction, you know? Everyone pitching in to help clean up the glass; tenderly picking the prints off the floor with the care that they so deserved. A warmth filled the space. Levity. People—critics, other artists, even some of the grumpy chauvinists who'd had me rattled earlier—came to express their shock, sorrow, regret that this had happened. That I would have to rehang all of the pictures. "*Believe me*," I'd said with a quiet smile, "*many more difficult things have happened to me.*" And this was true.

From across the gallery, I could feel his gaze. Soon enough Leslie was next to me, asking if I might want to join them for an "*impromptu meal.*"

The sushi manifested in waves, with barely a word to a waiter—the entire place in quiet deference to Jack's unspoken needs and wants. Bottle after bottle of champagne was opened and, as Jack became increasingly drunk, he somehow was both king and jester of his own court. Regaling us with serious conversation about art before digressing to raunchier jokes and gossip. Eventually, the other guests began making their farewells and I contemplated my own. How things might have been different had I just left? As if he sensed it, he asked if I'd like more champagne before refilling both of our glasses without waiting for an answer.

"That was something with your pictures coming off the wall like that," he said.

"Something is one word for it," I said. He didn't strike me as the kind of person who would understand about the energies. "Mainly it means a lot more work."

"Leslie thinks it's the heat in the building. Made them just pop off the walls like that."

"Maybe."

"It was bizarre. Everyone freaked out a bit. But not you."

"Well," I said, "I'm part witch, and witches are never surprised."

"Is that so?" he said and he turned his gargantuan self toward me. (OK, he was thinner then, but let me paint him the pig for a bit, OK?) Shifted his chair and everything. Much closer. I thought of Isaac. They were about the same age. But Isaac had a surfer's body. Ran every day. Not so with Jack. Up close, I could see a sadness in his eyes that Isaac never had. Somehow, I liked it. It made me feel that, beneath the bluster, there was a boy there. He dressed like a poor person, but his scent was of a rich one. He opened the champagne bottles with such ease, held his chopsticks like he'd been born in Asia and not Massachusetts. His pronunciation of the cities he'd traveled to—in Spain, Brazil, France—was perfect. He was, I had to admit, impressive. Complicated. Intriguing. But maybe also, slightly gross? Boarish. Disgusting in his table manners, brutish in his carriage. Revolting.

I wanted to push past it.

"Since I have your attention, why don't you tell me what you thought of my show?"

A moment of silence. I had him on the hook! He hadn't expected me to ask him so directly. I was going to keep him there. Let him wriggle like the fishes we used to catch on the Iowa River. I looked him in the eye and popped one of the remaining pieces of sushi in my mouth. Chewing, delicately, but never breaking his gaze. A staring contest. One that felt neither long nor short. Just nice. And then, after a few seconds—or maybe it was minutes—Jack Martin had the giggles.

"Well," he said, breathy and childish, "there's something to be said for body art."

And then we both laughed.

I pretended I was nonplussed, but I'd never met anyone like him. He was like the pitaya fruits I'd eaten in Mexico: hard and prickly on his outside, but inside, soft enough to scoop up with a spoon. He was not attractive: his face ruddy from sun and wine. But his speech was elegant and precise. A spider of language. Crafting sticky webs with words. Wrapping you in his threads. He would say he was just a poet or, as he preferred to call himself, a sculptor of words. And I don't know. It turned me on. True, he was old; too old, my sister would say. But I felt my bomba contract, sparked by the friction of his delicate language and his brutish self. His cold, brutal art. But also, it shrunk me a bit too, I must admit. How vast his existence had been and how narrow mine was by comparison.

You have to understand, for years I'd been starved! Sucking nutrients out of tasteless midwestern casseroles. Drinking bad American beer and cheap whiskey. Cuba had been my life and, up to now, this country a purgatory. In Cuba, I'd run free on Varadero Beach hand in hand with my cousins; I'd nap in the shade with my head on my yaya's lap, scream and laugh in the tongue I'd known since I was born. And then. And then I was sent to America and rendered invisible. Rendered lifeless. Alone. Everything around me muted, like a gray winter sky running into the pale tan of a frozen-over cornfield. And suddenly, here I was, finally before a gate to heaven. A portico. Behind me, a past where I felt trapped inside myself—my only chance to get out through my art. Before me, a future that felt limitless. From the time that I watched Cuba shrink to a speck in the ocean, I'd felt a knot in my chest. A thick snarl of feelings and nightmares: frustration, confinement, estrangement. And that night and in the weeks and months to come, Jack bored his fingers through the flesh of my chest, dug into the cavity just behind my heart, and found it. Untangled the bloody thing and unspooled it, revealing it to be a vast expanse of fabric. Helped me see that all that time, all that hurt that had been wadded up inside of me? Well, it was the cloth of my sails, the silk for my parachute. The apparatus for my escape from this small life. All I needed to do was catch some air, and Jack, like a god making wind, was more than happy to oblige.

Raquel

PROVIDENCE • SPRING 1998

"This is Marcus the Mack and the 360° Black Experience in Sound. Delroy's 'bout to rock you out with those soca jams, but we'll be at Lupo's Lounge for hip-hop night Thursday. We *will not* be at AS220 for Open Mic this Friday, because Raquel has a date—"

"Because it's Memorial Day," Raquel chimed in, laughing, but shooting him a dirty look.

"My last song is gonna soundtrack your summer," Marcus continued. "Drops Tuesday but you heard it first here: Timbaland. Baby Girl Aaliyah. And Raquel is sending this out to a very special dude—"

She glared at him and threw up her middle finger. In the background, Delroy and Betsaida were losing it, struggling to stifle their laughter.

"Nick," Marcus said into his mic, with his best seductive voice, "Rocky wants to know: 'Are *You* That Somebody'?"

And with that he clicked Play.

"Motherfucker!" Raquel screamed as she pulled off her headphones, and Marcus wiped away tears from finally letting out his stifled giggle. "He could've heard that, Marcus!"

"Sis," Delroy said with a laugh, "your man isn't listening to our show."

"I know that's right," Marcus said, and threw his hand out for a dap as he cleared Delroy's spot. "Rock, I know you're dickmatized and all, but your cute white boy doesn't dig you enough to suddenly spend his Sunday listening to 360. He's too busy listening to Hall and Oates."

"There's nothing wrong with blue-eyed soul," Raquel retorted. Secretly, though, she felt a snag on her heart knowing they were right. It had been almost a month that they'd been together, and he never mentioned the show despite knowing the import it held in her life. Or maybe he just never had a reason to bring it up? Maybe the dedication wasn't a bad thing.

"I don't get the baby thing," Betsaida said, deep in concentration, listening to the music. "Why did the song need a baby?"

Marcus rolled his eyes. "Because Timbaland's a genius, Bets! Does it sound cool or not?"

The song rolled out and a series of promos and ads came on: CVS, nightclubs, a new step aerobics chain. Raquel felt the need to correct the record.

"For what it's worth, I'm not dickmatized—"

"Oh!" Delroy jumped in. "So you admit to the fornication!"

"Fornication is about adultery, baby," Betsaida said. "She's just having plain ol' intercourse, like the rest of us."

"It's not plain when we do it, Mami," Delroy chimed in as he put on his headset.

"Actually, guys?" Raquel interjected, unable to contain herself. "This shit is like, real, I think. He asked me to dinner with his parents *before* going with him to Campus Dance—"

"Whaaaaat?!" Marcus and Betsaida exclaimed.

"Bup! Bup! Bup!" Delroy said into the mic. "Southern New England! Lesss get into it! Thirty minutes commercially uninterrupted Caribana heat!"

Beenie Man's "Girls Dem Sugar" filled the room and conversation be damned, the hit required a brief dance break. It was only respectful to the music.

"They're rich, right?" Betsaida asked over the music.

"I mean, he never showed me a fucking bank receipt, but yeah?"

Marcus stopped dancing, a look of concern on his face.

"What are you going to wear?"

Marcus was very into brands and knew Raquel mainly was worried about looking "elegant," which he found boring.

"I have this, like, black dress I wore last year."

"Last year you were selling tickets," he said with a skeptical look on his face. Delroy laughed, popped on "Heads High."

"I have a dress from when I thought I was gonna cross," Betsaida interjected, and Raquel couldn't believe she was talking about her sorority line drop. "I got it for their gala. Mi culo es bigger than yours, obviously, so you won't fill it out quite right, but . . ."

Fucking clear, Raquel thought to herself.

"Anyway, it's perfect. It's like silver, but all metallic, you know? Halter! Sexy."

A smile broke on her face.

"His parents are taking us to Al Forno before."

"Damn, Raquel," Marcus said, "that's serious shit. You were knockin' those girls in your class about marrying rich, but this dude seems like he's tryin' to lock it down."

"Fuck that," Raquel said and rolled her eyes. She didn't tell Marcus, or anyone, about what had happened in the girls' suite. About her confession. The shame of it was too much.

"Besides," Raquel said, "I don't think it's the same with white people. Not rich ones, anyway. They introduce everybody to their parents; it's not a thing."

"She's right," Delroy interjected. "I had dinner with my freshman roommate's parents like two or three times and I literally haven't spoken to the dude since we moved out."

Betsaida sucked her teeth, pulled an Arizona and a bag of chips from a tote bag.

"Maybe," she said, looking straight at Delroy, "but it's still not nothing. Some people have you going out with them for more than a year and still haven't introduced you to their parents, like they're ashamed of you or something—"

"You're reading into things that aren't there," Delroy replied, shaking his head.

"I study relationships, Delroy," Betsaida said. "Everything means something."

Marcus jumped up and tapped Raquel.

"So, we're gonna bounce," Raquel said, knowing it was just a matter of moments before they tried to drag the two of them into this. "I'll swing by this week for the dress, Bets."

* * *

MARCUS DROVE THEM to their favorite red sauce place on Federal Hill for dinner and gave her side eye when she only picked at the fried calamari she normally devoured. When she ordered a salad for an entrée, he surprised her by saying something.

"We're not going back to this, are we?"

"To what?" she said. "I just don't wanna be bloated for Campus Dance; it's in a week."

He nodded in recognition as he piled more calamari on his plate.

"OK, but I'm holding you to it," he said. "I promised your moms."

A rush of emotions—guilt, anger, anxiety—came upon her.

"She said something to you?" Raquel said, her voice a little tight, resenting her mother turning her friends into babysitters.

"When I came to pick you up in the fall," he said, "but don't be salty about it. You'd gotten all kinds of bony."

Raquel stayed silent. She knew it was not good what she had done, but also didn't like being told she had looked ugly. She thought of Betsaida's comment about the dress; no, her ass could not fill it out. She was not nearly as thin as she had been, but she understood that against Third World cultural standards, she was scrawny. In high school, she had been thick. Not like her sister, Toni, but her thighs were luscious with meat, her breasts larger, and her ass, in her summer shorts, garnered catcalls that terrified her more than they made her feel appreciated. She had enjoyed food then: pizza after school with friends, her mother's guisado. But at Brown, food for Raquel became something else. First, a source of stress and later, a thing that lent her a sense of control in an existence where she felt little of it.

She discovered how little she could eat accidentally. She would, as she had done since high school, begin her day with the biggest coffee with milk and sugar that she could order from Dunkin' Donuts. Her freshman year, she was really trying to make a go of it in the Psychology Department. Raquel had spent so much of her life focused on getting into college, she'd spent very little thinking or dreaming about what she'd do afterward. Confronted with the reality that her degree would carry the weight of a large debt, figuring that out suddenly felt imperative. Her sister had been forced to see a psychiatrist once, and Raquel remembered being impressed by the doctor's nice office suite and the way she had dressed. She'd always found people—and their behaviors—fascinating. Between the large prerequisite classes and sections for those classes, her two jobs on campus, and her half-hearted attempt to still be a part of the Latino Students Association, she found herself, three days a week, on the go from morning until quite late at night. One day as she was heading to bed, she realized she hadn't eaten and was surprised by how long the coffee had held her over. Fascinated by how—anxious as she was to do well in the classes, to ask the right questions, to take notes that would prove useful later—her nervousness unraveled her appetite.

Raquel was not suited to psychology. Yes, ultimately it was about people, but the preparation to provide such service required a medical understanding of the brain. She drowned in the deluge of new concepts; unable to parse why some things were illnesses and others were disorders. She ended up switching at the last minute to the pass/fail grading option, and still she struggled to get by. Heretofore, Raquel knew herself to be a success; a star of her high school. In all of this—the abysmal decline of her self-esteem most of all—she felt herself flailing, her conception of her very self slipping from her grasp.

What she realized she could control, however, was food. She could temper her hunger with coffee or water or cucumber slices. Food, and the avoidance of it, became a challenge to master. Could she subsist on one fat-free muffin a day? Or one hot dog ? Or a falafel salad, no pita? She could find something to applaud in how good she could get at not eating.

And, the shrinkage. A visual marker of her success in this one area of her life. But also, she realized, it meant she began—at least in her physical shape, if not her inner self—to more closely mirror the bodies of those around her. Of the mothers who moved their equally slender daughters into dorm rooms and hung their Laura Ashley curtains with matching bedding. Of the girls she would see in the art building when she went for her history of art class. Girls who, Raquel came to learn, mirrored the slender figures of the curators and gallerists and patrons of that world. And so, week by week, she began to transform her physical self to one that better conformed to an aesthetic attractive not just in the First World, but in the concrete world beyond the campus's borders. One that graced the covers of magazines and walked the streets of Manhattan's Upper East Side. That applauded tiny breasts and boyish hips and skinny legs. An aesthetic whose heroines were not Selena and JLo and Lil' Kim, but Carolyn Bessette and Kate Moss.

By the time she came home for spring break her freshman year, her clothes swam around her. Her mother, who had been quietly watching, observing her disappearing act, decided to become unquiet. "Estás hecha huesos!" she would scream. The anger in her voice was the only way she knew how to express her concern at Raquel's boniness. She would force-feed Raquel breakfast every morning, dinner every night, and ask for an account of what she'd eaten for lunch. The summer job, the one in the gift shop? Procured in no small part by her mother's desire to keep her close in order to keep Raquel eating.

This began a quiet battle that would play out for the next year. One between Raquel and her mother, yes, but also between Raquel and her inner self. One that ravenously consumed minutes, hours, and even collective days of her thoughts. The notion that less of her was worth more in the world had wormed its way into her brain and taken insidious hold over her perception of self. Despite knowing the starvation hallowed her, in the beginning, each pound gained back created in her a sense of fear. Fear of her own body, really. Despite knowing that food could soothe and nourish her, it became, for Raquel, something torturous; full of shame and complications. It was, ironically, only art history that began to unravel the cycle; something vast and new that she could master. The arguments in her papers the new things she could control. A new thing she could excel at. By the end of her second year, back at the gift shop, armed with the confidence of straight As, she relaxed. Allowed herself to feel not just hungry but worthy of being fed. By her mother's eggs in the morning, for the arroz con pollo in the evening—yes. She began to truly thicken again. To reclaim, with her body, space. She promised herself that she would not let this place suck her meat, her juiciness, off of her again.

And she wouldn't. She just needed to get past Campus Dance.

"Don't be mad," Marcus said. "She just said to make sure you were eating and to give her a call if it seemed like you weren't. This whole year went by and I never had to call her, so . . ."

The waitress came, set down Raquel's salad; and a massive platter of chicken parmesan and spaghetti in front of Marcus. It smelled delicious. A little bite of his food wouldn't kill her. She knew that. But also, she couldn't bring herself to give in to the point. It felt like an admission of guilt. Instead, she doused her salad in vinegar and olive oil; decided to change the subject.

"Do you think it's weird I'm meeting his parents so soon? It's only been like a month?"

"Nah," Marcus said. "I think you're right and white people just do shit differently. But, since you're asking my opinion, it is weird that you literally met the dude five seconds ago and are always at his house."

Raquel flinched, hearing it out loud like that. She could count on one hand the number of nights she had spent on her own, in her own room.

"We just really connected," Raquel said. She dipped a slice of bread into her salad dressing. "It's just because it's new."

Marcus was masticating his chicken parm and didn't even bother to swallow before he answered.

"You haven't come to Funk Night or Lido's or been by The Gate or the cluster—"

His voice was more matter-of-fact than bitchy, which almost made it worse.

"Nick has a laptop and a desktop, so—"

"And now you're canceling the open mic thing that *you* wanted to start."

"Oh, come on!" Raquel said, feeling defensive. "That's for Campus Dance."

"I get it," Marcus said, "I do. Just . . . all together, it paints a picture, you know?"

"A picture of?"

"A picture of somebody who forgets who they are and gloms onto their boyfriend's life."

They'd pondered this before. Watched it happen to others. Not just girls—anybody. Delroy and Bets, even. Where one day the person is a fully formed independent unit and before you know it, they are forever part of a "we." Disconnected from the rest of the world, existing in neither the First World nor the Third one, but one of their own.

"That isn't what's happening here."

"I hope not," Marcus said, "because you're dope as shit. I'm sure he's fine, but you and who you are is cool on your own."

She didn't know why, but she felt herself get a little hot. She took a sip of her Diet Coke.

"Don't worry about me." She smiled so he knew she wasn't mad. "It's new and he's graduating so he's had all these parties. Soon it will feel old; and this summer I'm gonna be so busy. The museum, my thesis, pimping out our apartment—"

"The apartment!" Marcus said, perking up. "I'm so pumped for this spot! I think we should chip in for good speakers. What do you think?"

* * *

SHE WAS EXHAUSTED when she got home. It was strange, she thought to herself, because Nick's apartment was so much nicer than her tiny single in Emery-Woolley. He had cable and tons of VHS tapes and a desktop he let her use. Plus a queen-sized futon and a full kitchen—even though, mainly, they went out to eat. Yet, the relief she felt walking into her cinder-block room with her skinny, university-issue bed and her nonexistent TV and the same stereo she'd had since her sophomore year of high school relaxed her immediately. Even now, with half her stuff in boxes. She absolutely loved her time with Nick, but when she did get to come back here—which was mainly on Sundays—she was relieved of needing to care about how he saw her. Here, she could play whatever music; keep the temperature how she liked it.

Tonight, she exhaled a deep sigh, turned on the radio to catch the slow jams show, and checked her machine. Tape full. She hit Play and began to brush out her long curly mane.

Raquel, hi. It's Mavette.

She had called at least once a day since the night of the dinner. Raquel had never been home when the calls came in and was grateful for it. She wasn't sure what she would even say. She was tempted to fast-forward, but in the two weeks that had passed, she recognized that she wasn't ready to cast Mavette as the villain. A coward, perhaps, but not a villain.

I stayed up for two days to finish the final paper for Temple's class. I just slipped it under his door and it was my last thing. I'm getting on a flight to Paris tonight. The other girls are coming next week, but . . . I don't know. I mean, I've called a million times, but I don't feel great about how things went that night and I'm really sorry I didn't tell them to shut the fuck up or something sooner and, well, I don't have your new address, so I'm just going to take your clothes over to BRU, OK? And I'll write you this summer, OK?

Beeeeeep.

Violently happy, cuz I love you.

Raquel looked at the clock, fast-forwarded. It was Nick. He would randomly do this, in the odd moments that they weren't together—typically Sundays—and fill up her answering machine with songs that made him think of her. It was cute. Beyond cute, actually. Her heart fluttered. Really. But her mother was due to call at nine and she still had to get through the rest of the messages and do her hair mask. She didn't need to listen to the rest of the song.

Raquel, how are you? This is John.

She hit Pause. What the fuck? John Temple was calling her? On a Sunday?

I doubt I mentioned this, but I'm moving out of my house this summer and in clearing out my things, I found a treasure trove for you. It's just great stuff: the catalog of Jack Martin's first solo show at Tilly Barber Fine Art, some write-ups from his Madrid show in '89. Those are in Spanish, but I figured you could get through them. In any case, I'll bring them to the office Friday.

John Temple, beyond strange. She made a note in her diary to stop in on Friday. Had she been able to call Mavette, the desire to gossip about this would have pushed her to a place of immediate forgiveness.

Beeep.

Yo, Rock, what's up! It's Julian. Hope you don't mind but I asked Niles to ask Astrid for your number. I didn't get a chance to tell you at that party: I'm staying up here this summer! Yeeaaah. Make it hot, Providence! I got a gig as a studio assistant for one of the painting instructors here. So let's do coffee? Breakfast? You tell me! Love that De La joint, by the way.

Her machine played "Ring, Ring, Ring." She appreciated that he appreciated that. It took a long time to get the audio clear enough for people to hear the instructions. There was no harm in coffee, right? Her mind flitted from there to Astrid. She'd seen her countless times since the night of the party (the night she and Nick finally did *it*), and they'd studied together at the slide table during their finals. The topic of Nick was never broached. Raquel, wondering if she'd imagined the whole thing, finally asked as they were leaving the library one night, "*Astrid, can we talk about your brother?*" To which, she very calmly said, "*Why? I stand by what I said.*"

Beeeep.

A coworker from the Avon asking if she could cover their shifts; two more—two!—full-length songs from Nick; end of tape. She couldn't imagine who she might have missed calls from because the machine had been full, but it did occur to her that she might have missed calls. She reminded herself that it was sweet of him. Sweet that he missed her.

She looked in the mirror, her heart-shaped face drowning in the cloud of her brushed-out curls, astonished at the length of her hair. She scooped some coconut oil in a bowl, squeezed in some honey, and popped it in her little microwave. At home, from when they were little, their mother used to do this for her and her sister every Sunday. Until the summer Toni cut off all her hair because she wanted finger waves. Her mother had not hit them very much as kids, but she beat Toni's ass because of that, and after, the very topic of hair caused such drama in the household that Raquel would just do it herself, locked in the bathroom. Still, she thought as she wet her mane with her spray bottle, the ritual of it made her feel closer to home. The very fragrance of the mask reducing the distance between mother and daughter. She glanced at the clock: 8:59; the phone started to ring.

"Mami?" she said.

"Hi, nena, how you doing?"

In the background she could hear the radio and New York 1.

"Mami, lower the TV. Or the radio. I can't hear you over both."

"They're doing a giveaway on Hot 97; a thousand dollars every hour. Me and Toni are taking turns trying to win."

"Mami, how are you gonna call the station if you're—"

She stopped herself; these were the kinds of things that she would say that always set her mother off. That would yield accusations of being stuck-up, of having changed. She didn't want to have that conversation right now. In the background, her mother turned off the news.

"Anyways," her mother said, "what are you up to? Did you eat today?"

"I went with Marcus and had a big chicken parm sandwich on Federal Hill."

"Muy bien, keep that juice," her mother said. Raquel noted the cheer in her voice.

"Somebody's in a good mood!" she said as she combed the mixture into her hair.

"Well, I got my grades back this week—"

After Raquel started college up here, her mother had gone back to school at night. Working, little by little, toward her associate's in nursing at CUNY, something they were all very proud of her for doing. The first semester had been a struggle and Raquel and Toni had to convince her to stick with it; Raquel could tell from her voice that this term had been a success.

"Oh yeah, and . . . ?" she said, joy in her voice.

"Straight As! Can you believe it? I mean, it's only two classes, pero!"

"Wepa! Go Mami, go Mami!"

"Dolores took us to Gargiulo's to celebrate."

"Look at Dolores, that baller. Did Toni go?"

Once Raquel got into Brown early admission, and it was clear the financial aid was going to work out well enough for her to actually attend, Raquel saw a pressure valve that she hadn't known was bottled in her mother slowly begin to release. As if, for seventeen years, she had been holding her breath. Hoping that her girls would turn out OK and, with this opportunity for Raquel, her prayers had been answered. Raquel hadn't realized that her own mother's life and wishes and . . . yearnings had been put on hold. Soon there was night school and random home improvements and Dolores. Her friend. It was clear that there was more, but her mother wouldn't name it. Perhaps in no small part because Toni, her little sister, didn't seem a fan.

"You know Toni," her mother said, and Raquel could hear the wind come out of her sails a little bit, "she's that age where she just wants to do her own thing. She's not like you, Raquel. I don't know, she's always out with that sucio—"

"Mami, you can't say someone's a sucio just because he's Dominican, it's—"

"Oh my God, the way you became the racism police since you went to that school."

"Mami, please," she said, "you were telling me about Toni."

Maybe because they'd spent so much time in the museum when they were kids, both Raquel and her sister were drawn to the arts.

But if Raquel had the focus and determination of an academic, Toni had the wildness of a real artist. An aspiring actress, she enrolled in the theater program at Brooklyn College and almost immediately met this Dominican guy in the Film Department who asked her to be in one of his shorts. Raquel had met him over the Christmas break. Aesthetically speaking, Toni, who was a dime, could do better. He looked like a poor man's Heavy D: pudgy, with thick horn-rimmed glasses and lots of Hilfiger shirts. But he wrote plays and poems and had a little hooptie and told jokes and what he lacked in looks, he made up for in personality. The last time Raquel had seen her, Toni was head over heels.

"She's carrying condoms in her pocketbook."

"Why were you in her purse though?" Raquel asked.

"I didn't go through shit; it's the clear Polo bag you got her for Christmas, Rocky," her mother said.

Raquel both admired and begrudged how disrespectful her sister Toni could be. For her part, Raquel had been paralyzed into submission by her mother's tirades and warnings about sex. Her rare moments of defiance—like when she dry-humped a guy at a party—were accompanied by such guilt and terror, she decided it was easier to comply. Toni, on the other hand, was a domestic insurrectionist. Not just about sex. Their mother loved her girls' long manes—Raquel's curly down her back, Toni's straight como una india—fetishized them even. As if each tendril was not a hair but a silken thread tying her daughters to her, to the womb that had once carried them. When Toni chopped her hair off it was the beginning of a personal mutiny: curfews broken, curse words screamed, boys and boys and more boys. There were occasional moments of peace—moments where the two were so close, Raquel felt the odd duck out—but most of the time she was in the middle, trying to broker an armistice, even if temporary.

"And I told her, nobody is going to cast a pregnant actress in anything. And she goes, 'You're always shitting on my dreams with your negativity.' And I said, 'Who's fucking negative? My life is about positivity. I'm just a realist.' How would she go to auditions if she's got a baby to look after? I'm getting my *own* life, I'm not trying to be a grandmother now."

"Mami, she could just get an abortion," Raquel said, knowing full well that Toni kept an emergency fund for expressly this purpose in her underwear drawer.

Her mother sucked her teeth.

"Shut your mouth! Babies are blessings!"

"Mami, if she's using condoms, then probably we don't need to worry—"

"They break! Or worse! Men do crazy things when they want to hold on to a woman. You don't even know."

In that moment Raquel decided that yet another week would go by without telling her mother about Nick. The time never felt quite right.

In the shower, as she washed the mask from her hair, she wondered if she should call her mother back. She was, as Marcus pointed out, practically cohabitating with this guy and she hadn't even mentioned to her mother that she had met someone. That she had a crush, even. Her mother's first question would inevitably be, "Are you having sex?" And if lying to her mother by omission made her feel guilty, straight-up deception felt, to Raquel, impossible. Still, this was more nuisance than anything else. Raquel had made it to college. *This* college. The worst of life's potential destruction had passed her, as far as her mother was concerned. No, what really stopped her from talking to her mother about Nick were all the questions that would come afterward. *Who is he? Where is he from? What do his parents do? What is he going to do?* All normal, valid questions for a mother to ask. The answers to which, in this particular case, might make many other mothers very happy. The Upper East Side; manage their money and their home; make art because he doesn't have to worry about money. But these were answers that would just beget more questions: questions infused with her mother's own inferiority complexes. *Are they snobs? People up there are snobby. I know, I work up there. What does that mean they manage their money? How is that a job?* The one thing her mother *would* probably accept was that he was an artist.

She wasn't going to call her mother back. Maybe later this week she would try to talk to Toni. Let her sister be the go-between. For a change. Toni's questions would be different; not better, but different. *Does he pay for things? Does he have a big dick? Has he taken you to any good parties? Would he be fun to go on a double date with?* Yes, all the time; I'm not sure I know; different parties; it depends on what you wanted to do on this double date.

Her mother, and to a lesser extent her sister, had conjured a narrative that this place had changed Raquel. Rendered her more judgmental of the life she had before. She did not believe this to be true, but carefully noted which moments her mother and Toni pointed out that revealed her new, changed nature. They validated and encouraged her friendships with Marcus and people from 360 because, when they'd met them in New York or on her family's rare visits up to campus, these people seemed "normal." She had gone all this time without ever bringing home a boy for them to meet and now for that person to be Nick? Well, she understood that they might see it as an affirmation of their worst fears about her. That she thought herself better than her old life. That she was trying to "date up."

She was not. (She didn't see Nick as "up," as much as she saw him as "in.")

She grabbed her shower caddy and headed back to her room. Janet Jackson was on the radio singing about getting so lonely.

Her old life was beginning to feel like a fever dream. Not just back in New York, not just back in Brooklyn. The life she had led, here in this very room, just a few weeks before. The solitude that so often smothered her now replaced with a different kind of asphyxia—the kind of searching for air underneath the weight of another person. Emotionally, physically, sexually.

Sex made her feel a different kind of loneliness. One that, for a few minutes afterward—during which she felt she could hide in the bathroom—filled her with sadness. She found Nick very attractive; the light blond hair on his muscular forearms, the feel of his hand on her back, his kiss. Sex, however, was different than what she thought it would be. Or perhaps the problem was she hadn't thought about it enough to begin with. She'd experienced—only a handful of times—the sense of arousal and pleasure with a guy. Had felt the sensation of climax, albeit not through actual sex. And the night that they first did it, she had felt turned on. Had been just buzzed enough to not overthink the pain or if she bled (she didn't) or if she would seem childish or not sexy enough for him. She was able to just feel lust. The desire for his skin to be on top of her skin. But in the times after—and it felt like so many times—she found that her arousal lay more in his desire for her and her ability to make him achieve pleasure than in that of her own. Her utility to him, his need for her—so corporal and primal—producing in her a desire to welcome him into her body more than any single physical need of her own. Perhaps this is why, in the rare moments she allowed herself to think about it, the actual act itself felt so much like an invasion; a robbery almost. An intrusion with the sole purpose of extracting, for him, an orgasm from her.

It would destroy him to think she wasn't enjoying herself. He would hate to think that she was acting. She didn't feel it was due to any fault of his, just her lack of experience. It was just that the sex itself—which she always hoped would make them feel closer—just created for her more distance. An urge to claim her body back as her own again.

It was only ten o'clock. Ivvone, the Christian girl who did the *Quiet Storm* show, was playing "Between the Sheets." Raquel's last final was in the morning. She felt prepared, but a little more work couldn't hurt. She turned on her reading lamp and went through her flash cards one last time before she decided to call it a night.

Anita

NEW YORK CITY • FALL 1985

Now, let me tell you about the day that I died. A night that, well—OK, obviously it didn't go as planned. But, in some funny way, I feel a twisted satisfaction about the whole thing. Because that day, I decided to burn a bridge. To never go back to how things were. And, in that context, it was a wild success.

I'm getting ahead of myself. Let's start here: being an artist is very lonely business. No one talks about that. All those years—my teenage years, my time as a young woman, the earliest days in New York—I was plagued by a sense of isolation. One I had attributed to being ripped from my home. But even after I finally went back to Cuba? Well, that fucking sense of solitude was still the undertaste that flavored so many of my days. This is the best that I can do to explain to you how and why Jack and I got back together. Again and again and again. Of course, in the moment, I didn't consciously know this. The problem with being alive, I can tell you now, is that it happens so fast, we don't have the time to make sense of it in the same way that you can once you're dead.

It was always hubris that made me think it would be different. Because how could it not be? How could I not learn anything new? How could I not grow and change, even if he didn't? And every time, it was always the same. Including the time in Rome when I agreed to marry him after he told me—and I believed him—that marriage would fix things! So, let me not waste your time on the details of my years with Jack. The cities change, the women mostly change, but honestly, who wants to hear the same story again and again and again? How he diminishes me and I get furious and he gets enraged at my fury and does something terrible, so I leave and he chases and I want to feel like I matter to someone so I take him back. And then he publicly humiliates me and I get furious and he gets enraged by my fury and does something terrible and so I leave and then he chases and I want to feel like I matter to someone so I take him back. No one wants to hear that story over and over again. Especially not me.

It was loneliness that made me go back, I eventually realized. I had friends. I had assistants who would help me in the studio. But my life was spent, you see, primarily in my head. Hours and days plotting and planning and researching and experimenting with materials and sketching and sketching and sketching. When I was in Rome, for instance: I would wake and, when I went to the studio, it was like entering a trance. Eight or nine or ten hours later, suddenly I was scrounging around for a dinner companion or maybe chatting up a stranger in a bar. Some days, the saddest days, maybe just eating some bread and butter and drinking wine by myself in my apartment. Or maybe I'd go to a party and get drunk and cause an argument just to feel like I'd made a dent in someone else's existence. But, more or less, these were tiny moments around the isolation my mind and body required to make my art.

It can feel so important to matter to someone. To just know there is someone who cares where your physical person is on this giant, wretched earth. To matter to another human being is the basis of having a life. I wanted a life. With Jack, I had one. I was accountable to someone and he was accountable to me. I had someone, even when we were far apart, who I could call for no other reason than to talk about my day because, even at his worst, even when his love carved deep grooves of pain through the softest parts of my flesh, I knew that he felt connected to me. And I to him. And I wanted to feel that tether. That tether salved the loneliness of creation.

But the repetition was exhausting! Oh, so exhausting. The weight of bearing all that humiliation. In each descending level of the cycle, I would find for myself a new level of debasement. Had I allowed him to shit in my mouth in the public square, Jack couldn't elicit the kind of shame my own acquiescence cultivated in me. His abuses, his infidelities, his acts of violence—big and small—they shaved away the epidermis of my soul, layer by layer, leaving me raw and rough and unrecognizable. Sometimes even to myself.

Still, his love wasn't killing me; I was killing me! Each reconciliation was to drink from a well-marked bottle of bleach! An open-eyed act of emotional suicide. One that felt intense and, in some twisted way, invigorating. Believing in a moment that you are truly, desperately loved? Well, that in its own way is a form of feeling alive.

So, I couldn't *just* leave. I had to burn the bridge, you see. So that *after* I got furious and he got enraged at my fury and did something terrible, I could leave but he *couldn't* follow. I had to find a way to part from him such that he would never want to see me again. That when I walked out the door, he would spit nails, breathe fire, curse the day I was born, wish me dead, roar like a trapped bear if he heard my name, and rage when he heard of my future successes.

But also, I had to decide to set the bridge on fire.

So, there were two decisions, really. The first was how to burn the bridge and the second was when, exactly, to start the inferno. Ironically, it was my pain that led me to the first and my glee that helped me arrive at the second.

We'd only been married about three months when I heard about the bitch in London. Jomar was there for a group show and saw them—saw them with his own two eyes—at Langan's, Jack's hands all over her. Soon enough, I learned about la sueca gigante, Ingrid, here in New York. He took her to parties with collectors! He took her to a dinner party once and Stephen, the Latin American curator from the Guggenheim, was also there. Of course, Stephen didn't tell me; he told Jomar—and who knows who the fuck else—who then told me. As if I didn't already know! But there was something about Stephen knowing that gutted me in a different way. The blade of infidelity given the double edge of how it inevitably impacted what people thought of me. *My* art. Who would not feel pity for a woman in my position? And neither my womanhood nor my work was about pity. I called my sister in hysterics, a call she had gotten so many times before, but she was the only person I allowed myself to be truly broken in front of. "*He said when he was a husband it was going to be different!*" I had cried to her; discovered a new layer of indignity at how foolish I had been to believe him. When suddenly something clicked. The next time I left, I wasn't a girlfriend walking out on a boyfriend. I was a wife leaving a husband. A woman seeking a divorce.

Worshipping money is a great way to be a good American, and in that regard, Jack was a regular Yankee Doodle Dandy. The more his pieces sold for, the better he felt about himself and his place in the world. But it wasn't *just* a love for money, it was a love for how he could control things with the money that he relished: the restaurants for those big dinners he loved to host, the wine and food at said dinners, where we took trips, what I wore on those trips. Whenever and wherever he could exert his influence or make a show of himself with his money, you could count on Jack doing so. I had grown up with nothing and, of all the things that affected me in my youth, impoverishment was not high on my list of complaints. I always figured it out. You could always get by. So, this thing with him was something that I hated—this pathetic petite bourgeoisie belief that money made him powerful. Now, I realized, if I wanted a divorce, as his wife, I could legally be entitled to siphon a bit of that money in my direction. Not because I needed it or even wanted it, but because this would be the dynamite on the bridge. He, this man of genius, having to give over the fortune he had made—with his own hands, every piece set down with his own two genius hands—to me? The loony Latina? The one who was only doing as well as she was because of her association with him? *That* was who he would have to give half of his money to? He would spit nails, breathe fire, curse the day I was born, wish me dead, roar like a trapped bear if he heard my name, and rage when he heard of my future successes!

And my, was I having successes! I meant what I said; artistically speaking, after Berkeley, I never did put Jack over anything. I worked and worked and got a few prestigious residencies, the Guggenheim Fellowship, and eventually, the Rome Prize—which was a very big deal and what brought me to Rome, a place where my soul found another home, for the first time. I had sold work to several museums, including the New Museum and the Whitney, and was getting public art commissions all around the world. I was in demand! I didn't need Jack's money. I didn't even want Jack's money. But I knew that if I took it, it would kill him, and in killing him, I could save me.

You can't fuck around with big plans like this. You strike and you miss? Well, suddenly you get him and Tilly sitting around at Nell's telling everyone I'm a fucking gold digger and them believing it because of the whole fucking hot, fiery, money-grubbing immigrant ex-wife story, which somehow had become a trope without it actually happening very much, as far as I could tell. No, I couldn't just go after the money with a long, drawn-out divorce. I had to do it in a way that made the case exactly what it was: very black and white.

"*Let's wear disguises!*" I said to Jomar. "*We can follow him around and take photos of him con la sueca gigante.*"

Jomar had laughed in my face. "*I think Jack will notice being trailed by a six-foot-tall skinny Black man and a five-foot Cuban. You're making some money now, hire a private detective.*" I felt he underestimated our ability to disguise ourselves but was intrigued by the idea. I had only thought about private eyes as television characters: Magnum P.I. and Jim Rockford. Had certainly never imagined being in a position to need one, but figured it was worth a shot. Jomar had a cousin who was a cop and he knew tons of retired detectives who went into that line of work. He gave me a bunch of names and I went with the one who sounded Latin: Mike Romero. As soon as we met and I told him I came from Cuba, he told me how he had come from D.R. and then we just switched to Spanish. By the end, he told me it would be his pleasure to bring this gringo fucking down.

But then, like I said, you also have to decide when to light the match.

It only took Romero a couple of weeks to get into rock-solid shape all the evidence of Jack's adultery that would deliver me freedom from this hamster wheel of humiliation my personal life had turned into. He'd been calling me, trying to get me to come in and see what he had documented and, I have to be honest: I dragged my feet returning his calls. There were still these good moments, you see. Moments when we'd be at dinner with five or six other people and someone was being a pretentious twat and we'd lock eyes across the table and know just what the other was thinking. Moments where he would say something about a film or a book that felt like he was telling me about my life, not a piece of art. Moments where I felt the warmth of togetherness you can only feel when you are accountable to someone.

One day, Rory called and said she felt it was time the museum had some of my work in their collection; did I have anything I could show her? We arranged to meet the next day and, emboldened for a second by the thought of all that my life could be—how I was just getting started—I called Miguel Romero and said I'd see him in the morning.

For a split second—a flash, really—I felt the cudgel of truth bash viciously against my heart. What I knew through instinct and hearsay was, in Romero's office, suddenly laid out as fact: photos and phone records and credit card receipts. But that pain was quickly replaced with a strange elation at my newfound power. Yesterday, Jack was a cheat and I was a pendeja, but now Jack was a cheat and I was a fucking wife emputada, not to be fucked with. I felt the power of this information—oh, this information that only I possessed!—rise up and sprout its wings, and I knew then, not exactly the moment that I was going to release them, but that when I did, the flapping of their alas would change destinies.

I wasn't, for the record, wrong.

Still, I hadn't intended to burn the bridge that day, nor did I expect it to engulf me in the flames, but here we are. I'm not always the best judge of things when I've lost my temper or when I've been drinking, and that night I did both.

I'd already told you the first part: the party at Tilly's. I guess what matters now is the after.

I'd had an amazing day, career-wise. Yes, I realized I would certainly soon be getting divorced, but I also had my first solo show in Rome offered to me and the acquisition from the Met. These were big deals! I was in the mood to celebrate. Then he fucking shat on me and did what he always did when his manhood felt compromised: found a hole to put his dick in that wasn't mine to prove a point about how important Jack Martin was. This was all normal stuff. Nothing new here. No reason to not bide my time, come up with a plan of where and when and how to manage my life in the aftermath of blowing us up. But then . . .

I was in the kitchen on the phone with my sister telling her—in Spanish, of course—what Miguel Romero, P.I., had found. She was raging worse than me, let me tell you! Telling me to send it in a letter, to not even be near him when I let him know, to just serve him with the papers. And I tried to explain to her that I couldn't do that; that it wouldn't be enough. Without telling him myself, to his face, he wouldn't hate me. Would, as his ego was inclined to do, feel confident that he could manipulate me and coerce me back into reconciliation. What I didn't confess to my sister was this: without a hideous scene, I was worried I *could* be coerced back. Bleach!! Jack had been in the living room watching an old movie, but suddenly he was charging! Screaming and cursing, my portfolio in his hands. He flung it at me in such a way that it struck me in the eye. Again, nothing new here. No, what made me spark—what made me take out the explosives—was what he said!

"What the fuck is this?" he yelled. "You're stealing from me now?"

My portfolio?! Oh, I felt a fury. But more importantly, the fucking accusation! This old, exhausted loser. The only way I could possibly be doing well is if I was stealing from him? What fucking nerve! I hung up on my sister, didn't even notice my eye throbbing the way that it was. I remembered my secret, felt the wings fluttering in my hands. A smile came over my face.

"Oh, siiii, Yack," I said, my Ricky Ricardo vastly improved from years of practice. "I sorry I steal from joo. This is why ayy no show joo my work."

He took the portfolio and showed me my tree trunk sculptures.

Pieces I'd designed after seeing the Taino carvings in Puerto Rico and Cuba.

"What's this then?" There was spit coming out of his mouth. His face was red from his wrath and I felt a quick rush of fear of him before I remembered the alas fluttering in my grip. And I started to laugh. Oh, I laughed at how fucked he was now! How very, very fucked. His own sense of self-import so perfectly being the thing that made me decide, in that very second, that I was going to put an end to us. And I just laughed and laughed.

"Do you know what Rory said when she saw these? They were important and relevant. Giancarlo said he'd never seen anything like them."

"They aren't classic though, not like my work," he said, and by this time I was calm. I said something about how easy it was for him to turn me into a talentless nobody in his mind because it allowed him to abuse me more easily. And as soon as I said it, I was sorry it had taken me seven years to figure out.

I took the portfolio, went into the bedroom, and started to throw my things in my bag to take back to my apartment after I struck the match to burn the bridge, when suddenly, I had an idea. I *could* just walk out with my bag and hand him Romero's file and tell him I wanted a divorce, *or* I could put on the electric blue thong Jack bought me for Valentine's Day and go out into the living room wearing nothing but that and the file, which I held behind my back.

"Jaaaack," I cooed in the way that I knew he liked, and stood in the living room doorway. "Jack, I don't want to fight anymore."

He sat up; pulled the recliner erect. He loved my tits. They were nothing but little beestings, really, but they always got him excited.

"I never want to fight with you, Anita," he said. He sounded almost as exhausted as I felt in that moment. So exhausted, I almost changed my mind. Almost.

"I love you, Jack," I said. And I did. But it was killing me! Swallowing bleach! Burying me alive while I still held breath!

He crossed the room toward me, lust in his eyes and forceful like a boar, and put one hand on my breast and the other on the small of my back, and as his tongue touched mine as it had done a thousand times before, I knew it would be the last time. I just didn't know why. I felt him feeling at the folder and without stopping kissing me for even a second, he asked what it was, and I whispered into his ear:

"It's what I'm going to show the judge when I take all of your precious money in divorce court."

That threw cold water on some things. But threw a fucking flame on others.

He stepped away from me and started flipping through the photos and the receipts and the call logs and all the other delightful bits of information Romero had gathered. I smiled.

"I can't take it another day. Now you know all that I know. I have a lawyer and I have proof. I want a divorce."

I could see him making the effort to hold his temper at bay.

"We aren't getting a fucking divorce, Anita," he said through gritted teeth.

"Why not, Jack? You don't love me. You don't love these other women either. You don't even love your art. But you love your fucking money and I'm going to love taking half of it."

He grew red like a wound then, was breathing like a bull—hard and through his nose—and his eyes lost something. Something strange came upon them, and now I felt fear. Not just for a fleeting moment, but deep and urgent. An animal in the woods spotted as prey. I wondered—in the split second between noticing this and him charging me, slamming my body hard—oh so hard!—against the doorway—why the fuck hadn't I listened to my sister? Why the fuck hadn't I sent a letter, or just packed my bag and said goodbye? Why the fuck did I always need to put on a fucking show? I thought this for mere seconds before my breath was knocked out of me. When I tried to get up, he kicked me, hard, in the chest. In the belly. I am sure that I screamed for him to stop. I am sure I screamed that I was sorry. That I hadn't meant any of it. The human mind is conditioned to survive and will say whatever it needs to do so. But it was too late. I had burned the bridge. It had been, it turns out, made of nothing but kindling and twine. There was no going back. No reconciliation. Just as I predicted.

I stumbled my way into the bedroom, crawled up on the bed, hoping it would stop, but he was just steps behind me. He punched me, hard, before he picked me up and I realized—my heart nearly stopped from the fear of it—that he was carrying me to the window. My eyes were cloudy with tears and blood but I opened them and looked into his eyes—right in those ice blue eyes—and screamed. *Noooooo!* Loud. In the desperate hope that it would pierce his rage, poke at his senses.

"No! No! No!"

But I wasn't loud enough.

I clawed his face as he put me on the windowsill. I clutched the frame like a desperate kitten. My fingers grasping with such ferocity I am sure I probably broke one or two and didn't feel a thing beyond terror. There was a brief moment where he debated it—seconds, really—but it slowed down enough that I could hear the car horns honking on Broadway. The warm breeze cool against the hot blood running down my forehead. I could hear my heart beating and his heavy breathing. I wanted to stay on that windowsill so badly. I wanted to do so many things with my life. I wanted to be so much and I was just starting to figure it out. I was just fucking figuring it out! But I was small and tired and he was big and full of venom and I had burned the bridge.

"No! No! No!"

I screamed again, but he couldn't hear me through his madness and I couldn't hear him through the blood throbbing hard against the walls of my brain.

All it took was a shove. No harder than a bully at a playground. And then there was wind. Breath sucked in that I knew would never be exhaled again. As I fell, I wondered if, when I landed, my eyes would be closed or open. I wanted to keep them open.

The fall was quick.

Jack's face in the window.

Quick.

The wind, punching a hole through my ribs.

Quick.

The building, a blur of concrete and reading lights and TVs in windows.

Quick.

Body bowed in two.

Quick.

The black tar of a roof and I willed myself not to die of a heart attack because I refused to give him the satisfaction of thinking for a moment that I died of fear and not impact.

Quick.

Only, I didn't land. I didn't crash.

Quick.

The plunge of breaking through a body of water.

The splash of me, I could feel extending at least to the fourteenth or fifteenth floor of Jack's apartment building. The sounds now not of fear or screams or cabs honking and Saturday night movies, but of a heartbeat. The fall slowed to a submersion, deeper and deeper, and, eyes open, I could see around me the schools of fish, glorious and multicolored. Above me, the sun, refracted off the top of the waves. Aquamarine. The water was warm, like a womb. And in that moment, I realized that it was. That the sound of the ocean waves was just Yemayá inhaling and exhaling. In and out. That she was the mother and I'd been returned to her; that she was blessing me not with an ending, but a new kind of start. I began to swim up toward the light and farther from the fish and the stingrays and wound my way around the seahorses and the jellyfish. The water got clearer and clearer until it was a blue I knew from a place at the root of my soul. In the shallows, I was able to put down my feet on the sand floor. Standing on the floor of Yemayá's world and looking at mine: Varadero Beach, just as I'd left it last.

II

PARTIES

Raquel

PROVIDENCE • SPRING 1998

John Temple's office was a mess; in fact, Raquel realized John Temple was a bit of a mess. His typical collegiate sartorial flair replaced with a Bad Brains T-shirt and some khakis. (This T-shirt, she decided, was the most edgy thing about him and once again she cursed Mavette for being such an asshole and depriving her the pleasure of someone to analyze this new fact about him with.) Around him were boxes of books and papers, some that looked old enough to have traveled with John Temple from his own college days.

"Apologies," he said, and Raquel noticed his stubble was at least two days longer than usual. "Like I mentioned, I'm moving, so just trying to reorganize some of this stuff."

"Yeah, no worries," she replied. "I just moved yesterday. It's exhausting."

"Now add twenty-five extra years of shit you've collected and a divorce and you'll get where I'm coming from."

Oh my God, she thought to herself, *John Temple is the sad divorced guy*. (She had not known he was married. He had, however, always seemed a bit sad.)

"I'm disorganized," he said now, going through some piles on his desk before pulling out a manila envelope, which he handed to Raquel, "but, I'm getting it together!"

She stifled a giggle because, in that moment, he looked like a gray-haired version of Nick, or countless other boys on campus. She wondered if perhaps the difference between youth and middle age was not simply having gray hair or stubble but wearing the pretense of having it together.

"When do you start with Belinda?"

She suppressed an eye roll. He wasn't going to let this Belinda Kim thing go.

"At the RISD Museum?" she corrected. "Tuesday! I'm excited. And I'm really appreciative of these."

"Really great stuff in there, you'll see," he said, gesturing to the folder. "I have other great Martin material, obviously, but most that you can find. That right there is the good stuff. Rare: sales sheets from gallery shows I've gone to over the years. And that first catalog especially—Tilly Barber's. Oh, it's probably the clearest articulation of why his work cut so deep in the first place."

He had such passion in his voice, he sounded like Julian when he told her about an obscure remix or Delroy when he'd get into talking deep cuts of reggae rockers. The genuine appreciation and joy in his voice, stripped bare of the academic talk. She had a strange moment of realization, as she saw his boxes and boxes of books, on top of all the other books already lining the shelves around his spacious office: she studied Jack Martin because he loved Jack Martin. She knew he was important because John Temple told her so. Who told John Temple?

"Profe—" she started. She corrected herself. "John, I have a question. What made you want to focus your work on minimalism? With all the art out there, why Martin?"

Professor Temple—who she had to admit, today, did look like more of a John—stared at her for a second before a broad grin broke out across his face.

"You know what's wild, Raquel?" His voice filled with true wonder. "That is the question every student should ask a professor and yet, no one has ever asked me before. And I don't even know the last time I thought about it, to be honest. It's just sort of . . . been my thing for so long, I stopped wondering why." His voice trailed off; he seemed lost in thought. "Honestly, that's probably true for a lot of things in life. But! What I can say with certainty is that I still love minimalism and all that it stands for."

He'd been standing all this time but now sat, not in his usual Eames chair but on the edge of his desk. His long legs dangling off, so close to Raquel, their feet could practically touch.

"The history of art—like culture in general—is really just a big long conversation among creators," he continued, leaning in with enthusiasm. "About aesthetics, but also about society and politics and the stuff of modern life. And I guess, to me, with what we call 'art,' maybe I see it as less a conversation and more . . . of a battle. Everybody is doing these grand-scale neoclassically perfect historical paintings and Delacroix comes in and is like, 'Hey, we're gonna add in feelings and romance.' And people get on board with that, and then eventually, that becomes establishment and somebody else, like Manet, comes around. And is like, 'Here's a grand-scale figurative painting, but it's of a naked lady having lunch with two modern gentlemen.' And there's scandal and outrage and excitement, until that becomes sort of normal, and then someone like Degas comes in."

It sounded like battle raps. Boogie Down Productions and the Juice Crew; Tupac vs. the late, great Christopher Wallace, a.k.a. Biggie Smalls (RIP); East Coast vs. West Coast; backpack rap vs. shiny suit music.

"Anyway, this goes on and on, as you know—this evolution, this throwing down of gauntlets by young men—and women—shaped by their society, their cultures, different nations, and we keep going and going until we're at Pollock and de Kooning and abstract expressionists. This is American Art, right? And it's just their personal demons and chaos and cults of personality in the world. Wild at first, but soon they too become establishment: the magazines, the fame, the giant museum shows. So, in the meantime—because you asked a personal question, so I'll keep it personal—I'm a kid in school in Connecticut and we're doing bomb drills, and then Kennedy is shot and Martin Luther King Jr., is shot. Then Vietnam and Kent State happened, like, the spring of my senior year at Milton. And the world around me was just chaos; it all felt really urgent, you know. And I remember coming down to the city for Columbus Day weekend with a buddy of mine from Yale. We went to see the Jack Martin show at the Guggenheim, and in the backdrop of all this chaos in the world, he stuck up a middle finger to abstract expressionists and was like, 'Nobody cares about your personal shit, we care about what's fucking real! And this is real—steel plates are real. Bricks are real. Wood beams are real.' And I remember walking into that show and feeling such a sense of calm that I hadn't felt in such a long time. It made sense, the art, but also the need for it in the world. An antidote. And they changed the conversation because it needed to be changed."

His passion and exuberance—completely at odds with what he reflected on the lecture hall stage—had carried him away. He was talking to Raquel, but she could also sense he was talking to himself. As if he seemed to realize this too, he buttoned himself back up. Leaned away from her and sat erect.

"Anyway, I went back up to Yale and decided this was what I was going to do. Because the history of art is an academic subject, but the artists who made these pieces were real people, existing in a society and reacting to that society, and the study of that, and the study of this particular era of it, felt important to me."

"That's really beautiful," Raquel said, and she genuinely meant it. There was a moment of quiet when she realized that he too was just a person. That somehow, the Art History Girls and everybody else had recognized that way, way sooner than she had. He was no god; just a kid like her or, more accurately, like Nick, who got really hooked on something he found cool.

"Have you ever met him?" she asked.

"Once or twice," John said, pleased with himself for the fact. "He's a taciturn character, but many geniuses are."

There was another moment of silence, this one more awkward than its predecessor.

"Raquel, would you like to grab a coffee? Maybe I can walk you through the catalogs?"

Her stomach flipped. Was this the pass that Marcus had predicted? Was he a fucking sucio? Or was he just wanting to continue the conversation? Was this just what normal students here did with faculty? Oh, how she didn't want to deal with this right now.

"I, um," Raquel said, trying to mask her befuddlement, "I wish I could, but, um, it's Campus Dance. I'm having dinner with Nick and his parents before we go—"

"Right, right," John Temple said, turning to reorganize his papers. And by his embarrassment she could tell that he had meant the invitation in the way Marcus had anticipated. Sad, divorced Professor Temple. "Campus Dance! A great night. I hope you and Nick have a fantastic time."

"Thanks so much," she said as she picked up her bag. "And thanks for all this great material!"

"If you get into any weeds this summer, email me! I should be around."

As she walked out of the art building, she wondered to herself why, exactly, she'd told him who she was going to Campus Dance with.

* * *

THEIR NEW APARTMENT was the ground floor of a clapboard house off of Ives Street that got tons of light. None of the student apartments in Providence were particularly nice—all just older places on the brink of falling apart. But it was still the nicest place Raquel had ever lived in. The apartment she grew up in was shadowed by the elevated train line, the whole place covered in dark brown wall-to-wall carpet that sucked up what little sun did get in. Even now, with the new apartment a mess of boxes, she felt her heart expand with pride and excitement: This was her place. Leased in her (and Marcus's) name. The first place of many. She would never need to live in an ugly apartment ever again. That was the gift of all this hard work, the chance to shed the skins you never liked too much in the first place.

She showered and did her makeup and then went back to her room to dress. The silver halter Betsaida had loaned her hung on the back of the door. The dress she was actually wearing was still wrapped in tissue paper and sitting inside the luxe paper shopping bag from Zuzu's Petals. Just as it was when Nick brought it to her yesterday. She hadn't bothered to unwrap it because as soon as Nick walked through the door and she saw the bag, she knew exactly what was inside.

"You didn't!" she'd said.

He'd simply smiled as he handed her the bag. (Oh, his spectacular, perfect smile. The teeth! So white and straight. She felt herself clench at the recollection of it.)

"You shouldn't have done this!" she said.

"Why not? You deserve to have all the beautiful things," he said as he pulled her close to him for a kiss.

"What did he do?" Marcus said from the kitchen where he was unpacking their measly supply of cups and dishes. "Besides not come help you move."

It was true; she had been kind of annoyed with Nick all morning. She'd slept in her own room to finish packing, but Nick had promised to meet at ten to help schlep the boxes from her dorm; split the contents of her life between Marcus's small sports car and his own Wagoneer. But at ten fifteen Marcus was waiting outside and Nick hadn't shown up. With her landline disconnected, she had no way of checking in. It took three round trips all the way to India Point and back to Pembroke campus to do what they could've done in one. Raquel hated inefficiency. But more than that, she hated being forgotten. Except clearly, she hadn't been.

"Man, I'm sorry to leave you hanging like that," Nick now said to Marcus. "I overslept and then, well, I'd had this idea to get Raquel this—"

"This fucking insane dress, Marcus!" she said, and started to pull it out to show him, but Nick gestured for her to stop, pulled the bag out of her hand.

"No," he said, gently, "let him see it when you're in it tomorrow! She looks amazing; you won't get over it."

"For tomorrow?" she asked, perplexed. "I have something Betsaida loaned me—"

"Raquel," he said a little incredulously, "this is Vivienne Tam."

It *was* a Vivienne Tam. It cost almost five hundred dollars. And it was so fucking cool. It was a long-sleeve sheer mesh dress with a painting of two Chinese dragons fighting; their faces across the bust, their long, elegant bodies and tails wrapping around the bodice and onto the back. She thought the artwork was Ming dynasty period, but she couldn't say for sure. She had only taken one Asian art history class. One day, Nick had driven her to work at the Avon and parked to run some errands on Thayer. They'd passed Zuzu's Petals and it was actually he who pointed the dress out to her in the window. "*That*," he said, "*would look phenomenal on you*." She laughed and said it was definitely an amazing dress, but she wouldn't even be able to afford a sock in that store. (This wasn't a lie. Her freshman year, she had gone in and they were selling cashmere socks for twenty dollars a pair. For socks!) At Nick's insistence, she went in to try it on and frankly, there was something liberating about entering this store, which she had put off-limits to herself and wasting the woman's time. The woman who opened her store on a college campus and dared sell twenty-dollar socks that make young students feel dumb for not being able to afford them. "*I don't know, maybe I'll think about it*," she feigned, though she really did love it—despite wondering if perhaps the mesh did emphasize her panza—and Nick came behind her, kissed her on the head, and said, "*It looks pretty amazing on you*."

Then she went to work and went about her life and, in the week or so that passed since that happened, had not thought of the dragon dress again until it was here, right before her. A present. With the request that she wear it for Campus Dance. Nick must have sensed her hesitation, because he said:

"You know, my mother just loves fashion, and she loves Asian art, and I just thought this would be such a great conversation starter at dinner tomorrow. Break the ice, you know?"

And with that, Raquel smiled and said thank you and how excited she was to wear it and how she couldn't wait for Marcus to see how dope this thing was.

Now, standing in her bedroom, she picked up the wrapped dress from the bag and opened the tissue and slipped it on. She could feel its expense against her skin immediately. She looked at herself in the full-length mirror. It was inarguably chic. Hip. Artistic and elegant all at once. She glanced at Betsaida's dress: a silver lamé hourglass evening dress. Absolutely what she would have chosen for herself for this occasion had she gone to a store, but she could see, when comparing the two garments now, that they were for two different occasions. Or, perhaps more accurately, two different dates to the same occasion. In Bets's dress, she would not fit in at the dinner table with Mr. and Mrs. Fitzsimmons; it would have been too loud, too flashy. She didn't even need to know what Nick's mother would be wearing to suddenly see it very clearly. She didn't need to show Nick the silver dress for him to know it too. He just wanted her to fit in.

She went to get the (only) evening bag she owned from her closet when she noticed something else still in the shopping bag. Pantyhose. The dress went to her ankles—who still wore pantyhose? Then she realized they were control top; extra firm, tummy control.

* * *

MRS. FITZSIMMONS WORE a boat-necked, cream knit floor-length gown from St. John that set off her red hair flawlessly. Raquel knew it was St. John because she recognized it from their advertisement in *Vogue*. She felt very grateful, both for knowing that fact—"*Mrs. Fitzsimmons, that St. John looks fabulous on you*"—as well as her present from Nick—"*And that Vivienne Tam on you, Raquel.*" She hadn't worn Betsaida's dress, but she came armed with her sage advice garnered from years of dinners with her wealthy white roommates' parents while at boarding school. "*Stick to academics*," Bets advised. "*Wow them with your smarts, because they think you were a diversity admit and will be extra impressed that you actually know shit.*" With this in mind, Raquel spun the comment on Vivienne Tam into a yarn about artworks and fashion and contemporary Chinese art, and, as Betsaida predicted, the Fitzsimmonses were duly impressed. "*Volunteer only positive attributes about your family, bob and weave around direct questions about your home life, and when backed into a corner, give compliments.*" Raquel offered them insight into her close relationship with her sister, an aspiring actress in New York, and her boyfriend, the filmmaker. "*What a wonderfully creative family*," Mr. Fitzsimmons had replied. "*Of course, you and Nick hit it off. I'm sadly the bean counter in our household.*" When asked for details about her mother, all Raquel mentioned was that she practically raised them in a museum and that she was enjoying life as an empty nester, having gone back to school. After they remarked how fabulous and commendable that was, Raquel pivoted this into a compliment for Mrs. Fitzsimmons. "*Fabulous for you! Nick told me how you went back and got your master's in art administration.*" The story of her return to school took them through the main course and, after the waiters came out with a tiramisu topped off with a flaming sparkler—*Happy Graduation Nick!* written in chocolate cursive on the plate—Raquel figured she would also throw some compliments Astrid's way. Astrid, who had failed to show up for dinner.

"Did Nick tell you that Astrid and I are fellows at the RISD Museum together?"

"Oh, thank goodness," Nick's father said. "Maybe being around someone so levelheaded will set her straight. Give her some of your and Nick's ambition."

Raquel was obviously not going to contradict this but felt it wrong. Astrid had lots of ambitions; lots of flights of fancy, but lots of ambitions.

"Don't get my mother started, Raquel," Nick said. "She's still upset about this summer."

The candlelight of the restaurant only slightly softened the tightening around Mrs. Fitzsimmons's jaw. She took a large sip of her martini.

"I set up a curatorial internship for my daughter in the Print and Photography Department of MoMA. Pulled every string, had countless lunches, wrote checks. All Astrid had to do was show up for an interview."

"They bought her a train ticket and everything," Nick chimed in. "She never showed."

"Raquel, do you know how embarrassing that is for me?" Mrs. Fitzsimmons asked. "I'm a trustee."

"It just goes to show," Mr. Fitzsimmons offered, "the deserving aren't always those born into opportunity. I can only imagine what someone like Raquel would have done with that same chance. Isn't that right, Raquel?"

"So true," Mrs. Fitzsimmons interjected. "Raquel, you must come by the apartment and see the collection. Nick told us you are studying Jack Martin; we have a marvelous piece."

At the table, Raquel marveled at this news and asked provocative questions about Jack Martin that she hoped made her seem both informed and moldable. Internally, she tried to untangle the knot of thoughts that had nested in the front of her head. Distressed at how misaligned the Fitzsimmonses' view of Astrid was from reality. The RISD fellowship application was intensely rigorous. Two letters of recommendation from faculty, a transcript, a previously graded paper, *and* a statement of purpose. It was striking to Raquel how little that effort was appreciated here. Outweighed by what? Rejection of prestige? Rejection of string pulling? Astrid was clearly in the wrong. But her behavior seemingly was more an act of rebellion than a character flaw. Yet, she couldn't find the voice to defend her friend. Why? Was she worried about finding herself on the other side of Nick's parents' favor? Then, there was the RISD fellowship itself. The implication that it was all well and good for Raquel, but someone like their daughter (or their son, she realized) could do—should do—better? Worse, she wondered, what was it about her that screamed out that she was not someone who had been born into opportunity? Certainly nothing she'd said. Certainly not how she dressed. Was it the way she looked? The way she spoke? Her name? Things their son had told them? Things that they simply presumed?

Everyone dove into the tiramisu except Raquel, who politely declined. The pantyhose were digging into her waist.

* * *

"YOU WERE AMAZING!" Nick said, the second they were out of earshot of Nick's parents. "They absolutely loved you, and how could they not?"

"Thank you," she said and gave him a kiss on the cheek. "And thanks for the dress."

They were standing on Brown Street, right outside the gates to the main green, and Raquel could hear the Providence Philharmonic from here. It was just a little bit chilly, but not so much as to ruin the crystal-clear night. Graduation weekend coincided with class reunions, and the university pulled out all the stops to make the campus look as idyllic as possible. The smell of finals was, ironically, the smell of fresh mulch being laid, hyacinth and daffodils being planted, freshly sodded and seeded grass. But tonight their fragrance filled Raquel not with the anxiety of exams but with excited anticipation. Mr. and Mrs. Fitzsimmons were picking up their drink tickets from the makeshift box office the school had set up and Raquel thought about how, just last year, she was on the other side of that window. The whole night, elegantly dressed alumni, coming up to buy drink tickets, getting progressively sloppier as the evening wore on, all of them having a ball. Her entire experience of the dance seen through a picture window; the best of the celebration having concluded by the time her shift ended. Now, for the first time, she'd get to see what was outside the frame; what all the fuss was about.

"All right, all right," Mr. Fitzsimmons said, cheerily. Since dessert, he had been giddy with excitement about Campus Dance, his enthusiasm only building up Raquel's own anticipation. "Nick, if you guys feel like hanging with some old people, we're at table seventy-five; but if I were you, I wouldn't hang out with old people. Here's some drink tickets, but you know how it goes—"

"The alumni will all buy us drinks," Nick said to Raquel. "It's tradition."

"The best tradition!" Mr. Fitzsimmons added. "Raquel, I can't believe you haven't come to this yet. It is one of the greatest parts about this place!"

Raquel wasn't going to burst his bubble by explaining that hardly any Third World students went to Campus Dance—at least not before their own senior year. Commencement weekend gigs paid double; it was too good a chance to make money. So Raquel had been around Campus Dance before, just not as a guest.

"Raquel," Mrs. Fitzsimmons said, a little slur in her speech from all the dinner cocktails, "when your time comes, try to marry someone who also went to Brown, because no one else will be able to match your enthusiasm. Though it is, I must admit, a marvelous event."

Nick linked his hand through hers.

"Let's get a drink."

When they stepped onto the green, her breath was taken away. For days, she had been crossing to get to List Art Building or the library and seen the bandstand being erected in front of University Hall, the hundreds of tables being set out, the thousands and thousands of lights strung across the vast expanses of the main and lower green; two football fields' worth of white paper lanterns. She had stood, watching in a riveted trance, as the guys from Facilities hung the illuminated sign that read 1998, the one she knew would be lit at midnight, as tradition as old as electricity itself dictated. Yet none of this prepared her for the night magic of it. Of nostalgia and the present moment, living, impossibly, side by side. The orchestra played Dizzy Gillespie and hundreds of couples flooded the dance floors. The bars—oh, and the bars were everywhere—were impossibly big. A dozen bartenders and who knew how many barbacks at each; and when you'd approach, older alumni would just stand there, tap you on the shoulder or clap you on the back and ask to get you a drink; they'd inquire about what you were studying, if you'd graduated, where you were headed after Brown. Everyone, if not a friend, a mutual part of something. And in every passing moment, as the night chilled, the drinks continued to warm her. The dozens upon dozens of moments when she'd walked past these buildings, feeling broken down or exhausted and unsure of her place, began to fade into darkness, replaced by the white, magical lights all around her.

After a while, Nick asked her to dance. The band was playing "A String of Pearls" and even though she was certain Nick wouldn't have the slightest idea of what to do if Busta Rhymes came on, here he led her confidently through what he explained was a Lindy.

"Don't forget," he said, "I've been coming to this thing since I was a kid."

"How establishment of my antiestablishment boo," she joked.

"You got me." Nick laughed. "The phonies have some savoir faire from time to time."

Another song came on that she didn't know and as Nick spun her around she caught a glimpse of something that took her by surprise: Claire dancing with an older man who Raquel quickly realized was her father. She felt her stomach drop; kept turning her head to assess the situation. They were near the twenty-fifth reunion tables, her father donning one of the dinner jackets everyone from the Class of '73 seemed to be wearing. (They were, Raquel thought, a particularly jovial group, judging by the number of drink tickets they'd been passing out at the bars.) She must have stared a bit too long, because from across the distance, Claire turned her head. Locked eyes with her.

"Ugh," Raquel said, taking Nick's hand as she stopped dancing. "Let's take a walk. One of the Art History Girls is here."

Raquel gestured with her head toward Claire and saw in Nick's eyes a moment of recognition.

"The queen of the phonies," he muttered under his breath.

The First World was, of course, full of microworlds. Some that she knew existed and others she'd just discovered, including that of Upper East Side private schools. Raquel tried to get them to leave and Nick yanked her back toward him on the dance floor.

"Raquel," he said, looking her in the eyes, "why should *you* leave when you're having a good time?"

Maybe it was the cocktails mixed with the sentimentality, but she felt herself full of emotion. She immediately returned to that night at the Art History Girls' suite. The wave of shame she had felt, bowing her head down and saying, despite every bone in her being not believing it was true, that she was sorry for stealing a spot. How they had said that wasn't good enough and kept blocking her way. How Mavette tried, finally, to get them to back off and they ignored her. And Raquel had felt the room closing in on her and wanted to get out of there, and suddenly found herself, eyes full of tears, dropped down on her knees, begging them to please just let her leave. How

Margot crouched down to look her in the eyes and said, "*Now say 'I'm a talentless nobody' and we'll let you go.*" And Raquel had said it. She demeaned herself and said that to them because she just wanted to get out of there. And how even then, it was only because Mavette shoved Margot out of the way and picked Raquel up off the floor that she had really been able to leave.

"You just don't understand," she said to Nick now, the sting of the tears hot like acid in her eyes, knowing Claire and who knows who else was watching them in the middle of this giant dance floor. "They were so awful to me."

"Which is why we shouldn't go anywhere," he said, "and why we should keep dancing. Because you have just as much a right to be here as she does."

He pulled her close to him and soon the dance floor broke out into applause as "It Had to Be You" began and the wet of her warm tears on Nick's neck released the scent of him and she breathed it in, deeply. Finding calm. It felt like everyone at Campus Dance then joined them on that dance floor but, there, in Nick's arms, she felt like they were the only two people in the entirety of the world. Nick spun her and twisted her and she felt, for the first time since she'd gotten to Brown, that he was right. This place was hers too. She had crossed through the looking glass and, on the other side, all of it belonged to her.

* * *

THAT NIGHT, THEY didn't go back to Nick's place or to hers, they went down to the Biltmore. They had one needless nightcap—martinis, because Raquel wanted to drink from those glasses—and laughed at all of the random, inebriated, and inappropriate conversations they'd stumbled into with alumni through the night. Of his father and mother doing the foxtrot on the dance floor, of the WASPiness of having so many people gathered for so many hours and never offering a speck of food but a bountiful supply of drinks. And then they took the brass-and-glass elevator of the neo-Federal landmark up to the thirty-third floor and, for the first time since they'd started having sex, Raquel felt herself release. She let herself feel the joy and the pleasure. Wanted more and more of him inside of her.

Jack

NEW YORK CITY • FALL 1985

It was a jovial affair, Giancarlo's gallery bathed in warm white light. Smartly dressed women and men sharing laughter and colloquies in Italian, English, and French. This is what Jack loved most about international shows. Yes, he'd carefully cultivated the image of the everyman artist, unconcerned with the material things. And, in many ways, he was that guy. He knew money didn't matter, but . . . refinement did. And openings, where he could just stand there, knowing everyone was gathered in *his* name, because of *his* art. Well, in those moments he appreciated that he'd traveled farther from Worcester, Massachusetts, than could be measured in miles. Yes, he might have calloused his hands once or twice at work, but this was by choice, not necessity. Not the way his father's hands had been, sacrificed to a lifetime of putting food on the table. Hands so rough, he once accidentally scratched his mother's porcelain face. (She hadn't protested, his mother.) "*Do whatever you can to have soft hands, Jack*," his father had said. "*My wife is a queen stuck with a brute's hands*." He'd never discouraged Jack from drawing or reading poetry; never thought it would make Jack a "sissy" or any of that shit that so many of his artist friends had suffered through. No, he wanted his son to have a soft hands kind of life. Cheered that on. And so, at these openings, Jack liked to linger in the corner a bit, watching.

Letting his chest puff a bit for having done right by his dad. His dad who would've felt out of place in Rome, let alone a gallery.

Around the room, mounted flush to the walls, were a series of plus signs, each formed from plates of different materials. One, squares of iron; another, mounted bricks. The third created from thin tiles of marble, and finally, one of wood. Just simple plus signs. Each deliberately set just a hair off from creating four equal quadrants. Just enough that you weren't sure if you were looking at a plus sign exactly, or was it a crucifix? (*What did a crucifix on a wall make you feel that a plus sign didn't?* he'd wondered.) It gave him a tickle to hear people debate what they were actually seeing contrasted against what he'd written in his artist statement:

> iron, bricks, marble and wood.
>
> Beginning. And. End.

Sometimes a pipe's just a pipe, right? And sometimes he'd find himself thinking about his time as an altar boy as a child. That was his business. A passing couple was having this cross–plus sign debate in French—he'd picked up a surprising amount over the course of his long career—when his eye caught on something. It was the wooden cross at the far end of the long gallery—unvarnished panels of oak, flaxen like Ingrid's hair, only now he saw—

RED.

Just a flash. Crimson.

Bright like a cardinal, but red where it shouldn't be. This show was white walls and warm light. The cool gray of iron, iridescent white marble smoked with silver. Not red. Nowhere red. He glanced again and it was gone. He was certain of what he'd seen. He excused himself from the person he'd been talking to and got a fresh glass of wine from the bar. Someone in the crowd called his name, he turned his head and—

RED. RED. RED.

Longer this time. Bright! A figure. A body.

A woman.

Then, nothing. Just the wood cross. Seven feet wide by seven feet tall, mounted flush against the wall. A red dress? A quickly turned head? The blurred vision of a depressingly aging man? Jack scanned the crowd to confirm this assessment and couldn't find her. Just the usual sea of black cocktail dresses. No woman draped in the shocking crimson that had sliced into his line of sight. He slowly made his way to the piece, dodging attempts to draw him into conversation. What had he seen?

Closer to the work, nothing was out of sorts. Just the clean cut of wood revealing its winding, senseless grain. A pattern so random, no man could make it, he thought.

From behind him, Giancarlo's laughter cut through the hum of the room, calling Jack's attention. He was chatting with the comely young poet who'd just arrived at the American Academy. Jack stood for a moment, admiring her. A dark blue dress with the thinnest of straps revealed cream-colored skin covered with freckles, chestnut hair just grazing the top of her breasts, braless under the sundress. She looked so perfectly . . . American. Exactly what he knew men in Europe imagined when they conjured the thought. Jack decided he would seduce her. Who could resist the man of the—

RED.

From the corner of his eye.

RED. RED. REDDDDDDDDDD.

(Anita.)

No. No. Could not be. A thing of madness.

He could not bring himself to turn his head, too frightened that he saw what he saw. What he must be imagining that he saw. He was frozen in place as the back of his neck goose-skinned, nerves tingling from the base of his brain down to his backside as he felt the pierce of a stare. (Her stare.) Eyes on him, boring through the back of his skull. The feeling of being looked at—not with admiration, but disdain—made his heart race. He knew he must look. Must see if he saw—he had—what he thought he saw.

He shuttered his eyes, commanded his neck to turn his head toward the cross. Willed his eyes to open, locking with hers in an instant. Anita. RED. Not as he saw her last in their apartment, but as she last was outside of it: Body mangled and bloodied, thirty floors below.

Hair matted with red, hot and wet and sticky, covering her face, but her eyes! Wide, wide open. Because even from that distance he could feel them staring up at him.

He sucked his breath, felt his chest cave in on itself. His hands covered his face, his only protection from the gape of her round, wide eyes.

Oh, but he could still see it. Still see her.

BRRuuuUM . . .

BRRuuuUM . . .

BRRuuuUM . . .

The buzzing—electric and loud—startled him, forced his eyes open when he desperately wanted to keep them shut. Desperately wanted to avoid the RED, but instead found. White. Bright and cold. The *BRRuuUM* droning on and on in the background. *Fuck. Fuck. Fuck*, he thinks. This is it. The passageway. The one to the other side. (His heart pounded; uncertain Saint Peter would be waiting at the end.) The light was too cold. Too fluorescent.

"Martin!" A baritone bellow, harsh and indifferent.

He closed his eyes again. This was not death.

Thwack, thwack, thwack, thwack. The rhythm of wood against iron.

This was jail.

"Martin?" the voice said, closer now. "Get your shit, dickweed, it's your lucky day. Somebody posted your fucking bail."

His lids fluttered open, the metal wire around the fluorescent light fixture so clear to him now. The pea-colored paint, peeling off the ceiling above him. So low he could touch it with his arm from his top bunk. To the left and right, the cinder-block walls, damp and clammy. The chill of the place cutting to the bone.

"Did you hear me? Most motherfuckers jump through the bars when they hear the word 'bail.' Or maybe you got a boyfriend in here you don't want to leave?"

Oh, that fucking fortune teller at their wedding had been right.

Jack sat up on the bunk and felt light-headed. He was fifty-seven years old and in that moment he felt it. The damp had made him stiff in his sleep.

His dream.

He remembered nothing. Not the fight, not the call to Tilly afterward, not the one to the police. He didn't remember the cops coming, the arrest. He barely remembered Anita. Suddenly she felt imagined too, though less the thing of nightmares than just a figment—wisp of a thing that she was—of his active imagination. He heard the keys turn in the lock of his cell and, with as much urgency as he could, gathered his few things—a sketch pad; renderings for his upcoming show in Paris—and followed the guard out.

"You're big news here," the guard told him as they walked. "It's not every day that somebody posts two hundred fifty grand in bail."

Jack, dozens of eyes clocking him through cell bars, choked out a reply.

"I've got good friends."

Oh, and they were good friends. In the parking lot, Tilly broke down, and in her embrace, which felt like a sister's and a mother's all at once, Jack finally let everything out. Under the auspices of the prison guards, amid the humiliating administrative work of restoring his freedom, he barely acknowledged her or their friend Gerry, who had driven her. Couldn't handle them bearing witness to his degradation. But now, in Tilly's arms, he released the anguish of the past three days in this place, and his brawny frame shook from it, Tilly's long, slender hands patting his broad shoulders again and again.

"We should go," Gerry interjected. "Ronald is expecting us."

This seemed to break Tilly from the spell. She pulled away from Jack, composed herself before heading toward the car. Mothering was over.

"We got you the best lawyer money could buy; he agreed to see us right away." She gestured for Jack to climb into the back seat. "You look exhausted. You can sleep on the way."

He obeyed, even as he protested.

"Who can sleep? The Paris show is in just a few weeks. I should have been there a week ago. This installation will be complicated."

"It was the Stellas who posted the bail," she said, ignoring him. "Please don't forget to call them."

He looked at her profile. She was such a handsome woman, even distressed.

"Fine, but when can I leave for Paris? Monday is the latest I think I can go."

She exhaled a sigh he recognized, the one reserved for midlevel artists not understanding why she was denying them a solo exhibition.

"Jack," Gerry said in a way he could tell had been rehearsed, "going to Paris is out of the question. Travel is out of the—"

"My shows are great because of the precision only I can bring. Tell him, Tilly."

Jack Martin, he wanted to make clear, didn't get to where he was in the art world by taking no for an answer.

"Jack," she said sharply, turning fully around to look him in the eye like he was a badly behaved child on a road trip. "Listen to me. You are out on bail on a charge for murder. Do you realize that? You have no passport. You aren't going to Paris. You aren't even going to Brooklyn until we get you through this trial."

Jack looked out the window. It was the first time Tilly was not taking his side. They were driving on the causeway, headed toward Queens, its low industrial landscape in the distance. This was bullshit and he didn't understand why they didn't understand. It's bad enough he's been through all this; bad enough he'd been in jail, lost his Anita. Now he would lose his art too?

He could hear Tilly and Gerry muttering: things Jack needed to do, stuff he needed to know about the days since *it* had happened. The three confusing days since Anita went out the window. But he shut them out, instead taking out his sketchbook and drawing, with as much precision and detail as he could, the plus signs that were to be installed in Paris.

"I got you a hotel, Jack, just for a few nights," Tilly was saying.

"I'll be fine at home," he said absentmindedly.

"It's not purely therapeutic," Gerry offered, "it's the optics. You have no idea the feminist nuts that have been camped out in front of your building."

"It's been all over the news, I'm afraid," Tilly said.

Jack understood now why Tilly had asked Gerry, specifically, to come with her; he was a public relations man. Had worked for Koch for a time and before that for Steve Rubell and the Studio 54 people. Tilly, always thinking ahead.

"These women are setting up street shrines, picketing. We don't want to leave any room open for public sympathies to build for their cause."

Jack had no idea why, but he thought of the doormen. What they must think of him. Anita and her theatrics. He shrugged it off. Returned to his crosses.

"Also, Jack," Tilly said, softly, "Anita's friends are putting together some kind of memorial for her."

"When?" he said, ripping the sketch out of his notebook to hand to Tilly. "Fax this to Thierry. I'll get him the others soon."

"Does it matter? It's not like you can go."

"I understand that I can't go to Paris, but I don't think they can legally stop me from going to my wife's fucking memorial. Or should I wait and ask the lawyer?"

He looked down at his sketchbook, the crosses all staring back at him, and his dream—the nightmare, really—came back to visit him. Oh, those damn eyes. A wave of nausea flooded over him. His head felt heavy and dry like a hangover, but this one from life. From his fucking miserable life.

"Wake me up when we get there," Jack announced. He closed his eyes.

* * *

THEY HAD GOTTEN married in the backyard of Giancarlo's house, a little ways outside of Rome. Oh, it had been perfect. All of it. The garden was out of a storybook—a low stone fence, wildflowers all around. Anita loved the flowers and they had made a print book together for all the guests. Her pages were all botanicals; his were all the stones. She wore a calf-length gown crocheted out of cotton by a woman she'd met during a long weekend they'd spent in Sicily. It was perfect against her tanned brown skin, her doll-like frame. She never really lost the girlishness of her body, though hearing that would upset her. She'd wanted curves so badly. "*Curves make you look more luscious when you dance*," she had told him. But he liked her size. His little broken wren. When she would cry to him—about her years in the orphanage, about his infidelities—he would make a nest of his big, long arms. Rest her. Feed her his love and lust through his mouth in words and kisses like little worms for a hungry fledgling. All with the goal of making her strong enough to fly.

They had no family at the event. It hadn't occurred to Jack to fly his aging parents across the ocean, and he and his sister were hardly close. Anita had called her father when Jack proposed so that Jack could ask his permission. A rare moment of traditionalism that surprised and intimidated him. But though he'd heard her talking to her mother and sister about the wedding over the phone—an English word slipping in here or there; he'd never grasped Spanish the same way he had French—she never made mention of them attending. In fact, on the day itself, she never even brought them up. She'd never, he felt, really forgiven them for sending her to America, for abandoning her. Giancarlo had offered to give her away but she shut him up. "*I'm here by sheer will of self. Nobody is giving me to anybody.*"

At the reception, as a surprise, Giancarlo hired a local fortune teller to read palms. Jack had been reluctant, but Anita was busy dancing and Giancarlo wouldn't let it go. Eventually Jack was so hammered that he relented. Giancarlo walked him to the corner of the garden where the little old man from the village sat. He took Jack's large, soft hands into his small ones, wrinkled from years and spotted by the sun. He turned them over, face up and outstretched. Jack remembered thinking he was standing before the apostle Thomas, allowing him to judge the veracity of his wounds. The man stared for a long moment before he clasped Jack's palms together in his, crossed himself, and spat over his shoulder three times. "*Che povera disgraziata creatura!*" he declared to Giancarlo. From then on, at nearly any and every cocktail party that they were at together, Giancarlo would tell that story: about the old man who called Jack Martin—the God of Minimalist Art—a poor wretched creature. "*Who, can you imagine, is less poor and wretched than this colossus!*" And every time, it would get a big laugh.

* * *

IN THE RECEPTION area of the attorney's office, Jack sat, recollecting his condemnation. Anita would never tell him what the fortune teller told her; her Italian was perfect and she had no witnesses. It had annoyed him then, and even more so now, for a reason he couldn't explain. As the moments passed, a sense of resolve came over him. Resolve to prove that prick of a palm reader wrong. When the receptionist told them Ron Rosen was ready to see them, Jack bolted up. Headed with determination into the well-appointed office, extended his arm, and took Ron's hand firmly into his.

"I'm Jack Martin and I'm innocent."

Jack never imagined needing to have a criminal attorney, never imagined what one would be like, but Ron Rosen seemed to fit the bill. He was incredibly fit, white-haired and tanned, in a suit that was tailored impeccably—something that made Jack relax; it showed he cared about details. But this was coupled with the demeanor of a boxer and a Bronx accent so thick, Jack felt confident that in another life—one that didn't go from City College to NYU Law, as the lavishly framed diplomas on the walls announced—he could have been breaking heads for Meyer Lansky. This felt, to Jack, like it would be helpful in a courtroom. As his client, however, after an hour of questioning, it was quite agitating.

"Your call to 911 was different from what you told the cops when they got there. That's not fantastic," Ron said.

"I was in shock," Jack said.

He had already played them the tape: Jack, through sobs, explaining that he and his wife had an argument, that there'd been a suicide.

"Over the phone you said that you'd fought, that she went to the bedroom, you went after her, and then she went out the window. But then, when the cops came, you said she'd stormed off to the bedroom and when you went to bed an hour or so later, she wasn't in there anymore."

"I didn't do it."

"I don't really care if you did or you didn't," Ron said. "I care that it makes some fucking sense, OK? What they have is the recording of the call—"

"I don't remember even making that call," Jack interjected, his voice rising.

"*And*, they have your phone records from that night, indicating that you made a call *before* you dialed 911."

"How many times do I need to tell you that I don't remember," Jack barked.

Ron Rosen looked over to Gerry.

"I need this, Gerry?" he asked.

"Mr. Rosen," Tilly said, calmly, "I have been Jack's gallerist and confidante for over twenty years. He'd been at my house with his wife earlier that evening. He was distraught and called me and I advised him to immediately hang up and call 911."

"I'm going to forget that you said that, Ms. Barber, because I don't think it's terrific that it took him forty-five more minutes to do that, do you?"

Jack looked away from Tilly's stare; did not want to register her surprise at that.

"I heard she wanted a divorce. Hired a private eye," Rosen continued.

"Bullshit," Jack said through gritted teeth. "Never."

"Her sister told the cops that Anita said as much over the phone earlier that night."

"My wife fucking loved me!"

"What would a private eye find out about you, I'm wondering," Ron Rosen goaded.

"You're missing the point," Jack barked. "What I explained to the cops when they got there is that I am much more successful than my wife and she was really struggling with that. That was what the quarrel was about and that's why—"

"Except that doesn't exactly pan out on paper."

"Oh, please," Gerry said, the defense in his voice. "This man's a titan! He's shown in every major museum, not just in New York but around the fucking world, Ron."

"I get that, I get it," Ron said. "I understand you are a great success, Mr. Martin. Like I said, I'm just trying to look at everything they are going to tell the jury. And that includes the fact that yes, you were exhibited by all the fancy museums, but your last big exhibition was at a state college almost five years ago—"

"With all due respect," Tilly interjected, a rarity, "that Berkeley show was very important."

"And that," Ron continued, ignoring her, "for the last few years, your work has been selling for less and less."

"Art is like fashion, Ronnie," Gerry interjected. "Things are hot and then they cool off and come back again."

Jack's irritation was growing into indignation. That he was paying his hard-earned fucking money for this man to insinuate he was on the decline?

"My wife was a nobody and a climber. If she hadn't been married to me, no one would have known who she was in the first place."

"Except that this isn't true either exactly," Ron replied. He picked up a piece of paper from his desk. Anita's fucking CV. "Let's see: 1980, Mellon residency in Miami. 1980, Guggenheim grant. 1982, recipient of the Rome Prize. Since then, commissions, museum acquisitions . . . I don't know about your world, but as an average Joe, that all sounds pretty impressive."

"You weren't fucking there," Jack yelled, jumping up from his seat. "And you didn't know her. Ruthlessly ambitious and blindly jealous of me. I told her she'd never have my career and she just couldn't live with the truth."

There was silence for a moment. Wherever there wasn't rich mahogany cabinetry in Ron Rosen's office, there were windows. Jack walked toward them for a moment, watched the traffic going up Park Avenue.

"Tracy," Ron said into his intercom, his voice notably softer, "can you order us some lunch? I think Mr. Martin could use a nice lunch."

Jack realized he was quite hungry; glanced at the bar cart in the corner and hoped he'd be offered a drink with the food. What he really needed, he realized now, was a fucking drink.

"Mr. Martin, listen," Ron said. "This isn't always easy work, but we've got to do it. What they've done well, at least in the public arena, is make it hard to buy that your wife was suicidal with her career on the rise and her future plans discussed with friends. So, I'm thinking we need to paint a picture of a woman more . . . unhinged."

Jack grimaced. Anita was no crazier than any other artist. More passionate, maybe, but not crazier.

"Tilly was telling me that she was into witchcraft?"

"Santeria," Jack replied. "It's a Cuban thing."

"Between that and her acting bonkers at Tilly's party," Gerry added.

"She was acting like Anita," Jack said.

"Are you working for or against me here?" Ron said.

"He's working *with* you," Tilly answered.

"Great. So, this thing your wife was into?"

"Santeria, it's a religion. It was more of a fascin—"

"Tilly says there's blood and chickens and shit? That she studied with witches in Cuba or something?"

Jack nodded and a big smile broke out on Ron's face.

"Perfect. We're gonna convince them that Santeria sent her out that window."

Anita

CUBA • FALL 1980

Now we are at a crossroads.

The only way for you to understand what comes next is for you to know what came first: going home to Cuba. Not the time when Jack pushed me and I died and ended up in Varadero. No, the time, years before that. When I went through the air the other way: on a plane, and finally saw again the place I'd been dreaming of for nearly twenty years.

Pero coño, here's the thing: I don't want to talk to you about Cuba.

Because what do you know of it? Of the joy and horror of arriving at the place you'd counted on to answer all the nagging questions of your soul, only to find more questions? To get to the destination your inner compass has been driving you back to, screaming to you was home, only to discover that you didn't really belong? Not anymore. Not really. What do you know of that? Sure, maybe you too know heartbreak and betrayal and loneliness. Fine. I'll give you that. But what do you know of Cuba? My Cuba.

And if you *do* know of Cuba—if you know of exile and separation—you certainly don't need me to tell you about it. You don't need me to tell you about the Castro of it all. How you don't want to distill an entire country down to just one man's existence, but how Castro won't tolerate anything less. If you know Cuba, you won't need me to explain your parents raging at you for going back, not understanding how and why you needed to return! How it beckoned to you for so long, the taboo be damned! If you know Cuba, you won't need me to tell you how America makes you feel so Cuban you bleed cafecitos and rum, and then you get back home and discover you might as well be an apple fucking pie for how American you've become. If you know Cuba you will know the heartbreak of reuniting with family who have become strangers. No, if you know Cuba, you won't need me to tell you about any of this. And if you don't know, and really want to, at least have the decency to ask me in Spanish.

In Spanish I'll tell you about what it was like to feel the sand of Varadero—fine and silky and sticky like sugar—wedged into the crevices of your toes. The same way it did when I was twelve years old. In Spanish, I'll tell you about smelling the air again: thick with salt, wet with palm leaves, bright with the smell of diesel, and rich from the metal of the red earth. In Spanish I might tell you about Yemayá, my orisha; the mother of all orishas. And how she claimed me there, like she's claimed so many of her other children. And if I *trust* you, well, then I might tell you how I learned to hold ceremony, how it taught me patience and a different kind of work. In Spanish I might tell you of how, until my year in Cuba, I'd only known the iconography of this faith, but none of the true meaning. And how I started my spiritual journey under a ceiba tree—my destiny, really—at El Templete, when a man I didn't know told me to walk around the tree three times and make a wish. If you want to know about all that, then ask me in Spanish. Then, at least, I can give these things the poetry with which they were meant to be told.

But we're talking in English. So, I'll leave my return to the most salient details: Marco, my art, and how I came to stay—not for a week as was intended, but a year. A full year of finding myself. A full year away from Jack.

The homegoing was part of—as all things Cuban-American are—a political gesture. An American delegation of artists was invited to soften relations between the two countries that we were a part of. The first night, they welcomed us with a grand dinner on the lawn of the Hotel Nacional. Government officials and American and Cuban artists broke bread, reunited under this common bond of our vocation. And at the end, we lined up and took a picture. All of us smiling. Very polite. But, underneath the pomp, the whole thing was strangely heartbreaking. How American the Americans among us were! Constantly wanting and taking more: food, wine, information. Myself included; maybe me most of all! All this fucking time, thumping my chest about my Cuban-ness only to discover that I'd not been impervious to twenty-five years of America. None of us had. "*But can you make a living?*" "*Who buys your art?*" "*Can you travel to promote your work?*" The inability to measure the value of our work without commerce, money, prestige. We didn't talk about love or happiness or family, but of our ambitions and successes. None of the Cubans at the table had heard of half the credentials we'd spent all night bragging about holding. But that didn't stop us from boasting nonetheless. Why? Because at home everyone told us we were shit, and the only way we'd found to believe otherwise was to wrap ourselves in tiny moments of white validation.

Also, truth be told, we couldn't really *talk* to the Cuban artists. That became clear. They gave us answers cloaked in propaganda. Answers manicured for the government officials among us. Truth was in their eyes, not their words. And I liked the mischief I saw in Marco's eyes immediately. Jomar, who'd come as my guest, befriended him during cocktails and by the time we were getting dessert—as exhausted by the policed small talk as we were—he leaned toward me and whispered, "*Are you game for an excursion later?*" And of course, I said yes.

We rendezvoused at his art studio in Habana Vieja, a long, narrow space with large windows that opened out and let in all the music of the street. The walls were lined with Marco's paintings, all landscapes. Even in the dim light, it was easy to see that they were magnificent, moody things. Ah! How we drank that night. Glass after glass of rum. We laughed plenty, but what I really remember was how we cried. Me about my father's wrath, his fury with this very trip. Jomar for the family who disowned him when he came out as gay. Marco, in whispers, told of his boyfriend who was hauled off to jail simply for acting on his natural desires. Then Marco said, "*Can I show you what I'm really working on?*" And disappeared into a hallway and returned with two large canvases: gorgeous monochromatic blue nudes, all of the same man. The only color in their lips: red and petal pink and luscious and wet-looking. "*My old boyfriend*," he said with a smile. "*I paint him and it makes me miss him less.*" They were stunning things, the backdrops abstract and smooth, the flesh of the bodies full of life and brushwork and the colors—every shade from azure to electric to midnight pulsing with intensity. They took your breath away. I felt a deep melancholy overcome me and Jomar must have had the same thought because he was animated before he suddenly went solemn.

"You can show these?" he asked, incredulously.

"Are you kidding?" Marco said with a laugh. "As it is, my landscapes are almost too queer for the government galleries."

His rolling hills *were* quite sensuous.

"Then, what do you do with them?" I asked.

"I show them now," he said, "for friends. I don't know. Maybe if someone wanted to buy one, I'd sell, but even then . . ."

Jomar wanted to do just that, right then and there, but Marco said no. We thought it was some act of false modesty or Cuban pride at an act of charity, but then he told us that he was afraid. It was too risky. If our bags were searched as we left and they discovered it—discovered what he was really painting—he wouldn't get to show in the few galleries that did sell his work. If they saw what he was really painting, maybe the punishment would be even worse.

"Like I said, I make them for me," he said. "It's worth the paint to tell my truth."

Ah! I couldn't sleep that night. Or for many nights afterward. This casual remark by Marco having exposed the fraud of my very self! My work had not been about my truth for a very long time. New York, I realized, made a liar out of me. My work that got me there? The shit I did in Iowa? Yeah, sure. The performance of it was. The ideas! The spirit! But the images? The stills? The fucking frames Isaac had designed that popped off the walls? All of that was packaging, not designed to tell the truth but to win approval. From whom? Buyers? Tilly? Jack fucking Martin?

After Havana, the government sent us up to Jaruco, to a nature preserve. Our hotel there sat high on a hill, overlooking the vast wilds below. Sleep was impossible and when it did creep upon me, the nightmares came with it. One in particular that made me bolt upright in bed. (Yes, I remember it. No, I won't tell you.) I need to get outside when I'm troubled. It wasn't yet dawn but I went on a walk. Took myself outside so that I could go in. I went out along the red dirt road that stretched in front of the hotel, all of it surrounded by forest. Barefoot, so my soles could feel the earth. The energy!

A rain started—unexpected and quick—and the road went muddy. The smell of wet earth reminded me of the Iowa River. I remembered the silt of it that I buried myself in for my art. But as I walked there, the terra of Cuba on my toes, I realized that the truth of that piece was a desperation. To do with my body what I had yearned to do with my life: Fit in. Belong. Be accepted by "my country." Time and again—in a classroom, at a party, with my foster parents—I'd been told I wasn't enough. That I was too much. And so I tried to fit in literally. Wedge between rocks and river. Render myself barely visible. And I realized—in a way that newly pained me—that the reaction to those images? Tilly rejecting them. The "establishment" rejecting them. It felt like . . . Well, it felt like even when I bury myself in your fucking soil, I'm still not American enough.

I was disgusted with myself for trying so hard. Felt a need—an urge really—to make amends. To prostrate myself, in some way, for having gone to such pains to become one with a place that rejected me over and over and over again. To give myself back to the place that had birthed me; this place that politics and man—American man—had pulled me asunder from. On the side of the road with the rain beating down, I peeled off my wet clothes. Stripped my body bare and began to cover myself. Covered myself with the red earth of Cuba. On my knees, I raked my hands through the mud, carved out two handfuls of brick-shaded clay and slathered it on my breasts. Covered my thighs, my arms. I combed it thick through my hair, letting it permeate my scalp, the rain, softer now, running it wet down my back into the crack of my backside—cool and cold. I scratched into the earth so it melded into my nail beds, deep under every single fingernail. So deep it hurt. I frosted my face with the mud like a cake. Rolled my tongue over my lips and took in the taste that was older than me or my mother or Castro or the Spanish conquistadors. I tasted the mineral and salt of it; the taste of Taino land on my lips. And it tasted so good. This return to myself. And then, when I was reddened and fully covered with home—on the inside and out—I stood up and let the rain wash it all off of me and I felt truly cleansed. Bathed with the same kind of peace I would feel when I made a piece of art. And I had. There were no stills to document it. No video to take back home and try to hawk to this gallery or that. But I had made my first silueta at home and, like Marco, I had made it just for me.

The trip, the official trip, was meant to be seven days. But I was not going back.

Not then anyway.

For some, the distance between deciding and doing is a wide gulf. I'm fortunate not to be one of those people. Later that morning, while the rest of our delegation was gossiping over breakfast, I took a seat beside Rezza, the guide the Cuban Arts Ministry had assigned to us.

"This is a magical experience," I said. "Truly inspiring."

"The ministry will be happy to hear that. We wanted you to see that vibrant culture is still thriving here in Cuba."

"I'd love to make some artwork here."

"Well, perhaps you will be able to come back," Rezza said.

"I was thinking now," I replied. "Not right now, of course. But why abandon inspiration?"

Rezza was funny, I have to hand it to him. He seemed like a government shill, but he was quick on the uptake.

"You want to extend your stay."

"Who wouldn't want to stay here?" I said with a smile.

"It's not possible," he said.

Here's what I'd already discovered in Cuba: nearly everything that seemed impossible—making salacious art, speaking your mind, owning Miami Sound Machine records—had a work-around. For a price, of course.

"Rezza," I said, and though he was much younger than I was, I made sure to touch his arm and smile, "thousands of Cubans are trying to get off this island every day; here's one who wants to stay home."

Rezza looked at me, then took a sip of his coffee.

"If I could help you, it would be expensive," he said, before quickly adding, "and that isn't me, I want you to know. You can't stay without a visa extension and the guy in that office is a fucking capitalist pig."

"I have five hundred dollars in cash."

He laughed then. "Anita, you don't think we all know about your rich American boyfriend in New York?"

Even here somehow everything became about Jack. And then it hit me.

"I have something worth more than what the capitalist pig could even imagine," I said. I began to unwind the back off the Bulgari earrings Jack had given me. I put them in Rezza's hand and looked one last time at the gift that had cost me so much. "The rubies alone should more than cover his inconvenience. And I know you don't care about money, but find a way to keep some of it for yourself, my friend."

"I can't promise anything," he said, but I saw him smile a bit as he closed his fist around the jewels.

"But you'll try," I said.

And that was how I came to stay in Cuba for the next year. How I came to know my grandmother, my cousins, my family again. How I came to know my orishas. That was how I came to make my cave sculptures all over the island and my beach figures on the shores of Varadero. And more than half of the things washed away or were worn away over time, or maybe some of them are still there. I don't know. I didn't care.

Raquel

PROVIDENCE • SUMMER 1998

Raquel had just brought Belinda Kim her morning coffee and was trying her hardest not to gush too much about her weekend in Newport with Nick when the phone at her desk (her own desk!) began to ring. It was only 8:00 a.m.—Belinda had surprised her by coming in early—and Raquel was puzzled as to who would possibly be calling already.

"I'm so sorry," she said, more apologetically than necessary as she scurried to the cubicle outside Belinda's office, where she'd spent her days over the last month.

"Belinda Kim's office, this is Raquel."

"Oye. You're alive," her mother said.

Fuck! They'd gotten back so late, she'd completely forgotten about her mother's Sunday call. She pushed away her guilt and replaced it with defensiveness.

"Why are you calling me at work, though?" she said, a snip in her voice.

"Watch that attitude, Rocky," her mother huffed. "Three years I call you every Sunday at nine. You never miss a call. Excuse me for wanting to make sure everything is OK. I tried you at home—"

"I was out till late last night and left for work mad early," Raquel said quickly, hoping Betsaida hadn't mentioned not having seen

Raquel in a week. "Listen, Mami, sorry I missed our call. But I'm at work. I can't talk."

Her mother sucked her teeth.

"I know where you are; *I* called you," she said, exasperation in her voice. "It's my day off, I'm not trying to shoot the shit either. I just had some news. But, I get it, if you're busy."

Raquel rolled her eyes. The dramatics.

"Mami, *please* tell me your news."

"We won!" she said, the triumph in her voice.

"Won what?" Raquel said.

"The thousand dollars from Hot 97!" she replied, as though they had just been talking about it and Raquel hadn't followed the conversation properly. "I swear, when your sister and I get along, we're unstoppable."

"That's great, Mami," Raquel said, because it was.

"Anyway, we were trying to call you last night because we're gonna use some of it to come visit. Next weekend. I took Saturday off." Raquel froze. Dropped the phone cord she'd been playing with and sat straight up at her desk. Her mother continued, unaware, excitement building in her voice. "We'll do it up! Rent a car; go to the beach. Toni says they're supposed to be real pretty up there. Maybe hit up Foxwoods."

Her mother started laughing; she loved a little gambling. Raquel knew that to seem anything but enraptured about this idea would not just crush her mother but start a minor war. And she missed them. She had never gone this long without seeing them and was excited to show them her first, real place of her own. But now there was no way to not tell them about Nick. And once they knew about Nick, they would want to meet Nick. And the thought of all of this gave her a headache and she definitely wasn't going to get into it now, not while she was at work. So instead she said,

"That sounds dope."

"Mira, we're gonna pick up the car after I get off work Friday, so we'll be to you by dinner. Maybe we'll get lobster!"

"Maine has the lobsters, Ma. Rhode Island has calamari."

"Bueno, we'll have that too."

Raquel checked to see if Belinda needed a coffee refresh and then went to the ladies' room. She always came in early when she stayed at Nick's because it helped her avoid the awkward issue of shitting in his apartment. It was ridiculous; everyone poops. At her mother's house, Toni would leave the door open and continue conversations from the toilet. There was no such comfort at Nick's. She felt burdened, strangely, by the notion of how aesthetic Nick was. After poring over images of paintings, photographs, and architecture, day after day these last few years, Raquel could see how transformed her own aesthetic sensibilities had become. More keen to readily notice moments of accidental beauty, yes; but also every imperfection. For Nick, steeped in and reared around exquisite things his whole life, she imagined this would be doubly true. She would think sometimes of how perfectly lacquered and impeccably stacked those tires had been at his show; how flawlessly white they had been—not a scuff or blemish anywhere. Of course, the eye that cared so deeply about every detail like that would notice a little pooch in a dress, a blemish on a chin before her period, the frizz of hair ends overdue for a trim. They weren't criticisms. He just wanted to make her the most magnificent version of herself that she could be. *That she deserved to be*, he would say. So, she tried, to the best of her ability, to show him that side of herself: devoting close attention to perfection of her breath, nails, skin, and bikini line. Squeezing in jogs along India Point in the mornings while he slept. Enduring grapefruit and cottage cheese lunches. And, not shitting in his house.

She didn't fully comprehend what prevented her from telling her family about Nick. She had tried, several times, to use Toni as an intermediary, but free-spirited and rebellious as her sister was, she began to feel that, on paper, Nick would seem suspect to her sister. *So, he's rich, but would he be as successful if he was Joe Schmoe from Bushwick?* she could hear Toni saying—a question that Raquel wouldn't fully know how to respond to. Nick had an impeccable sense for the visual. He also had the financial resources to fabricate into reality nearly any specter that popped into his mind. But she still (very quietly) felt that his work wasn't about anything, except—as he himself had admitted about his senior show—looking cool. Of course, she never said this. After that first night, when he would show her sketches for his installation in progress or the paintings he was working on in a studio his parents rented for him in the Jewelry District, he would preempt her questions by launching into a diatribe regarding the concept behind the work. Raquel would nod and smile; careful to mind the frailty of both his ego and the intellectual conceits behind most of his art. That he had sold work to a major museum already was, naturally, a testament to his strong aesthetic. That his mother was a major donor there, she knew, would raise one of Toni's overplucked and preternaturally suspicious eyebrows. In any case, there was no point in using Toni as a middleman if she wasn't going to be a total ambassador.

Perhaps, she now thought, this would work out for the best. She'd come clean on Friday over dinner and they could meet him on Saturday. Keep to a minimum the amount of time for their preconceptions to fill in the blanks about who someone "like" Nick was and just let Nick—handsome, charming, witty—speak for himself. It would all be fine. Truly. She was overthinking this.

She flushed the toilet, washed her hands, and smoothed the flyaway hairs from the part in her hair; adjusted her low, tight chignon. Nick loved her hair this way, told her it made her look more French. A silly compliment, but she wondered at the time if Mavette would agree. In the mirror she put on lipstick, one she and Nick had picked together at Filene's during a day trip to Boston (he eagerly supported her luxury cosmetics habit). It was more orange than the deep wine color Mavette wore, but it complemented her. She smoothed her skirt, feeling a minor wave of pleasure as she noted the way it hung a bit lower on her hip now than when she wore it last, two weeks prior. It would be the first thing her mother noticed. Would she also be able to tell she wasn't a virgin anymore? If she couldn't, she bet Toni would.

The rest of the morning was a thrill: Belinda presented her vision for their figurative exhibition, *The Body Is Not Silent*, to the lead curator for the museum and the marketing team and was met with great enthusiasm. Raquel felt a deep sense of satisfaction for her small role preparing the presentation and awe as she watched her boss in front of her colleagues. Belinda was slight—perhaps under five feet—but she commanded a massive presence in any room she entered. She was the only nonwhite person in the museum who wasn't security or, like Raquel, an intern. But she walked around like she owned the place. Though what she wanted to execute was far loftier than the directive prescribed, Raquel watched as she masterfully sold her vision of an interdepartmental show celebrating the figurative in art history. Belinda, Raquel discovered, was more like her than she could have anticipated in her first interview. Born in Chinatown and raised in Queens, she hadn't gone to prep schools like Betsaida or Marcus, but to public school like Raquel. She'd won a scholarship to Princeton, where she'd intended to focus on Chinese and Asian art history, but, after taking a course on Postimpressionists, found herself gobsmacked by the discourse around Gauguin's Tahitian work. Where her classmates saw exotic beauty and a sense of alienation, she saw a pervert with mental illness objectifying Pacific Islanders as sex objects. "*What I realized, Raquel*," she said one day, "*was that I was just as entitled to be part of the Western art history conversation as I was to the Eastern art history conversation. In fact, perhaps my perspective as a woman of color made my voice more necessary in the first*." Her thesis: one of the first biographically grounded critiques of Gauguin's work through a feminist (womanist, Dr. Kim would say) and racial lens, went on to be published by *ARTnews* and created a national conversation in the academy. Belinda Kim was a pioneer and Raquel was in wonder. Raquel was determined, before the summer was over, to ask Belinda where her confidence came from.

Before lunch, Raquel checked her school email. It was chock full of reminders from the university to preregister for this or that, but also contained an email from her sister with the same information that her mother had relayed over the phone, *Bonjour from Nice* from Mavette . . . and a subject-less email from Marcus.Rhodes@mtv.com. She couldn't bring herself to open Marcus's email yet, so she clicked on the one from Mavette.

Hiiiiiii,

How are things? Still happy in love? How is this woman you're working for? Things here are OK. I mean, it's stunning. You have to come next year. I'm reading The God of Small Things. Have you read it? It's sad and dark and beautiful. Or maybe I'm just grateful to have time to read a novel again.

The "project" is coming along, I guess. The girls met these German brothers whose father runs some kind of national bank and keeps a big yacht out here. They invite us to Lake Como with them. The yacht is nice, but they are dull and I'm not sure I am going to tag along. I went on a few dates with this British guy whose mom is one of my dad's clients (Asian art fetishist), and I could say he's just like Hugh Grant, only younger, except I think he's more like a frat guy with an accent and better clothes?

Please write back this time.

Amitiés,
M

P.S. I just want to say again, I am so sorry.

P.P.S. Have you seen Niles out and about?

Raquel sighed. Mavette had written a couple of times now. The first a long and profuse apology; an acknowledgment that Raquel deserved that spot. That she had no idea Claire had applied and gotten dinged the very first round of the RISD application. And Raquel wanted—desperately—to reply each time. To tell her of John Temple and his sad divorce; about Nick and meeting his parents; their open invitation to tour their private collection. To further evangelize Belinda Kim's brilliance. She wanted to tell Mavette to forget about Niles. Tell her how she saw him often, actually, as he snuck in and out of Astrid's room, or as Astrid herself shuttled back and forth to whatever place he was staying. The two of them seemed to have fallen into their own drug-hazed world. Raquel would start to reply with all of this in mind and then, inevitably, she would remember the night of the dinner and that Mavette was not someone to be trusted.

She felt a melancholy come over her and then a bit of dread. She could avoid Mavette, far away on some boat in the South of France, but she couldn't avoid Marcus. Marcus who, when she called him on Saturday evening, from a pay phone near Bowen's Wharf, to say that Nick had surprised her and taken her off to Newport, remained silent. Quiet, as she explained that it was only supposed to have been a day trip, but Nick's family friends invited them sailing the next day and she'd never been on a sailboat. Marcus, who was utterly silent as she assured him he would be able to do the show without her, of course; that she was certain he would understand her desire to have this very cool experience that she might never get to have again. Marcus, who, when she stopped talking, just said, "Is that all?" and, after she said yes, hung up without even saying goodbye. The silence said everything about his exasperation with her and her choices and with the place she had given Nick in her life. She felt terrible in that moment, and then she felt frustrated. Frustrated that he couldn't just be happy for her; that she had finally found someone who needed and valued her. That he couldn't just let her be in love and a little reckless and a little irresponsible. Then she hung up, told Nick that everything was cool, and pushed Marcus and the station and all of it out of her mind. Drank beers with Nick in a pub he knew about while he ate clams and she pretended to. Felt the sun kiss her face on the boat the next day as she sipped prosecco. Nick's arms wrapped firmly around her waist as she watched the wind catch the white sails, pushing them farther out into Narragansett Bay, while Nick pointed out the various landmarks on the shore. Mansions and parks and places she'd never heard the names of before, somehow all ingrained in his mind.

She clicked on the message.

Raquel,

I spent the entire drive back to New York last night trying to decide what, exactly, to say to you. What you did was profoundly uncool. Not just missing the show, which you claim is one of the most important things to you, but being so flippant and last minute about the whole thing. More concerning is that you seem blind to the way you have let this dude completely re-prioritize your life. In short, it's fucking wack.

Commit to the show. Commit to Open Mic. Commit to the shit you committed to.

Marcus

After work, Raquel stopped at the Rock on her way back up the hill to put in the interlibrary loan request for a Jack Martin catalog from an exhibition at the Museo Reina Sofia in Spain. Her original thesis topic was not a difficult case to make: the line from his early work to brutalist architecture made of thick dots; the conversation that then ensued between him and the brutalists throughout the seventies was a visually strong one. It was also boring. She had gone back and found the article Belinda Kim had published based on her thesis and it practically lit up the page with its passion and conviction. It was written from the heart, something Belinda had cared deeply about. Raquel's topic, if she were to really examine it, had been selected not because of her own passion but because of John Temple's. Drawn less from a desire to expand her knowledge than to show deference to her mentor. To keep, if she had to be honest, the flaps of the tent open for her. Her internship with Belinda made her realize that she didn't want to just write a good paper but one that she felt captured a fire in her as well. She felt certain that it couldn't be this. She was anxious that dropping Jack Martin as a topic altogether would run her afoul of John Temple. And so, searching for a new angle, she familiarized herself with his more contemporary work, which she discovered was surprisingly sparse. According to his CV, after two intensely prolific decades, he produced nothing for almost three years outside of a small show at Tilly Barber in 1987, which Raquel could barely find a record of. He went dark again for another year or so before a massive exhibition in Spain. She was hoping the catalog might lend some insight she could latch on to and make a paper about; some grand shift in his work that was a nod to changing times, perhaps.

She hit Play again on the Jurassic 5 album; she couldn't understand what Marcus didn't dig about this.

Marcus. Before she left the office, she'd sent a short but sincere apology. She knew better than to overly explain herself. Actions were what mattered to Marcus. The problem with his email was that it was true. Mainly. It wasn't so much that she reprioritized her life because of Nick, as that he made it very challenging to *not* prioritize him. She'd had an amazing day in Newport with him on Saturday and was curious to go out on a sailboat. But, she was also perfectly happy to go back as they'd planned and do the radio show and she'd said as much. Because she knew it would be a drama with Marcus and also, she loved doing the show. "*Have you ever been on a sailboat?*" Nick had asked, his tone of voice clearly assuming that she hadn't. She felt a little annoyed in that moment because no, she hadn't been, but it wasn't completely out of the question. Their high school prom had been on a yacht. Why couldn't she have also had a chance to go on a sailboat? She answered honestly: no, and then surprised herself by saying, "*I'm sure I'll have another chance.*" Which, for some reason, made him go pouty. "*I'm sure you will. With somebody. Someday.*" And she had to explain that wasn't what she'd meant, just that they should stick with the plan and go back.

Now, when she revisited it outside the immediacy of the moment, she realized what he had done: turned it into an issue about her. Her depriving herself. Him just wanting to do nice things for her and her refusal to accept his kindness. "*Why won't you let me give you this experience?*" He had an uncanny ability to turn things into personal rejections and because that was so far from what Raquel intended, it never felt worth the conflict to push back. It wasn't the first time he had sort of done this. The other time that immediately came back to her now was in his painting studio; when he'd convinced her to let him go down on her, even though she was horrified at the idea of undressing in a public space. Somehow, it went from his supposed desire to pleasure her into her refusal to make a memory with him; his injury so deep she felt obliged to soothe him with her accord. So,

Marcus was right that Nick *had*, slowly, one grievance or incident at a time, caused a shift in how she prioritized her time, but not because she ceased to care about the things that mattered to her before. It was that Nick made it intensely difficult to not put him first.

* * *

THE EVENING SUN painted Thayer Street with a honey brush, casting Nick in a golden light that stopped Raquel's heart for a split second. As if he'd appeared right out of a magazine: sitting casually reading at a sidewalk café, thick blond hair pushed off his face, peering over his Ray-Bans, white button-down with a couple of paint splatters—the sleeves rolled up with ease showcasing his muscular forearms tanned from their time out on the boat. For a second she could hardly believe she was the girl who would be sitting across from him, but then the thought put a smile on her face nearly as wide as the one Nick had when he spotted her.

"Hey!" he said. He rose and pulled her into his arms. "I've been dying for you to get here."

"Somebody's in a good mood," she said. He'd been a little testy in the morning, suddenly anxious about the presentation he was supposed to give to the city council about his installation that day. "I'm guessing they liked the piece."

"Loved it! But that's just the gravy," he said. He sat down and pulled a bottle of champagne from the ice bucket near them. "I got representation today."

"Fuck yeah!" Raquel said. The week prior he'd gone down to the city armed with his portfolio and had meetings with several of the edgier galleries popping up in Chelsea: Bronwyn Keenan and Artworks and Matthew Marks. The people representing the kids coming out of Royal College and the Yale MFA program. Nick felt (and Raquel supported the idea, even if she didn't fully agree) that his work was at the same level. Whatever was said during his meeting, he never revealed, but he'd returned to Providence miserable, oscillating from taciturn to inconsolable. Raquel stayed up late one night poring over issues of *Artforum*, compiling a list of all the other new smaller galleries he had yet to write to. She thought it would make him feel better, but instead it caused a tantrum. That she didn't believe he could get blue-chip representation, that she wanted him to settle. It was a volatile (and exhausting) couple of days until the trip to Newport.

"You haven't heard the best part." He poured them both champagne. "It's Tilly Barber Fine Art."

"As in Lee Meisel's dealer?" Raquel said, careful to come across as impressed rather than incredulous.

"As in fucking Jack Martin's dealer," Nick said, more than a little satisfied with himself.

"Cheers to fucking that!" She raised her glass.

"And you wanted me to go begging around Canal Street."

"That wasn't what I was trying to say," she said, keeping the smile on her face. This was a big deal for him. This was a big deal, period. "But, you know what? It doesn't matter now anyway, because look at you. At one of the most legendary galleries in New York."

The waitress approached.

"Everything good over here, hon?" she said to Nick. "You want to put in some food?"

"Absolutely," he said, "Let's get the grilled calamari to start and then I'll have the Paragon Burger with cheese and she'll have the Caesar with grilled chick—"

"Actually," Raquel said, feeling ravenous after having skipped lunch, "I'll have the Paragon Burger too. No cheese."

"You can just have a bite of mine," Nick said to her, and then to the waitress, "She'll just have a bite of mine."

The waitress hovered for a second, looking at Raquel for confirmation, and Raquel found herself unable to speak, hot with shock and shame. She sipped her champagne.

"Thanks," Nick said to the waitress, with finality.

When she was out of earshot, Raquel leaned in toward him.

"What the fuck was that?" she asked.

"What? We'll share," he said, putting his hand over hers.

"That was embarrassing," she said, pulling it away. "I can pick what I want to eat."

"You always get the salad. You'll be happy you had the salad later."

"Why?" she said. He looked at her a bit quizzically. "Why will I be happy later?"

He smiled, cocked his head a bit.

"Don't make me *that* guy. I'm just trying to help."

"Help?" she said.

"Yes," he said, smile still on his face. "You're the one who asked if you looked OK when we were out on the boat—and you did. You looked great. But if you're nervous about your weight, why get the burger and then overthink it later?"

She scrutinized him for a second; this wasn't a conversation that they'd ever had before and yet something about it felt familiar and she couldn't tell what it was. The way that his words were somehow true but also not. She had been nervous—being on display with friends of his—to make a good impression. To seem as attractive a girl as she knew people expected Nick to be with. She just wanted to check that he thought she looked good. She felt her appetite leave her completely.

"Raquel," Nick said, reaching under the table to squeeze her leg; his hand soft, but his grip firm in a way that sent a shiver up her thigh and to her breasts. "You know how hot I think you are."

She felt herself blush at this. Being desired created a sense of desire in her. She was going to let it go. He was just being a guy. Clumsy. Well-intentioned.

"So, tell me," she said. "Did they invite you to do a group show? What's the next step?"

"I mean, the conversation didn't get that far, exactly."

Raquel was about to ask what, exactly, was promised to him when a Jeep blasting "Ghetto Supastar" stopped at the red light and she heard Delroy shout her name. She looked up to see Betsaida in the passenger seat.

"What's up!" Raquel shouted as she rose from the table. "Why aren't you in Boston?"

"Played hooky," Delroy said, barely lowering the music. "You inspired me."

Raquel and Betsaida laughed and Raquel tried to grasp Nick's hand to bring him to the car and introduce him, but he resisted and, just as quickly as they'd arrived, the light changed and they were pulling away.

"Raquel," Betsaida shouted from the window as the car drove off. "Your moms was looking for you."

Her mother. So much had happened since the morning, she'd almost forgotten. She wrapped her arms around Nick's neck.

"That's my roommate, Betsaida," Raquel said as she kissed his cheek before heading back to her seat.

"I figured," Nick said as he portioned some of the calamari onto each of their salad plates after the waitress came out with their food.

"Speaking of my mom, her and my sister are coming up this weekend." Raquel picked at her salad. A smile came over her face thinking of how the trip came to pass. "They won this radio contest and the money is burning a hole in their pocket or something."

"My parents invited us to the Hamptons."

"Oh," she said. Had he mentioned that? He hadn't mentioned that. She knew they had a place there; Astrid told her it was sick. Right on the beach. She was curious what all the hoopla about the Hamptons was, but he'd never mentioned any kind of plan. "Well, a different weekend. My mom never comes and they want to see my place."

"I don't know what other weekends my parents will be out there."

"Nick," she said, "don't take this the wrong way, but your parents don't have jobs."

"Ouch," Nick said.

"I'm not being snarky, just honest. My mom and my sister got time off already, so I can't tell them no. Especially not to go to the Hamptons to be with someone else's family."

Nick picked at his fries. The sulk. She hated the sulk.

"Besides," she said, grabbing his hand from across the table and kissing his palm, "they're dying to meet you. I know they are going to love you."

His ego couldn't handle the real truth, that all this time had gone by without anyone even knowing that he existed. That meeting him would be a shock second only to hearing about him for the very first time on Friday.

"Maybe I can even bring them by your studio," Raquel suggested. "My family loves art."

This last bit, at least, was totally true.

"Sure," Nick said, smiling back. "That'll be great."

Later, when they were walking home, it struck her that he never suggested that her family come out to the Hamptons with them.

Jack

NEW YORK CITY • FALL 1985

Oh, Tilly. Always right. The moment Jack arrived at the service it was obvious that it was a terrible fucking idea, but he'd never even entertained not going. What, he thought, could make a man look more guilty than missing his own wife's memorial? And he was not guilty, he explained, again and again. And she was, he felt the need to remind everyone, his wife. Not his girlfriend. Not his lover. His fucking wife. No one deserved, he felt, to be there more. If she was going to be remembered, he would not allow himself to be erased from her life. In another time, she would have been known as Mrs. Jack Martin. And of course, he was not so backward as to want that kind of thing, but why agree to something as conventional as marriage if you didn't somewhat believe in those roles? So yes, she was Anita de Monte—now a martyr for the feminist cause. (Because the feminists . . . ugh, the feminists were *very* angry. And they did not believe that Jack was innocent. No, they did not.) But she was *also* the wife of Jack Martin, and that should not be forgotten.

For this reason, he had, wrongly, assumed that the place would be equally full of his friends and champions: the famous artists and gallerists and curators and dealers and collectors that he and Anita had had countless dinners with over the years. That they would come to comfort him—the grieving widower. That they would come to show that they believed him. That they knew that she had simply gone out the window. He could never possibly push her. They would come to show they did not care about the scratches on his face that the *New York Post* reported. They did not care that the *Daily News* said he called Tilly a full hour before he called the police. They believed him when he said he truly did not know what happened: he blacked out from the trauma of it all. He assumed the place would be full of people who saw him as he clearly was: a man mourning his wife who died suddenly in a terrible accident.

Tilly tried to tell him that these friends would never show up here, that it wasn't personal. Did not mean that they weren't on his side. Just that no one in their right mind would go out of their way to attach themselves to such a spectacle. This was not his memorial for Anita, Tilly tried to explain. This was a publicity circus organized by feminist zealots trying to turn an accident into a political crime. An exploitation of one couple's personal tragedy populated by the tuft-hunters on the periphery of the art world that Anita associated with. Jockeying for relevance by association. His presence, Tilly had forewarned, would only make for a third ring. And still. Still he was shocked that Tilly wouldn't go. ("*I refuse to be a lion tamer*," she had snapped. "*If you insist upon going, go it alone.*")

But of course, he couldn't go it alone. He was missing his Anita. He knew her family would be there. Knew that they felt he was surely responsible. They never said so, but he could tell what they thought; their silence spoke volumes. Quiet during the many, many phone calls he'd made to assure them that, despite what her friends were saying, despite how it sounded in the news, he had nothing to do with it. Quiet as he tried to explain that, to his best recollection, she had just gone out the window. He knew he could not face them and their judgment (their terrible, terrible judgment!) alone. And because Tilly wouldn't come, he asked Ingrid.

People would obviously talk about this. Whisper. But his and Ingrid's intimacies were already such an open secret, it would hardly come as a surprise to anyone. It was his talking with Ingrid *that* night—before *it* happened—that set Anita off in the first place. But needing Ingrid did not take away the love he'd had for Anita. Oh, how he loved her—her smallness, her brashness, her unlikability, really, or maybe it was her charm in being so fucking unlikable. She made him better. More youthful. More like the version of himself that he always boasted about being: the proletarian, the activist, the man of passion, the artisan of the fine arts. She made, for him, all these things feel real. More than a persona. It was who he really was with Anita. And now she was gone.

He'd had the sense to arrive early, and even then, it still created a spectacle. Outside the Americas Society—of course, this is where they decided to have it, as if to underline the Latin-ness of the whole thing—Jomar Burgos was smoking with two other queers. Even though Jack kept his focus straight ahead, he could still register the shock on Jomar's face when he realized it was Jack and Ingrid coming out of the car. The Spanish patter, cruel and quick, began immediately among them. Inside, a cluster of mourners gathered in the lobby parted before him like some sort of derelict Moses. Their silence, on the other hand, continued well after he passed, their eyes piercing as he and Ingrid ascended the stairs.

Since the arrest, he'd been surprised by how easy it was to render himself impervious to such scorn. For weeks now the protesters had made it impossible for him to get in and out of his building without them surrounding him, screaming in his face that he was a murderer. Plastering the neighborhood with his mug shot in makeshift WANTED posters. His friends worried about how he was holding up against it, but the truth was, he was fine. Because they didn't really matter. He understood that. They—like critics, like uncooperative gallerists, like early collectors who tried to commission work from him and then made "suggestions"—needed to be drowned out. Because all they could do was distract from what really mattered: his vision.

In the beginning he hid from them, the protesters. He ducked through the secret entrance, the one that led through the parking garage directly into his lobby. He would nod at the doormen, both of them pretending that they didn't see the women marching in circles outside the building, carrying posters with Anita's photo and homemade picket signs demanding "justice" for her. One day, though, he decided: He hadn't done anything. It was an accident. They could believe whatever they wanted, but they were not going to have him sneaking around. His absence, he explained to Tilly, was just ammunition for them. And this time—this one time—perhaps, he was right. The more he passed them, unflinching in his expression, immutable in his resolve to go about his day, the more the angry women diffused. He was, he reminded himself as he hoisted his frame up the Americas Society's winding staircase, made of strong New England stock. This would not fucking bring him down.

The room itself was long and narrow; a selection of Anita's works hung around the walls. He entered and locked eyes with Leslie—one of the people responsible for this thing—almost immediately.

She was leaning over and speaking to a slight older woman in the front row. Anita's mother, Jack thought. He had never actually met her. Seven years of this outrageous dance with Anita—the back-and-forth, the breakups and reconciliations—and he'd never actually met her mother. Anita had built a citadel around this aspect of her life—Cuba, her parents, most of her childhood in Iowa—and he never tried to breach it. It hadn't struck him as odd when Anita was alive, but now, it felt shameful somehow. Leslie excused herself quickly and rushed to the doorway where Jack and Ingrid stood.

"What the fuck, Jack?" she whispered. She turned to Ingrid. "Excuse us."

Ingrid, the dear that she was—always so understanding, so cooperative—headed toward the rear and found herself a seat.

"I'm here for my wife's memorial," Jack said, refusing to let Leslie bully him.

"No one wants you here," she hissed.

"Anita would want me here."

"And she'd want your fucking mistress here too, I suppose?" Leslie said with a glare.

He could see how much she detested him and he would be lying if he said that it didn't hurt. Leslie and Arnold were friends; had been his friends for years. They were the reason he'd even met Anita.

"Leslie," he said. He heard the pleading in his own voice. "Don't tell me you think I did this."

But he could see plainly that she did, her neck and face flushed a bright red as her chin began to tremble. She was fighting back tears.

"I don't know what to think," she said. "But I know she would never jump out that window. And everyone here knows that too."

Tilly. Always right. His presence wasn't going to prove anything to anyone. He could see that now. "*Let me and Gerry work on shaping people's opinions, Jack*," Tilly had warned him. Since he'd been released on bail, Gerry kept the press largely at bay. There was a big *New York* magazine story coming, but Gerry assured him it would be "*as balanced as can be.*" He and Tilly were having drinks and dinners with as much of the "legitimate" art world as they could. Museum directors, blue-chip artists, critics, and magazine editors—anyone the reporter might possibly speak with, stirring up support for Jack. Or, if not support, fear of retribution for speaking out against him. "*She was an erratic Hispanic*," Tilly said to him and he gave her a look, one that hinted to her that she was going too far. She shrugged and reminded him, "*Those were your words, not mine.*" And again, Tilly was right. He had long known it could never work between them; cool, calm New England and hot, chaotic Cuba. Not in a million years. He was just never able to quit it. Unable to admit defeat. Too attached to her to be apart.

"I'm just going to sit in the back, Leslie. I just want to hear people remember her."

And this was true.

Leslie walked away from him then, off to console someone who'd entered while they were talking. Off to play hostess. The fucking irony, he thought to himself, Leslie at the helm of this thing. Anita could barely stand her.

The place was standing room only, but around Jack formed a cavity; everyone avoiding him like rot. Mourners extended far into the hallway, their voices and *Shhhh*s audible from inside the room. But on either side of them, the row in front, the row behind, the seats were empty. At least twenty seats. Twenty people who would rather stand in a hallway than sit near Jack Martin.

None of the speakers acknowledged him in their remarks. No one mentioned that she was a wife, that she had been loved. He could hardly believe it. Jack heard some people whispering about wanting to mount a retrospective of her work and felt himself sick and sad and lonely at the idea of it. He had kept her portfolio. Before the police came, he had stashed it behind the washer/dryer along with the file of shit that started the whole row. (It was hardly evidence! It had been an accident!) But he hated the idea of her sister getting it or the police keeping it and him never being able to look at it again. But, in the weeks that had passed? Well, instead of feeling closer to her, looking at her art made him feel a chasm between them. The same kind of aching he would feel when she would leave to actually make art. Her work literally pulled her out of his arms, out of his bed. Honestly, even the terrible thing that happened, when he thought about it, only happened because of her work.

* * *

THEY HAD MADE one piece together. It was the summer of '80? He'd been commissioned to create something for the Biennale in Mexico City; something outdoors and he was inspired, in no small part, by the pyramids there. He loved the neolithic. He had a plan for what he wanted to do. A very clear vision. And then they were having dinner at the Italian place Anita liked with Ira and his wife. Anita had arrived late and when she did so, Ira congratulated her on being awarded the Guggenheim Fellowship. Jack had no idea that she'd even applied and somehow Ira Pascal knew this before he did? (They weren't yet married then, but they were very much together.) She said that she was going to take the money and travel and work around the Caribbean for a year—how she was going to create works near indigenous burial sites or some crap, and that she'd already been connecting with artists and collaborators in various countries. He'd felt his heart sink before his temper rose. Unable to congratulate her, he was so blinded with anger that she had done all of this without him. Had not factored him into her equation at all. Just dismissed him. Not just in the applying, but that she'd already formed a plan. A plan to be away from him. Not for just a little bit of time, but *for a year*. A year, he thought as he fumed over dinner, is not a trip, but a reimagining of a life. A total relocation.

Her ego (her huge ego), of course, could not let go that he would not congratulate her. She began to egg him on, cajoling him, and he would not be cajoled. "*Isn't it just marvelous, Jack? This is a very prestigious prize, Jack, did you know that?*" she purred as she poured herself more champagne and he ordered himself a scotch on the rocks. When the entrées came, there she was, just crowing—gloating, really—over how competitive the field had been this year. And worse, Ira and his wife were fully wrapped up in it, did not even question what this meant for Jack. He couldn't remember what the last straw had been, but he heard himself bark at her, "*If you mention the fucking Guggenheim one more time tonight, I swear I'm throwing this bowl of pasta right at your head.*" And she had shut up—for a split second—and then picked up the bottle of champagne and refilled Ira's and Dana's glasses as well as her own and raised it up. She looked him right in the eye, smiled, and said, "*Let's toast to my Guggenheim!*" And it was just reflex. It was that fast; the bowl was in the air, she ducked so fast it just missed her head. Dana screamed. Ira yelled, "*What the fuck, Jack!*" and the bowl shattered, and the spaghetti really did get thrown against the wall. There was the terrible, terrible silence while the whole place watched her pick up her purse and coat and walk silently out the door.

She had gone to her own place that night.

She would never give up that apartment. Even after they got married. It was a shitty walk-up on Varick Street near the Holland Tunnel. It had a little window seat that looked out onto a narrow alley, a terrible Murphy bed, and an irregular shape that she said made her feel like they had sculpted it from the leftover space in the building so that it was just big enough for her. That night, she had gone to her apartment—this, he knew, was why she never gave it up—and she stayed longer than she had stayed in a while. And after almost two weeks he finally showed up, bearing not gifts—no, by this point, she'd soured on his gifts—but what she loved most. An opportunity.

He handed her a first-class ticket to Mexico City. She had glanced at it, refused to even take it from his hands. "*I'm done being the great artist's companion*," she'd said. (As if Berkeley hadn't made that clear enough already.) But he explained that this wasn't going to be that, that he'd spoken to the curators and suggested that he create an installation with his partner, Anita de Monte. That her nature-based works and his building materials, together, would be the perfect statement to the past and future of Mexico City itself. It was a group show in a major international museum and a piece co-created with him, a legend. It immediately elevated her public profile. "*I suppose*," she said, "*that I can postpone my trip for a bit*."

If he had to be honest, including her had been a desperate gesture on his part. Just a means to reconcile, to keep her from leaving. It was the first and last time he would allow that desperation to contaminate his art. His original idea was for him to create pyramids from bars of gold and silver. And then Anita proposed something that, at first, he thought was clever: to make them out of bricks so that she could design plantings that would overgrow the sculpture, that it would create greater tension between the idea of nature versus man. (The idea, he wanted to explain to her, was simply the observation of bricks in the out-of-doors. Nothing more, nothing less. But he went along with it.) The exhibition was up for three months and in the course of the time his large, twenty-foot-tall pyramids of brick and stones, laid with such precision by him and him alone, were overgrown with marigolds, yucca, and *Passiflora*. Wild, massive beast mounds of flowers. Everyone delighted in them; the Latin media especially, who adored talking to Anita.

He detested it. She'd poisoned his vision. Gone in, taken charge, and wrested the piece of art, and the spotlight, for herself. As the show wore on and the flowers burgeoned, they began to asphyxiate the bricks with their fragrance and he felt a distance growing between them. Mexico City ended worse than . . . well, worse than any fight except when *it* happened. (Though, he really didn't remember what happened that night. He'd blacked out. Completely.) She ran off in the cloak of dark without so much as a goodbye—before the closing even.

When he returned to New York, no one had seen her. A month or so later there was a postcard from Miami telling him she was headed to Cuba. When the show closed, he called his attorney and formally disavowed the piece. He nullified any right to reproduce its image or re-create it in any future retrospectives of his work.

* * *

SOMEONE WAS PLAYING something on a cello and Jack knew this was one of Leslie's ideas. Anita would have hated it, found it pretentious. There was a moment of silence and then Jack saw Anita's sister rise from the front row and stand in the center of the room. She looked like Anita, but stretched out; a good half foot taller than his wife had been; a more gaunt face, or maybe she was just sad? They'd only had dinner a handful of times in the years he and Anita were together. Anita always preferred to speak Spanish with her sister and Jack had never found the woman, or her husband, interesting enough to protest. Still, in this moment, he very much wanted her to recognize him, acknowledge his presence in the room. He looked directly at her, sat up in his seat a bit, shifted away from Ingrid even, but she looked toward every part of the room except toward him. That fucking Cuban willfulness. The reverent silence for her remarks became awkward, before a murmur arose, as Anita's sister stood at the front, avoiding his eyes. People began to (finally) look his way as they whispered. The buzz of the space turning hostile as it became evident that this witch was not going to speak with him in the room. Oh, Tilly, always right. A fucking circus. He grabbed Ingrid's hand and walked them out as quickly and quietly as possible.

As soon as the door closed behind them, he could hear Anita's bitch of a sister begin.

Outside, Jack had to sit for a moment. The body heat and judgment so close on him he struggled for breath. Ingrid suggested they cut through the park, a way for him to get some air, and though it sounded like a good idea, he almost immediately regretted it. Ingrid was chattering on, attempting to distract him from his thoughts, when he recognized that they were on the same path he'd walked during his first real date with Anita. They'd gone to the Guggenheim, and then for a stroll, and he remembered she was talking about a piece she was going to make inspired by a dream: how she'd been alone in the forest and seen people in the trees. She'd stood up against a great big sycamore, perfectly still, her eyes darting around as she showed him how they had watched her in her vision. He remembered thinking her so terribly cute, this tiny thing exploding with life. And it filled him with lust; he'd been desperate to get lunch over with and get her into his bed. Now, though, it filled him with melancholy. A deep sadness that she was gone. He felt tears start to well and stopped for a second on the pathway, stared out at the bank of the reservoir. Let himself just feel for a moment. Ingrid's voice trailed off awkwardly as she followed suit. Unsure, he was certain, what to do with this sorrow he'd loathed to let show.

And then he saw it. There was a rock formation near the water's edge. A figure—a woman's figure—alighted on one of the large boulders up top. She sat straight up and, despite the distance, he felt it clearly. She was staring right at him.

"Do you see her?" he said.

"Who, Jack?" Ingrid was standing behind him, but she stepped to his side now, her hand going to his shoulder.

"Under the willow. On the rock." He pointed in the direction of the water, but he'd already begun to pull away from Ingrid, heading off the paved walk. He cut across a slope of planted hydrangea and azalea bushes to the path around the reservoir. He stopped for a closer look. It was, indeed, a woman. Naked, or nearly so. Her body painted with clay. Staring. At him?

"She's naked," he called up toward Ingrid. "Can you spot her? On the rock?"

"She's sunbathing," Ingrid said, as she made her way down the dirt slope toward Jack. She wasn't even looking at her, Jack could tell. If she had been she'd never think this woman was sunbathing. She was covered in mud.

"She's staring at me," Jack said. He felt the tightness in his voice.

Ingrid laughed. "All the girls do, don't they?"

But Jack didn't like her joke. He felt uneasy. He raised his arm slightly, lifted his hand toward his face, and, with great hesitance, rotated his wrist to create the slightest of waves. Immediately, the woman on the rock returned the gesture. Her face, faint given the distance, but Jack could tell there was no smile there. It chilled him, this smile-less wave. This madness. This fucking madness.

"It's them!" he said, as he headed closer—first in a walk, and then, as his revelation of what was happening crystallized, he broke into a full, lumbering trot. "These bitches are playing a trick."

"Jack!" Ingrid said. "Please stop. What are you talking about?"

As he approached, he caught the second one. Oh, this fucking trickery! He would make these bitches pay! The second one, also naked, also covered in mud, was standing up against the tree. She, unlike the other devil, was smiling. Perfectly still, up against the trunk of the willow tree, nothing but her eye and the pink of her mouth showing. Just like in Anita's photos. Oh, these clever fucking "feminists." He was just paces from them now on the path, and he had to fight his urge to go up and grab them, physically toss them from their fucking roosts.

"I see you, you cunts!" he screamed. "This is harassment! Do you hear me?"

He decided to confront the one on the rock; she was closest. He climbed over the low fence that separated the reservoir from the path and began to ascend the rock pile where this bitch was perched.

"Jack!" Ingrid screamed. "What the hell are you doing?"

"They can't get away with this, Ingrid! I am entitled to live my life."

He was so fucking fat. He hated how he'd let himself get. He was out of breath and barely able to lift his weight, and of course this bitch couldn't even do him the decency of just telling him he was a sonofabitch. She was going to make him climb all the way up to her. Ingrid was screaming in the background for him to come down, but he was almost there, to the boulder where this sow was sitting, fucking with him. But when he got to the top, she was gone. She had just been there and now she was gone. And he couldn't have been imagining it. It wasn't just her. It was the other one, too! But when he looked toward the tree, she also was gone. He stood in the expansiveness of Central Park, the wide sky up above, and felt it all close in on him. Felt the breath leave his lungs and then his brain, as his lumbering body lost its footing and tumbled off the rock formation.

III

VISITS

Raquel

PROVIDENCE • SUMMER 1998

"Mira, que flaca!" her mother said when Raquel opened the door. She leaned in to kiss her. "I thought you told me you'd been eating?"

"Hello to you too!" Raquel said, though all afternoon she'd been anticipating this. Steeling herself for the sharp edge of her mother's raw words.

"Rockyyyy," she bellowed as she beelined toward the kitchen, hands full of shopping bags, "we've talked about this. It's a slippery slope."

"It's summertime, Mami," her sister interjected, giving Raquel a hug as she walked through the living room and followed her mother into the kitchen. She plopped down in the little nook Raquel had found so charming. "Nobody wants to eat in the summer but you, Ms. Thicc. This place is mad cute, Rocky."

"I still need to show you the rest," Raquel said, grateful for her sister's presence. "We have a back porch!"

Her mother was at the counter, unpacking Bustelo and plantain and Utz chips, opening cabinet after cabinet, trying to make heads or tails out of the place. Raquel was surprised how examined it made her feel, to have her mother riffling through *her* kitchen.

"No wonder you're so skinny, there's no food in here."

"I can put that stuff away, Mami," Raquel said, steering her mother away from the cabinets and toward the table.

"I'm just trying to find your pantry."

"Just relax. Have a beer. Let me show you around."

"Sure," her mother said, but her body language was defensive. Raquel decided to ignore it, grabbed a beer for her mother from the fridge.

"What's up with your hair?" her mother said, lips pursed in disapproval.

Raquel was still dressed for work—black pencil skirt, black tank top, her hair pulled back into the chic bun that had become what she thought was her signature look that summer. The look that kept her "hot and sticky" hair out of Nick's face and, as he told her, showed off her beauty.

"Oh my God," Raquel said as she handed her mother the drink. "Is this going to be the whole weekend? You picking at me?"

"I'm not picking on you," her mother said. "You have beautiful hair!"

"It's a chignon," Raquel said, now feeling defensive.

"It looks like you clean houses for a living."

"Enough! Enough!" Toni interjected, before turning to her mother. "*You* need to calm down and stop taking your insecurities out on innocent people—"

"Mira, the way my kids talk to me, wow—"

"Instead of picking on her, tell Raquel what you told me in the car."

"What are you, Toni, a narc?" her mother said, turning her body away in a huff, like a defiant pug, as she muttered about her disrespectful daughters. Her face as lovely or as miserable as whatever feeling she wore inside herself.

"Raquel, Mami's having feelings about you having your own place and growing away from her—"

"You don't need to put words into my mouth, Toni," her mother yelled. "I can talk for myself."

But actually, her voice was breaking. Her gray eyes were glassy and her lips started trembling and Raquel felt her heart breaking a little bit because she could feel all the things in her mother's chest pushing up and not knowing how to find their way out. The frustration at feelings unable to attach themselves to words. How many of their fights had been the result of this same incapacity? Raquel sat at the table next to her mother and put her petite hand on her mother's plump forearm.

"Mami, it's OK," she said. "Just say whatever you want to say."

"It's just that . . ." her mother said. Now she was fully choking on her tears. "If you can do all this for yourself, what do you need me for anymore?"

The question punched Raquel in the chest; knocked the air out of her. She threw herself onto her mother.

"No, Mami," she said, tears now welling in her own eyes. "Don't say that."

And she *didn't* want her to say it, because it hurt too much to hear the truth. To watch her absorb what Raquel had felt for three years now: she didn't really need her. Not to cook for her or clothe her or pay a bill or remind her to succeed or do her homework. She wished—actively, often—that her mother could be someone she could call for help. That she could understand her ambitions, the world she was in, day in and day out. Wished, often, that her mother could comfort her or give her advice but knew she was ill-equipped. Raquel was on her own in that regard. The apartment was just a symbol of what she already knew: she could live without her mother. And she hated that, but she hated it more that her mother knew it now too. She draped her body on top of her mother, to calm and quiet her, to muffle the sound of the veracity of it all.

"Because if you two don't need me anymore," her mother said now, heaving with sobs, "I don't know what to do with myself. You're my whole life."

Toni, tears streaming down her heart-shaped face, now wrapped her arms around both women.

"Mami, don't be crazy," she said. "We'll always need you."

But Raquel couldn't lie and instead she just said, "You'll sit back and relax and be proud of what you did. Of the two women you raised all by yourself."

But that just made their mother cry more, and now—not even fifteen minutes into their visit—all three Toro women were collapsed on one another, sobbing and muttering how much they loved one another and apologies and how fantastic the apartment was, and what a nice job Raquel had done decorating it, "nice and classy." Indeed, who knows how long they would have stayed in this tear-stained, love-filled heap had Marcus, fresh from his own drive up from the city, not walked in.

"Well, hello, ladies," Marcus said, awkwardly. "Am I interrupting something?"

"Maaarcuuuus," Toni called out, in her best Eartha-Kitt-as-Lady-Eloise voice, giving them all a fit of the giggles. The kind that only releases after tears.

"What up, Antonia?" Marcus said and as the women untangled themselves from one another, Toni and her mother rose to give him a hug. "And how are you, Ms. Toro?"

"Loving the place, Marcus! Felicidades!"

"The drive OK?" Raquel asked. She was unsure if they'd reconciled. She had emailed her apology to Marcus. Then emailed him separately to tell him her family would be there that weekend, and all she got was a one-word "Cool," which she knew he meant. Marcus was an only child and sort of loved being in the midst of her family dramatics, plus her sister basically fell over herself flirting with him, which she knew his ego appreciated.

"Did you know that there's a new fucking hip-hop station here?" he said, outrage in his voice. "Hot 106. Like, they didn't even try to be original. I got to that fucked-up spot where you lose Hot 97 and thought, Lemme listen to some classic rock, and all of a sudden I hear Lord Tariq and Peter Gunz."

Raquel shrugged her shoulders. Resisted the urge—given their recent squabble—to say she tried to tell him this back in the spring. Hip-hop was getting so commercial, it was basically turning into pop. Either way, it was clear the beef between them was squashed.

"Three sixty is more than just hip-hop," she reminded him.

"Marcus, come to dinner with us," her mother interjected. "We're getting lobster."

"Calamari," Raquel said before adding, "We're gonna go to that place on the water across the river."

"We're gonna get all of it," Toni said, "including oysters. They're supposed to be an aphrodisiac. Did you know that, Marcus?"

Pobrecito, Poor Man's Heavy D, Raquel thought. And their mother was worried that *he* was the sucio!

By the time they arrived, the moon and the string lights on the restaurant patio made the lackluster Providence River look picturesque. Her mother ordered everything, including lobster, which she then made a big show about. ("*Oh, you* do *have lobster here in Rhode Island. How nice.*") She even let them all get daiquiris. Everyone was in a festive, albeit bitchy, mood. Her mother bitched about how hard nursing school was, Marcus bitched about Hot 106, Toni bitched about their mother, and Raquel mainly just weighed in on the topic at hand. Just as she was wondering how best to bring up Nick, Marcus asked about their plans for the weekend. Their visitors eagerly itemized their plans: breakfast at Bickford's, the beach for the day with Betsaida (who was in a spat with Delroy and in town for the weekend), maybe Foxwoods, and then Louie's and the station on Sunday before they headed back.

"When are you guys meeting Nick?" Marcus asked, as he shoved a fried oyster in his mouth.

Though it was a perfectly normal question and there was no way at all for Marcus to know that she had gone all this time (all this time) without telling them—but that, of course, she planned to tell them tonight and bring them by his studio tomorrow morning—she still felt the flame of anger spark inside her.

"Who's Nick?" her mother and Toni asked, practically in unison.

Marcus let out his awkward, high-pitched giggle, the same one he'd made when she got caught with her foot in her mouth the night she met Nick.

"Raquel?" he asked, leaning into his fuckup now. "Who's Nick?"

"I swear the point was to tell you tonight and then introduce you tomorrow," Raquel said, "but Nick's my boyfriend."

"You got a boyfriend since Monday morning?" Mami asked. Toni laughed.

"No, Mami," her sister said, before practically singing in elation, "but I bet that's why she missed your call on Sunday."

Raquel rolled her eyes, sucked her teeth. Whose side was Toni on?

"So, wait?" her mother said. "You got a boyfriend since two weeks ago?"

"It's only been a few weeks," Raquel said sheepishly.

"A few weeks in dog years," Marcus added. "They are together all the time."

"Snitches get stitches, Marcus," she muttered under her breath.

"Like sleeping together, together?" her mother added, looking Raquel in the eye and making her feel like she wanted the earth to swallow her up. Toni exhaled dramatically through her nose, her tiny septum ring vibrating from the force of the performance.

"She's twenty years old, Ma. It'd be weird if they *weren't* sleeping together."

"What did I say?" her mother said, defensive now. "She can do whatever she wants. It's her life to mess up."

"That's why I didn't tell you," Raquel said, surprised at the bite in her own voice. "Everything becomes a premonition for disaster."

There was some silence around the table and her mother played with her food before Toni spoke.

"Well, Mami, now you know why she's lost weight," she said mischievously. "All that physical activity."

She and Marcus giggled. Even her mother had to stifle a smile while Raquel felt her face burn in humiliation. The last thing she wanted or needed was for her family to think of her having sex.

"So, what's he like?" her mother asked, forcing some cheer into her voice. "Where's he from? Tell us all the things."

"He's from New York. He just graduated. He's an artist. A sculptor. He actually had something bought by the Guggenheim."

"Damn," Toni said, impressed.

"His stuff is dope," Marcus said, "though Raquel doesn't think so."

"I just didn't get it at first," Raquel said, aware that she was lying, but this was not the time for nuance. "Anyway, we'll go by his studio to say hi before the beach."

Raquel explained the meet cute as though it was the most casual thing in the world—introducing her family to her first-ever real boyfriend. A boyfriend who would do nothing more than reaffirm every one of her mother's fears that she was choosing a future life far removed from the one they had had together. A casual description of an introduction she had played and replayed in her mind all week.

"Why doesn't he just come?" her mother said. Her mother was of the kind of mindset that the more was always the merrier. "Saying hello doesn't sound like much of a chance to get to know him."

"He works on Saturdays," Raquel said, and then quickly added, "on his art."

The truth was, she'd never invited him to the beach and he'd never asked if or when he could spend some time with them.

"Where in the city is he from?" her mother asked, and Raquel could tell she was trying to put a story together. Assemble these tidbits into an entire telenovela. She wasn't going to give in so easily. Let them meet him—and see how charming and handsome and doting on Raquel he could be—and then form their opinions.

"Manhattan," Raquel replied, and then quickly turned her attention to Toni. "So what's going on with your boo's film?" And in the shorthand parlance of their family, it was clear that the topic was closed.

That night after everyone else had gone to sleep, the two sisters sat watching *X-Files* reruns into the wee hours of the morning. They were in the middle of the cockroach episode when Toni turned to her sister.

"So, why'd you keep your boyfriend a secret?"

"I didn't keep him a secret per se," Raquel started.

"Please, bullshit someone else."

"Why don't you ever hang out with Mami and her girlfriend?"

"This, again?" Toni said, exasperated. "Because Dolores is fucking boring and a show-off and it's easier to avoid hanging out with her than to go and have Mami complain that I'm not nice to her 'friend.'"

"So, there's your answer," Raquel said. "Sometimes avoidance is easier with Mami."

"In the short term," Toni said. "In the long run, it's always worse."

"She thinks you're embarrassed," Raquel said.

"That she has a girlfriend?" Toni said. "She needs to stop projecting. I'm in theater! What do I care? I'd dislike Dolores even if she had a dick."

The two girls laughed at this.

"He's really rich," Raquel said. "Nick, I mean."

"Good. Let him buy you things."

"He has, but it's weirder in practice than it sounds."

She didn't want to taint her sister before she met him, so she stopped herself from saying more. Didn't tell Toni how it at once made her feel both special and also defective. As if with each dress or pair of earrings or shoes or blouse or suggestion for how she wear her hair, he was helping to "improve her." The implication being, of course, that the original version was somehow not enough.

"I think I could learn to live with it," Toni replied. For a second their focus returned to the TV before Toni grabbed her arm and turned to fully face her sister. "Wait? Is he white?"

"Yeah," Raquel said, understating what she knew her sister would observe once she met him: super, super white. Like *Mayflower* boat white.

"Is that why you're getting so skinny again?"

"You told Mami," Raquel said, putting the volume up on the TV and turning away from her sister. "It's the summer, nobody likes to eat."

She quickly pushed the recollection of purging her po-boy sandwich in the restaurant bathroom out of her mind. (That wasn't something she normally did; she'd just felt literally ill having eaten so much to shut her mother up.)

"White guys like bony girls," Toni said. "Everybody knows that."

"Not Josh Cangelosi. Josh was white and he liked you."

Josh was one of Toni's boyfriends in high school.

"Josh was a pizza bagel—his dad was literally, like, from Italy. His mom was mad thick. They appreciate women with some meat on their bones."

* * *

NICK'S STUDIO WAS in a former brick factory in the Jewelry District that had been converted for artists' use. He was sharing it—at least for the summer—with a locally famous mural artist who'd been commissioned to create a series of portraits for a wealthy investor who brought something called high-speed Internet to Boston and apparently made a killing. The murals were, from what Raquel could surmise, images of his many pets. They were also remarkably better than what Nick had been working on and, as she and her small entourage exited the parked rental car, Raquel's anxiety temporarily shifted from the forthcoming familial introduction to how to prevent them from accidentally gushing over the wrong artist's work.

"So, Nick shares his studio with this painter who does really sensational portraits," she said, "but Nick is working on these cool sculptures that the city is going to auction off to raise money for kids' art programs."

They were a boisterous group as they made their way up the four flights of stairs to Nick's studio; Betsaida regaling them with stories of growing up in Providence. Despite her mother's general reservations about Dominicans, Betsaida immediately charmed her; she was declared "down to earth," which Raquel knew was, in this context, the highest possible compliment. That Bets woke up early to prepare food for them to bring to the beach only raised her esteem, and the camaraderie around the crowded house that morning had soothed Raquel. Watching her two worlds interact so seamlessly, seeing so many people that she loved in one space—her space—temporarily dissolved this nagging loneliness that seemed to follow her everywhere. With the door to the studio in sight, a nervous feeling churned in her stomach. Her mother had no poker face and her sister might have one that Nick would buy, but that she—Raquel—would know how to read. He was just *so* sensitive and these sculptures were simply not very good. Or maybe they were and it was just a matter of taste. Tilly Barber didn't sign just anyone, she kept reminding herself.

"Hello!" she called out as she opened the door. "We're here."

"I know," Nick said as he walked toward her. "I could hear you all coming from down the block."

He slipped his arm around her waist and kissed her cheek before she felt him tug at her hair, which hung loose down her back.

"Not very practical for the beach," he whispered.

"This is my mom, Irma," she said, ignoring him, as her mom reached out her hand. "And my sister, Toni—"

Toni winked.

"And this is Betsaida," she said.

"Of course," Nick said, all smiles. "Ms. Toro, your daughter is the most brilliant and delightful woman. You must be so proud."

"Thank you," she said, smiling. "Rocky's always had a good head on her shoulders."

There was an awkward moment of silence that Raquel desperately wanted Nick to fill; something proactive she wanted him to say, though she was unsure of what it would be. It wasn't like he could comment on her mother's St. John's dress. She glanced at her mother and sister and saw them for the first time not as the familiar entities she'd been surrounded by her entire life, but with fresh eyes. No, his eyes. His eyes on her mother and her curly mullet, the Betty Boop cover-up and her board shorts, her freckled face and pretty gray eyes set off by the circles under them. What was Nick making of Toni, with her quasi-Gothic bob and thick figure busting out of the tank dress she wore over her bikini? Of the terrible tribal tattoo she'd gotten on her ankle. The Revlon Toast of New York lipstick that had become nearly as permanent as the ink. They did not actually fit into any mold or aesthetic story Raquel had seen on this campus, period. Betsaida looked positively preppy in comparison, with her Brown University T-shirt, naked face, and Aquafored lips. She had been so riddled with anxiety about how her family would receive him—the very first boy in her life—she hadn't stopped to think about what he would make of them. (Or maybe, if she were being honest, she was too frightened to think about it.) She wanted not to care what he thought. That it didn't matter that he was seeing them as an extension of her, but suddenly she felt both nervous and anxious over what, exactly, that would mean.

"So, Raquel told us about your piece at the Guggenheim," her mother said, finally breaking the silence. "Very impressive for such a young man. Was it similar to these?"

Her mother gestured to the three slightly larger than life-size sculptures around the room: each of a gondola and, the main variation between them, varying gondoliers. Raquel felt then a bit of relief—her mother's edges were rough, but she was a smart cookie. Knew how to turn on the charms. (But why was it her mother performing for him, she thought? Shouldn't it be him endearing himself to her?)

"Oh, no, no," he said, "the stuff I sold to the Guggenheim was different. Drawings."

"Oh, you draw too," Toni said with enthusiasm.

"Yeah, but I'm leaning into sculpture these days."

Raquel's shoulders tensed; give them something to fucking work with here.

"Well, these look cool," her mother said.

"Thanks," Nick said, the smile so fixed now, Raquel felt it start to feel fake.

"They remind me a little bit of the Segals by Christopher Street," Toni said.

"Mira!" her mom said, walking toward one of them now. "I was trying to think of what they reminded me of! You're so right."

She was so right, Raquel thought. It was partly why she hated them. They were derivative. As if to counter this thought, Raquel suddenly found herself saying:

"Nick is moving back to New York at the end of the summer. He got signed by one of the biggest galleries in the art world; they represent Jack Martin."

Nick pulled her closer to him, kissed her on the top of her head.

"OK, even I've heard of him," Betsaida said, impressed. "The steel plates, right? I don't get it at all, mind you, but I know who he is."

"There's nothing to get," Raquel's mom chimed in. "The point is to appreciate the materials and do they change the space or not."

"Damn Rocky, Mami's about to bogart your art history degree," Toni added.

Everyone laughed but Raquel tried not to notice how stiff Nick's smile was.

"I'm just repeating what they told us on the staff tour we got before that sculpture show last year," her mom said. She seemed relaxed, the ice broken somehow. "Nick, you should come with us. Hang at the beach."

"Oh, thank you, Ms. Toro," he said. "But I just came in to say hello to you ladies and then I'm getting in my car and heading to my parents' place in the Hamptons."

"The Hamptons," her mother muttered, and Raquel was torn between her surprise at this news and her embarrassment at her mother's response. (You *never* acknowledge the money. Never.)

"You're leaving?" Raquel asked, hearing the consternation in her voice.

"Yeah," he said, a little sheepishly. "I decided last night. You're tied up here, and they missed me. They were super bummed you couldn't come."

Nick grabbed her hand now, turned to face her mother. "My parents *love* Raquel—"

"You've met his parents?" Raquel's mom interjected.

The Hamptons. The parents. Oh, the dramatics this would drum up. She couldn't get this over with quickly enough.

"Oh, yeah," Nick said, "they took us to this amazing dinner and then we all went to Campus Dance together. My dad went here, so he loves all that tradition stuff."

"Of course," Toni said, and Raquel felt her suspicious eyes. "Who wouldn't?"

Raquel tried to make eye contact with her mother, but she wouldn't even look at her.

"Nick, nice to meet you," her mother said, offering her hand out again. "But you've got a big drive, and we should get going. Hopefully we'll see you again. For longer next time."

"Oh, definitely," Nick said. "Girls like Raquel are hard to come by."

"I know," her mother said.

After Raquel let everyone else go ahead with promises to meet them at the car, Nick leaned in and kissed her, aggressively, pushing his hand up under her T-shirt.

"Stop," she whispered as she gently pushed him away. "My mom is right outside."

He leaned in again and she pulled herself away.

"Why didn't you tell me you were going to the Hamptons?"

"I seemed like a low priority to you this weekend."

Why did he always do this? The sulking.

"You guys have a great time," he continued. She didn't know why she suddenly felt overcome with a sense of insecurity.

"When are you coming back?" she asked, the question hanging in the air with an excessive amount of gravity.

"I dunno. Maybe Monday? Tuesday? Maybe I'll head into New York for a day to see if I can meet with Tilly."

"Oh," she said.

"What? You have shit all weekend and I have to start getting the rest of my life in order."

Was that a life with her? she wondered. He'd just said that it would be. Just said that girls like her were hard to come by. She didn't understand why she felt so uneasy. She got closer to him now, leaned in, and kissed him. Tried to put all of her body and feeling into it.

"Don't," he said, pushing her away gently. "I'll just get worked up and, like you said, your mom is waiting."

"OK," she said.

"I'll call you when I'm back."

* * *

THE WHOLE DRIVE to the beach, to Raquel's relief, nobody brought up Nick. She knew that this wasn't necessarily a good sign—that when they liked someone or something, like Betsaida or Marcus or oysters Rockefeller (her mother had licked her fingers over these and declared them "delectable")—they were very verbal about their opinion.

He hadn't done anything wrong, but he certainly hadn't done anything right exactly either. One of the things Raquel appreciated the most about Nick when they first met (and even now, when, admittedly, it sometimes felt cloying) was how he made her feel special, valued. That was not the vibe he gave off today to her family. It felt obligatory. Forced. She felt hurt for them, but also defensive of him. This wasn't who he really was. It was just a bad day. When she'd seen him last on Friday morning, he was admittedly sulky about a whole weekend apart but normal. Today, though, it felt like something had shifted. Still, he came. He didn't even need to do that much, she realized. He'd gotten up early to meet them, even knowing he wasn't staying in town. He could have, she surmised, left last night for the Hamptons. But he didn't. He stayed to meet her family. Because that was important to her. So what that it didn't go well? There'd be a second chance to make a different impression.

The beach was nothing like the beach in New York; blankets practically piled on top of each other. Family running into family, just the accents and skin colors and music delineating one group from the next. In Rhode Island, the beach was vast. The sand was pale and soft and the water, cool and briny. When you could see buildings, they weren't housing projects or cheap old condos but historic buildings and lighthouses. "This shit is straight out of a J.Crew catalog," Toni'd exclaimed when they walked onto the pristine corn-colored sand. It was. Somehow it was pretty and preppy but not pretentious. The kind of America they sing about in classic rock songs. Everything Raquel had wanted from college, but without the sense of otherness. Far less vibrant and diverse than New York, but with a beauty that she felt—and could see her mom and Toni felt—grateful to experience. They lay out and played Frisbee with a group of frat guys from URI who were near them—something Raquel would never have done with frat guys from Brown. When it was time for lunch, they dug into the spaghetti Betsaida had made. ("*Weird choice, but strangely satisfying?*" her mother had declared, before later whispering to Raquel while Betsaida went in for a dip, "*I told you, Dominicans are mad strange.*") They listened to music and tried to play cards, but it was too windy. Toni tried to read their tarot, but she was too bad at it. It was a gorgeous afternoon.

Just as they were trying to decide if they should pack it up or go in for one last dip, someone called her name. Assuming there was another Raquel, she ignored it.

"Broccoli!" the voice called out now, and when Raquel looked up, there was Julian, with some other dude, walking toward them. She remembered his message from right before the end of the year. She'd never called him back. She hadn't, she realized, thought about him much at all.

"Julian," she called back. "Whaddup!"

He approached and introductions were made all around, the other dude being a very hot, slightly older Latino-looking guy named Sam whom Julian introduced as his cousin. ("*Play cousins*," he added when they all looked confused.) Raquel's mom offered the guys beers (she was acting like a straight-up underage alcohol pimp this weekend) and, unprompted, Toni took one look at Sam and declared, "We definitely shouldn't leave yet."

"Julian and I know each other from my one failed actual art class," Raquel said, which made them both start laughing. "I tried to paint Duran Duran—"

"You did? I loved that friggin' dog," her mother exclaimed. "He was the sweetest—"

"Not the way I painted him," the memory of how upset she'd been now truly hilarious to her. "It's a long story, but let's just say he ended up looking like a pile of broccoli."

"Broccoli with eyes," Julian added. "She got so pissed about her crit, she threw the painting away after."

"These things are brutal!" Raquel lamented. "You don't even understand."

"Wait," her mother said. "You threw a painting of Duran Duran away?"

"It's at the house," Raquel said. "Julian saved it for me."

"I dumpster dove for her. That's what it took for her to be my friend. She can be a little stuck-up sometimes, you know?"

And Toni and her mother laughed because, yes, they understood.

Sam was quiet but not for a lack of Toni asking him questions. He was getting his master's at UConn, was visiting for the weekend. Julian told everybody about how he was actually a great R&B singer and Julian was trying to make him beats, which then begat even more questions: about Julian and his music, about Julian and his mixtapes. They were having such a good time, Raquel didn't even care when her mother invited them to dinner.

"Ah, Ms. Toro, I wish we could, but it's our night to grind in my little makeshift studio."

"No, do your thing, nene," she said. "Some other time. If you're ever in New York."

"True dat," he said and gave her mother a kiss on the cheek.

They were walking away, and Raquel couldn't tell if it was how sweet the gesture of him saving *Duran Duran* suddenly seemed to her now that the bitterness of the moment had passed, but she felt herself sad to watch him go. Regretful that she'd never returned his call. She promised herself to email him Monday to make a plan.

As soon as he was out of earshot, Raquel was inundated.

"Yo," Betsaida said, "Julian is mad cool."

"Such a fun dude," Toni chimed in.

"Yeah," Raquel said, "sweet guy. I hadn't seen him all summer."

"Now *that* is a good guy," her mother said, in a final, definitive statement. The implied second clause of the sentence—*not like that fucking cabrón you took us to meet this morning*—didn't need to be uttered.

After the beach, Toni insisted they go to an oyster house they had passed and they gorged themselves (well, everyone but Raquel, who claimed to be full from the spaghetti) on baked oysters, bourbon oysters, clams, and all the seafood they could manage to stuff into their little mouths. Raquel was confident that Toni and her mother had to have spent more than they won in the Hot 97 contest. She tried to pay the bill (the truth was, Nick paid for so much of her life these days, she'd never been so flush), but they wouldn't let her. "Think of what you saved us on hotels!" her mother said.

It was dark by the time they started driving back. Toni took the wheel because Mami had one daiquiri too many at dinner and, coupled with the sun, she was already snoozing beside Betsaida in the back. Hot 106 had switched to R&B now (*Just like fucking 360*, Raquel thought) and they had been talking about Toni and her boyfriend and if she still really liked him or not ("*I think the answer is not*," Raquel said) when Toni stated:

"He's not good enough for you."

Raquel felt her tears well up immediately. She didn't want to have this conversation.

When she didn't reply, Toni continued.

"You think he's doing you some sort of favor by being with you—"

"Oh my God, what are you, Mami now?" Raquel hissed. "Everything's the worst side of everything."

"Sometimes she's right!"

"You don't understand how it is here," Raquel said. "Me and Bets and Marcus and everybody like us, we're like, here, but we're also *not* here. Like we got in but then we aren't welcome. He helps me. When I'm with him, I'm fully here."

She tried to fight the tears but they weren't staying away.

"You're right. I don't know what it's like here. I go to dumb Brooklyn College and Mami works in a cafeteria and goes to BMCC. But we know good people, and he's not good people."

"It was a bad meeting."

"You look at him like he's a prize at a carnival and you're the dumb bitch who won the stuffed dog with her only token. And he looks at us like we're there to clean his studio."

"But that's not how he looks at me," Raquel said.

"Does it matter?" Toni said, and Raquel could hear the anger in her voice. "We're all from the same house."

And Raquel didn't know what to say to this because it was true. They were all from the same house. She had just been the one who wanted to get out.

Jack

NEW YORK CITY • WINTER 1987

As Jack pulled off the highway and onto the country road, he allowed the faintest of smiles to creep onto his face. The result was more smirk than smile, really; the muscles required to express the contentment and—dare he say it?—near happiness he felt had long atrophied. Life, of late, giving little occasion to use them. The winter snows and melts and frosts had encased the wooded roadside in ice; the bare birches and maples glistened in the strained rays of winter light. He rolled the window of Gerry's car down a bit—just a bit—to inhale the scent of the cold, the crisp transporting him to the snow-filled backyard of his parents' clapboard home in Massachusetts. The smirk widening. Ingrid, who sensed his mood shifts like a loyal spaniel, turned up the volume on *Graceland*; put her long-fingered hand on his knee, squeezed it. Another sensation he hadn't felt in ages: the surge of blood to his crotch, the slightest stiffening of his cock. The smile grew wider still as he thought perhaps this afternoon might end up being spent in what would surely be plush down bedding he'd likely helped to underwrite in the "country house" that Ron Rosen, his lawyer, had lent him for the long weekend.

Not that he wasn't grateful. He'd been about to fucking crack, and Ron had seen it and took action. He was a pain in the ass, a thorn in his side, and a literal excavation drain on his bank account. But he was a world-class reader of people, which was in part what made him a stellar attorney. It had been more than a year of absolute living hell: of prepping for depositions, of being deposed by absolute morons in the DA's office, of listening to depositions by Anita's friends—so many of whom used to kiss his ass to win his favor, now painting him as some kind of monster. Worse, a monster in decline. As if he—a literal living legend of the fine arts—could "decline." The insinuations of these people—all losers and climbers themselves—that he somehow felt jealous of her? How was he not supposed to be enraged? How was he not supposed to be angry? And then to listen to her sister! Oh, that mousy cunt. How little she had to say to him in his presence and how much she suddenly had to say to the attorneys about verbal abuse and temper tantrums and frightened calls from her sister in the middle of the night. It was absolutely ridiculous and Ron had agreed and called it all hearsay and promised he'd have it ruled inadmissible. But still!

Still, when he heard her saying that she'd warned Anita to break it off with Jack in a public place because "she knew," he felt the steam rising to his top like the pressure valve on an old boiler. And when he looked up and saw Ron's paralegal's eyes wet with tears and contempt, he raged. "*What the fuck are you crying over, you bitch?*" he'd hissed and hurled the closest thing to him on the conference table desk—a coffee mug—over her head, where it then smashed on a wall. Ron, really, truly a gem, didn't throw him out of his office. He just escorted that nitwit out of the conference room where he could hear her *really* sobbing. And Jack felt bad for throwing the mug, but not for being angry because she was being paid to be there to support *him*. Not to be another woman making Anita into some martyr. As if, other than his being famous, there was anything different about their marriage than anyone else's. When Ron walked back in, he was carrying two scotches—one neat, for Jack, and the other on the rocks—and said that he thought it would be a good idea to get Jack out of the city. He petitioned the court for permission, pleading that it was a mental health issue and assuring them he would be confined to Ron's very own cabin. That without a brief escape, he might not be able to handle the strain of a trial.

This wasn't hyperbole. Since *it* happened his life had gone from bad to worse to nearly insufferable and he'd simply had no release. No. Fucking. Release. He had no space or ability or demand for his art—not under this cloud of scandal. His mind was too crowded and his spirit too pumped with adrenaline and anxiety about this torment the DA was putting him through to even write his poems. He had spent the better part of his fifty-eight years traveling the world, often at a moment's notice, and now he couldn't even leave Manhattan. His whole world shrank to his apartment, Ingrid's place at the Chelsea, and Ron's office. Yes, he still had Tilly and the artists he'd come up with—friends he trusted with whom he would go to dinner—but relative to his previous life, he'd become a recluse. He'd venture out to dinner parties but avoided anything like an opening because he could feel the eyes on him. Not of admiration or intimidation of his import but of pity. Or worse than that, disdain. This fucking situation with Anita hovering over him like a cloud. Even the release of fucking—a reliable source of validation and joy and triumph for him even longer than his art career had been—was taken away from him. Though he could never admit why to anyone. The why a hideous beast so chilling to him, he locked it in a corner of his mind under tight key. Indeed, it was only the spark of a lustful thought—of the recollection of feeling himself over Ingrid's soft and slender body—that would rouse it, cause it to scratch and rattle in its cage.

* * *

THE FIRST TIME was a week or so after Anita's memorial. Those bitches in the park—he knew what he saw, even if Ingrid insisted he'd imagined it—got him so riled that he lost his footing. Gashed his head so bad, he needed seven stitches. At the hospital Ingrid had launched into a story about his being under stress and taking a hike and growing light-headed on an unusually warm autumn day. He nodded and agreed to it, but he told Tilly what really happened. He told Ron too. Raged about it, actually. And his rage just kept building. Every time he felt the throb and itch of the stitches closing, tight against his skull, he himself throbbed and itched to find those two nasty terrorists and make them pay.

The tabloids were still lurking in those days. He couldn't afford, he knew, to be so on edge; his temper was simply too volatile. Though his head pounded and he felt himself depleted, a few nights later, he rolled over as Ingrid slept; put his mouth over a nipple just barely visible through her thin negligée, slid his hand under the silk of her underwear. Oh, and how she had responded in kind, kissing him with such depth of passion and yearning, the heat of it made the pain of his head fade into memory. They used to spend entire days in bed, but since the night *it* happened sex came in fits and starts. She'd begun, he could tell, to take it personally. But this night, he managed to channel his anger—his pain at all that he'd been forced to endure—into pure passion. He pulled her long blond hair gently as he entered her and she moaned in a way that made him feel needed and missed and important. But he soon found himself winded at the weight of himself (what he'd managed to do with no problem at all in the weeks since *it* happened was to eat). He lay on his back and drew Ingrid on top of him, lay resplendent at the sight of her perfect, cream-colored breasts. It was everything and more than it had ever been with her, the pleasure so exquisite he wondered why he'd denied himself. He was close to climax, but wanted this to last forever; he went into himself to will it so when—

Plop.

Amid the moisture of bodies in pleasure, he felt—keenly—the sensation of a drop—cold like chilled water, but heavier, somehow—land on his chest. He kept his eyes closed, intent on staying in the moment, dug his genius hands into the flesh of Ingrid's thighs.

Plop.

His neck this time. He called Ingrid's name. Moaned in praise of her beauty.

Plop. Plop.

Cold, wet, heavy on his face. He instinctively wiped himself, placed his hands back on Ingrid's hips and coaxed her to move faster. She leaned down to kiss him, the tips of her hair soaked wet from their passion. He felt a fresh wave of lust, inspired that he had made her quite so wild. His eyes were still closed as he tried to make it all last just a bit longer.

"Look at me, Jack," she whispered, "and tell me you love me."

Just her voice made him want to come, but he did as she commanded and fluttered his eyes open.

"Ingrid, I . . ."

His pronouncement was drowned out by screams. His screams. Bloodcurdling things, Ingrid would later tell him. He himself heard nothing. Was enveloped in the horror of what was hovering above him: Anita's broken body. Joints askew, limbs going this way and that. A macabre ceiling fan. Black and blue where her flesh was meant to be. Dripping, dripping, dripping blood—it flowed like the steady trickle of a broken faucet—most of which had primarily collected in Ingrid's tow-headed locks, drenching them in slick crimson paint that had dripped down her back. Her hips, where he'd been holding her in her straddle over him, marked by his bloody fingertips. The blood not hot with life, but cold and congealing and putrid with death. His horror at the sight of it, the feel of it now that he understood what had lubricated their lovemaking, pumped panic through his body and he hurled Ingrid off of him and onto the floor. Without her between them, though, he could see without obstruction the most horrific aspect of it all: Anita's face. Body dead but eyes alive and wide open, face in exactly the smug smile that she would sometimes get when she felt she'd bested him in a fight that would make him want to slap it off of her (but he never did).

Every time he fucked, or thought about fucking, he thought of Anita. Every time he thought of Anita, she showed up. With that piece-of-shit grin. The blood to his dismay was imagined. A conjuring of spirit or memory of her lying there (flattened, really) on the roof. (The photos the police made him look at again and again and again.) But what he knew—what no one could say otherwise to him and he'd never believed shit like this before—was that Anita was *there*. Every time. Oh, and it was just like her, that bitch. Who, when alive, loved nothing more than to ridicule his sexual appetites. Of course this was how she would torment him. As if her existence wasn't the cause of his torment all day and every day of his life now since *it* happened. Try as he might to block her from his consciousness, each and every time she would be there. In a corner, against a door. Peeking out from under the bed. Those eyes and that smile and sometimes a twisted broken leg for, he assumed, good measure. And he didn't want to be scared, but he was. He was! She terrified him because of how real she was. Her presence. Because if she was in the room, then where else could she be?

He hadn't performed successfully since that night. But now, driving Gerry's car, he didn't know what it was—maybe the sound of the Paul Simon cassette on the stereo, or the freedom of driving itself, or being back in cold, wooded country like he knew when he was a boy, or steadfast, loyal Ingrid—something about this weekend filled him with hope that this awful specter of Anita was gone. It was the hope that made him particularly hard. The smile on his face grew wider.

* * *

THE HOUSE, OVERLOOKING a pristine lake, was better than Ron had promised, and the sex more exhilarating than he had even remembered. No blood, no shit-eating grins, not those goddamned brown eyes darting this way and that or the cold chill that, once he came to recognize her presence in the room, would goosepimple his skin. Just Ingrid, vigorous with life after walking across the frozen pond while he watched from the sideline, taking photos (was it really frozen solid?). Just Ingrid: under him, over him, beside him, all over the course of several glorious hours. He made them a spaghetti carbonara and they drank between them several bottles of wine by the fire while they played Monopoly and—absolutely uncharacteristic of him, but totally appropriate for the lightness he felt that afternoon—he joined Ingrid as she danced to the Paul Simon album she was obsessed with. She looked so happy and the zydeco reminded him of a weekend in New Orleans when he was young; he was happier than he had felt in a longer time than he cared to remember. Eventually, exhausted from the day and the excitement and all of the (magnificent) lovemaking, they collapsed for the night in Ron Rosen's (perfectly luxurious) Egyptian bedding.

He'd been in deep sleep when Ingrid woke him.

"Jack," she said, worry in her voice.

"What?" He turned on the light.

"I think something got into the house."

"What do you mean?"

"I saw something fly, out of the corner of my eye."

"A bird?"

"I don't know," she said, "but it must be?"

"We probably left something open," he said, though he couldn't think what, as the night was particularly cold, even for his New England blood. He looked around the room and could see nothing. Maybe it had gone into the den or the kitchen. "Stay here."

He put on his slippers and began to make his way down the hall toward the living area. Even half asleep, he found himself humming "Graceland"—they'd played it about a dozen times that day and damn if that wasn't an earworm.

"Jack," Ingrid called from the bedroom, "did you turn the stereo on?"

He hadn't realized the music was playing on the stereo. He was nowhere near the stereo. No one else was in the house, but the volume, he now realized, went from low to audible to pulsing to Paul Simon practically screaming to them that losing love was like a window in the heart. He could hear Ingrid shouting but couldn't make out what over the music. The den was as dark as they'd left it; dirty wineglasses and abandoned board game just discernible in the moonlight coming from the window.

It swept in from the built-in where the stereo was—fast. Its wings black and thick like leather. It didn't fly so much as soar through the lofted ceilings of the space. A bat. Accidentally found its way through the chimney flue, he supposed. Landed on the stereo and turned it on? He couldn't quite figure that part out, but man could never truly know animal. The bat was up at the top of the ceiling now, easy to spot against the blond-wood beams. He stood paralyzed; racking his brain for how best to handle this. The animal—frightened—could accidentally bite them. Could be rabid. But no exterminator would come at this hour. He lowered the stereo.

"Ingrid," he shouted, "stay in the bed—"

The bat swooped down and nearly clipped his ear. Changed directions and disappeared into the built-in again. "Graceland" had ended, but the cassette was rewinding itself before it stopped and he watched the Play button depress on its own. Watched as the volume dial turned itself, slowly, back up. His skin grew clammy despite the cold, rose into gooseflesh.

"Jack!" Ingrid called, and he realized she was coming into the living room.

"Stay in the fucking bedroom!" he shouted.

"What's happening?"

"It's a bat, Ingrid." But even as he said it, he didn't quite believe it. Didn't believe it at all.

Ingrid didn't fucking listen. There she was, beside him. Shouting over the music before getting frustrated. She went toward the stereo to lower the volume and the bat flew out of the built-in, sending Ingrid screaming before it nose-dived back and orbited her, frantically, several times.

"Just stand still, Ingrid."

But Ingrid would not stand still. She was running in circles now and—he couldn't believe what he was seeing—the bat was fucking chasing her. He ran to open windows and doors, all the while screaming to Ingrid to just stand still. He would drive the bat out of the windows. He was certain it was rabid and had to at least try to get it out. Jack grabbed the Monopoly board from the table, intended to guide the creature toward the open window with it. But just as he neared Ingrid, the bat plunged toward her, nipping the nape of her neck before flapping its wings and diving in—ferocious and swift—to her scalp, which it bit again and again. Jack grew closer, whacked it with the Monopoly board—but it was no use. The beast now turned on him. Rapid. Rabid. Swooping low and biting his thick fleshy thighs exposed in his underwear and then his bare belly and then it swept up to his face, which he went to protect with his hands. A chill came over him beyond his natural fear. Because he knew this was not just an animal. The bat was fucking relentless—it nipped at his hands most of all, bite after bite after bite, and Jack attempted to run, but its wings kept flapping and flapping. *Whoosh. Whoosh. Whoosh.* And it did something Jack didn't even know bats could do: it hovered in place, right near his face. In the background, over Paul Simon, Ingrid was sobbing. Jack was flooded with the sense that if he didn't look at this bat, didn't acknowledge its menacing presence, it would never let them be. He lowered his hands and opened his eyes and found before them, in the tiny feral face of this animal, Anita's eyes. And he swore that if a bat could smirk, this one did. But it was only a glimpse before it plunged in toward him and dug its tiny fangs into the flesh of his nose.

Anita

THE CEIBA TREE

What can I say? Can a girl not have a little fun? Don't I deserve a little nip at that sow? And, really? ¿Qué clase de puta aparece en el funeral de la esposa? Why not wear a red dress too while you're at it. She had it coming. And as for Jack . . . well, look. If he doesn't deserve it, who does?

That was a big night for me. Death reveals itself slowly. Till that night, I hadn't been able to take physical form. I could haunt, in the purely metaphysical sense. But that night was the first time I was able to corporeally harm his world and it was exhilarating. A night full of possibilities . . .

The ceiba showed up out of nowhere on the beach one day. Or maybe it just felt like one day. . . . Time is funny here. Jack threw me out the window and I went through the roof of the building and came out on the shore of my beautiful Varadero and there was sun and music—but from where, I have no idea. No one was at the beach but me. The little bars along the shore were open but empty. Which was nice, because normally, in the busy season? Well, you could wait forever for a table by the shore. Just for a little ham sandwich and a piña colada. But now I had the place all to myself. I never felt like sleeping, so it was only when sunset eventually turned to dusk and I started walking—hoping to find my yaya's house—that I saw the ceiba tree, big and shadowy, just off the dunes and the clusters of sea grape and hibiscus. I had never seen a ceiba this old—the roots stopped me in awe, with the hills and valleys that they created. The thorns of the thing ancient, horn shaped, like a thousand little rhinoceros tusks, climbing their way toward the sky. The roots spread out to at least twice my size, the crown of leaves above—so high you began to lose perspective when you looked up. The eyes of its thick trunk, staring out, big and wide. But not ominous. Kind, the way you hope a mother's are. I found myself a comfortable spot nestled between two surface roots, watching as the last of the sun went down past the horizon and the blue darkened from dusk to navy. You could see the stars emerge through the branches up above; the moonlight eventually catching on the silken threads of the ceiba flowers, as the bats came in and out to rest. Hanging themselves upside down, finding comfort in the vastness of the tree.

I have no idea how much time had passed when suddenly "Jack" cracked in my mind like a firework and a feeling blanketed me—one of indignation. Suddenly—despite not having climbed a tree since I was a young girl and cried from the height of it—I had the urge to scale the thing. No fear, just an instinct, primal, to go up, up, up. I was wearing nothing but the blue lingerie I'd been in when I went to tell Jack about the divorce, the detective, the evidence—all of it. No shoes, no shirt to cover my arms or shorts to protect my legs—yet somehow I found myself ascending the thorny trunk without harm. My hands and feet moving so fast it was as if I'd grown up inside the crown of a tree. As if I wasn't afraid to get on a ladder and change a bulb. Going up, past the eyes that looked at me and told me it would be fine. Going up until the roots, wide as a house moments before, were just a small hand, gnarly at the knuckles from hundreds of years of digging into the red soil, several stories below. When I got to the crown, the branches were thicker, the leaves denser than they'd appeared from the ground. The silk of the tree stuck to my skin; the pink of its flowers tinted my arms and legs. And just as I could see the sky—the dark azure of the night sky—I realized it wasn't a sky at all. It was a ceiling. A dim, vast room made of cinder blocks and catwalks. It took me a moment to recognize I was in jail. And then *crack!* It went off again. Loud and clear: "Jack!" and a smile broke out on my face.

Oh, the great fucking Jack Martin, lying in a cell like the other (non-genius) murderers! How delightful! How wonderfully, fucking delightful to imagine. Only I didn't have to imagine! I was there!!!! I was there!!!! Oh, I cackled in the moonlight that poked through the tiny windows. Or maybe I cackled by the light of the emergency exits. It doesn't matter. No one could hear me. That much became clear. I laughed as loud as I could, first because it was genuinely funny; then just to see. One man came to the edge of his cell. Looked around. He heard me but didn't see me. Figured it must have been a dream, or his imagination, or the voices in his head. Or maybe he knew? Maybe he knew he could hear ghosts. Maybe, had that happened now, I'd have gone to see how much he could hear and see and understand. Maybe now, knowing what I do, I would have stuck around. Maybe now, with some time on my hands, I would have spent some time with him.

But I didn't.

All I cared for was Jack. Peeking through the bars of each cell, moving on. It was different now, walking and being. It was not coming from a place in my mind per se; there were no thoughts or reflections or analysis of what I was seeing or what I was doing or even what I was proceeding to next. I would just feel things. In the cells, I saw mostly young men, many who looked like they could be my cousins or my uncles, and in the air I felt sadness and frustration and anger and some lust and lots and lots of longing for people who would never come. It was a heavy place. Gray, but not soft or comforting. Muddy and directionless. There was the occasional note of brightness here or there. A burst of excitement, anticipation, delight. Maybe from someone who was going home? Who knows. Then, from above me, I felt a hot red that was turning into purple. The color of a child who'd held its breath too long with anger. And I knew that if I followed that sense of rage, Jack would be on the other side of it. And he was.

He was so big on that tiny twin cot, his weight causing it to sag down below into the airspace of the sleeping man underneath him. I didn't walk through the bars so much as I was able to squeeze through. Boneless, like a mouse. No one told me, I just knew I could do it. I had to step on the other man's bunk, but he didn't notice and I realized I didn't have any weight anymore. Anyway, I climbed up to Jack's bunk and I squeezed myself next to him. I lay on my side looking at him sleeping, the way I had so many nights before, and I felt every emotion he was having, even there, in his sleep. (Oh, the way we feel when we are sleeping; all the things you have well up inside you during the day, but without the veil of politeness for "civil society.")

His body emanated grievance and vengeance. Angrier with me now than he had been the last time he saw me alive. He felt sorry for himself. Wasn't thinking of what I went through at all! Wasn't thinking of all that I now wasn't going to be able to do! I thought, at least guilt, like in that Poe story, would weigh on him. I should have known.

My nose was so close to him that I realized I mustn't be breathing because he would have felt it on his face. I suppose I didn't need to breathe anymore. Still, I decided to try. I closed my eyes and focused and said to myself, *Blow!*, and pursed my lips and felt a little something come out and watched Jack stir before he pulled the sad little blanket they had given him a little closer. Cold. I guess my breath was cold.

If I focused, I could see his dreams. There, he was seeking solace in his "greatness." Imagined himself in a future outside of here being celebrated at yet another party. He almost wore a smile of smug satisfaction. I conjured myself up there. Appearing when he least expected it. Not as I was, but as he last saw me, mangled and bloody. Bones shattered inside skin and skin that had been punctured like a plastic bag, that allowed my blood to leak out all over the place. Ah! But he didn't know! He didn't know that the *real* me had gone through the roof of the other building and come out in Varadero! I imagined myself hanging on one of his crosses and smiling at him; getting another chance to ruin his night. Like he had done to mine so many times before! And suddenly, as I was imagining it, he stirred—jolted really. Writhed a bit. And the feeling coming off of him changed. Pity and rage replaced by . . . Fear. Oh. Yes.

His fear felt nice.

From what I could best figure, it was people who conjured me up or down the ceiba. The call most loud and urgent and when someone was talking about me, or my work, in a way that I'd really like. Or that I really wouldn't. I would hear a name and then feel their feeling: sadness or anger or longing was the most common. And I would go up, up, up. Never fully certain as to where until I arrived. Being unable to actually do anything about what I was seeing or they were feeling—unable to do anything about my anger—I often felt frustrated. And I would think of the ceiba and soon enough find myself back in the branches, scaling my way down, down, down, back to the massive roots. At first, it brought me only back to Varadero, but then one day, after I visited my sister who was helping Leslie—Leslie of all people!—plan my memorial, I found myself down in the backyard of our old house in Havana, where I could walk into our old rooms. Another time, I descended the ceiba and found myself back in Rome. Not just anywhere, but behind the American Academy. Oh, how I loved to lie in this one grove of trees and stare at the sky and sort through the problems with my artwork that simply couldn't be fixed in the studio. I found so much peace there.

The ceiba never sent me down to America. Only to places that made me happy.

In the early days—days! What do those even mean anymore! In the immediate aftermath of my life, my calendar was very full. I was inundated with names and emotions and I would go here and there and listen and learn and sometimes, especially if they were, like my sister and my parents, very sad, I would come into their dreams. Stepping into the dreams was easy and it was only Jack who got the nasty ones. Though, truth be told, I spent a few nights sleeping next to a critic who printed a terrible review of some of my wood sculptures from my time in Rome. I didn't realize it, but I had so much power back then.

The power took time to understand.

Who could sense my visits and who could not didn't always play out the way that one would think it would. Jomar, a brujo, not only could feel when I was there, sometimes he would talk to me. That was nice. My sister, on the other hand, couldn't. Her daughter, on the other hand, could. She didn't know what or who it was, just that she felt "something." Leslie, her husband, Giancarlo—who was far more bereaved than I had ever expected—almost none of the art world people, for all of their leaning into intuition, ever had the vaguest sense of my presence.

But, wait? Where was I? Ah! The night I came to Jack as a bat! Right!

I'd been fucking with Jack's sex life for a while. This felt, to me, like a just punishment. I loved to watch him long and then regret. I loved to take away from him the one thing he felt validated him, besides his art. But then, Jack did something that made me want to spit nails, breathe fire, curse the day he was born, wish him dead, roar like a trapped bear, and rage, not only at his successes but at the simple fact that he walked this fucking earth and I didn't.

I needed to raise the stakes.

I was under the ceiba and heard my sister's name, draped in anguish and pain. I climbed faster than I knew possible: hand over hand and foot over foot, hoisting myself around the rhinoceros thorns until I was up at the crown of the tree and then in my sister's kitchen. She was on the phone, her face contorted from torment and a letter in her hand. At the table, my brother-in-law sat, rage steaming off him like a boiling pot of stew.

"How does he have any right to do this?" she was screaming into the phone.

It was a bit hard to make out, but the person on the other end—a lawyer, I quickly came to understand—told her that *he doesn't necessarily have a right to do it, but he has a right to try*. The rest was for a judge to decide.

"So everything is up to fucking judges now?" she shouted, and I knew she was talking about Jack. His lawyer—who thought about me constantly; I was able to visit him all the time—had argued that her testimony was hearsay. Mike Romero, private detective; the divorce; and taking his money and all the things I told her the night that I died? The judge ruled it all inadmissible. There was no way to prove Jack knew what I'd known. And without that, well, it was harder to prove motive. "I will not allow him to fuck with this show. The least Anita deserves is to have this."

My sister had always supported me being an artist, but honestly, I never thought she appreciated my art. My aesthetic. Our yaya painted. Landscapes and still lifes and other safe things. She grew up loving things like that. The Dutch masters, Frida Kahlo's portraits. My work, she told me once, "frightened" her. She said it had so much rage.

But after Jack pushed me out the window, something shifted in her. Her first concern was for my studio: the contents of both my apartment and the one in Rome. She changed the locks on the Varick Street place and sent her husband on the first flight they could book. She would spend hours just sitting there, on the floor of my apartment, staring at the prints of the photographs of my happenings. Thumbing through the sketches. Sometimes when she sat there, she would weep and I could feel her, not so much sad as she was comforted. And it was because of the energy. I was in those pieces! I was in the tree trunks in Rome and the sand sculptures and the videos of the girl on fire in the cornfield. I was alive in my art. So maybe she couldn't feel my ghost in a room, but she could feel my vitality in my art. And she was committed to keeping it out in the world, since I was no longer able to. And in that way, she fought for my life in my afterlife.

At first, there was overwhelming interest in mounting a retrospective of my work. Every faction of the art world that wasn't siding with Jack was jockeying to take the reins of it. Jomar and the Latins on one side, Leslie and the feminists on the other. Each expecting my sister to name them custodian of it all, neither group anticipating her—art world outsider, schoolteacher, suburban mom—to buck their assertions and anoint herself as the guardian of my legacy. "*Anita*," she told them, "*was not an artist defined by one thing except for her spirit.*" She also wouldn't settle. Jomar and Leslie, who eventually found a way to work together, introduced her to gallerists—places with far more prestige than Leslie's place. Each time my sister said no. "*My sister's work is in the collections of the Met, the Tate, MoMA. She's a museum-caliber artist, she deserves a museum retrospective.*"

She pushed and prodded and made the case, again and again and again, until finally she arranged not only a retrospective at the Museum of Contemporary Art of the Americas, but for the show to travel to small museums in Philadelphia, Chicago, Miami. A gorgeous catalog—that Giancarlo helped to edit—was being produced and the show itself was meant to open . . . soon.

"So what do I let him do?" my sister was screaming into the phone. "Bury her work? Let people forget what he did?"

Then she began crying—tears of rage, really—but her words stopped making sense. Her curses and laments to the lawyer became tear-soaked and muddled with Spanish about Jack being a son of a bitch and worse than the devil himself. My brother-in-law—a sweet gringo she'd picked up in Chicago who, unlike my husband, had learned the language—got up and took the phone from her hands and it was only when my sister walked away, dropping the letter on the table and pacing frantically, that I was able to fully understand the calamity of the moment.

FROM THE OFFICES OF WRIGLEY, ROSS & MURPHY, LLP

KEITH MURPHY, ESQ. PARTNER,

Wrigley, Ross & Murphy, LLP

200 Fifth Avenue, Suite 1500, New York, New York

Date: January 15, 1987

Re: Unauthorized Disclosure of Intellectual Property

Dear Ms. de Monte,

We have reason to believe that you are in direct violation of reproducing, showcasing, transporting and handling artwork and archives that are deemed intellectual property belonging to Anita de Monte, spouse of our client, John Christopher Martin, II.

The infringing actions include the following:

- Illegally acting as executor of the Estate of Anita de Monte
- Illegally taking into your possession the artwork created by and belonging to Anita de Monte

- Improperly lending the artworks of the Estate of Anita de Monte to the Museum of Contemporary Art of the Americas
- Illegally authorizing the reproduction of said artworks in publicity and marketing materials
- Illegally gaining, financially, off of sales and reproductions of the artworks of Anita de Monte
- Improperly storing and caring for the artworks in the Estate of Anita de Monte

IT IS REQUIRED THAT YOU CEASE AND DESIST THE FOLLOWING:

- The exhibition, marketing and promotion of the forthcoming show "Anita de Monte: Earth and Body"

And after that I didn't care what the fuck else the thing said because he was trying to stop my show! Icing me out of the conversation! Keep my work—keep me—hidden away in a closet!! Oh, the rage I felt! I knocked over everything—all the other pieces of mail that had sat unopened after this piece had been opened! My sister's telephone book earmarked with her attorney's information! My phone book, which she seemed to always keep by her side these days! I threw it all to the floor, pounded the table, and my brother-in-law's coffee cup rattled a bit! My sister—sweet, earthbound thing that she is—ran to the window, which was opened a crack. Certain it was a draft. But it was no draft! Oh, no draft at all! Just my sheer, sheer fucking wrath!!!!

On the phone my brother-in-law was insisting to the attorney that they would simply violate the cease and desist and suffer the consequences. This only made my sister more bereft. "*Consequences? We are always the ones to suffer the consequences. The only ones!*" She then started cursing me in Spanish about not leaving a will and how my disorganization always ended up falling in her hands to fix. (Not true, really, but this was hardly the time to nitpick.) Continued ranting about how she knew Jack was going to make trouble about this when he refused to hand over my portfolio. Wondered why he had waited until now? On the phone the lawyer spoke in even tones. I got close to the receiver to hear what he had to say.

"Legally speaking, him being a suspect in your sister-in-law's murder—"

"He killed her," my brother-in-law said, and I nodded in silent agreement because this was true.

"Well, he doesn't have a strong case to win control of her estate, will or no will."

"Great."

"Still," the lawyer said, "you might want to take this particular case to the court of public opinion. I know someone at the *Post* I can introduce you to."

I felt so much frustration with my inability to do anything that I closed my eyes extra tight and found myself back at the crown of the ceiba tree. Only this time, as I made my descent, I heard somebody whistle at me,

"*Phwwwwwhht.*"

And when I looked over, it was one of the bats that came to rest between the boughs at night. Even with his face upside down as it was, I could see that he was handsome. Not like a rat, like a man. I'd never looked at them that closely before. Then again, they'd never tried to make conversation either.

"You don't have to go back like that, you know," he said.

"Like what?" I said, because I really didn't know what he meant.

"Like that. Invisible. You have power. Not everybody does. I think you can make it."

"Make what?"

"Some of us can go back up like this," he said, and his eyes were very enchanting. Familiar. A strange blue-green I didn't even know bats' eyes could have.

"Like bats?"

"Bats can keep their form. Their physicality beyond the ceiba. They can travel back and forth. Be visible. Then invisible. Fly both here and there."

I stopped to consider it. An exciting prospect.

"They," the bat said to me, "can bite."

Very exciting.

"Why are you telling me this now?" I asked. Suspicious. All this silence and suddenly the bats were giving me advice?

"Because now is when you needed to hear it," he said, and I looked at him a little skeptically. "Fine. Because you were very nice to someone very special to me."

"Who?" I asked.

"Marco."

And suddenly I knew who it was. He was Marco's lover. The one we saw in the paintings. The one he painted over and over again—further heartbroken by news of his dying in jail. Whose death finally motivated Marco to leave Cuba. Marco, who I helped get set up in Miami. Marco, who for a time dated Jomar but was too heartbroken over the loss of this bat to move on. Oh, we'd lost touch, but he'd become very well known in Miami. His portraits of the men of South Beach becoming hot commodities there, but none more valuable than the innumerous paintings he did of his deceased love.

"Do you visit Marco?"

"Sometimes," he said. "I bring him mice. To let him know I still love him. I leave them at the door."

And his almond-shaped blue-green eyes got glassy.

"But mainly, I taunt the jailers who killed me," he said, before adding with pride, "Once, I flew into Fidel's house and ruined a dinner party. That was satisfying."

I just nodded in quiet agreement. My head was full of questions, but I didn't want him to think I was being impolite.

"How do I do it?" I finally asked. "How do I become a bat?"

* * *

MANY PEOPLE DON'T know this, but bats cannot fly the way normal birds do. Normal birds can just stand on their delicate little feet, widen out their wings, give a couple of flaps, and find themselves soaring in the air. One moment grounded, the next propelling themselves, higher and higher up into the sky. Ascension, the motivation. But not the bat; their wings are too heavy to build momentum. For the bat, the only way to soar is to first allow yourself to fall. To disorient yourself to the world and hang upside down, and, when you feel certain that you want to go up, allow yourself to actually go down. To release what branch you are clinging to and to drop. Plummet. Plunge. Not up, but down. Having full faith that when you spread your wings—your strong, majestic, perfectly constructed wings—you will catch wind and fly. Higher than you ever knew you could go, to anywhere you wanted to be.

Raquel

PROVIDENCE • SUMMER 1998

"Belinda Kim's office; this is Raquel speaking."

"Raquel, darling," came the voice from the phone, and she felt her stomach flip at the immediate recognition that it belonged to Mrs. Fitzsimmons.

"Oh. Linda, hi."

Raquel could hardly hide her surprise or confusion.

"I'm sorry to bother you at work, dear, but we're headed up to a wedding in Barrington—child of an old family friend—and we figured we'd stop and have a drink with you kids on our way. This evening? The University Club? It's right near Nick's studio and you and Astrid can walk over after work."

Raquel twisted the phone cord around her fingers while she spoke; she pulled it tighter for a moment, felt the rush of blood in her fingertips before she finally managed to exhale and utter, "Mrs. Fitzsimmons—"

"Darling, Linda! I've told you."

"Right, yes. Linda. Sorry." Raquel felt her quickened pulse; completely flustered how to handle this moment, which would surely prove to be one of the most awkward of her life. "The thing is. Ugh. This is kind of embarrassing. The thing is, I would love to see you and Mr. Fitzsimmons and say hello, but it feels a little inappropriate—"

"Inappropriate? Why on earth—"

"Well, it's just that I think Nick and I have . . . well, I . . ." She stopped and took a breath. How could she be both quietly dumped and in the position of having to tell his mother? "Actually, I haven't seen or heard from Nick in a week so I don't think Nick would want me—"

"Nonsense, Raquel," Mrs. Fitzsimmons purred into the phone. Raquel was shocked and surprised by her certainty about a matter whose uncertainty had been plaguing Raquel for days. "Why on earth do you think I'm ringing you up?"

"Excuse me?" Raquel said with some trepidation. "Nick knows you're calling me?"

"Nicholas asked me to call!" she said with a laugh. "I know I shouldn't interfere in the business of two young people in love, but, you've probably guessed, I have a soft spot for my son."

"But why wouldn't he just—"

"Call you himself?" Mrs. Fitzsimmons said, amused. "Raquel, love, Nick is a wonderful young man, but even the best of them can become little boys sometimes. Trust me, I'm married to his father. You two just have one of these soul connections, but that can be overwhelming and I think he just needed a breather and then was too embarrassed by his behavior—"

"So he asked you to apologize for him?"

"No, not apologize. That wouldn't be my place to do, now would it?" Mrs. Fitzsimmons said, as if that were a line of etiquette she would not breach. "He'll need to grovel or send flowers or whatever you kids do now. But, he just thought I could help you two . . . reengage."

"I see," Raquel said, though she wasn't sure that she did.

"He figured you couldn't refuse me, dear," she said, "and I hope that you won't."

There was silence for a second as Raquel wasn't sure what to say. She wasn't wrong. Raquel didn't know how to say no to someone's mother making such an earnest call.

"Terrific," Mrs. Fitzsimmons said. "We'll see you this evening then. Have a lovely day at work, darling."

And with that, Mrs. Fitzsimmons hung up.

For days, she had tormented herself: alternating between frantically checking her messages and emails for a sign of Nick and replaying every moment of their last interaction to try to parse what had happened. What exactly had she done that was so egregious that he would not only lie to her, he'd disappear on her like that. Without a call, an email, a note, or anything. And it was all just resolved, seemingly, with a phone call from his mother.

Ever since they walked out of his studio Saturday morning, she'd had a gnawing feeling that something was off. A feeling confirmed on Sunday evening when, after her mother and Toni left, after the station, en route to get pizza from Fellini's, they drove past Nick's house on Wickenden, and Raquel saw his car parked outside. His car that was supposed to be in the Hamptons. Raquel could barely contain herself while Marcus waited for his pizza (she immediately lost what little appetite she had), and found a pay phone. When she called his number and he answered, she hung up. Sick to her stomach and desperate to get back to the apartment to check the answering machine for the inevitable (she hoped) message explaining why he was back so soon and asking when they could see each other. Only, when Raquel got home, the message wasn't there. (And, what is worse, she never *really* thought that it would be. There was a knowing that sank into the depths of herself, the second she spotted the car, that something was off. Before she saw the car even.) She was inconsolable, despite Marcus and Betsaida assuring her that he would call the next day. Which only made her more hysterical because she knew that he wouldn't.

And he didn't. Or the day after, or the day after that. Raquel could see Betsaida, wondering if he'd called; could sense that she knew he hadn't. Could read his absence on Raquel's face; in her eyes, darkened under the sockets from tossing and turning and red from tears. Raquel's humiliation would not allow her to confide her torment to Bets. Nor could she bring herself to call her mother or Toni, already predisposed to disliking him. When he came around (He would come around! Of course he would come around. They were in love!), she didn't want to work twice as hard to get them to like him. Astrid had made it clear that she wanted nothing to do with this subject. Their conversations at work-time lunches were restricted carefully to museum gossip and art history talk.

As a means of avoidance and distraction, she had thrown herself into her thesis research. With her music blasting to silence her mind, she'd spent every moment of these days deep in the stacks of the Rock and the RISD library. From the second she got out of work until the moment security threw her out. She had, she realized, uncovered something potentially fascinating.

After showing nonstop for two decades, Jack Martin seemingly stopped working in the mid-'80s. Four full years without a major exhibition and the only thing in between was a one-off at Tilly Barber Fine Art—and her smallest gallery at that. She'd been curious if and how this absence from producing—or at least producing for public consumption—might have evolved his work. When she finally got her hands on the massive catalog from his 1989 show in Spain—the exhibition consisted of a dozen or so massive works—she'd flipped through the pages, secretly hoping to find some innovation; some radical change in his style or materials. Instead, she discovered more of the same, same, same that had come before: Rows. Lines. Columns. Grids. Lumber. Brick. Gold brick. Ingots. Fishing weights. Sheets of metal. Iron beams. *And then.* About forty pages in, she saw something wild: a circle. Steel beams set in a radial dial like the sun. The centerfold featured a sprawling sea of ingots, set seemingly at random on the floor of a large open gallery, but in the center of the room was a clearing, in a shape that was amoeba-like—almost figurative. And while many of the pieces were, yes, exactly the same as what he was doing before, there were at least three that were radically different. Rounder. Softer. Outside of an advertisement in an old *Artforum*, she couldn't find a record of the '87 Tilly Barber show anywhere. Then she remembered the materials John Temple had given her and she found it: the sales sheet with thumbnails from the small gallery show. And there they were again, albeit on a smaller scale: circular patterns, almost vagina-like shapes. And that was it. Just those two shows and then it just stopped. Back to the beginning he went. (Well, not the beginning. There weren't any poems framed as artwork. Oh, how ridiculously pretentious Raquel found them. The more Belinda Kim exposed her to conceptual art happening outside this canon, the more indulgent she found it.)

What had caused the change? Was it something that was happening in the world? Environmentalism? Feminism? The text held so little for her, but she kept digging and digging. In *Artforums*, on microfiche. In catalogs of exhibitions his contemporaries and rivals were in at the time. PhD thesis citations. She searched high and low. And there was nothing. It was intriguing, but where was the scholarship to support it? And without the scholarship, what was a year of her life dedicated to Jack Martin? Another dead end. She contemplated abandoning the thesis altogether, but she couldn't quit. She just had to find some thread of connection. A stellar thesis on Martin would cement her, surely, as John Temple's star protégée. A role that, no matter how tedious, was worth the dividends it could pay for her by way of recommendations and introductions after graduation.

After Mrs. Fitzsimmons's call, Raquel's mind was once again racing; her stomach a nexus of nerves, sick with anticipation or dread, or was it excitement at the prospect of seeing Nick again? Relieved things weren't over between them but also unsettled. Hurt at his lack of care for her heart. A week of torment and just like that, it's over? No. Even Mrs. Fitzsimmons said she was owed an apology. But Raquel didn't just want a sorry, she realized. She wanted an explanation. His mother had said he got overwhelmed or anxious? But by what? Was it her family? Was it the way they reacted to his art? Was it that he wasn't the focus of her attention for once? Did he need endless devotion?

With her work done for the day and nothing to do but wait for Astrid to finish proofing exhibition labels—Astrid, who had no desire to come to the University Club, but Raquel made her promise—Raquel had been sitting in silence, driving herself insane. She decided to focus on the other artist in her life who tormented her: Jack Martin. She pulled from her bag a large early 1970s catalog from his land art era—a brief but prolific period when he was creating grand-scale out-of-doors projects; mostly public commissions. But even against the rolling hills of nature, Martin never wavered. Straight lines begat more straight lines. Nothing like what she had seen in Spain. She had just let out an exasperated sigh when Belinda Kim stepped out of her office.

"TGIF, Raquel!" Belinda said with a laugh. "Whatever's got you sighing like this will still be frustrating you on Monday."

"Ugh, I know, that's the problem," Raquel said as she closed her book. "I'd hoped to get a head start on my thesis and I'm just a little stuck."

Belinda looked at the catalog before tossing Raquel a skeptical glance.

"Minimalism?"

"Jack Martin, actually," Raquel said, wishing in that moment that she was working on something that Belinda might be more interested in.

"Your thesis is on Jack Martin?" Belinda said, disdain in her voice.

"I could see how his stuff isn't your thing, but Professor—"

"Who cares about his fucking work?" Belinda said. Raquel realized she'd never heard her curse before. Her New York–ness came out thick with the word. "He's a fucking murderer—"

"Wait? What?" Raquel said, her face almost smirking because this sounded so preposterous.

Belinda looked at her, stunned.

"Do not tell me they are teaching him at Brown University of all places without *at least* telling you what he did to her."

"To who?" Raquel said.

Belinda Kim stood there as if Raquel had punched her. Her posture changed; her purse slackened on her arm.

"Oh my God," she said, more to herself than to Raquel. "Jack Martin was married to an artist—an incredibly talented artist—Anita de Monte, and he killed her—"

"What?" Raquel said. They had literally had one entire week of lectures on the minimalists, an entire section devoted to nothing but Jack Martin—starting with his humble Massachusetts roots and his early days as a merchant marine—and there was not one mention of murder. Or even accusations of murder. She'd read dozens of museum catalogs and interviews and profiles of him in academic texts and archived art magazines. Nothing. "But I've been—"

"There was a big trial, they tried to make her sound like a lunatic, like she was into voodoo or something, barred her sister and her family from testifying, and a judge let him off—"

"I've been researching all summer and never knew he'd married again—"

"Because they wiped her away! Oh, just like Leslie had said that they would." She touched her head in frustration. "I was just a grad student when it happened and we were just so outraged. Outraged! A woman—an artist—killed and you would think civilized society would shun this man! Ostracize him. But no! They rallied around him. Protected him. Gave him giant shows around the world. He got even bigger! And Leslie Golub, her dealer, she wrote an op-ed about how he was using his power to erase Anita and people said she was insane. Except that, here you are: a young Latina at an Ivy League school utterly unaware that the man you're devoting your senior year to took the life of a woman not much different than you."

Belinda had tears in her eyes now and Raquel felt unsure of what to do.

"I protested outside the courthouse! Put up signs in the streets! It felt like a statement about all of us—all of us on the outside trying to make them see us. And the worst part is, now I'm on the inside, and I don't even know the last time I thought of Anita de Monte."

"Belinda," Raquel said, feeling responsible for getting her so upset. "I'm so sorry, I didn't mean to—"

"No, Raquel. I'm sorry. That all these years later, so little has changed." Belinda looked at her watch. "I have to go. If you have time this weekend, you should look her up."

* * *

RAQUEL PULLED A compact from her bag, dabbed the oil from her skin, refreshed her lipstick, and smoothed the frizz around her temples. She and Astrid were standing outside the University Club, and she felt her heart beating loudly in her chest.

"Why are you being so weird?" Astrid said as she pulled her toward the heavy wooden doors of the old private club.

"Seriously?" Raquel asked, stopping in her tracks. "You haven't noticed that I haven't been around the house all week?"

"Unlike my mother, I don't want anything to do with this mess."

"It's not a mess," Raquel said, defensively. "Your brother's just been in a mood lately."

"No, my brother is just being himself and he's finally letting you see it," Astrid said, as she led them through the lobby.

Raquel had passed the stately University Club many times, but nothing prepared her for how stunning it was on the inside: walls of carved mahogany, the air thick with the scent of lilies from the oversized flower arrangements adorning tables and alcoves. Everyone dressed to the WASPy nines, just for an afternoon cocktail.

"Oh darling, you came!" Mrs. Fitzsimmons called out when she saw the girls. Her red hair was perfectly coiffed and she was wearing another St. John's dress. She already had two empty martini glasses in front of her, while Mr. Fitzsimmons was nursing what seemed to be an Arnold Palmer. Nick, Raquel noted with some anxiety, was nowhere to be seen.

"She's absolutely talking to you," Astrid muttered under her breath and, though she had heard how Mrs. Fitzsimmons spoke *of* Astrid, was still shocked when she rose up and embraced Raquel before offering her daughter (her own daughter!) an air kiss.

"Don't you look so chic!" she said, as she turned to her husband and said, "Clarke, doesn't Raquel look so chic?"

"Very elegant, Raquel," Mr. Fitzsimmons muttered.

"And so slim!" she said to Raquel. "What have you been doing? You look fantastic."

"I've been running a bit."

"Fabulous! Clarke, get the girls cocktails. Order something for Nick too. What does Nick like, dear?"

"Scotch on the rocks," Raquel said. It was his new thing, something about being "done with school" now.

"I'll have a lemonade, Dad," Astrid called out to her father.

"Skipping a chance for inebriation?" Nick said as he approached their table. "That doesn't seem like you."

He gave Raquel a kiss on the cheek, and while she knew she was the one who should be aggrieved, angry even, she felt the knot in her stomach ease.

"I have a urinary tract infection," Astrid said, matter-of-factly. "I'm on meds."

"Really Astrid," Mrs. Fitzsimmons said. "Is that polite conversation?"

"Is it? I don't know."

"Why does she have to be like this?" Mrs. Fitzsimmons asked Raquel and Nick, as if Astrid wasn't there. Raquel wanted to change the subject.

"Well, I don't know if this is polite conversation, exactly, but you won't believe what I learned at work today."

"Nick," Mrs. Fitzsimmons said, "doesn't Raquel look just sensational? And she's slimmed down so much."

Now she was talking as if Raquel wasn't there.

"She looks marvelous," Nick said, putting his arm around her.

The waitress returned with the cocktails just then, and Mrs. Fitzsimmons proceeded to slurp her next martini. Her diet, it seemed to Raquel, might not involve much food, but she did not limit her alcohol consumption.

"Be careful, dear, we still have a long night," her husband cautioned, "though I'd be right there with your mother if I didn't have to drive. Roger Brown's son's marrying some religious zealot who doesn't believe in dancing. It was a giant fight just to have an open bar, apparently."

"Thank God Roger won," Mrs. Fitzsimmons said and raised her glass.

"What did you learn at work today?" Astrid asked Raquel. She was happy to be reminded. Eager to share this bit of uncommon knowledge she thought the Fitzsimmonses, especially, would find both interesting and cosmopolitan. Very *Vanity Fair*.

"Well," she said, giving her dishiest voice, "I'm writing my thesis about Jack Martin—"

"Genius! An American genius," Mrs. Fitzsimmons declared, clearly a bit drunk, and Raquel tried to recall if she'd drunk this much when she'd met her last.

"We're fortunate enough to have a piece of his," Mr. Fitzsimmons added. Raquel was about to comment on this but Mrs. Fitzsimmons continued.

"We did a big retrospective for him at MoMA a few years ago—a quirky character—"

"Dear," Mr. Fitzsimmons interrupted, "Raquel was telling a story."

"Oh, yes."

"Anyway, today my boss told me that he killed his wife!"

"What?" Astrid said.

"That's insane," Nick said.

"Stood trial for murder and everything."

"Allegedly," Mrs. Fitzsimmons said, her mouth in a thin, flat line.

"Allegedly, what?" Astrid said.

"Allegedly murdered his wife," Mrs. Fitzsimmons said. "No one really knows what happened. Some say it was suicide."

"You knew about this?" Nick said, surprise in his voice.

"Like your mother said, we knew him a bit. Besides, it was hardly a secret," Mr. Fitzsimmons said. "It was all over the tabloids."

"It was?" Raquel said.

"This is crazy," Astrid said. "They never mention this in class and we talk about Martin all the time."

"That was Belinda's point," Raquel said.

"Well, the man was acquitted, so why does it matter?" Mrs. Fitzsimmons remarked, irritation in her voice.

"It matters," Astrid said to her mother very pointedly, "because she was a human being and we've been studying someone who might be a domestic abuser!"

"Oh really, Astrid," Mrs. Fitzsimmons said. "You sound like the women who tried to bring him down. The time that they gave this man!"

"She was an artist too," Raquel said, more to Astrid and Nick than anyone.

"She was hardly anyone of consequence," Mrs. Fitzsimmons said, rather firmly. "It's not like he threw Frida Kahlo out a window."

"Jesus, Mom," Nick said, "does it matter if she was good or not?"

"Wait? What? He threw his wife out of a fucking window?" Astrid asked Raquel.

"I didn't ask how it happened," Raquel said.

"I knew her," Mrs. Fitzsimmons said, testily. "She was a horrid woman. Loud, pushy Cuban thing and not a lot of talent. People only took her seriously because of Jack and I never knew what he saw in her. Raquel, you have to understand, it was a different time—but Jack invited her into spaces Latin people would never be welcomed into. And she always had to make a spectacle of herself. I don't like to say that people deserve things that happen to them, but not many people were sorry to see her go."

There was a moment of shocked silence. Raquel sipped her drink though she actually felt quite sick.

"I think," Mr. Fitzsimmons said, "what Linda is trying to say is that she's had one cocktail too many. Nick, how is the commission coming?"

And, with tremendous animation, Nick launched into his struggle and turmoil with *The Great Gondoliers*, as he had subsequently titled the show, and talk of the opening weekend and Mrs. Fitzsimmons's quest to try to help find him a good loft in Soho for September. Raquel was happy to fade into the background. To live in the space Astrid had grown to inhabit. Wondered quietly to herself if Mrs. Fitzsimmons found her sufficiently grateful for the chance to spend time with them. To be in *this* room.

When it was time for Mr. and Mrs. Fitzsimmons to leave, Linda once again complimented Raquel on being so "slim and chic" as she kissed her goodbye.

"Don't let this curator make you too radical, Raquel," she said. "A couple of letters of recommendation and an intro from me, and you could have a job at MoMA like that—"

And she made a sloppy attempt at a drunken snap.

"Oh, you're too kind," Raquel said.

"Nicholas, walk us to the car," she commanded her son, and waved goodbye to her daughter.

"She'll do it too," Astrid said when they were out of sight.

"What?" Raquel said.

"She'll do anything to make him happy. Get you a job, buy you clothes, whatever he wants—"

"Wait, she knows he's bought me clothes?"

"Of course. Unlike me, he actually talks to our mother. Besides, how do you think he pays for everything?"

"Why would he ask for money for that?"

"Why I think or what he said?"

Raquel thought about this for a second.

"I want to know what he said."

"That you're beautiful and deserve beautiful things."

* * *

WITH THE BUFFER of the Fitzsimmons family having been removed, Nick and Raquel now stood on the sidewalk outside the University Club, awkwardly facing each other. The air thick with humidity and the tension between them.

"Hi," Nick said, extending a wave. The gesture so timid and ridiculous after all they'd shared between them that Raquel involuntarily smiled.

"That's more like it," Nick said, pleased with himself. He walked toward her, put his arms around her waist.

"Why'd you have your mom call me?" she said, pulling away a bit. She felt uneasy. (Who just disappears like that?)

"She wanted to see you," he said, as though it was a perfectly normal thing.

"Why didn't you just invite me?" Raquel asked, watching as Nick started and stopped himself from answering a couple of times. Felt her frustration build with his inability to own his behavior. "OK, better question. Where the fuck have you been?"

"Well, I told you—"

She pushed herself away from him completely now. Anger flushing her hot in a rush.

"I saw your car out on Wickenden on Sunday. I called; you answered—"

"You prank—"

"Please," she said, her hand going up in protest. "You never went to the Hamptons."

He retreated. Shrugged his shoulders. Looked down on the ground.

"I realized by the time I got something to eat, got there, and then left, that it was dumb."

"So you were here since Saturday and didn't try to see me."

"You were busy, you said as much—"

"With my family. Who you barely acknowledged—"

"That's not fair, Raquel. I was there by eight a.m., I smiled at everyone, I—"

"You want a gold star for that?" she erupted. "At least I engage with your mother."

"Because she can give you something to engage with!" Nick yelled.

Raquel's eyes went wide with indignation. She turned on her heel and walked away from him as fast as she could up the hill. The evening sun baked down on her, the humidity making her feel she was carving her way through the air. Her urgency to escape him felt desperate, but her body—weak from lack of sleep and food; weak from anxiety caused by him—unable to keep up with the demand. She slowed, not so much because of Nick's cries of "Raquel!" but her own inability to outpace them, eventually steadying herself under the shade of a tree. Taking a seat on the front step of one of the old department buildings.

She was nauseous with heat and heartache and some strange sense of opprobrium. Was it the way Nick spoke about her family or that he put to words the way she herself saw them? Even the mild recognition of that made her sick to her stomach, wishing she could chase the feeling away. Instead, it quickened. Found other similar floating emotions and recollections in her mind—a magnet gathering tiny scattered metal shards into one heavy mound. She remembered how quickly she wanted her mother and Toni to leave when they came to her first Parents' Weekend, or how she never told them about any of the other campus events happening after that. The way she would cringe at the Met when her mother would tell curators that her daughter went to

Brown, the loud and boastful way she said it. How Raquel could see on their faces that they didn't believe her, or if they did, dismissed Raquel as an affirmative action admit, something she herself was never confident wasn't at least a bit true. She didn't think this would be how Nick saw her family, because she felt Nick understood her. She had been grateful to Nick for that and now, it turns out, he was her worst fear personified—a mirror to her own view.

He sat down next to her, put his arm around her shoulders to comfort her, and it was only then that she realized she was crying.

"I shouldn't have said that in that way," he said.

If he was waiting for her to say it was fine, she didn't.

"It's never mattered to me that you didn't grow up the way I did," he said.

"And now it does?" she said.

"No, no, I didn't say that," he said, "it's just that it didn't mean anything. Like you are here, I am here. We ended up in the same place. You are pretty and smart and if I would have told my parents that you'd gone to Brearley, they would have believed me—"

"What did you tell them?"

"Can I finish my point?" he snapped. "It's just when I met your mom and sister—I don't know, they are totally great, I'm sure. It was just sort of . . . well, I guess it was the first time that I realized we are both from New York, but not the same New York."

Wow, she thought to herself, *he really had no idea*. Every day she stared at that different experience—his experience—like it was a Christmas display in a department store. It never occurred to her that people like Nick never thought of her experience at all.

"We're from different New Yorks, different campuses. Everything about us is different," she said flatly. "Sorry to burst your bubble."

"No, but that's the thing," he said. "That's what I thought too. I got kind of freaked out, you know. Because I told my mom the other day—and it's the reason why I asked her to call you, because I didn't know how to make it right, or how to start again, but I knew I had to—because no one has supported me the way that you have.

Nobody's believed in me the way that you have. And you're not a phony. You're the real deal, so I know you mean it."

She cringed a bit at this; she did support him, but because she loved him.

"I don't think," he continued, "back in the city or wherever, I could find anyone else like you for the long haul, you know. I just got scared, like, 'Oh my God, we're so different. How could this ever really work?'"

She felt confused, the perception of her specialness muddled with his condescension, leaving her unsure which to latch on to.

"And then?" she asked. She stared at him, blinking away her tears.

"I realized something. You—the person that I know, that I see every day, that I love—you chose to be here. You're like, amazing. No one helped you and you ended up here. You chose this life as your future—"

"That doesn't mean I don't love my family!" she said, defensive.

"Of course not," he said, "but you wanted something better than that."

"I wanted something different."

"You could have gone to a state school like what's-her-face."

She hated and loved that he brought that up. Hated that he somehow twisted that story to buttress a point, but loved that he listened to her so carefully. That he paid such attention to her. That what he was telling her was true. She did want better.

"I wouldn't be here if it wasn't for my mother," she said plainly because it was true. "And I don't like you trying to make me feel embarrassed of her."

"I never want that," he said. "I'm just trying to tell you why I disappeared, but also why I had to come back."

"And so what did you conclude?" she said.

"It doesn't matter where you came from. It matters that we both want to go to the same places. With you next to me, I know I'll be unstoppable. And with me? Well, maybe everything doesn't need to be so hard."

She felt herself exhale at this. Found herself believing in their possibilities. And as Nick leaned toward her, Raquel forgot about his mother and her mother and Jack Martin and letters of recommendation and just surrendered to his kiss. Inhaled him, just as she had the very first time. Ignored, the best she could, the salty brine of her own tears.

Jack

NEW YORK CITY • WINTER 1987

"Am I your fucking counsel, or am I your fucking counsel?" Ron Rosen screamed, pacing behind his desk, wielding a *New York Post* around like a fire-and-brimstone preacher's Bible.

"About the murder trial, yes," Jack said, smug.

"For fuck's sake," Gerry said, and even Tilly, Jack noticed, sighed with more than a little exasperation.

ADDING INSULT
TO
(FATAL) INJURY

The headline read; left aligned next to a photo of Anita in front of one of her tree trunk sculptures from Rome ("You didn't invent trees, Jack") and Jack's own mug shot. Beneath that the subheading was: *Jealous hubby on trial for wife's murder tries to put kibosh on museum celebrating rising star's work.*

Jack Martin, jealous hubby.

When Ron saw it on the newsstand, he fumed: calling not just Jack, but Tilly—who had technically hired him—and Gerry—who had brought Jack to him in the first place—to his office for an emergency meeting. Jack, who had no intention of letting Ron Rosen dress him down for taking charge of his life, had planned on being a no-show.

"*Jack*," Tilly implored, "*Ron is not messing around. He can fire you, you know*." That, Jack knew, would be bad. The trial started in just a matter of weeks and Ron was a good lawyer. A smart lawyer. In another circumstance, Ron might have become a friend or drinking companion, even. But Jack did not like being yelled at. Even if he had possibly misstepped.

"I don't even know where to begin with the levels of fuckery happening here," Ron said. The veins in his thick neck throbbed with his vexation. "You're just a few weeks from a trial where your sister-in-law is gonna be sitting and crying in the front row every day and you decide *now* is when you want to fight her for control of your wife's estate?"

"She's birdbrained, a plebeian. She doesn't know the first thing about art or the art world or how to care for—"

"And you hired a lawyer other than me, without consulting me, to handle this for you, completely ignoring how this might impact your trial. Your murder trial—"

"She went out the window," Jack said. "I didn't murder anybody."

Ron looked to Gerry. "I've had three paralegals quit on me because of this jackass. I see he's fraying at the edges, I go to judges, let him use my country house—"

"You had a bat—"

"I've never had bats in that fucking house, Jack. Never."

Tilly cleared her throat, shifted upright in her chair.

"Ron, we need to know that you aren't going to walk away from us," Tilly said. "Not now. Jack is going to fall in line. Isn't that right, Jack?"

"I'll cooperate," Jack said, but he couldn't help himself and added, "But really, this woman doesn't know her ass from her elbow when it comes to Anita's—"

"Jesus, Jack," Gerry exclaimed, "I am not a lawyer here, but I know media and I know common sense. The woman managed to get her sister a traveling exhibition, she doesn't seem like a birdbrain to me. Your story doesn't hold water. Not on Page Six."

"It looks petty. And their entire prosecution hangs on this idea that you were jealous of her success," Ron interjected.

"What success?" he said. "A couple of prizes and a show here and there?"

"Well, that's what I wanted to argue in court, Jack, but you went and sent that cease and desist! What innocent bereaved widower wouldn't want to see his wife's legacy honored?"

This momentarily muzzled Jack. This logical assessment of what a loving bereaved husband might do. None of them understood what Jack did: it was hard to be loving and bereaved when you hated the bitch's guts. Oh, he hadn't hated her that night—the night *it* happened—but he had grown to detest her and the way she tormented him. Day and night. He was desperate when he sent the cease and desist. Desperate to make her go away. To put her and her work in a closet forever and never let her see the light of day again.

From the second he heard whispers of a retrospective, it distressed him. Yes, he supposed there was a world where Ron Rosen lived where he should be happy for her art to be celebrated. But for Jack, seeing her art had become a living reminder of this cloud hovering over his head. Her imagined "legacy" tainting his legitimate one. Every time Anita came up—the topic of her, the subject matter of her art with the blood and the bodies and all of it—it was a flashing green light to talk about him, Jack Martin. Not as the leader of one of the most important art movements since the Second World War, but as the (suspected) murderer. And he hated that. He found himself obsessed with this show: the possibility of it, the status of it. At every dinner he would casually fish for information. Pump his close friends for any gossip or updates. And he didn't know if it was his preoccupation with it, or . . . something else, but the moment he found out it was happening: not just happening, but would travel! Would have a catalog! Would be a MAJOR ART WORLD HAPPENING (really? body art?), well, he felt as if Anita—the ghost, the bitch spirit who had been fucking with him ceaselessly since *it* happened—seemed to get stronger.

He swore she was screwing with his sketchbooks, crossing out certain ideas he'd written out, circling others. He tried to write a poem at one point and he saw, in a different hand than his, just the word: *Ha!* next to it. Then, one day he recognized what he knew to be her handwriting in there on a brand-new, clean page, up at the top. Just his name. Like she was going to write him a note. *Jack* . . . Like she was going to write him a note and decided not to bother. (Why had she decided not to bother?) When he heard that they'd managed to get her catalog published by Rizzoli, she began coming to him. Every night. Only not in his dreams. He would waken to the noise of slurping and chomping from the kitchen and wander out and see her—always bloodied and broken—munching away on a fruit, the whole place sickly sweet with the smell of guavas. He was sure it had been a dream until one day he noticed a guava on the counter. He wouldn't even know where to buy a fucking guava and when he confronted Ingrid about it (albeit a bit antagonistically), she insisted she didn't even know what she was looking at. Still, he hadn't even thought about Anita's estate in ages.

Until, one day, while flipping through the new *Artforum*, he saw an advertisement for her exhibition. It was still months away and yet, here they were, already promoting it. He phoned Ron and Tilly cursing about how the dates of her show overlapped with his trial. Railing how they needed to do something, to stop it! Everyone said to just ignore it. But how could he ignore it? Certainly not, when, just two days later, her portfolio—the one he had hidden the night *it* happened, the one he told the police and her sister that he'd never seen—was lying out and open on his kitchen table. Not behind the washing machine where it had been tucked away since that night more than a year ago. But out on the kitchen table! How was that fucking possible?

He didn't understand the supernatural. Not in the least. But he understood his fucking wife and she was a self-involved narcissist. An attention whore. She fed off of this kind of thing and he became certain—oh, how everyone would tell him that he was insane if he confessed to his thoughts—that it was the attention that was making her stronger. And so he decided to pull the plug on the show. To pull the plug on her. He found some hack lawyer he knew who would do him a favor and send the sister the cease and desist. And he thought it would work. Felt relief. Happiness.

Then there was the bat. And the bat bites and the rabies shots and the scars on his hands (his genius hands) that he was sure would never go away, despite how much vitamin E he rubbed on them at night. The fucking bat. The bat that perched outside of his bedroom window every night since she bit him. The window where *it* happened. The bat that made Ingrid—sweet, loyal Ingrid—stop being sweet or loyal. She refused to set foot in his apartment again once she saw the thing—black and shiny—hanging upside down in the window. Saying something in Swedish that he didn't understand, but got the distinct impression was not good, as she hastily threw her things in a bag and left. Ceased even picking up his calls. The bat.

He knew it was no bat. In the middle of the night he would wake and see it there. See those fucking eyes and that goddamned smirk and he knew it was her.

But who would believe that?

All they knew was the aftermath of the bat. The *Post* headline and the *Daily News* story and the mucking up of optics and defense strategies and the possibility of jail. (Not jail! No.) Without understanding the bat and all that had come before it, you couldn't possibly understand why he didn't care—sitting there in Ron's office—about seeming remorseful. He just wanted her gone.

"Well, what can we do to fix it?" Jack said. This was, he knew, the closest he would get to apologizing.

"From a PR perspective?" Gerry asked. "I think you issue a statement giving the Museum of Contemporary Art of the Americas show your blessing. That you never intended to block this important celebration of Anita's legacy, and just wanted to secure the manner in which her work is treated going forward."

He looked Gerry in the eye with more than a little disgust.

"How can I get a fair shake if the trial is going on and a few blocks away a jury sees her presented as some kind of martyr?"

Ron had been staring out his large office windows contemplatively, but he turned to them now, taking a seat at his oversized desk.

"It might be worthwhile to seek a postponement. Or, perhaps there's another option to consider."

"Which is?" Tilly asked.

"I've been thinking—even before this, to be honest—that maybe a trial by a jury of your peers isn't the best thing for you, Jack."

Jack looked at him quizzically. "The alternative being?"

"Well, there are women on a jury. Women with husbands and boyfriends and ex-husbands and ex-boyfriends. Feminists. Sympathizers. I've seen the way the younger women in this office have reacted to this case, to be frank. And so have you. The other option is a trial by judge. We can take that option."

"And you think that will help to get him off?" Tilly said.

"Without looking even worse?" Gerry asked.

"Optics? Who knows. Innocence? I feel a little more confident about that. Eight out of ten judges in the district are men. Successful men. Men with wives. Men who have problems with their wives. You're not the easiest pill to swallow, Jack, but you might have a better chance with one man than a handful of ladies."

"Well, if he's found innocent, it all goes away. Who cares how it looks now," Tilly said. "I think you should do it, Jack."

But what Jack knew that Tilly didn't was that even if he was found innocent, the whole thing would not go away.

* * *

JACK FELT DEEPLY unsettled after the meeting. Not about the trial decision but about issuing the statement. About the exhibition. About the catalog. If he was living with her now—not just the idea of her, but the physical fucking manifestation of her—and the show hadn't even opened yet, what would she be capable of once it did?

And then there was the other part, the tiny nagging voice that was not just afraid for his own sanity but of something worse than all of that. Frightened that the true curse of Anita's death, the real witchcraft of it all, was that her most evil (truly fucking evil) desire for him might come to pass: irrelevance. That in all this time while he'd been unable to make anything or show anything, while he had nothing on the horizon of his own at all, it was Anita, enshrined by this scandal, who would be skyrocketing into relevance. All while he faded from people's minds, hiding as if he had something to be ashamed of. Hiding as if *it* hadn't been an accident. This fear horrified him more than anything the bat could do. (Mostly.)

He had to be cooperative. But, also, as an artist, he needed to be happy. Productive. People would understand that. Tilly would understand that.

He called her and asked her to meet him at La Goulue that evening for dinner. He'd taken to socializing uptown since *it* happened. Finding himself less the center of gossip, the pace of the place more befitting his new (slower) speed.

He arrived and discovered that Tilly was early and had ordered his favorite champagne for them.

"I was glad you called, Jack," she said. "I was worried about you after this morning."

"Rosen is OK," Jack said. "He's just doing his job."

"He's very good. You just have to cooperate and soon enough this will be behind you."

"That's part of what I'm worried about," he said, "that by the time this is behind me, I'll be behind me."

"We've talked about this. I don't want you to show and not sell. I'm just not sure what the market will be with this hanging over you. A soft show—"

"I don't give a fuck about the market. I want to work," he barked.

Tilly took a sip of her champagne, put some butter on a piece of bread. Her silence was not dismissive but contemplative. He felt his own temperature go down in the presence of her serenity.

"We can stage something small, at the original space on Greene Street," she said. "I can look tonight to see when I have an opening."

"No," Jack said, very firmly. "I want to show when Anita is showing."

"Is that what this is about, Jack? Some kind of a pissing contest?" she asked, and Jack was startled by her use of such a vulgar expression.

"No," he said. "Not at all. But after all the work I've put in over all these years—all this work *you've* done—we're supposed to sit by and let some dimwit DA stand there and paint a picture that *she* had a career that *I* would envy?"

He could see that something in this struck a chord in Tilly.

"All I'm saying is, Tilly," he continued, "let me have the space and let the public decide for themselves who's the genius."

The waiter came then and Jack didn't even need the menu—escargots, moules a go-go, and steak tartare. All of Tilly's favorites.

"I can see the value in that, Jack," Tilly said. "It will be a lot of work to pull it all together so quickly. But if you can be ready, I can be ready."

"I can be ready."

She smiled at him gently. Oh, how she reminded him of his sweet mother.

"Are you happy?" she asked, lighting a cigarette.

"Mainly, yes."

"What else is bothering you?"

"Well, it's sort of a big ask."

"If I can do it, I will."

"The trial will be over by the time Anita's show opens in Philly. If I'm found guilty—"

"Please, Jack, don't even say it."

"If I'm found guilty, my show with you will be the last one I'm likely to do."

He saw that hit her like a smack. Her face contorted in displeasure at the very idea.

"But," he said, "if I'm found innocent—especially if it's a trial by judge—all anyone will be talking about is not my new work, or the shows you'll be able to book for me overseas again, or anything. All they will be talking about is her and that *it* happened. It will follow me for the next year. Maybe longer."

"I don't think it has to be like that."

The tartare was set out in front of them and he scooped a giant gob of the raw red meat onto the toasted French bread. Put it in his mouth in one bite.

"Oh, come on, Tilly," he said as he chewed.

She was staring at him; he knew she hated his table manners but would never say so.

"What would you like for me to do about it?" she asked, some annoyance in her voice. "These are major museums. Call them and ask them to upend their entire calendar?"

"They are not major museums!" he hissed. "They are regional shitholes that can't get A-list talent. That's why they took this show in the first place."

"Jack . . ." Tilly said.

"What? You represent the kinds of artists these places wished they had—on loan, in their collections, for their big exhibitions. You're a person of great influence, Tilly."

"For supporting artists, not for institutional intimidation."

"This *is* supporting an artist," he said, as he put his hand over hers, "the one whose entire career you've helped to build. Are we going to let one very unfortunate accident undo our legacy?"

Anita

TILLY'S APARTMENT • WINTER 1987

Oh, and she did it!! Puta madre! Did his bidding! A handmaid of the devil. A woman bewitched. She knew it was wrong and still! Still! She made call after call to curators and journalists! First, suggesting gently that perhaps this was a bad time for the show for "the art world," in general. "*Of course, no one wants Anita to be recognized for her work more than I do—but is this the best timing? A little bit of distance would allow the art world to heal.*" Oh, and I know she said these things, because I was there! I was sitting right there on her desk in her office, propped up on the countertop of that fucking claustrophobic galley kitchen, sitting on her piano bench. Listening to it all! And I got there not because Jack called me but because of her! Her and her seemingly troubled thoughts. I was minding my own business, lying out at Varadero in the sun, when I heard the ceiba call. It said her name loud and clear—Tilly—and it came with a wave of upset and sadness and shame and loyalty—oh, the weight of the loyalty—and I climbed and climbed and I was in her loft as I heard her make call after call and pour drink after drink as she did so.

The museum in Chicago folded right away. Oh, the cowards! The fucking fools!!! I raged. I had no intention of presenting myself to Tilly. Had hoped to simply listen. Observe her in this act of moral disgrace. But as soon as I heard the pause, the silence on the other end of the phone when she said, "*Don't you think it might be good to make some space for the art world to heal?*" Oh! She didn't even need to say Jack's name! Didn't need to twist an arm or be a heavy or anything at all. There was just some silence, in which she sipped her drink—and, a funny habit she somehow never did in public, scraped the polish off her nails with her teeth. Waited. Leaned over the counter of the galley kitchen and peered out to the rest of her loft, as if looking for something. And then I heard the coward on the other line! Oh, the fucking institutionalist!!! The pig! "Well . . . Our next show was from our collection, so we can just slide some things around." And Tilly let out a sigh, not of relief but one that I could feel—I could smell—was of repugnance. Of self-disgrace. Because she knew what she was doing was wrong! She knew it! But she stood up straight again, swallowed, and said, "Well, it's so wonderful of you to be so considerate." And then she said goodbye, like the polite WASP that she is. She hung up the receiver and I took the tumbler from the counter where her scotch had been and I flung it against the front door! I threw it with such force it shattered! The lead crystal that had probably been in her family for generations—destroyed! Destroyed! Like she was trying to destroy my work being in the world! And that bitch didn't miss a beat.

"Anita?" she said.

How did she know it was me? How did she know it was fucking me?! Her knowing made me angry! She, of all people, shouldn't understand. She, who set out to erase me? And I wailed! I don't know why. You cannot understand the stab to my soul this was, this woman who could have helped me time and again, being my undoing even in death? And it stung! Stung worse because she knew it was wrong. She didn't want to do it. She knew that even if he hadn't thrown me out the window, even if she hated me, I didn't deserve to be erased. And her complicity made me all the more vexed!

She picked up the phone to call the curator from Philadelphia next and I hung up the receiver. I saw her—those watery blue eyes—go wide in surprise and then unwide in recognition, as she saw the lever depress and then come up again. Heard the line go from a *brrrring*,

brrrring brrring to a *behbehbehbehbeh*. She tried again and I hung up again. She tried again and I hung up again.

In my frustration I thought of my ceiba tree, found myself back in its thick green crown, descending until I was able to find a bough sturdy enough for me. I wrapped my ankles around a branch and allowed myself to hang—upside down, so that my hair hung, long, long, long like Rapunzel's braid, below me. I crossed my arms (soon to be wings!) over my chest and closed my eyes and breathed in and out. Out and in. I tried to wipe Tilly and Jack and my sister and my art out of my mind, for just a moment—just long enough to feel free. And when I did, when I was fearless, I allowed myself to drop. Felt the kiss of cool wind around me as I spread my arms, heard the flap of air catching them, and suddenly I was—

Swoop.

Flying through the open window of Tilly's loft, soaring over the same place that I'd danced in the night I died.

Swoop.

Circling Tilly on the phone in the living room now, dropping the receiver as she noticed I was in the room.

Swoop.

Down, toward this imperturbable bitch, who somehow managed to politely end her call. "I'll have to ring you back, Philip, but I hope you'll consider a postponement."

Oh, but I knew it wouldn't be a postponement! I knew it was going to be the end. I knew! I knew! I knew! And in that moment I realized it was not thoughts. It was not memories. It was not my mother's tears or my niece and nephews displaying my photograph that made me powerful. That made me vibrant.

It was my art!

It was my art out in the world.

Because when my art was in the world, so was I. My energy! My spirit!

Swoop.

I came in toward the bun on her head and began picking and picking and picking.

"Anita!" she said, sternly. "Anita. You are upset. But this isn't going to solve anything."

Swoop.

I went up toward the ceiling—the very high ceiling—and then I dove—fast, fast, fast—down toward her hands, protecting her hair. Sank my fangs into her bony fingers and thrilled in hearing her scream. Hovered over her to watch the blood come. Then dove! Dove in again—not at her plain face or her hands, like Jack—but at her perfectly neat blouse, at her unwrinkled skirt, at what remained of her hair. She loved to be perfect and *I* was going to make her a mess! I was going to make her a mess for having no heart! Oh, she was heartless!

"Anita!"

How did she know it was me? Jack had not told her. I was certain. How did she know it was me!

"Anita! It's done. It's done. All the calls were made. If they didn't say yes tonight, they will say yes in the next few days. It's done."

I flew into the kitchen and willed more glasses onto the floor, onto walls. I flew over the piano and flapped my wings against photographs of her and Jack and her at Miss Porter's and her at Radcliffe and her being perfect! Being perfect! Being perfect! I scattered them all to the floor with the power of my wings. I flew over her armchair, her velvet sofa, her elegant Turkish rugs, and I let myself shit guano all over them. Stenchy, acidic feces all over her house! I flew over her head and shat over that too.

"It isn't right, Anita, but it just is," she said, and I could feel the sorrow. I could feel the regret. But regret with inaction is just a swallowed apology. "I know you are mad. I know we never got along. But you have to understand, you are dead and Jack is alive."

And I couldn't believe what I was hearing. I couldn't believe she could truly be so clueless, so naïve—as though the issue here was me not knowing that I was dead. I knew I was dead! Of course, I was dead! And though I couldn't talk and though whatever I said would be too high-pitched for her to hear, even if, by some miracle, Tilly could speak bat, I had to say it to her. I had to let her know.

Swoop.

I hovered in her face. Right up close. As close as I could get. And I looked into her watery blue eyes with my glassy brown ones, that I hoped she would remember. And I screamed,

"But I want to be alive!"

"I want to be alive!"

"I want to be alive!"

Raquel

PROVIDENCE • SUMMER 1998

Thirty-three stories. On the corner of Broadway and Eighth Street. Her body landed, broken, on the roof of a deli. A deli Raquel had gone to many times during her high school years to get a Snapple or a soda on a hot Saturday spent wandering the stores of Greenwich Village. The woman's face—this young, beautiful face—had been plastered on the covers of the *Daily News*, the *New York Post*. Newspapers that surely would have been in Raquel's house. Nineteen eighty-five. She would have been only seven years old when it happened. Too young to register the headline. Too young to likely have any interest in it even if she had. She wouldn't have understood then the magnitude and significance of the story. The headlines—"Death in the Art World; Sculptor Kills Wife"—flattening what Raquel already knew, even in her limited experience, was a far more nuanced story. A more heartbreaking one.

A Latina girl, like herself. This one raised in an orphanage with barely a penny to her name; came to New York to try to make it in this lily-white art world. What she lacked in connections she made up for in ambitions. Big ambitions. And she was breaking through! She fell in love with someone who had it all: fame, money, access, maleness, whiteness. It would have seemed like a fantasy. To feel like you are on the outside of things and have someone so deeply on the inside take you behind the glass. A chance, Raquel understood, to maybe have things be a little easier when, likely, they'd always been hard. A chance, Raquel thought, to "marry well." To have a "better life." She wondered, in fact, if he had promised her that; if he'd promised to "help her." But instead of easier, instead of better, she ended up dead. Thrown out of a thirty-third-story window by the man she'd loved. The man she'd married. And that same person took what little she had—what little she'd been able to accomplish relative to him—and took it from her.

Because then, she didn't just die. It was as if she never even existed at all. It was the second death of Anita de Monte.

What had Mrs. Fitzsimmons said? That Jack Martin's wife was lucky that he'd let her into those rooms. How lucky could she have been if she was dead?

The morning after her reconciliation with Nick, the morning after she learned about Anita de Monte, Raquel woke up early, an intense sense of unease vibrating inside her. The whole week prior she had longed to be back here; back at Nick's, sleeping beside him. And last night it had felt very right. The makeup sex, the walk to get Thai food afterward. Their easy conversation as they ate their takeout in the park. But this morning her first thought had been of his mother. Raquel was horrified—disgusted even—with the way Nick's mother had spoken about this woman. Jack Martin's wife. Even if she hated her, who could say someone deserves to be dead? Thrown, as Mrs. Fitzsimmons implied, out a window. Who on earth could deserve that? She cringed when she remembered how Mrs. Fitzsimmons had conjured up Frida Kahlo. Remembered the implication that she, Raquel, was somehow a better person than this poor woman who had been dead for years because, why? Because Raquel was polite? Because she seemed gracious for the fact of a family like theirs was welcoming someone like her to their table? Why had it even occurred to this woman to compare the two of them? Just because they were both Latina?

Raquel wanted to know the full story; headed straight to the library. To discover all that she could about the case as well as to decipher how on earth she had spent hours upon hours reading about

Jack Martin's life and work and never come across her. But she could not remember her name! Not while she was brushing her teeth, not as she waited in line for her coffee. Only as she was ascending the library steps did it come to her: Anita de Monte.

Nick's father had said it was a big news story, so she decided to start there; went over to the research computers, ran a LexisNexis search, and was stunned by both the volume of results yielded and the short time span they ran. She started in the beginning: a review of her first New York show from the *Village Voice* in 1978; another around the same time in *Art in America*; a mention of her in a group show in *Ms.* magazine. Then nothing much for a couple of years before an article on her and Jack Martin creating a piece in tandem for a museum show in Mexico City—a wild, crazy thing. She had never seen this piece when looking through his scholarship—somewhere, seemingly, there were pyramids, but in the photo, all you could see were wild mountains of flowers. Gorgeous and overgrown. Nothing at all like his work. The ninety-degree angles and rigid lines he was known for, obliterated by the wild, feminine. The idea of nature besting man for a moment made her smile. She didn't know if it was his idea or hers, but she liked it. She found a short profile of her from 1982 after winning the Rome Prize, and another from the *Miami Herald*. She'd carved a goddess into the base of an old ceiba tree there and the local santeros had turned it into an altar.

And then she died.

For a brief moment, people were very interested in everything about her. Who she was: a feminist artist. Where she was from: Cuba by way of an orphanage in Iowa; sent there by her parents on Peter Pan. If she was successful or not: this depended, it seemed, on who you asked. The crime itself was covered in all of New York's tabloids and the *New York Times*. But it was never written about in an art section or a trade publication. She only found one obituary, written by her gallerist for an art magazine and published as an op-ed. As if her death was a matter of opinion. The aftermath—which clearly rocked the art world and divided it in two—was in all the city long forms. What was notable was how many more people were interested in her story once she was dead than they were at all when she was alive, producing art. This pained Raquel; gave her a physical feeling of anguish. Perhaps because they only ever studied white artists—men, particularly—Raquel had not been prepared for the full-throated racism voiced by Jack Martin supporters, and so many of them women. Yes, her advocates had been women, but her detractors surely were too. A "loony Latina"! A "kook"! An "immigrant climber"! "Cult-art"! "Voodoo"! "Cuban art"—the identity rendered as an insult in and of itself. Oh, some of the things people said were vicious; and that was what they were willing to put in print. She wondered if Nick's mother was one of these women, or if she just spoke about her behind her back?

Anita came across as strong. And strong-willed. And yet, Raquel wondered, did she ever even stand a chance? If they so openly closed ranks after something as heinous as her death, Raquel could only imagine the barricades they erected in her path during life. How she'd likely been reminded again and again and again that she was "lucky" to be there. How often they'd let her know, in ways great and small, that she did not belong.

At one point, it seemed Martin made headlines again for trying to impede an exhibition of her work. Then, there was some coverage of the trial, but not very much. It was, she gathered from going through the papers, eclipsed by a different assailant of women: an investment banker who had killed his girlfriend on a bench in Central Park. He was, Raquel had to admit, much better looking than Jack Martin, and who didn't love to hate an investment banker? There was only the smallest of items about the not-guilty verdict. The whole thing, then, just faded from the public consciousness. At least by way of media accounts, Anita de Monte was never heard from again.

Raquel felt a pang of guilt. She looked at the clock on the wall and realized that she'd been there for five hours; five hours of a deep dive into Anita de Monte's death and she'd never done her the decency of looking at her work. All the library had in its possession was one book; one catalog of an exhibition at the Museum of Contemporary Art of the Americas. There were a few other publications she had been featured in, a dozen or so master's theses and dissertations at other universities that had been written about her—all of these the librarian put in requests for interlibrary loans for her. But today the only thing she could get her hands on was this lone tome. She ventured down the two flights of stairs to the bowels of the library where the art books were kept and began hunting for the call number.

It was a perfect square, red linen bound. If it had a dust jacket once, it no longer did. Most of the images were reproduced in black and white, but the centerfold was made of color plates—striking, shocking images that stopped Raquel in her tracks. They spoke to something inside of her she had not ever seen in a piece of art: Of belonging, of embodying place. Of being part of something larger than you. They spoke a visual language that Raquel knew but didn't comprehend how. One she felt she had, perhaps, been born knowing. What she was seeing was unlike anything she'd been exposed to in the classroom; was more conversant with stuff happening out in the world today, and yet also somehow fresher than that too. It was vibrant. It was loud. Combusting. Raging. Her life and all of her pain jumping off of the page.

Anita

NEW YORK CITY • SPRING 1987

Let me say this: my friends know how to throw a fucking party! It was as if someone—Jomar—heard me bitch about everything I hated about art parties and then made sure that the Museum of Contemporary Art of the Americas didn't do any of them. There was a little Cuban combo playing—people danced!—ample wine, and plenty of food! I knew my sister would be sure that there was food.

I had come by then to resign myself to the limited sentiments of death: rage and anger, freedom and exaltation, release—release is a big one. But the night my show opened I felt something I hadn't felt yet: Melancholy. That I wasn't there in the room. That I was in the past tense. It is, I will admit, easier to be pissed about what happened to me. Easier to fly through the sky and scream and rail in high-pitched cries that make dogs bark and wake up neighbors. Easier to stalk Tilly and fly around her apartment every time she would actually get to sleep. Easier to follow Jack around and bite all the bitches he tries to fuck now that la sueca vaca left him. But there? In that magnificent room, with all my pictures on the wall? I felt *almost* alive, you see. And feeling almost alive was, in some way, harder than just being dead.

And I felt all their energy! Oh, such much energy! Surrounded by so many people. Many who I loved, many who I liked. Many who

I frankly couldn't stand and knew couldn't stand me—alive or otherwise—but I appreciated that they put on a nice cocktail dress and heels or a dinner jacket and at least thought I was important enough to celebrate. I was important enough!

Oh, had I been able to really be there! Oh, I would have made the band play "Fever" and done my best La Lupe impersonation! I would have worn a blond wig and smoked with a cigarette holder. Or maybe gone and had my hair blown pin straight at the salon, like Cher. I would have worn the dress with the silver paillettes. Or no! Who am I kidding! My first retrospective at a museum? An actual museum? Oh, I would have bought something new. I would have made Jomar come with me to Saks or Bendel or maybe a vintage store in the Village—I don't know! But I would have worn something fabulous. Something fabulous that *I* bought. Not that Jack and some boring old white lady at Bergdorf decided I should wear. I would have worn big dangly earrings. Or hoops. Shiny and gold. The kind that catch the light. I would have bought new heels; ones with straps that wrap around your ankles. The type that make it easier to dance! I would have drunk so much that I would've told people what I *really* thought of them—and I could have, because it was a retrospective of *my* work!

But I wasn't there. I mean, my work was. So I was. But, I wasn't.

Oh, the yearning! The *yearning* to be there, walking around the room instead of broken and burned to ash, confined to life in a canister in my mother's china cabinet. Well, it was hard. It was so much easier to be around the people who banished me to this existence. Easier to rage, easier to rail. Harder to hear people miss me. To hear them see totally new things in my work. Harder to hear people remember what a fabulous, annoying bitch I was. To hear people lament and complain about the fact that the traveling show had been indefinitely postponed.

I was so grateful. For the night, for the work my friends and my sister had done to make it happen. And when it was over, I brought them all little mice. The way Marco's lover told me to do. I don't know. I doubt they knew it was from me. Or maybe they didn't realize it was even a present. But, my yaya used to always tell us, it was the thought that counted.

I didn't know these were my glory days! I had no idea that, even dead, one day you are strong and another you are suddenly weak. I didn't know he could keep on hurting me—pummeling me and destroying me—even from the other side. Even from the fucking other side!

* * *

THE DAY THAT they were packing up my show—packing me up from the light, from the public, from the conversation—I went to the museum, of course. I lurked, close, as the art handlers pulled my children from the walls; felt overwhelmed by their indifference to what it was that they were wrapping up and shipping off. Me, Jack, fucking Jasper Johns . . . you could tell it didn't mean shit to them besides a paycheck. And as I watched the last of the crates get loaded out of the museum, I felt a new level of venom. A new pulsing desire to cause damage. To cause pain. To terrorize. To hurt! Flesh and hearts and spirits and souls! I wanted to nip the ankles of all the curators who acquiesced to Tilly; to terrorize these art handlers for their indifference with my babies! My babies! I wanted to bite at Jack's dick and pummel his fat face with my thick black wings. I climbed up the ceiba, fast, fast, fast. I wrapped my ankle around a bough and let myself hang. I steadied my breath and crossed my arms before my chest. And then I let go. And even though I spread my wings right when I always did, seconds later I was plummeting to the ground. Bumping my back—hard!—against the momentous roots of the ceiba.

I was not a bat. I was just dead me.

I climbed back up. Fast. Fast. Fast. Wrapped my ankles around the branch again and let my hair hang, long, long, long as I dangled upside down and just as I was about to let go . . .

"You've lost it," a voice came from above me. Way high in the ceiba.

He was an old fat bat named Roberto who hung around my tree sometimes. Mostly it was a transient population, no one stayed for very long, but the last time he visited, Roberto had made himself known. Constantly bragging about his legacy: a house he'd built all on his own near a river in northern Mexico for his family to pass on from generation to generation. He'd died a natural death, which was annoying because he didn't want to scare or hurt or haunt. He just wanted to hover. And he would talk about all the parties and weddings and quinceañeras his family would have at his house that he would attend and I wanted to just say: Good for you, Roberto. Good for fucking you!

"You lost it," he said again, when I didn't reward him with attention immediately.

"What are you saying to me, you old bat?" I yelled back. I was in a terrible mood.

"I may be an old bat," he said, and he did at least have the decency to drop down a few branches to look me in the eye when he said this. "But now *you* are nothing at all. Just dead like everybody else. So there."

"And what's so special about you?" I asked, because really?

"I designed and built an exquisite home that is the envy of the region! A house that has kept my family—and my spirit—alive for four generations—"

Four generations, I thought. *That is a long time.*

"And you've been dead for what, five minutes?" he asked.

"I'm not really sure how long it's been—"

"Point is, people like me can teach people like you a thing or two. If you weren't so arrogant."

And I thought that perhaps he did have a point. I really had no idea what I was doing here. Had no idea why one day I could fly and the next I couldn't. Had no idea how to get it back. I pulled myself upright.

"Roberto, I'm sorry," I said. "My name is Anita and I would appreciate your help."

And so Roberto explained to me that all spirits could visit dreams and climb the ceiba, but that only artists and muses could become bats. But only for as long as their art was serving its purpose: being out in the world. Of living! Roberto could fly because his house—*his* creation—was alive! And *my* art was in packing crates en route to an art storage facility that my sister could barely afford in Parsippany, New Jersey.

There went my power.

"But, not all of it, of course," Roberto explained. "Thought is a very powerful thing; how do you think I've gotten so big and fat? My family thinks of me all the time. Even negative thoughts are power."

"Power to do what, exactly?"

"Well," Roberto said, "you can still move things."

You know, moving things around doesn't sound like a big deal, but it can make a person crazy if you knew the right things to move. And, well, no one knows a husband like his wife, and no one knew what made Jack crazier than me.

Jack

MADRID, SPAIN • SUMMER 1989

A TRIUMPHANT RETURN TO THE WORLD STAGE

If you happen to be in Europe this summer or fall, do yourself a favor and carve time in your itinerary to get to Madrid. The magnificent Jack Martin show at Museo Reina Sofia, which opened yesterday to great anticipation, is well worth the trip. The sprawling site-specific production marks his first major exhibition of new works since 1985. It is nothing short of a triumph. In his absence from the public stage—Martin did not produce or exhibit due to personal challenges—he has fermented a new vitality in his long-running minimalist project.

Martin is a master of using the mundane and elemental—bricks, beams, blocks of wood—and not so much transforming it as using it to transform: a space, our aesthetic sense of what is beautiful, our very conceptions and conceits of what is art. The mode, as the noted minimalist and Martin scholar, John Temple, has expounded on many times, "was born from the chaos of the struggle for civil rights, the eruption of protests against violence in Vietnam, a way to bring aesthetic order into a world exploding, not through excess, but through reduction." The eighties have been nothing if not a time of excess and elaboration. So perhaps this is why, after a period of seeming peripheral to the issues of the

> moment, minimalism—and specifically minimalism in the capable hands of Jack Martin—feels relevant yet again.
>
> Still, the power in what he has done is that it has the restraint of his old work while embracing a changed world. The rigid grid formations and linear columns of yesterday have made way for massive blocks of timber arranged in radial dials, ingots in amoeba shapes, and gold bars set in alluring ovals. Somehow, the softness of these formations against the rigidity of the materials that are forming them creates a tension that feels not only alive but reminiscent of the many binary oppositions of our society today: liberty and constraint, masculine and feminine, the individual against the collective.

Jack couldn't read another word; threw the paper down onto the café table in a huff. Frustrated and disgusted. His face was as dour as his hangover from the night before; a condition not helping matters in the least.

"What?" Tilly said, a pile of newspapers she'd brought from the kiosk near their hotel in front of her. "It's a magnificent review. So is this one—though my German is shit, so I have no idea what *Der Spiegel* wrote, but it's got *brillante* in front of *kunst* a bunch of times and deductive reasoning says that seems positive."

Tilly was effervescent. Happier, even, than when the judge acquitted Jack. This show—and the satellite exhibitions at her gallery in New York and his other gallerists in London and Rome—if received well, was going to put him back on the map. Make him relevant again. Drive demand for his work, which had all but collapsed. The flood of the seventies waned into the trickle of the early eighties, the trickle transforming to drought, with a pity sale here or there, by some longtime collector who felt sorry for Jack and his troubles. It was, at first, a matter of mode. Art is, if nothing else, always about the next thing. He knew that. But then after *it* happened, he was a pariah. No one would touch him. Europe—they care less about that kind of personal messiness there—was receptive, but he couldn't travel. Not for the longest time. Tilly had really kept him afloat—finding him the occasional private commission, allowing him the full gallery during the time of the trial. But this show, the Reina Sofia show, was meant to be his big comeback. "*World-class*," she had said.

And so here he was, back at the center of the universe. Last night was, in most respects, as if he had turned back the hands of time. Nineteen seventy-nine, instead of eighty-nine. Save, of course, ten or so pounds. The room—and the art world—orbiting around him again. Tilly, delighted and stripped of all the heavy grimness of these last four years. A new, vivacious young woman on his arm, in his bed. His art, the talk of the town and, he knew from the buzz in the air, by the morning, the talk of the world. Or at least the part of the world that mattered to him.

The problem, of course, was that the art wasn't his. Oh, yes, technically. His physical hands, as they always were, the only ones to touch the materials. The ones to set them out. But not the ones to move them. No, those were invisible. Bodiless. Devilish fucking hands. And they worked so quickly! They worked so quickly, those fucking phantom hands. Faster and stronger than he could ever be. Tainting his vision, pissing on his lines and structure and order with her ovals. Her circles. Her "amoeba shapes." Oh, he knew what she was doing. He knew exactly what she was doing and he couldn't seem to fucking stop her. She'd done it before when he was showing at Tilly's. Every day after the gallery closed he noticed things were moved. Rearranged. Tilly had assumed he was just being "creative" and "exacting" after not having worked in so long. And what could he say to her? He couldn't tell anyone. Not without getting himself committed.

"Really, Jack," Tilly said as she sipped on her espresso, "if it's your hangover that's making you so grumpy, order a beer or something. I hate to see you missing the chance to bask in all that we've worked so hard for."

He tried to force a smile. Tilly truly did deserve to celebrate this moment. Yes, the trial, the not working (the visions, the fucking terrifying visions), the stress and strain of it all had been hard on *him*. But Tilly's shoulders had been carrying much of this too: of his career, of his public image, and—what he knew that she didn't, of course—of his sanity. Because it was Tilly who made Anita—the physical form of her at least, the version of her that terrified him most of all, vengeful little rodent that she was—go away. And because, as shameful and shredding-of-the-soul painful as it was to see his vision—his elegant, clean genius—tainted by Anita, it was still preferable to seeing her, night after night with those eyes and that fucking grin, hanging outside his bedroom window. *That* bedroom window. Hanging in wait, never sure what she might do.

"It's a tremendous triumph, and you architected it all," he said and forced a smile. "We should have champagne—"

She laughed, conspiratorially. "It's still breakfast time!"

The last four years had taken a toll on her. Still a classic beauty, but her eyes wore more lines than they had, he could see that. Her neck, she, as of late, almost always kept covered under a scarf of some sort. An accessory of age, she'd told him once. He gestured for a waiter and he could feel her studying him. No secrets between them. Except for the one. The big one.

"Monica seems lovely," Tilly said, hunting, he could see, for the source of his malcontent.

Monica had replaced Megan, who had replaced Ingrid. She was lovely; a PhD student at Columbia studying antiquities.

"She's terrific; had a wonderful time last night."

Tilly sighed. "Why aren't you happy?"

I am angry, Jack thought, *that the ghost of my dead wife fucks with my artwork by inserting vagina shapes and areolas and women's silhouettes and I am pissed that the pieces she fucked with got better reviews than I've gotten in ten years. That, Tilly, is why I am grouchy today.*

"If you must know . . . A rave is a rave, but, I suppose I'm bothered by how effusive the vitality of my 'new' work seems to be. As if my old work is now, well, not vital."

Tilly smirked. "Jack, that's pompous even for you. The new work is great—a new direction."

"But what if it's not?" Jack said, with urgency. "I'm not sure I personally even like it—"

"You've never shown a thing that you didn't feel confident about in your life," Tilly said.

"Well, I'm not sure this is a new direction. In fact, I'm hoping that it isn't."

"You aren't making any sense," Tilly said, in a rare moment of irritation before she composed herself. "How about this: let's cross that bridge when we get to it—about formations and shapes. Right now, let's savor what you've done. You, after all, are the captain of this genius ship."

I'm not so sure about that.

"Thank you," he said. Finally the waiter appeared, and the champagne was procured and pastries inhaled and more coffee ordered and, with some alcohol in his system, his anxiety about the show dissipated a bit. (It was worse than fucking Mexico City.) What he should do is bask in the light this will put on him; the light he had been longing for. There were six magnificent, tremendous pieces. He should not dwell on the three that she'd managed to sully. He should focus on how the world was so happy to have him back. How he was so happy to be back.

What he wouldn't do to get rid of Anita.

They were sitting quietly, like a married couple—only better, because Jack still loved Tilly with all of his heart—poring over the various papers. Tilly reading tidbits of reviews she particularly liked, Jack looking—searching—desperately for a comment or a photograph about anything but the three tainted pieces.

"Oh," Tilly exclaimed, her hand rising to her mouth.

"What? Nasty critic?"

"No, no. A great review," she said flatly. Before she looked at him with pursed lips and shook her head as she handed him the paper. "Well, we were going to hear about it eventually."

The arts section of the *Guardian*, folded to the headline of his review. To his delight, there was an insert of the large walls of bricks he had installed in one of the galleries. (One Anita had not touched.) Up at the top right was an ad; white sans serif font set in a black box:

The Winter Gallery
Presents
JACK MARTIN
Sculptures
Now through November

The gallery show, he thought to himself, was nothing new—all re-creations of pieces he'd done in the past—and still Anita had found a way to fuck with him while he was installing them. Twisting a gold brick to just the slightest angle. Moving one—just one—of his perfectly lined up grids of twelve 12 x 12 steel plates, out of line by just a hair. Just so much that no one else might even notice. But him. Oh, he had wasted hours—hours!—fighting with her over that one damn steel plate. He would fix it and then, as he would walk a pace to survey the correction, he could hear it—sliding, oxidized steel on poured concrete floor. Once, twice, a dozen, two dozen—oh, he'd lost count of how many times they went back and forth there. Him, wanting her to know he knew it was her—screaming and cursing her name! Only to later—at nearly the break of day—leave the gallery recognizing that she would take even greater pleasure in that. Further enjoy his knowing that she was the source of his misery.

He would have to check that plate before the show opened. He was certain she'd moved it again—

"Jack!" Tilly said, snapping her fingers. "Are you looking?"

Only then did he spot it. Just below his own ad, another. A smaller box, white with black print:

Rothschilds' Auctioneers
Presents
Body Art
from the collection of
Arlene Spier
Featuring works by Anita de Monte
On view, 2-10 October;
Auction, 10 October; 7PM

"The blatant opportunism of the whole thing is just disgraceful," Tilly said when she could see by the look on his face that he had seen the ad. "People will only remember who she is when they see your name!"

But for the first time when it came to matters such as these, he felt not indignation but dread. From shortly after *it* happened until they closed her exhibition downtown, Anita had made his life a living hell. He had suspected (hoped) that if her work went away, so would she, but even he hadn't thought it would be quite so effective. This was the first time he'd heard of her being shown again—and in such a prominent space—and he felt himself terrified of what this might bode. It was suddenly clear to him how she had been able to fuck with his work in the first place. He felt confident the attention charged her; felt certain now that he saw it in black and white: just the preparations for this auction had given her more power! She'd been a bat before; what if she came back as a cat? Or a dog? She'd bitten and battered. She'd lurked, she'd tormented. She'd done all that with just those tiny fangs, that short wingspan. What could she do with real teeth?

"This can't happen," Jack said aloud, though he didn't mean to.

"Be reasonable," Tilly said. "It's mildly unpleasant, but really? You've made a comeback. You are, once again, way bigger than—"

"That isn't it," he said, his voice hushed, picturing her artworks framed and hanging on the walls. The whole room of gawkers or collectors—or, God forbid, museum curators looking to hang her on their walls permanently! "If I tell you something very private—something I've never told anyone—will you promise not to use it against me?"

And he noticed that normally unflappable Tilly suddenly appeared quite flappable.

"At this point, doesn't that go without saying?"

"At first I thought it was just stress; that I would see things because of stress," he said before he took a breath and started again. "She's not really gone. Anita, I mean. I . . . I . . . Well, some strange things—things related to her, began going missing in the apartment. Or if not missing, moved. Important things. And she can move big things too. I don't want to say what—"

That was too much to say, he thought to himself.

"But suffice it to say pretty big things. She is strong. Strong! And then. Oh, it sounds so fucking nuts, but do you remember the time I went up to use Ron's cabin—"

"The bat," Tilly said, perfectly calmly.

"I sound insane, but I swear to God, it was her. The bat was her. The eyes and the face. And it was a bat—I mean, I got bit and everything, now a bunch of times. But she *is* the bat. And I just had this feeling, I had this feeling that if we could make her art go away, I could make her go away. And she had been. She'd been mainly gone. Only lately she's been back. Not the bat, but the other stuff. And . . . and I know this sounds ludicrous, but I can't help but feel it's because she knows. She knows this auction is coming up. And even if this has nothing to do with how or why . . . Tilly, I'm afraid to take my chances."

He could hear the desperation in his voice; looked up now, ready for her assessment, frightened at what he might see in her eyes. That after all this ordeal behind him, after all of this, she might now have him committed or worse—drop him as a client. But instead, the eyes that met his were full of knowing.

"She could never get enough attention, could she?" Tilly said.

"I need you to make her go away. Make her art go away," Jack said. "Please."

"I'll see what I can do."

Anita

UNDER THE CEIBA TREE

I'd forgotten those pieces were out there; forgotten about the little old lady who looked like a homeless person who'd shown up the night of my very first show—I'd called her a cheese eater because I thought she just came for the free food. And then a few days later, after I'd rehung the thing, Leslie phoned to say that someone had come in and bought two pieces from each part of the series. The little old lady. She died in some cramped apartment filled with old newspapers and furniture and art by everyone: Basquiat and Haring and Cindy's early work and . . . me.

Imagine my surprise when I heard my name, and felt the thrill of excitement and discovery! And I listened and heard the word "auction," and I got up that ceiba so fast and found myself in the auctioneer's office. Oh, the feeling when I saw my babies that I hadn't seen in all those years! Their life blood pulsing with the energy of my twenty-seven-year-old self. A version of me before Jack pulled me apart and I tried to stick myself back together again. And the auctioneer was so taken with them. With me! With the sudden recollection of the story of how I died and an honest appreciation of my work.

And I heard the auctioneer on the phone with the old lady's family; how he had a strategy for selling some of the art: to get it more value and more publicity. And when I heard that, I felt myself grow stronger.

Oh, not strong enough to take form—try though I might to fall off the tree and fly—but I could feel myself, could feel the force strong enough to fuck with Jack. And every night I went into that museum in Madrid and I tormented him! In London it was even more maddening, my intrusion even more subtle. In a way I knew only he would notice. I don't know. Maybe I went too far? But no, it wasn't far enough! Far enough would be to drive him mad. Have him running through the streets in his underwear like his hair was on fire, babbling in tongues about phantom bats and freezing his balls off on a winter day in New York. Far enough would be . . .

It doesn't matter. They stopped it all. Stopped it all. Stopped. It. All. Bought up all the pieces in the auction, canceled the exhibition. Back into the crates I went.

Ay puñeta!!! Coño! How many times can a person die? How many deaths can one soul endure? She buried me fucking alive! Hijos de su puta madre, los dos! They buried it all! Oh, the levers they can pull. The tricks! The tricks! The whole lot of my works scooped up by some lackey doing Jack's bidding. All in exchange for one piece of Jack's. He sent them three squares of steel to put on the floor of the foyer in their Park Avenue apartment. Three squares of steel! In exchange for my blood, sweat, and tears.

Forget about flying. I could barely move an envelope in Jack's house. That man, when he decided, was stubborn as a fucking mule. He shut me out of his brain completely. Cut me from his thoughts. The animal! The brute! Maybe, sometimes, at my sister's or Jomar's, where they kept a piece or two of mine out on display, where they would look at it and commune with me—my energy—maybe there I might be able to move a glass or change the location of a picture. Just to let them know I was there. Occasionally, there'd be a poet or a feminist studies major who'd stumble on my story or my work—pore over the body work, always interested in the blood and feathers, never paying attention to the sculptures, which I personally think are more sophisticated but, whatever! But at least they were looking at the work, and every once in a while, I could move a book on their library carrel or flip a page—just to focus their attention. But as far as Jack and my art? I was buried. Left to just listen and hear people talk about *wishing* I'd be rediscovered.

Jack made it impossible. Jack and that comemierda Tilly. For the tenth anniversary of my death—ten years! Oh, the time is funny here—the usual suspects wanted to put on an exhibit. Nothing complicated. Mainly stuff in my estate—things stuck in Parsippany—and Jack caught wind of it. This time, with his ducks in a row and his legal troubles—about me! His "legal troubles" about murdering me!—behind him, he made a legitimate case to take control of my estate. Can you imagine? Oh! He who had been cockblocking my work, having his friends buy up anything and everything that came on the auction block or the resale market—having them buy pieces just for the sole purpose of keeping them in hiding! This same brutish monster had the nerve to argue that my sister wasn't a good steward of my work because I'd "faded from the public eye" under her guardianship. I faded from the public eye, you cocksucker? Because you buried me! You threw me out a fucking window and then you buried me alive!

It was a wonder I could haunt a dream or even skulk around a kitchen. All of my power, kept in a jail. A jail of Jack's making, rigid with lines and made from beams of steel.

Raquel

PROVIDENCE • SUMMER 1998

To: Mavette
From: Raquel
Subject: Soap!

Dear Mavette,

What a lovely surprise the soap and stationery were! Even the box was beautiful with all the postmarks. How did you know that I love (LOVE!) fancy soaps? Anyway, it was the perfect thing to get and on the perfect day too. (I was so down.)

I know my last email was brief. To be honest, I've had a hard time making sense of that night and what it meant for our friendship, which I had very much begun to value. But I've appreciated hearing from you. And I've missed you. I don't know, it's just been such a weird summer. Wonderful in some ways, strange in others.

You'd asked how love was and, well, I'm not sure. Love is hard. Well, I guess you knew that already. Everything had been amazing—better than amazing—with Nick and lately, they just haven't been. And I can't tell if something has changed or if it's how he sees me that's changed. It went from feeling like he was the person who understood me the most to feeling like I'm not sure if he likes me, or an idea of me. It's hard to explain.

Like, he had his big opening at WaterFire for these sculptures he did (you'll see them when you get back; you can't miss them). He was nervous and testy for days before—and I wanted to give him some space because clearly nothing I said or did was going to make him feel better. But then he said I wasn't being supportive. And, at the opening, well . . . Nick's very particular and he wanted me to wear a specific dress and have my hair a certain way and, I don't know, I started to feel like a doll a little bit. Actually, he has good taste. But, when we got to the party, he sort of just kept talking to everyone—which makes sense, it's his night, right? But then, it was like he would turn to me like he was giving me permission to talk and be like, "Don't you think so, Raquel?" Like he was pulling a little string or something. I don't know. It was just weird.

Or it wasn't weird and I'm just reading too much Naomi Wolf. I don't know.

I keep reminding myself he's an artist, he's temperamental, he needs support, he's about to make this big life change. He says he's in this with me for the long haul, but, it's hard to explain . . . I'm not sure if he actually loves *me*, or the picture we paint as a couple. Or maybe the issue is we're more different than I realized.

Yikes. I'm sorry to vent, but to tell you the truth, my friends—and even my family—aren't exactly fans of his. In your letter you wrote that you've been surrounded by people all summer, but have never felt more alone. I completely understand that. And sorry you feel that way. Honestly, nothing is that great with anybody or anything right now, except at the museum. (Belinda Kim is like no one else I've met before and pretty much this has been the antithesis of everything that we've complained about in the department.)

I'm sure it will all be OK; just growing pains in a relationship, right? In the meantime, I'm trying to focus on my thesis and the job and getting out of here!

And listen, let's make last year water under the bridge. I can't wait to hang out more (but, sorry, obviously without the rest of the "package"). Nick's mom rented him a loft off of the West Side Highway, so we'll have to go into the city together to visit.

I hope the quest is going well (seriously—who am I to judge?) and that you're enjoying Italy.

XOXO
Raquel

P.S. In answer to your question, I think Astrid is seeing a couple of people. She does her own thing and I haven't seen Niles in a month or so.

P.P.S. Oh my God, I almost forgot to tell you—John Temple is getting a divorce!!! And he has such a sad, sad divorce beard and I think he's living in those depressing apartment buildings down by the Kentucky Fried Chicken. I saw him out of the window of Marcus's car carrying grocery bags.

Raquel's finger hovered over the mouse as she debated whether to hit the Send button or not. Despite having reconciled, things between her and Nick had not been quite back to normal these past few weeks and the reception for *The Great Gondoliers* had only brought to a head a strange tension that had emerged between them. One that seemed to volley from one to the other as the quiet keeper of grievances. She had donned the DKNY dress he'd bought her for the occasion, hair back in the chignon he preferred, and inexplicably he was upset that her hair wasn't down. He did nothing but complain about her hair when it got in her face or his face and suddenly, he wanted her hair down? When she asked why, he said that it brought out her "ethnic beauty" and that soured her mood; made her feel like an accessory to a statement he wanted to make about himself. But, worse, at the reception, if Raquel tried to have any sort of conversation with anyone apart from him, Nick would immediately come and cut her off—making an offhanded comment about how it was *his* night. Making her feel, at best, like a prop and, at worst, an opportunist. They didn't fight, they didn't yell, but afterward, when they got home that night, the sex was awful. The gentleness, the care, was gone. She felt herself a vessel, an object in his room, this one for pleasure. Was it the way he acted when he was inside her? Or after, when he got up and went to the bathroom first, almost as if she was not even there.

She could not stop thinking of how he had talked about her family; how she felt that cascade upon her. Could not push away the sense that since meeting them, Nick saw her differently. Not as a peer, but as someone *almost* a peer. It was hard to divorce his mother's talk of gratitude and "rooms" from his suggestions about what she wore or what she ate or what she should be reading or listening to. And so she found herself more rankled by these things, and yet, still, she ached to please him for reasons she couldn't quite express. A strange sense of indebtedness for having opened her world up so much; for the promise of all the ways it could open further still.

She had hoped things would be better after the exhibition, but with his time in Providence coming to a close, he seemed both irritable and strangely cloying, now more than ever. If she lingered at the station, if she spent a day—a Saturday, as she did, after his mother's visit—in the library; time spent away from him seemed, suddenly, a referendum on her support of Nick and his work and her belief in their relationship. And she did believe in their relationship! In fact, it was this belief that kept her around even when she suspected that what they needed was space. Even when, with all the nitpicking, she sometimes wondered why, exactly, he wanted her around in the first place. Still, she kept wishing and trying and doing everything she could to turn back the hands of time. To when it was fun and wonderful together. Desperate to get back. Feeling, she knew, that both of them believed it was possible. And if they believed it, they could do it.

Perhaps this is why she had been so reluctant to utter any of their problems out loud. Also, who would listen? Everyone around her was looking for an excuse to get her to break up with Nick. When she got the soap from Mavette, she read it as a welcome sign that she should reach out. Tell someone about her anguish. Her uncertainty. She hit Send.

* * *

"WHAT'S ALL THIS?" she said with a laugh.

She'd walked out of the museum to find Nick, leaning against his idling car with a massive stuffed puppy dog in his arms. The kind you'd get at a cheesy flower shop or a fair.

"We're going to the dogs, baby," he said, in his best (terrible) attempt at a New England accent. "I thought it'd be fun to go to the greyhound track. Bet on some hounds!"

"Is that humane?" she asked, more seeking permission than an out. Raquel had never been to the greyhound races; had just heard of them, but was intrigued.

"They're dogs running around in circles," he said. "Don't overthink it. Besides, I've been a fucking pill these last couple of weeks and we could use a little fun, don't you think?"

"We sure fucking could!" she said, and threw her arms around him with a laugh and a kiss. It was like he had read her mind, or at least her email.

The whole thing was cheesy and hilarious. They were such fish out of water in the Southern New England dog racing scene that it made them both relax. Enjoy experiencing, for the first time, something totally new to each of them. Made Raquel feel, again, that they were equals.

They'd been betting on the same dogs for most of the races—Raquel realizing that perhaps she'd inherited some of her mother's love of gambling as, time after time, her picks kept winning. And then the last race, Nick decided he wanted to go with a top seed—a contender named Murphy—but Raquel fell hard for an older, haggard-looking dog named Ay Bendito. It was, she decided, the most hilarious name for an animal since her mother's dog, Duran Duran, and figured—given the pool of money they'd already won—Ay Bendito was worth losing twenty bucks to support a fellow Puerto Rican underdog.

Only he didn't lose! When they got shot out of the holding pens, he looked worse for the wear—Murphy was out, chasing the mechanical rabbit, leagues ahead of him. But then, on the second bend, something kicked in for Ay Bendito and he ran after that machine bunny like he had real meat on his bones and Ay Bendito hadn't eaten in weeks. Neither of them, nor any of the old men and ladies around them, could believe it, and everyone was screaming and hugging and laughing.

Afterward, Raquel bought them all rum shots at the dingy track bar with her winnings and it was, they agreed on the drive home, the best night they'd had together in ages.

"Let's go to Legs and Eggs in the morning!" Raquel declared when they got back to Nick's apartment. She fanned out her stack of small bills with a wide smile.

"First a dog track, now a strip club? I'm turning you into a degenerate, Toro!" he joked.

Raquel didn't know if she was high off her earnings or that her little dog that could actually did, or that for the first time in what felt like weeks they had just enjoyed each other, but she found herself feeling confident. And, dare she say, sexy?

"Or," she said with a raise of her eyebrow, "I could strip for you here . . ."

"Really now?" Nick said.

She put the volume up on the stereo, shook her hair from her bun like she'd seen girls do in those old hair band music videos, and, between fits of giggles, did her best impersonation of a lap dance, before Nick, with a series of kisses, put her out of her performative misery.

They made love that night the way they did when she first thought maybe this could be OK. That maybe this could be more than just pretending to like it for his sake. She always found it better when she was on top and the whole day had given her the confidence to ask for what she wanted. It was hot in the old apartment and, even with the window AC blasting, they were drenched with sweat. Slipping around each other. She grabbed onto Nick's shoulders to stabilize herself. Her hair, damp and cascading over his face. She leaned in to give him a kiss.

"Raquel!" he said sharply, and she pulled herself off of him. "Please. The hair!"

She got up off the bed, apologetically at first, to look for a hair tie. Her hair *was* so long. Nearly past her butt, she realized. She caught a glimpse of herself, naked, surrounded by it, in the mirror over Nick's dresser and stopped in her tracks. What was all of this? This attachment to her mother's tastes? This same attachment that had kept her a virgin for all this time? Afraid of sex. Afraid of men. Afraid of someone knowing her? Was it a mantle to be proud of or a veil? Covering and hiding her. From life. From change.

"Do you know what I think?" Raquel said to him, a provocation in her voice.

"What?" he said. She could tell by the cock of his brow and the look of him, lying there on his futon, naked, that he was intrigued.

"I think you should cut my hair."

"What?" Nick said, fully sitting up now.

"You hate how long it is—"

"I never said—"

"Don't fucking lie," she said, smiling. Somehow very confident about this decision. "I'm twenty years old, I can't go around like I'm in grade school with hair down my back my whole life. Give it a trim so it stops annoying you and when I'm back home in a couple weeks, I'll have my mom's person shape it up."

"Well," he said, as he climbed up off the bed and walked up behind her, "I am a sculptor, so you'd be in good hands."

They both laughed at this. He looked at her in the mirror, began playing with her hair like she was in a salon chair.

"So what are you thinking? A bob? Bangs? How much can I take off?"

"Hmmm," she said. "I was thinking about this much . . ."

She gestured with her hands about half a foot, but Nick spread them out wider, at least double that.

"That much?" she said, incredulous. She couldn't even remember the last time she'd had a real length taken off her hair. Usually her mother would just snip the ends.

"You must have three and half feet of hair on your head," he said, with a laugh. "Are you getting a haircut or what?"

She closed her eyes in disbelief.

"OK, twelve inches," she said. She was really going to do this. "Aargggh!" She let out a little scream.

"I think I need to take a shot first," she declared.

"Definitely a good idea," Nick said.

They threw on clothes and Nick changed the music on the stereo.

Raquel began to brush the curls out of her long mane as Nick prepared their midnight salon. Vodka and glasses retrieved from the kitchen, a chair from the dining room, a towel to serve as her smock, and a set of pristine silver scissors from his drawing table. Back in his room, with Raquel's hair all combed out and wetted, Nick poured them shots.

"OK, here we go," he said.

"Twelve inches," she said, as they clinked glasses and downed the shots.

Raquel sat on the chair in front of the mirror as Nick grabbed a comb, took a section from the front of her head near her face, pulled it semi-taut, and cut about a foot off the end. Raquel watched the long, wavy, wet clump hit the floor and felt a little queasy. She couldn't believe she was doing it.

"I think I need another shot," she said.

"Raquel, come on, it's not that big a deal. You can barely tell the difference," and he tried to illustrate it to her, but she was already out of the chair. Pouring herself another drink. She downed it, looked at the scissors and the clump of hair on the floor. It really was just symbolic, she realized. It looked like a lot, but nobody—except maybe her mother—would end up really noticing the difference. And maybe Nick.

She turned the chair away from the mirror. Sat back down and closed her eyes.

"The only way I'll keep going is if I can't see," she said.

Even over the sound of the music, she could hear the metallic clip of the scissor blades, as the haircut began to take on a rhythm of its own: the comb piercing her mane, the pull of the hair, the snip of the scissor. Comb. Pull. *Snip.* Comb. Pull. *Snip.* Comb. Pull. *Snip.* Nick's body so close to hers, but also, her having no real sense of where he was. He first began working in an orderly fashion; she could sense him on her left side or her right. Could feel where on her scalp the pull was. But then, he began working more haphazardly. She'd feel the tug at the top of her head, then the back, then down at the nape.

"Everything OK up there, Edward Scissorhands?" she joked. He chuckled.

"Couldn't you have just cut straight across?" she asked. "It's not like a real haircut."

"That would look crazy in real life," he said. "I've watched my mom's hairdresser cut her hair a million times. You don't do it like that."

"Charlie Don't Surf" came on; she hummed along, to distract herself. Maybe he did know what he was doing. He seemed so confident. Comb. Pull. *Snip*. Comb. Pull. *Snip*. She felt the comb, then the tug on a section of hair toward the back of her head, but when she felt the snip, the blade of the scissor brushed against her ear. The sound, loud. Louder than it had been.

"What are you doing?" she said, and she could hear the panic in her voice.

"It's coming out wonderful," he said. She felt the comb, tug, and could sense the tension of the pull was much too close to her scalp now, and just as she tried to jerk her head away—*Snip*. She leapt from the chair, grabbed at her hair, and screamed.

"Shhhhh! Shhhh!" Nick hushed her.

But it was too late, she'd turned around and looked in the mirror, looked around the floor, at the layers and piles of foot-long sections of hair. At its longest, her hair was at about the nape of her neck, but when she felt the back of her head—the section that made her jump up—it was shorter. Not more than a few inches away from her scalp. The tears scorched hot, streamed down so fast.

"What did you do?" she yelped.

"It's just hair, Raquel," Nick said calmly.

"What did you do?"

"If you don't like it, it will grow back."

"We said twelve inches!"

She was screaming so loud, Astrid came running in.

"What the fuck is happening?" she said, sleepily as she tried to take in the scene.

"We said twelve fucking inches! Why did you do this?" Raquel wailed as she pounced on him, pummeling him as Astrid attempted to pull her away.

"Are you two on fucking drugs?" Astrid said.

"I took off twelve inches," Nick said flatly, "and you could barely notice it, so I took off twelve—"

Raquel was balling now, collapsed on the floor, surrounded by her pile of hair, which she was attempting to gather, the wet strands sticking to the floor and her arms and hands as she combed through them with her fingers.

"That wasn't what we said," Raquel cried, snot bubbling from her nose and choking her voice. "That wasn't what we said!"

"You wanted a change. I just wanted to help you take a risk—"

"Why?" she wailed. "Why?"

She felt something had been removed from her, something deeper than her hair. She saw in each strand a memory of the life she'd had before. Of her life as her mother's daughter, lying in wet heaps on the floor of a rental apartment that wasn't even hers. Removed from her body. Separate and now part of the past. Years gone in minutes. Cut off—carelessly, without her permission. She felt cold and naked and terribly alone.

"I'm sorry!" she wailed. The apology screamed out to her mother, far away.

Astrid was down on the ground now, beside her.

"It's OK," she hushed. "It's OK. It will grow back—"

But hearing that only made the truth cut harder. She could grow back new hair, but this hair—the hair that had been grown and nurtured and loved by her mother, in that dark apartment near the elevated train, that had been pulled up for gym class and blown straight for dances and school pictures and graduations—this hair was gone.

* * *

THE SUNLIGHT IN the window woke her up in the morning. She was lying on Nick's futon, Astrid asleep beside her. The chair and the towel, vanished. Someone (Astrid, she knew) had gathered up all the hair and very neatly put it in a large ziplock bag on the dresser, beside the pair of scissors. She got up and looked at herself in the mirror. Dry, it was even worse than she'd imagined—the curls had sprung up, making it look even shorter. Tighter, she realized, because they weren't elongated by their own weight. Sitting differently one part of her head versus the other. She found herself hideous. Unrecognizable. She tried to comb it all back into a tight bun, but it wouldn't quite go, the parts at the back of her head where Nick had cut the closest curled up and nestled close to her scalp. She took the scissors in her hands and cut a piece from the top as close as she could to where the curl broke. She cut another and another. Not with emotion, but purpose.

"Raquel," Astrid said, "what are you doing?"

"I can't go out like this," she said with resolve. "So, just trying to make myself not look like total shit."

They sat in silence as Raquel moved methodically around the crown of her head. When she got to the back she turned to Astrid.

"Can you help me?"

Astrid nodded yes. Raquel walked with the scissors to the futon and sat on the edge of it. Astrid stood on her knees and gingerly took the scissors and began cutting.

"I don't want to mess it up," Astrid said.

Too late.

"Just cut it close. Maybe I can get away with a whole *Rosemary's Baby* look."

She wanted to cry, but the tears had all fallen out with her hair.

When Astrid was done, Raquel stood up, put on her jeans, which were on the floor, and picked up her bag off Nick's desk chair.

"I can save this for you," Astrid asked.

"Put it all in the trash," Raquel said. "It's garbage, isn't it?"

And she walked out the door.

IV

RETROSPECTIVE

Anita

NEW YORK CITY • SUMMER 1998

Generally speaking, death has become more boring than one of Tilly's parties. That impossible distinction of the passage of time. One day into the next. Lately, I think I've become depressed. I don't want to visit anyone. Not my sister. Not my niece, who always senses that I'm there. Not Jomar.

Jack almost never thinks of me. Can you believe that? Tolstoy apparently proven wrong about a guilty conscience. I've said it before, Jack's heart was as cold as his work. It only warmed when he was fucking.

Something funny happened recently though. It bordered on interesting. Or at least curious. I heard a name from the tree; one that was only vaguely familiar, coupled with feelings of sycophancy, climbing, dissatisfaction. I was going to let it pass, sit here on the beach eating guavas and feeling sorry for myself, when I felt something else: Energy! My spirit! My babies!

I climbed up the tree—fast! Fast! Fast! It had been a while—and found myself in a long marble-floored hallway in a penthouse overlooking Central Park. I was behind a woman—a skinny Upper East Side bitch. Everything about her stereotypical to the point of boring: Chanel flats, shift dress, pearls. Except for her hair. Where all the other girls went blond, this lady had gone red. Lucille Ball, fire-engine red. Coiffed to the nines. Anyway, she walked into a large room with canvases in art bins and flat cabinets for photographs and went to a drawer and lo and behold, what did she take out? The pieces that the old lady had bought! Just stood there and flipped through them, completely indifferent.

And then I recognized her—the name. She was one of Tilly's people. Would always be around her art openings. Always kissing Jack's ass. This was the lackey that bought the images for him. And this is where they ended up. Another fucking storage space. A slightly better location than the locker in Parsippany my sister got.

And just like that, back in the drawer my babies went. And death went back to what it had become for me: the same old, same old.

Raquel

PROVIDENCE • SUMMER 1998

It was early when Raquel walked out of Nick's apartment. As she stepped out the front door and onto the porch, she stopped for a moment before she very intentionally pulled it closed behind her. Many things, these last few months—so swept up in the whirlwind of it all—had been undertaken by her nearly unconsciously. Sleepovers and day trips and invites to parties and blow jobs and sex acts that she blindly said yes to because she thought herself lucky for having been asked. (Not just asked; asked by him!) She wanted to remember the act of shutting this doorway—the feeling of the knob in her hand, the look of the peeling paint—and of knowing, in the base of herself, that no matter what happened next, no matter what Nick said or did, or what she said or did, that she shouldn't walk through this portal again. That this should be the last time.

She had no ability, in that moment, to disentangle the reason she felt that way, just that it was more than the fact that he had cut off all her hair. More than that he had tricked her. More than the simple fact of him being a dick.

She walked into the Coffee Exchange and, driven more by defiance than actual hunger, ordered a chocolate croissant and an iced mocha. She remembered once she sat down that she actually hated the Coffee Exchange—the too-cool-for-school staff and the wannabe artists the place attracted—and had only gone there every day because Nick thought it had atmosphere. She didn't know what to do with herself. She couldn't go back to her own house; couldn't bear to see the shock on Betsaida and Marcus's faces when they saw her hair (or lack thereof). She decided to walk to India Point Park; pulled out her book of CDs and sought comfort in the only woman who was always more heartbroken than any other person could possibly be: Mary J. Blige. (Misery, she realized, really did love company.)

A thought as she crossed the highway overpass: Nick often told her that she was special and important, but there was always an "almost," if not spoken, clearly implied. That if she just did or didn't do this thing or that, or wore this, or didn't eat that, she could be something she had long strived for but had a nagging suspicion might not be possible to achieve: "perfect." Only, what made it more fucked up was that she'd believed, nearly as much as he did, that he knew how to help her. That his suggestions, his implications, his aesthetics were superior to her own instincts and desires. That his preferences were more important than her preferences; his needs more important than her wants. The haircut was, in some absurdist way, simply a draconian conclusion of a dynamic that had already been set into place. Arranged by him, but reinforced by her. That he thought he could do something so dramatic—so violating—and get away with it; presume her to be grateful for it, even—was only possible because he had told her, in ways great and small, that he knew best and she had signaled that he was correct.

The croissant was buttery but not too sweet. She forced herself to keep eating despite the knot of humiliation lodged thick and deep in her throat. She realized that there were a lot of songs about cheating and unreliability and all of those things, but very few about shame. Feeling ashamed of yourself for letting someone think that they were better than you.

What was she going to tell her mother? Her mother who would never in a million years believe that she wanted short hair. Would remember how she herself had acquiesced that, despite Toni's right to cut off all her hair, she didn't particularly like the look of it.

The thought of her mother sparked that of another: Nick's. She felt a hot flash of embarrassment at how keen she'd been to impress that horrific woman. So eager to lap up her favor.

Oh, Nick might have deemed her mother unsophisticated or (falsely) presumed her unintelligent because of how she looked and talked, but Raquel deemed his mother cruel. Heartless and cold. Who, she thought, treats their daughter that way? Nick might have thought he was of superior stock to Raquel; that being here, among people like him and his family, was an "opportunity" for her, but Raquel was suddenly aware of how wrong thinking that was. How whatever her mother might lack in polish, she made up for in integrity. In being loving. In supporting her daughters moving forward even if that meant away from her. The thought brought the tears back to her eyes. Imagining her mother seeing her short hair turned the trickle into a stream. She would be horrified and Raquel would have to tell her that she was lucky to walk away only losing her hair.

On the river, the crew team was training, running a drill. One boat speeding past the other, quickly declaring victory. Even in a team, one person, she supposed, always ended up on top. She thought of Jack Martin. Ay Bendito won last night, but that was a fluke. Most of the time it was people like Jack who were the victors; the underdog, forgotten. Wiped away like Anita.

She decided to go to the library. To look again, at the work of Anita de Monte.

* * *

STARING AT THE catalog anew, at the other images that had been waiting on her carrel, Raquel realized that part of why de Monte's work struck her as so dynamic and fresh was that she had genuinely never seen anything like it before. Not in school; not in the museum. She had not been taught to appreciate it. Not the way she had Mondrian and Kandinsky and Picasso. She realized that so much of what she thought was good art had simply been that which had been elevated by John Temple, because it was understood by and spoke to and created by men just like John. And that in the omission of things that were made by or understood by or in conversation with people like her, Raquel had, unconsciously, begun to see those things as lesser. And that revelation sparked one that was even more painful: the reason that Raquel subconsciously believed that Nick knew "better" than her was that it was Nick's point of view that had been affirmed and internalized by the white walls of every museum or gallery they had ever been told was worth looking at.

She stared at the color plates, went through each image, slowly, page by page. Taking them in, not so much to try to understand them but to let them talk to her. To hear what it was Anita de Monte was saying. To see if there was any wisdom she could pass along. And whether it was staring at the pieces or just the emotion that came to fill the space of sitting in silence deep in the library, what began to churn up in her was an anger. Raw and salted anger. A blister desperate to burst. The root of the rage was nothing in particular and everything all at once: Jack Martin, Nick Fitzsimmons, his mother, her shorn hair, this fucking school, the First World, the Art World, the Art History Department, the Art History Girls, her bony legs, her still too fat stomach, Mavette not sticking up for her, her not sticking up for herself, her ridiculous knockoff Prada bag, the real Gucci one Nick replaced it with, her letting Nick replace it. But most of all, she felt a deep ire for Professor John Temple. Because he let his passions dictate her passions and she'd never questioned it. Because she had trusted him. And all this time he knew she had been searching, looking for any small reflection of herself in the art world, and all this time he knew about Anita de Monte and never said a fucking thing.

She slammed the catalog shut and carried it with her upstairs to the computer cluster. It was Saturday afternoon and she was the only one there. Her inbox full of art happenings in Providence, university updates about financial aid for the coming year, and an email from

Mavette. One that she would, she decided, read later. Right now she had to send an email. Before she lost her nerve.

To: John Temple
From: Raquel Toro
Subject: Jack Martin's Murder Trial

Dear Professor Temple:

I recently learned that in 1985 Jack Martin pushed his wife out of the 33rd-floor window of his New York apartment building and was arrested on charges of murder. Though I understand he was found not guilty in a trial by judge, I would like to meet with you to discuss the impact the omission of this information has on both my thesis and our curriculum as a whole. While this biographical fact may or may not have impacted his art and art-making process, it surely has important art historical implications as the victim of his crime was an artist on the rise and her sudden death cut that career—and the impact it may have had on the progress of Latino art-making in America—short.

My museum commitments keep me fairly occupied from nine to five, but I will gladly schedule time to step out at your convenience to discuss.

Sincerely,
Raquel Toro

It was evening time when Raquel got back to the apartment. She had hoped that, by some way of miracle, no one would be home, but she could hear Brownstone blasting from the stereo through the open living-room window, Betsaida telling a story even louder than that. She stopped at her door, took a deep breath, and stepped inside.

"Hey," she said.

"¡Ay, Dios! ¿Qué fockin' hiciste con tu pelo?" Betsaida exclaimed.

Marcus and Delroy were also there, both of them open-mouthed at Raquel's new look.

"It's a little shorter than I'd wanted . . ." Raquel started to say, but seeing them see her proved to be too much and her eyes flooded with tears. She didn't know how to explain herself, was too ashamed of her complicity in the humiliating matter to be able to tell anyone. Ever. The swallowing of that choked her words.

Betsaida moved toward her, put her arm around her, and sat her on the sofa.

"It's OK, it's OK," she said, patting her back as she sobbed, "we were just surprised is all."

"I look ugly," Raquel gasped between sobs. "I look ugly and it will never grow back the same."

"You don't look ugly," Betsaida said. "You have a beautiful face. It just will take some getting used to."

"And a better haircut," Marcus said.

"Marcus, what the fuck?" Betsaida yelled.

"What? Short hair is dope, but that's a jacked-up haircut."

Raquel stopped midtears and looked at him.

"It's absolutely a crazy, jacked-up haircut," she said, and started to giggle.

"Like a bootleg T-Boz," Marcus added.

"Toni Wackston," Raquel quipped and then they all started to laugh and rechristen her with monikers inspired by shorn celebrities. Raquel relaxed for a bit, realizing that they were not going to ask her how the bad haircut had come to pass. At least not now.

Betsaida was on the phone making arrangements for her cousin, a hairdresser, to hook Raquel up ASAP, when Raquel spied a dozen red roses on the kitchen table. A queasy feeling rose up in her.

"What's with the flowers?" she asked.

"Your boy brought them," Delroy replied, flatly.

"He called a couple of times and then showed up with those this afternoon," Marcus said. "There's a card too."

Raquel realized then that no one was going to ask her what happened because they all already knew. Not the particulars, of course. But the broadest and most important strokes: Nick was clearly sorry for something and Raquel was very unhappy about her unfortunate haircut. In some ways, she thought to herself, the story really was that simple. She walked toward the kitchen table and saw her name in his handwriting on the card. It wasn't a card as much as it was a piece of folded paper on which he had drawn a stylized image of them, kissing, surrounded by hearts and a blazing sun. On the inside, with impeccable penmanship, he wrote:

My beloved Raquel,

I'm so sorry. I just wanted to push you to do something bold that you were too afraid to do. I never thought it would make you this upset. Please forgive me.

Love,
Nick

She read the note over two or three times, chewing on each word, trying to understand where, exactly, the gristle was that made it so hard to swallow. The illustration. She looked at it again: the rays of the sun emanating from between the crown of their two heads and then her long, long hair cascading in spirals down, down, down and off the page. Even he couldn't picture her without her hair!

"Fuck you, you fucking shit!" she screamed and picked up the roses and hurled them across the room, the cheap glass of the florist's vase shattering against the stove where it landed. Imitation crystal and water and petals all over the shiny blond-wood plank floors; the smell of rosewater syncretizing with Raquel's sense of abasement.

Betsaida hung up the phone and Marcus and Delroy were lingering in the doorway, staring.

"I'm sorry, guys," Raquel said quietly, embarrassment having replaced her rage. "I'll clean this up."

"No," Betsaida said, "let them do it. You and I are going out."

"Your cousin can see me?"

"Tomorrow. Ahora mismo tú necesitas una limpia."

Jack

NEW YORK CITY • SPRING 1994

Jack was on top of the world. MoMA. Fucking MoMA. It's a funny thing, in a life full of storied accomplishments, there are the few that can still stand out as special. Personal milestones, if you will. He remembered himself as a younger man coming to see Pollock here and feeling that hunger in the pit of his stomach to see his own work on these walls. His sculptures in these hallowed halls. Oh, he'd been shown in hundreds of museums around the world, was in more permanent collections than any of his peers. He'd had six different retrospectives in his career and he wasn't even seventy years old. An early piece of his just sold at Christie's for nearly one million dollars. He was a success, by any definition. But to go from looking at these walls and yearning for your chance, to seeing the whole place—the whole fucking place—full of your creations? Knowing that he, even at his age, had still set out nearly each and every brick, beam, plank, and plate in the place? (Nearly, he admitted sadly, because at Tilly's insistence he'd begun to employ art assistants. Training them, as she had suggested, for the future. In his meticulous methodology and process for setting each piece.) Seeing his legacy—these pieces, he realized, were his legacy—celebrated on such a scale at an institution that had shaped him so profoundly? It was a level of fulfillment and satisfaction he hadn't felt in a long time.

The opening was glamorous. Full of friends and former rivals, most of whom he realized were getting too old to bother rivaling with. There was a string quartet playing the score from *The Remains of the Day* (oh, he had loved that film) and though he had brought Camilla (a new gallerist Tilly had hired to oversee her expansion into London), there were more than a few beautiful young women all too eager to get a few minutes talking with the man of the hour. It was a true New York affair—Graydon Carter was there, all the critics of course, even John-John and his new, very fetching girlfriend. Tall and blond, she reminded him of Ingrid (oh, sweet Ingrid; how he missed her).

He was having a drink with Camilla and some Argentine novelist when Tilly approached him.

"Dear, can I bring you over to say hello to some people?" she said.

"That's part of the show," he said cheerily, taking her arm and allowing himself to be led through the crowd.

"You really are in a good mood," she said. "It's Linda Fitzsimmons. She did us that favor a few years back . . ."

Oh fuck, fuck, fuck.

"Tilly, no."

Did she not know that he had put this in an iron box? The thought of *her.* The simple fact of *her*. Locked her away and dug a grave deep enough for twelve men. Covered it with worm-filled dirt and then poured concrete over that. Oh, how hard he had tried to keep her at bay. Now here was Tilly with a jackhammer, trying to get her out?

"I don't want to think about it," he said, and stopped in his place. Dug in his heels.

The night ruined.

"Jack," Tilly said firmly, "nobody does. But Linda's an old friend who did us a favor, who is a board member here, and now her son wants to be an artist. She just wants a chance to brag. So, come on."

And soon enough he found himself in front of an attractive woman with Titian red hair and a vaguely familiar face beside her smiling, besotted husband.

"Linda, Clarke," Tilly said, cheerily, "here he is."

"Jack," Linda said as she air kissed both his cheeks. "So wonderful to see you again."

"Oh yes, it's been a while."

"Not since you installed that fantastic piece in our foyer. It completely transformed the entrance."

Jack bristled. Forgotten he'd been suckered into gifting them something. It was simple. Clever. Three steel plates arranged such that they created a triangle in the center of the circular portico.

"Glad you're enjoying it. Tilly said your son is an artist now?"

"Nicholas Fitzsimmons! You'll be hearing his name soon enough, Jack. That, I promise you. He thought about going to RISD, but he's a true intellectual. Loves your word sculptures. Can't get enough of them. He's starting Brown in the fall and can take—"

The poems. The kid loved the poems.

"Terrific. Good for him," he said, trying to feign enthusiasm.

"Yes," her husband offered. "We're very proud of him. Darling, don't forget to tell Jack about the other thing."

"The other thi—" she said, seeming a little drunk.

"About the loan?"

"Oh God, yes." Linda leaned in conspiratorially. "We got a call from a small museum in Vancouver asking if we'd be able to lend those pieces we picked up at that auction. You remember?" she said.

"Of course we remember," Tilly said, not even hiding her displeasure.

"They are mounting an exhibition next year," Linda whispered, and Jack wanted to smack the shit out of her. This woman of so little significance—relished being in the middle of something relevant for a change. "It's the anniversary, you know."

Jack could not commit an act of violence at his own opening, but he felt his grip on his wineglass tighten.

"Of course," the sow continued, "we said absolutely not. Not under any circumstances."

"Well," Tilly said, gesturing her farewells, "of course, that's appreciated."

"Of course," Mrs. Fitzsimmons said, "I just wanted to let you know."

They were barely out of earshot when Tilly said, "I'll call Ron's office in the morning and figure out what our options are."

And he knew that she would. But what was done was done. His perfect night soiled by *her*.

Raquel

PROVIDENCE • SUMMER 1998

By the time Raquel arrived at the station the next day, she felt like a new woman. Or more accurately, like a better version of her old self. Not herself before the haircut, or before Nick, but a version that existed long before that, even. Raquel before she even got here. One that had not suffered a bruised ego and feelings of deficiency and a debilitating sense of anxiety. One who was not terrified of getting something wrong or missing a step or who held, even loosely, the axiom that she was undeserving. She felt more like the younger Raquel who'd been hungry and curious and eager to get out into the world; who never entertained the fact that she might not be enough for it once she arrived.

She of course attributed this all to Betsaida, who, as she drove with her in Delroy's car across town to her tia's house, gave her the gift of silence. Just put on some music and let Raquel stare out the window and cry to herself. She appreciated Bets's ability to see the depth of her brokenness in that moment but not need to understand it all. It made her feel comfortable and safe. Raquel's mother made limpias a regular part of her life. Indeed, it was in the living room of her preferred santera—a woman in Bushwick—that she met Dolores, who was far more knowledgeable and serious about the faith than her mother ever had been. In some regard, Raquel had looked upon the entire thing—the superstitious beliefs, the ritual, the offerings and giving of money to ladies in random apartments with no vestments or clerical authority—well, it had felt to Raquel low-class. Somewhere in the same neighborhood as scratch-off tickets and selling Amway. She would never say anything, maybe just make a remark or two that her mother should watch herself from being had, but she'd held those thoughts in her heart. But when Betsaida looked at her in the kitchen and told her she needed a limpia, no thought but gratitude crossed her mind.

She had been feeling, she realized on the drive over, out of control. Her childhood and teen years had been a camera lens opening onto the world. Year on year, the aperture widening. But college had thrust her into a new landscape, one that required a completely new lens. She herself had barely been certain of the kind of film she had been making. She had just begun to sort things out; found some kind of truth—a lonely truth, but a truth nonetheless. And suddenly, the film changed again. This time the lens didn't get wider but closed tighter and tighter until the scene was about one actor and one actor only: Nick. The insertion of him in her life—of his proclivities and routines and habits and her desire to affirm and accommodate them—left her feeling unsure, uncertain. Her eagerness to perform—at work, with him—had overwhelmed her. She had lost hold of whatever it was that had been guiding her until now. The last time she felt herself so unmoored, it was food and the removal of it from her life that helped hew her to some sense of control of herself. Until, of course, it didn't. This time, all it had done was leave her thinner. Thinner the way that Nick had preferred.

Betsaida's Titi Jael lived over a coffee shop in Warwick. Despite Betsaida telling her that Titi Jael was her mother's youngest sister, Raquel still found herself surprised by the woman who opened the door. She had expected an old lady who barely spoke English, and instead found in front of her a very attractive, forty-something, well-dressed older version of Betsaida. She worked as a court translator. Her apartment was decorated very stylishly—"*Minus these things my ex-husband didn't take back yet*," she said to Raquel when she complimented the place. The house was empty when they got there, save for the delicious smell of habichuelas that filled the space. "*You're lucky my kids aren't here yet,*" she said, and it was only because Bets had explained that she never had kids but had taken on lots of "godchildren of her faith" that Raquel understood. Jael made Bets a plate of food and sent her out to the living room before she sat Raquel down at her dining-room table. She had an altar set up in a built-in bookcase there, with a Virgin Mary statue and a few other saints Raquel probably once knew but had long since forgotten.

"Yemayá," Jael said to Raquel, watching her look at the altar. "She's my lady."

"I didn't know young people could do this," Raquel said.

"You thought only viejitos could be santeros?" Jael said with a laugh. "Nah, I been studying from my welo since I was a kid. Have you had a limpia before, nena?"

Raquel shook her head no.

"My mom goes all the time though," she said.

"Well, everybody's are a little different, but basically I read your cards to see what's really wrong with you and then I give your spirit a bath—but it's also a literal bath."

"I know what's wrong with me," Raquel said, and Jael sucked her teeth, just the way Bets always did.

"Probably what's wrong with you is that you always think you know what's wrong with you," Jael said. She began shuffling and reshuffling a deck of cards.

Raquel felt butterflies fluttering in her stomach watching the cards being laid out, row after row, no idea of what they meant. She was certain that it would be advice about Nick and love and if she should forgive him or not, but in actuality, romance did not come up at all.

"So," Jael said, very matter-of-factly, as if she was diagnosing a hangnail or pink eye, "you have good intuition, but too often you lead with your brain and not your gut. You've let your confidence be shaken by people who don't deserve to shake your confidence. You've swallowed this idea that there's some people whose approval or validation will fill you, but in the process you've lost your ability to validate yourself. To feel that that's enough. You elevate the position of others by allowing them to use your back as a step, but then are blind to people around you who see your worth. You feel lonely because you have blinders on, not because you are unloved."

"Fuck," Raquel said.

"Fixable," Jael said. "Ellegua says leaving the house is a risk, an adventure. You're in a dark valley, but the point is you come out a lot wiser. You have a lot of gifts and you have a lot of guardians on the other side."

"My abuela died a few years ago," Raquel said.

Jael laid out a few more cards.

"Yeah, she's strong. But there seems like someone else maybe, too? A stranger. Spirits are funny things, who they attach to, who they don't. Better a guardian than a ghost, you know?"

"Is there a difference?" Raquel asked.

"Yeah," Jael said, without elaborating. "The point is, me, this guardian, your wela, we're all just here trying to get you to see your own light, because it's strong enough to guide you."

"Anything else?" she said, hoping for some message about Nick.

"Be more compassionate to your mother. Like all mothers, she just tries her best."

And then Jael took her to a shower and bathed her in eucalyptus water and beat her back with the branches while she uttered an incantation that Raquel couldn't fully make out. She cleansed her with Agua de Florida and rose water and pulled all of the greens and petals and remnants of the bath and put them in a plastic bag with the clothes Raquel had been wearing, which she had cut into shreds, and told Raquel to throw them away in a trash can at least four blocks from her house. She gave her a vela and told her to leave out two glasses of water—one for her wela and one for the stranger. "*To let them know that they are welcome*," she said. "*Whoever they are.*"

As soon as they left, Betsaida asked her how she felt.

"Lighter," she said, "and hungrier."

Betsaida laughed.

"Wait until tonight! You're gonna sleep so good!"

And she did.

In the morning she treated Bets to breakfast before they again got back in Delroy's car, this time to her cousin's hair salon. The girl was,

Raquel thought, a fucking magician. She somehow transformed her haphazard cut into something stylish—including some little highlights. "The grow-out is gonna be a bitch," she warned her, but in that moment, Raquel didn't want to focus on the challenges of the future. She was going to enjoy looking good in the now.

"You were my fairy godmother this weekend," Raquel said on the car ride home.

"It's what friends do, right?" Betsaida said, and Raquel knew the answer was yes but what had she done to earn this level of generosity?

"This was above and beyond," Raquel said.

"Well, hopefully one day you can return the kindness when I need it," Bets said. "The truth is, I just really get it. You fall for someone, you get so into them your whole world shrinks, and suddenly you barely have a life besides them."

She somehow was articulating exactly what had welled up for Raquel once or twice in the salon chair. The shock of the haircut subsiding, it started to dawn on her that her life—the one she had redesigned around Nick—didn't exist anymore.

"But Delroy is dope, you love him."

"You love Nick, right?" Bets said, and looked at her from the corner of her eye. "Delroy *is* dope, mainly, but I think it's all just dumb luck. My father is a dick and my mother's life is miserable because of it, but that's who she fell for. I don't think you can help it—women especially."

At the station, Raquel was surprised at how much more fun being there was without the nagging knowledge that Nick resented her absence; her being away from him.

"If you play "The Boy Is Mine" today, Marcus, I'm gonna fucking scream," she said to him as they were heading into the second half of their show.

"Give the people what they want, Rock."

"Give the people exactly what they can get on Hot 106?" she retorted. He huffed.

"Just *try* one of my songs?" she said. "Playing more independent stuff is going to be what keeps our audience. Makes our hip-hop show distinct."

"You can't dance to it," Marcus said.

"People can absolutely dance to this," she said, riffling through the handful of CDs she'd been trying to push on him for the last two weeks. "Track six. Q-Tip, Mos Def. Totally accessible."

He made a screw face but took the CD nonetheless. When the Total track was over he got on the air.

"All right, we've been digging in the crates over here and Rocky's got something to play for you all. It's off Rawkus Records and it's called "Body Rock." Let us know if you dig it or if you'd rather be singing along with Brandy and Monica."

He hit Play. A few bars in and the phone lines started lighting up; Raquel handled incoming and proceeded to field an abundance of calls from dudes excited to hear "something fresh" on the actual radio. She was stuck with a long-winded caller saluting them for saying no to shiny suit rap when the door to the station opened and Mavette walked in.

"What the fuck!" Raquel screamed and ran up to hug her.

"Does no one check their fucking email?" Mavette said, before she quickly added, "Oh my God, you cut off all your hair."

"A long story about short hair," she said, breathing in Mavette's familiar scent of cloves and her French perfume, only noticing that she'd been crying when they broke from their embrace. "Mavette, what's wrong?"

"Ladies," Marcus said, "we're trying to produce radio over here."

"I walked in on Niles fucking someone else," Mavette said, ignoring him.

"Damn," Marcus said.

Raquel felt a flutter in her stomach. Should she have told her about Astrid and Niles?

"Don't worry, it wasn't Astrid," Mavette said flatly, and when registering the look of surprise on Raquel's face, she added, "I don't know why you always think I don't know anything."

She had a large weekend bag over her shoulder and threw it in a corner, before collapsing into one of the studio's chairs as if she'd hung out there a dozen times before. Marcus hit Play on another track.

"What did you do?" he asked Mavette.

"What do you mean what did I do? I said I was sorry and I closed the door and very quickly walked away. So, I guess he didn't read his email either. Or maybe he did and didn't care."

Her email. Raquel had been in such a state when she had checked her email last, she never remembered to go back and read Mavette's.

"So, what did it say?" she asked.

"Well, now it's almost embarrassing," Mavette said. "Can I smoke in here?"

"No," Marcus and Raquel said in unison.

"Fucking America," Mavette muttered. "The email said that the project was officially over, things had taken a turn for the weird, and I was back to following my heart. That we had flown back early and I was headed here to get back together with Niles and hopefully spend some time with you."

"Fuck," Raquel said.

"Yeah," Mavette said, patting the edges of her eyes to try to stop her tears.

"Ladies. Seriously," Marcus said, and when Raquel mouthed to him not to be a fuckwit, he gave her the finger before he was back on the air. As he talked up their upcoming Labor Day weekend cookout event and other promotions, Mavette continued.

"Anyway, I thought I'd be staying at Niles's place, but now I guess I'll just crash with you. Is that cool?"

For a split second Raquel thought of all the reasons she could say no: that she was tired; that Mavette hadn't completely earned her way out of the doghouse; that she too was nursing a broken heart; that her house was crowded. But then it occurred to her that Mavette could have stayed in a hotel—the Biltmore even—without a second thought. She thought about the blinders Jael told her she was wearing and, removing them for a moment, saw clearly that what Mavette needed was not a place to sleep but a friend. And Raquel said, of course, yes.

* * *

Over dinner at Paragon, where Mavette treated them to a bottle of wine, she explained to Raquel and Marcus how the summer-long experiment of searching for monied romantic prospects ended in dramatic and surprising glory.

"We were supposed to split our time between France, the Vineyard, and the Hamptons, but very quickly we realized that, in fact, if you are looking for young men with generational wealth, it's like shooting fish in a bucket over there—"

"I don't think that's how the saying goes," Marcus added. Mavette just shrugged.

"So, we just kind of kept meeting these different rich Euros and they'd take us dancing or invite us to go out on their boat or to another resort town, and we'd follow."

"Must be nice," Raquel said, reactively, because she immediately thought that it sounded exhausting.

"Anyway, a week ago, we'd been out with this whole crew of rich Germans—"

"The ones you emailed me about? With the boat in Como?"

"No, different rich Germans. Anyway, I was trying to sleep—it was really, really late—but my room was off the common room and there was music playing loud, but more than anything it was the moaning."

"Moaning?" Raquel said.

"You know, *moaning*," Mavette said, before exhaling her cigarette for dramatic effect. "Anyway, I came out—honestly more out of curiosity, but as I got closer, I could hear very clearly that it was Margot, and just as I was about to go back to my room to give her privacy, I heard her calling Claire's name."

"No!"

"What? I thought you were there to find husbands?" Marcus said.

"Well, that's what I thought too! And that's what I said when I walked in there—"

"Wait," Raquel said, "you walked in on them?"

"Of course! They convinced me to break up with a man I was in love with—"

"Who is sleeping with someone else," Marcus interjected.

"Besides the point. They sold me on the stupidity of love and the wisdom of marrying for fiscal and social security, but the whole time they knew they weren't really sacrificing anything, because they had this relationship with each other! I felt duped and I told them so."

Raquel wanted to take a bit of gossipy delight in this tale, but instead it made her feel sad. That they didn't feel they could just be open about how they felt.

"What did they say?" Raquel said.

"Well, then it turned hysterical. Tears. All of it. And, you might not know this about me, but I hate crying. Even when I'm the one doing it. They went on about how they really do believe in marrying for security, and how Margot's father was way too conservative to ever accept her wanting to be with a woman, even if it was Claire. And I told them how they needed to stop being so juvenile and own who they were—"

"That's a bit harsh," Raquel said. "My mother is a grown woman with adult children and she still has a hard time calling her girlfriend her girlfriend."

"Your mother is gay?" Mavette said. "So progressive."

"Just who she is," Raquel said. "Also, she works in the lunchroom at the Met, not as a curator. Just to clarify."

"Oh," Mavette said.

Raquel was done with trying to be someone besides herself.

"Anyway, the point is," Raquel continued, "Margot knows her own parents. She probably has a decent sense of things."

"Well," Mavette said now, a look of guilt washing over her face, "that's the thing. I convinced them both to just go up to their parents and tell them how they feel about each other and not live a lie. And that their parents should be happy that they both found someone so accomplished and smart."

"And?" Marcus said, leaning in, riveted.

"We all flew back to the States and went to Claire's parents' house and it was, as I expected, a nonissue. But when we went out to the Vineyard to Margot's, it was World War Three. Disinheritance, tears, screaming. I've never seen WASPs be so emotional."

"Wow," Raquel said, feeling an alarming amount of sympathy for Margot.

"Anyway, I went back to the city with Claire and literally, by the time we arrived, Margot's mother was on the phone to Claire's mother saying how while they don't approve of lesbians in general, they recognize that Claire is exceptional and from a good family and that they should all get together to discuss it."

"Fuck outta here," Marcus said. "Just like that."

"Just like that," Mavette said. "But you know Claire's father is, like, number two at Goldman Sachs."

"And?"

"Margot's father is the CEO of a telecom firm they'd like to take public."

Marcus and Raquel stared at her blankly.

"So," Mavette said, with exasperation, "at the end of the day, it's a good family merger."

* * *

AFTER MARCUS HEADED back to the city for his second-to-last week at MTV, Raquel, Mavette, and Betsaida split a box of wine and talked late into the night about the science of breakups, about love, politics, of knowing better and not listening to yourself, Anita de Monte and Jack Martin, racism in their departments, sex, and if it mattered and why. When her mother called for their usual Sunday catch-up, Raquel told her about the limpia and then softened the blow of chopping off all of her hair by delivering what she correctly anticipated would be received as a welcome surprise: her breakup with Nick. ("Nena, vales más que el oro.") Later, though, when she got really, really drunk, she told the girls the whole story about what happened. For the rest of her life, only Astrid, Mavette, and Betsaida would know how and why she'd come to have short hair.

* * *

ON MONDAY MORNING, Raquel headed to work early, armed with the Anita de Monte catalog, only to find Belinda Kim already there.

"Oh my gosh, Belinda," Raquel said, abashed at having arrived after her boss. "Let me get you coffee!"

"No, no! Don't worry about it!" Belinda said, waving her in; a cheer and excitement in her voice. "Come over here. I want to show you something."

Once Raquel discovered Anita de Monte—or rather, after Belinda put her on Raquel's radar—a new bond formed between the two women. Raquel had come into work gushing. About how raw and pure her art was. About the way that it made her feel inside. About how she'd thought she was the only person like her—Latin, female—to have ever tried to permeate this world and how dumb she felt now not realizing that there was a whole history of women who had come before her. An entire conversation that she just hadn't been aware of. How foolish she confessed to feeling, for silently assuming no one like her had ever created world-class art simply because no one in the front of a classroom had told her about it. How mad at herself she was for never seeking out Anita or any of the other people whose work had probably been forgotten.

"Be angry at the system, Raquel," Belinda had told her that day, "and then see how you can fix it. I've been very hell-bent on showcasing emerging artists from underseen backgrounds, but I've not paid enough attention to connecting the dots. To correcting this lie that you were taught and that I was taught: that art started with some white guys in ancient Greece and was passed on and made better and better exclusively at the hands of white men. I rejected that narrative, but I haven't done my right part to amend it."

Since then, Belinda Kim had taken Raquel's art historical reeducation to be her personal project. She brought her catalogs featuring Anita de Monte's work, yes. But she also exposed her to works by

Jomar Burgos, Carmen Herrera, Juan Sánchez, and Soraida Martinez, which Raquel took in with pure delight—each artist expanding and reconciling the aesthetics she'd come to value at the Met and at Brown with her sensibilities of home. And she was deeply grateful.

Raquel now eagerly threw her book and bag down and joined Belinda in her office, where she was hovering over an aerial photograph of a walkway.

"I had lunch with Roger the other day. From the Photography Department," Belinda said, focused, "and was just telling him about your enthusiasm for Anita de Monte and he said he was fairly certain he had some of her photos in his collection."

"Really?" Raquel said, astounded, looking at the piece with new interest.

"They shouldn't really be there; they belong here—they're not so much photographs as documentations of a land art piece she did here at RISD. I mean, you won't recognize it. It was on a plot that's the modern gallery now, but take a look. I think we should include it in the figurative show. It's a bit of a stretch—"

But as Raquel looked at it—a piece done in grass, designed around a stone walking path—she could unmistakably delineate the presence of a figure sculpted into the earth, over which Anita had grown grass.

"No," she said, with a confidence that surprised her, "no, I see it very clearly here."

"Yes," Belinda said, "that's how I saw it, but good to see your eyes do too."

They did, in part because she realized that she had seen the figurative shape before. When she was staring at the Spanish exhibition catalog trying to spark her interest in Jack Martin.

Anita

PROVIDENCE • SUMMER 1998

Oh, hello, little baby.

I had, I'm embarrassed to admit, forgotten about this one! Jack, of course, was always getting called to do site-specific commissions. Giant things paid for by municipalities populated by the wealthy. They almost always left everyone scratching their heads and drumming up enraged local headlines about "What IS Art?" and "$600,000 for Bricks?" And it all made Jack delighted because his art was generating controversy and nothing drove up prices more than controversy. But, after the exhibition in Mexico, a small museum in Rhode Island asked me to make a piece on the grounds of the campus that surrounded it. It was such a picturesque kind of place; it reminded me of where she went to school in *Love Story*, you know? And I was inside the museum, looking out a window onto this little pathway, and I saw it clearly as a spine; the grass clearing around it as a tumbling pile of hair, and could imagine the outline for body. Simple clean lines rising up out of the earth, two loooong beautiful curved lines on either side of the path. Mounds of earth that I covered with sod. A woman on the walk. It was subtle and alluring and I wondered often if the students and professors passing would ever notice they were crossing over a woman's back. Almost appreciated that they might not realize it. It felt poetic, since people use women's backs as bridges every day without ever thinking twice.

I heard the crack of names I didn't know from the ceiba, but the feelings: remorse, admiration, righteous anger. Oh, they were good feelings. And there it was! On a big table, being taken out of a box and unwrapped carefully—oh, so tenderly!—in glycine paper. Out! Being seen! By two people, but still! Free! In, I realized, a museum of all places! And then I heard the older woman tell the younger woman that it was going to be put in a show. A fucking show! I would be in the world again. My energy, out there! My vision, visible! If I could have cried, I would have.

I had taken it for granted before—the moments when part of me was able to stay alive. All I could do was rage at what I felt was my right! My right to be seen! But now, after so long, after being buried and buried and buried again, these women were unearthing me! Unearthing me. And I felt, for the first time since I had been dead, joy. Gratitude. With no melancholy. Just the thrill of fucking existence again!

Then I saw the younger girl—oh, she reminded me of my cousin Lupe, her tiny little face and her closely cropped hair because she was always getting into tangles and sand and would play with little boys and bring back lice. The young girl looked like she was going to weep, and I could feel her. I could feel that this meant something to her; it meant something to both of them, but it meant something deep in the girl. I drew closer to her, while she was looking at the piece, because I could sense her thinking.

"I've seen this shape before," she said.

Oh, she couldn't have seen it. Could she?

"Some of her later sculptures, maybe?" the older woman said.

"No, no. I remember because it was . . . strange," she said and she exited the room with an intensity to her stride, was riffling around on a desk. When she came back she was flipping through a catalog. Jack's show at Reina Sofia!

Did she notice? Could it be? Oh, she was just a young girl; a graduate student, maybe? What did it matter, really. And yet it did, it did, it did! I felt myself electric-sizzle, tingle, hair-on-end at the prospect. Could it be that *someone* saw what I'd done? Someone saw *me* there!

Her hands were moving through the pages to the centerfold shot—an overhead image of the fucking ball bearings piece. Oh, how I had driven him crazy with the ball bearings! Mad! Loony! Because I am dead, I am fast! Fast! Fast! Because he's old and living and drinks too much and eats fatty foods, he is slow, slow, slow, and he could not keep up with me there. The exhibition hall was big. Vast. Infinite feeling. And there were thousands of them. Thousands of tiny little ball bearings all cast in different sizes of silver to his very exact, very genius specifications. Each and every one set by him and his genius hands. Set to seem at "random"—chaos, accidents, spills—but in reality meticulously plotted by him to turn the big, hard, vast hall into a place of tiny, careful tedium. (He was always intrigued by the tension of opposites. Perhaps that's why he liked me.) And he would place them and I would move them. And he would place them and I would move them. Again and again and again. Until finally I had created a clearing in the center of the room, a clearing that came in a shape that I just could feeeeel. One that was in my soul. One that was of me. One that was me. The outline of a woman—abstract, of course. An amoeba to some. A body to others. But the girl saw it. She saw it in the photo from his catalog. Oh, that fuck! How I should have had catalogs of my shows! How I should have still been making. Creating. My fucking art!

"I was struggling to find an angle on this thesis that I was passionate about," the young woman said, nearly breathless with excitement, "and then I noticed this image. And it was just so striking because I immediately saw a figure in the void of the ball bearings—"

"I don't think I've ever seen this piece, Raquel," the older woman said, mesmerized.

"The whole show is kind of weird for him," and she began to show the other woman the other pieces—the ones I had fucked with. The pieces I rearranged—quick, quick, quick. Sisyphus, I rendered him.

Yes, I did. He fumed. He cursed. He swore my name into the air and the guards of the museum thought him insane. (Ugh, or worse, bereaved. He was not bereaved.) The show was too big for him to stop me. He could not keep up nor could he stand guard. He would leave from setting up for the night and in the morning I would have had my way with his work. I would have defiled it in his eyes! I would have left my little spiritual fingertips all over each and every piece of metal, of wood, of clay, of stone. Even if just to fuck with him by an inch! But I never thought—never had even hoped in a million years, especially after they buried me—that anyone would see me in there.

The older woman took the catalog from the girl, looked at the dates.

"It's the first big show he did after he killed her."

Yes! Yes! Yes!

"I remember seeing the reviews and thinking, of course he was getting welcomed like the prodigal son over in Europe. We would have been out in the streets if it happened here."

Ah, she was one of the girls! The ones who stood outside of the building and the courtroom. Making Jack miserable. I, of course, liked her immediately.

It was exciting to be in the room; exciting to hear these two strangers appreciate me—my pieces. To hear this older woman miss me. To see this young woman so touched at seeing my work. Up close. So close.

After a bit, the younger woman, seeming very satisfied, went back to her desk, but not before sending my piece—my art!—to the framing department to prepare it for the exhibition. I followed it, the photograph of my land piece, to the framers and sat with it for a bit. And remembered Jack.

If past was prologue, some of my strength would be back. Just the prospect of the auction had enabled me to fuck with a giant exhibition. And yet. I don't know. There were so many feelings around that young girl: feelings that were familiar to me from when I was alive. There was loneliness and heartbreak and restlessness and not knowing if she was understood and also ambition! Oh, the girl throbbed with wild ambition! Of wanting to change things. Of wanting to fuck shit up. And, I don't know. I've got good hunches about things. I decided to stay with her.

It was wild, the two of them! The other woman, Belinda, was a curator. Raquel her assistant, or a grad student or some combination of both. I couldn't figure that out and I'm not sure it matters. But it put a smile on my face; two Third World women in charge of a whole department. Yes, a tiny museum, but still. If a man was in that room, nobody would be talking about me. Pulling my work—my baby—from storage! If it was a white lady in that room, she might care, or be too busy championing this one or that, to understand that it was my brown roots—the ones that went all the way down to the soil of Cuba, that allowed me to be erased. Oh, had I been pretty and blond like towering Ingrid, it's not that he wouldn't have killed me, but the "sisterhood"—that lily-white sisterhood that cared about nothing but themselves, the things that benefited themselves—would never allow me to be forgotten. Discarded! No, the Tillys of the world were complicit in it! Midwives! They burned their bras and then they stopped giving a fuck about anyone's tits but their own.

I went back to the big office. The nice one with a window. I watched Belinda write a note on a thing—I don't know what it is or what it was, but I could read it. There was a box and it said SUBJECT and there I saw her type: Anita de Monte.

My name! I drew closer.

> Ladies,
>
> I have found myself of late reconsidering the forgotten work of Anita de Monte. I've recently discovered that we have documentation of a piece of her land art in our collection. Her estate has been tied up in legal for ages, from what I remember, but I'm curious if any of your museums, like ours, have any of her work in your collections. If so, perhaps we could discuss . . .

I, as you can imagine, liked the sound of this. She was looking for more of my work! Well, I knew all the people who had more of my work! All the places too! On her desk was an address book, and as she typed, I flipped the pages . . . over to S. And there she was! Rory! Rory! She had drawings. Beautiful drawings. Drawings from my wedding book that I'd made with Jack too. I slid the address book over to the center of Belinda's meticulously kept desk. And just like that, when she turned around, she spotted it. Seemed confused that it was out of place, but then, I watched her look at the page. She registered a thought and the feeling that I had from her was determination and "why not!" when I saw her pick up the phone and dial! Coño! I was back!

"Hello, this is Belinda Kim, the curator for contemporary art at the RISD Museum, calling for Rory Simms," she said. "No, she wasn't expecting me to call. Could you tell her that I'm calling about Anita de Monte?"

Oh! Would she call back? Would she call back? I was dying to know! I felt like I was on pins and needles and needles and pins. Rory had always liked me, I thought. Jack told me not to overstate things, that she was likely just being polite, but he didn't understand the bond. The bond of always being the only ones in these all-white rooms. How she would feel she was choking in them sometimes, and how she knew I understood.

The young girl—Raquel—was a hard worker. Trying to stay focused on the task at hand and, I could tell, desperate to keep diving into this Jack Martin mystery at hand. When she left for lunch I stayed behind. Flipped through my own catalog—I'd never actually seen it before and it made me sad and wistful and frustrated and happy—so many of my little ones together. And I remembered every dream that had inspired each piece, each trip to Cuba that sparked an idea, of where I was when I conceived the notion behind each object I'd created. All of them vessels for my spirit, my experiences, my life journey. There was one sculpture I'd remembered them showing. One I thought it was important for the girl to see. I left it open on her chair and waited.

Oh, she was smart as a whip, this one! Smart! Smart! Smart! Had good eyes, as we used to say. She saw it immediately. Looked at it for just a second, and then pulled open Jack's Spanish exhibition catalog and went through, with some determination, until she stopped, and got to the radiant dial piece! That one was more of a struggle! The beams were so heavy. Even for me. I had moved them to that formation because the shape of it pleased me and I knew would annoy him. Even I didn't realize how loud the echo of my own work was.

The subconscious. It is a strange place.

Later, Raquel went to gather her things and say goodbye to her boss.

"Belinda," she said, very confident, "I'm heading out, but I've been thinking about my thesis."

"Jack Martin?"

Pig! Pig! Pig!

"Well, I've been trying to find an angle that I feel passionate about and it's been difficult. I think I found one."

"Want to run it by me?"

"Yes. I'd noticed before you told me about Anita de Monte that there was a gap in his work. And that his work was remarkably different—even just this one time, at this show. Now, it's very clear that the gap was after her death and the trial and that the difference, I believe, was her influence on him."

It was, cariña, more than influence.

"That's bold and risky. Martin's whole thing is—"

"That none of it is about anything. I know. Which is why I wanted to talk to you. I don't think that Professor Temple would be the best adviser for this—"

"I don't know him but, considering what I've heard, no."

"And I'm wondering if you might advise me instead."

* * *

SHE LEFT THE museum ecstatic; the feeling coming off her was joy! Pure joy! Fire! Ambition again, but now with a streak of revenge. She was going to prove someone wrong and I felt the strong desire to help her. And I thought to myself: *yes! Yes! Yes!* And I just remembered looking at her, how passionate about it I had been. About art and my art and what was happening with it and defending it and making it intellectually sound and visually compelling and—oh, the nights we would have, drinking and dancing and fighting! Fighting about what was true and who was a hack and what was fucking bullshit! And we would yell and not speak for days and what the fuck is wrong with conflict sometimes? It makes your brain better!! It makes you fight harder, it makes you more convinced in what you believe and who you are! I could see this young girl had fight in her. And after being so bored for so long, I found this very interesting.

We were walking for a ways when I saw the smile on her face fall and what I felt coming off of her was this: shame, embarrassment, anger, hurt, humiliation. Oh, I knew those feelings well. I knew them so well and I knew before I even saw the person she was looking at that it was heartbreak that had caused them.

He was very handsome and very full of himself. Good-looking, but common. Light eyes that made me feel distrust because they reminded me of Jack and the way he'd looked at me just before he pushed me out the window. But I realized that was silly and prejudiced and you can't hate everyone with light blue eyes just because someone with light blue eyes happened to kill you—I mean, it's a pretty good excuse, but I hate that kind of laziness. No, when I looked in his eyes, what I saw was the most dangerous thing of all in a man: insecurity. Because they will crawl over and push down anyone around them in their desperate thrashing to find themselves comfortably affirmed at the top.

There were tears and he was sobbing and then she was crying and screaming about feeling humiliated and trusting him and pronouncements of how he was only trying to help. Always, always, "trying to help." Then, I'm sorries and pleas of I love you . . . and more tears. More tears. And he tried to kiss her and she pushed him away, and he screamed on the street about how he would do whatever it took to win her back. And it's so funny how, even when it isn't your life, you can see the pattern. The same story again and again and again. How he diminishes her and she gets furious and then she leaves and then he chases and she wants to feel like she matters to someone and so she takes him back. And from him I felt the longing, the longing to keep her; half as a person and half as an object. An object he didn't want to lose. (Boys hate to lose their toys.) And I knew then, from the feelings of fear radiating from him, how one day he would grow up and these insecurities in his young heart would become entrenched. And how her loneliness would never be abated by him, just exacerbated. And how because of this it would escalate until he would humiliate her and she would get furious and at some point he would feel indignant over her fury! Do something so terrible she would have to leave, and then he would chase and she'd want to feel like she mattered to someone and so she would take him back.

And my heart couldn't take it. Could not take someone else living through that. Dying through that. And I didn't know what to do and so I pushed him—so hard—and he ran into her and she stumbled back and dropped her bag and her books—my book, Jack's book, her notebook—slid out and they went to pick up her things and for a second I thought I was going to make it worse and not better, because I saw her soften and I saw her get choked up again and I thought he was going to kiss her and she was going to dissolve, the way we so often do.

The way we so often do.

"If you want me to consider giving you another chance, you can't stay at Tilly Barber."

What? Was I hearing things? What did Tilly have to do with these children?

"I don't understand."

"You said you would do anything to get me back. And I'm telling you I don't want you represented by that gallery."

Oh my God, he's an artist too. I should have hit him harder.

"That's ludicrous," he said.

"The thing your mother told us about? Jack Martin throwing his wife out the window? She made the joke about Frida Kahlo—?"

"She was just drunk when she said it."

"She's a fucking racist."

"My mother loves you!"

"And that means she isn't a bigot?" she said.

There was a silence between them for a moment before she said,

"If you won't leave Tilly, there's nothing else to say. As far as I'm concerned, Tilly Barber has made money off a murderer for the past thirteen years."

You don't know the half of it, I thought.

"What does that have to do with me?" he said, and I could see the snot starting to come from his little nose. Oh, she probably doesn't realize that he's just a boy. Just really a boy.

"You keep talking about building a life together. I don't want a life with someone who isn't bothered by that. I don't want someone who doesn't care that a woman was murdered by her husband and everyone looked the other way so they could keep making money off of him. So that they could keep their fake fucking world in place."

I was riveted. Transfixed. He was wailing like a kindergartner now. I felt badly for him.

Except that I didn't. Not in the least.

"I can't leave Tilly, Raquel, because my mother pulled every string she could to get her to represent me," he eventually said. "She's a friend of my mom's from a long time ago; she couldn't say no."

He was really sobbing now, actually. Now I understood the insecurity.

"You and my mom are the only ones who believe in me, Raquel. I can't lose you."

And he had the nerve to seek comfort from her. To lean in and ask for something to which—I surely felt—he had no right. Not this snotty-nosed boy! But instead of pulling him in, she pushed him away. Put out her fucking hand and stopped him and she looked—oh, not sad. She looked pissed. I saw spit and venom in her eye and I knew this look! I knew this fucking look!

"You've been so obsessed with 'helping' me and you actually have no idea how to help yourself."

And then she walked away.

Raquel

PROVIDENCE • FALL 1998

The morning was when Raquel missed him the most. In the haze of sleep and before rational thoughts and recollections could flood out her dreams. The absence of warm breath on her neck, of leg hair against her smooth skin, of his hand grasping her waist. It always took a second to realize the void of his body next to her, to recognize the room she awoke in was her own, and a pit of sadness would churn like acid in her stomach, scream to her brain that no one else would love her the way that he did. That no one would want her the way he did. No one would make her feel so chosen and special. It came in waves, like morning sickness: cresting and drowning her and then subsiding. Eventually, she would lie there and remember there was more to her life than Nick. That missing was normal, that missing was part of the process. That missing, as her mother had reminded her, did not mean mistake.

And then she would remember all that she wanted to accomplish. And she would feel a sense of purpose and determination that would pull her out of bed. It blossomed into excitement by the time she was in the shower; an eagerness to devour as much of the day before her as she could.

And then the wave would crest again. When she would check her email and wish that there was one from him. When she would hear a particular song come on or pass a certain corner.

It was, she knew, for the best. When she saw him the first time after the night of the haircut, her heart cut to anger. Until he began to cry. And she realized in that moment that though her initial attraction to him was the pull of all that he seemed to see in her, what kept her—what made her feel "important"—was how much he needed her. To tell him that he was good. To tell him that his work was good. She realized that she had felt dispensable here at this university. A background actor in a film about other people, and he had made her central. Important. Accountable.

But at what cost?

Deep down, even though she was, if not growing to not love her short hair, but to at least appreciate her own face and the prettiness of it without the frame of her tresses, she felt he had wanted to make her ugly. Or feel ugly. She began to believe he wanted to hobble her at the knees, make her feel grateful for his love. She didn't think it immediately, but in the two weeks since she'd seen him last, in the moments after the wave subsided, she found herself replaying all the occasions when he'd made her feel less-than. The way he had spoken of and to her family. Consciously or not, all of it was to make her feel that, yes, she was special, but that *only* he could see her that way. She began to feel that by playing up her insecurities he made himself feel more secure. Oh, how right Toni had been that she'd seen him as a prize! Now, she began to see him as a scared person. Frightened of being left, of not being in control, of not being good enough. And she realized that, yes, while she was often anxious about falling short in her life, she was not a person who was scared. Not to stand on her own. To leave home, to chase ambitions, to endure solitude in pursuit of a different future. One without a net.

She threw out the Tilly Barber thing on a lark; had no intention of making that a condition of getting back together. Was surprised at her own self for uttering it in the first place. But maybe it was because she knew that he would never do it. Had the knee-jerk inclination that when given a choice of the right or wrong thing to do, he wouldn't have the courage to choose correctly. Not if it held a cost for him.

Of course, that the cost was higher because it would involve him betting on himself, cultivating his art, improving himself and his work and not just leaning—out of fear—into whatever connections his mother had or bought for him? Well, that just made it clearer to her. Yes, she longed for him, but she clung to this knowledge when the waves of missing threatened to wash her away and back toward him.

Not that she didn't have her weak moments. The one email she tried to send to him—to tell him how lonely she felt without him in the mornings—bounced back to her. They'd emailed a million times before but somehow she'd put an extra letter in his first name. She checked her answering machine and heard the start of "Hyperballad"—knew it must be him calling—but then the tape fast-forwarded and ate itself and since she wasn't completely sure it was him, decided to just let it go. Astrid begrudgingly handed her a note from him to her at work. She slipped it in her notebook to read when she was alone only to be unable to find it later. Raquel wasn't a superstitious person, but she started to wonder if it was some kind of sign. Because really, when she stopped herself and thought about it, what more could he have to say? Sorry? For the hair? For the intention behind the hair? For the trust he broke? For not being half the person that maybe (just maybe) she actually was?

She missed him, but hoped—was assured by Betsaida, by her mother, by Toni, by drunken Mavette, drowning in the sea of her own regrets and semipermanently parked on Raquel's sofa—that in time it would pass.

* * *

John Temple's reply to her email had been terse. He informed Raquel that he was traveling and wouldn't be available until just after Labor Day when he offered her exactly one time slot to come by his office and discuss her "personal concern." Raquel replied that she would be there. And though her internship had ended, and the part-time position Belinda had wrangled for her to continue assisting her in the fall had not yet begun, Raquel was sure to dress to be taken seriously. While normally she would have cribbed and taken notes and made sure she had her facts and dates and critical references cited, she had immersed herself so fully in Jack Martin all summer, and Anita de Monte these last few weeks, that she felt confident about her points. Also, some things were much less about academics and much more a matter of principle.

John Temple's office door was open and Raquel eschewed her usual rigid politeness of waiting to be acknowledged and announced herself as she walked in.

"Hi, Professor Temple," she said, taking her customary seat. She noticed for the first time how the room smelled faintly like stale cigarettes.

"Raquel!" he said, surprise in his voice.

"You said two, right?" before she realized that it wasn't she who had surprised him, but this iteration of her. She gestured toward her hair. "It's been a summer of change."

"I can see that," he said, the normal warmth absent from his voice. She had expected him to make conversation with her about her fellowship and the summer at the museum, but instead he just got right to the heart of the matter. "Well, I suppose we should discuss your email."

"Jack Martin, yes."

"What should I say?" he said, not bothering to hide his annoyance. "The simplest answer is that he was found innocent in a court trial and that it wasn't relevant to his art-making nor does it take away from his genius or importance, so why would it be relevant to mention in class?"

She had anticipated him saying some version of this.

"Why does it matter that van Gogh cut his ear off, or that Kandinsky was spiritual, or that Lautrec was practically a dwarf, ostracized by his family, or that—"

"Because it was relevant to the way that they saw the world and therefore their work—"

"Chuck Close is in a wheelchair," she interjected, "and has said it's had no effect on the trajectory of his work, but you mentioned it in your lectures anyway."

"Well, that is a matter of opinion," John Temple said. "Artists are the most notorious liars about their intentions—"

"Except Jack Martin?" she said, and she struggled to manage her breathing to keep her voice as flat as possible. To establish a barrier to keep passion from seeping into the vibrato.

"His work has remained consistent and part of the same conversation for decades," John Temple replied, "so even if he's totally full of shit about it being about nothing, it didn't suddenly become about grieving his wife."

She grimaced visibly at his putting it that way. As if Martin was a poor old widower. As if, as she'd read in multiple accounts of the aftermath, he didn't bring his lover to Anita's memorial! As if he hadn't waited hours—hours—to call the cops. She didn't want to make this about a tabloid story though. She wanted to keep it to what John Temple cared about: Jack Martin's work.

"What if I don't agree with that?" she said. She went into her bag and pulled out not the full catalogs but just two photocopies. One of the ball bearings piece at the Reina Sofia and the other of one of Anita de Monte's sculptures done in the caves of Cuba. She handed them to him.

"Fine, perhaps he was influenced by the primitive. He was very interested in Neolithic—"

"No, no, no," Raquel said, shaking her head and now actually unable to mask her emotions about the matter. Because he was doing it again—removing her from the story. Removing her from the history. "This is Cuban. And it isn't some primitive sculpture. This is Anita de Monte. From 1981."

And she could see by the look on his face that he had never seen it before. Was barely familiar with her work. That she hadn't even seemed important enough for him to familiarize himself with. Because she had nothing in common with him. She was an inconvenient blip in his ability to cement his idol's place in the canon.

"I want to write my thesis about how Anita de Monte's art, for a brief period following her death, influenced Jack Martin."

"I hate to burst your bubble, Raquel, but I just don't think there's the scholarship out there to support this."

"Then I'll make it."

"What do you mean?"

"In my opinion, which I understand is completely subjective, it's morally wrong to be teaching Jack Martin while omitting the inherently negative impact he had on the trajectory of art history—"

"She was a minor artist."

"Like I said, this is an opinion," Raquel continued. "But I think it's also ethically wrong, as an educator and as an institution, to lionize someone as a genius and not tell us that he's a perpetrator of domestic violence."

"Should we stop teaching Jack Martin because he had a tendency to fight with his wife?" John Temple said with a laugh. "Because we'd have to throw out Pollock and about half the curriculum too."

"Please don't put words in my mouth," she said. "That would be ridiculous. But the same way that you acknowledge that Balthus's paintings are questionable—"

"Because that's plain as day. The man paints nothing but lewd girls."

"And also obscures his biography," Raquel said. "The same way you insert relevant biographical details about these other artists—somewhere, at some time, you should present that information about Jack Martin."

She did not want to begin to debate with him about how the sheer reliance on hypermasculine materials might be a nod to the same sort of machismo associated with abusive partners (thank you, Betsaida).

"So, that's your opinion on my curriculum," he said. "And what about your thesis?"

"I told you. I want to investigate the influence of Anita de Monte on Jack Martin's art. Specifically in the period after her murder. If I can create the scholarship that ties her work to his body of work, well, she won't be able to be forgotten anymore. Not here or anywhere else."

Now she watched him grimace.

"This is exactly what I was trying to warn you about in the spring, Raquel. Getting all wound up in this identity politics. It's just poisoning the well—"

"Then what am I doing here?" she said, unable to contain her emotions any longer. "Why am I here? Did the school just let me in to fill a quota and make everyone feel better for being so open-minded? Am I supposed to just churn out the same thoughts as everyone else? To worship the same gods you did? I'm told time and again that my culture, my background, aren't worthy of study or time. Was I supposed to come here and pretend to have had the same life you did? Parrot the same opinions? The same perspectives? Or am I here to fucking change things? Because otherwise, what was the point of the whole thing—of letting me in, letting us all in? To just put out more tanned versions of all the other people coming in and out of those gates every four years?"

She knew it was wrong to curse. To get emotional. She knew that was bad as a woman. As a Latina woman. As a poor woman. That what she knew was passion, he would see as inferior upbringing or inarticulateness or anger management issues. And yet she did not care. She was angry. And hurt. Hurt that time and again—with Bearden, with Betty Sayre, with her independent study—she had been seeking. Seeking sovereignty with someone—anyone—that she encountered in the classroom; in this building. In any of her classes. Someone who validated her place there; who didn't just make it seem like she was the first person of her kind to invent fire, let in from some sort of performative nod about "reflecting America." All she had been seeking was what he himself had found in Jack Martin: someone who helped her make sense of the world. And that world was shaped by being a fatherless Toro, descended from a homeland she barely knew, left largely alone to make her way through this vast white landscape. And all this time, while he reminded her she was Latin while also reminding her it didn't matter, he was hiding the knowledge that a woman like her had existed. In fact, she realized, her Latin-ness mattered so little, it could allow you to be wiped clear from history. She had idolized John Temple, sat in awe of his genius. And now she saw him as selfish and self-indulgent. And so she didn't care how he saw her.

Then John Temple surprised her.

"I don't know the answer to that, Raquel," John Temple said. He picked up his Dunhills and she prayed he wouldn't ask her for another fucking smoke. "I think when I was a kid, all I thought about was rebelling against 'The Man,' you know. I never thought I'd become him."

"Belinda Kim has said she's willing to advise my thesis. I would need your permission since she's not faculty."

"I'm open to still advising you," he said.

"I appreciate that," she said, with no hesitation at all, "but I think Belinda's familiarity with de Monte's work will just make it a better fit."

"Understood," he said. "You have my blessing."

She rose.

"Thank you for your time," she said.

"Thank you, Raquel, for your honesty," he replied.

She felt very much that he meant it.

Jack

NEW YORK CITY • WINTER 1999

"Well, why don't you tell us what you have in mind," Tilly said, "because Jack's had a zillion retrospectives and they are a tremendous undertaking for him physically."

He hated when she spoke about him this way. As if he were an invalid. Yes, since his stroke, things had been harder for him physically. But mentally, creatively, he was as sharp as ever. It did help, he would admit, that he had Ingrid with him. Loyal, sweet Ingrid. All these years later, hearing about his illness and rushing to the hospital. Helping him convalesce. Helping him return to himself.

He hadn't shown in a year when the DIAL Center—one of the largest and most prestigious outdoor art centers—called, requesting a meeting.

"Well, of course," said Dan, the director of DIAL, a foppish Brit in his forties. "We are very aware that Mr. Martin was an important but sometimes forgotten figure in the land art movement."

Oh, Bobby Smithson!! That fucker! How he had hijacked the whole scene. How he discounted all that Jack had done. And then disappeared. Not everyone has the longevity that he's managed to have.

"I appreciate that," Jack said, with his best ability. The stroke had left him with not exactly the same speech capability as before.

"We want to give Jack Martin the largest exhibition of outdoor land art and minimalist sculpture that's ever been staged. New works, re-creations. All of it. And we've already partnered with two world-class institutions—outside of Zurich and Johannesburg—that want to take it on as a traveling show. Jack Martin with no confines of scale beyond what God has given him."

There was a delicious pause as Jack savored this. The old ambrosial scent of being appreciated alongside the wet, electric prospect of the new. The big. The important.

"Yes," he said, emphatically. "Fuck yes."

A beeping noise began to go off and the eagerness dropped from his face as Ingrid emerged from the kitchen.

"Apologies," she said to the others, and handed him a water glass and three pills. One by one, with such loving care. Oh, how he hated the pills but how he loved that she'd come back. He took them all at once, slammed the water quickly. Shoved the glass back to her swiftly so that this moment of sad humiliation—aging in public—could be over.

"Well," Dan said, "we're thrilled and of course we'll do a full catalog, with introductory essays and scholarship and perhaps even a preface written by you."

"Oh, never," he said, despite the idea intriguing him. "I'm a poet, not a prose writer."

"Well, perhaps a new poem then."

"Let's have some champagne!" Jack said. "And we can talk word sculptures."

"Jack," Tilly said, rigidity in her voice. He was meant to be curbing his drinking and that made him feel old and he did not want to feel old right now. He called out to Ingrid to bring them some Perrier-Jouët.

A bottle was popped, glasses were poured, and a toast was made to Jack's health and his long and brilliant career. Jack smiled as he raised the glass, but as he took the flute to his lips, his buttocks clenched, the nerve running up his back tingling all the way up to his goose-fleshed neck. The glass, seconds before heavy crystal in his hands, was suddenly weightless. Held no longer by his fingers, but controlled by another force altogether. A force that turned the stem of the glass up, up, up. Faster and faster until the champagne spilled from the mouth of the glass, past his lips, dribbling down his chin and onto his lap completely.

And just as quickly, whatever had seized hold of the glass let it go and the flute fell down, with a laden thud, onto his Turkish rug.

"Oh, Jack," Ingrid exclaimed, staring at his wet lap, unable to hide her pity. He could hear the fuss of rushing for a towel and embarrassed declarations about this sort of thing happening now and again since his stroke. All the kinds of vexing comments that normally would have made him storm and charge like a bull. But now, he just stared straight ahead. His focus solely on trying, desperately, to ignore the specter of bruised and mangled Anita hovering in front of his chair with her shit-eating grin.

Raquel

PROVIDENCE • SPRING 1999

"It's my particular pleasure to introduce our last honors thesis presentation for the evening," John Temple said to the lecture hall full of parents and faculty and curious classmates. Raquel, seated in the front row beside Astrid and the other honors graduates of the department, took a very deep breath. Astrid, done with her talk about geisha in woodblock prints, gave her hand a tight squeeze. She had decided she was going to do this talk just as if she was speaking to her mother—which, in a way, she was. Her strength, John Temple had once said, was her ability to make the seemingly obscure quite clear. She didn't want nerves to mangle that skill.

"Raquel Toro's honors thesis, 'Form and Figure: Revisiting Jack Martin and Anita de Monte,' is not only the recipient of the Department Chair's Prize; its findings will soon be a feature story for *Art in America*, coauthored by Raquel's adviser, Dr. Belinda Kim of the RISD Museum, where Raquel was a fellow and the assistant curator of the upcoming exhibition, *Excavating Anita*, the first show of de Monte's work comprised entirely of pieces on loan from museum collections. Please welcome Raquel Toro."

And while the rest of the audience broke out into polite applause, Raquel took great pleasure that those in her row—Toni, her mother, and Dolores—were raucous. Stood and whooped and shouted "Rocky!" as she ascended to the stage; the last reminder she needed that the best way to do this was to just be herself.

"Thank you everyone for coming," she said as the lights dimmed. "First slide, please. I'd venture to guess that most of you, if not intimately familiar, would likely recognize a Jack Martin sculpture if you saw one. He is perhaps the most celebrated living artist in the world; known as much for his ethos of art being about nothing as he is for his art itself. But I suspect many of you, like I was, are less familiar with the art of his wife, Anita de Monte. Next slide, please."

What pleased her the most, when it was over and everyone had spilled into the lobby for the departmental reception, was not so much the attention that she received but the conversations that she was hearing. A room full of people talking about Anita de Monte. Her death, yes, but also her art. Her life. His life. A life that for decades everyone was told had no impact on what he made. And now, here people were, openly questioning that. Sure, it was just fifty or sixty people, but even that small number meant something.

"Nena," her mother said, "that was better than a telenovela. It had everything—art, love, heartbreak."

"It would make a great play," Toni said. "Obviously, I wanna play Anita."

"Obviously," Raquel said, rolling her eyes.

"Raquel," John Temple said as he approached them, champagne flute in hand. "A toast to a marvelous job and a marvelous year!"

Raquel could see that it was genuine; met his flute with hers.

"Thanks so much. I was nervous," she admitted, before turning to introductions. "John, this is my sister, Toni; and mom, Irma; and her girlfriend, Dolores."

Raquel could see her mother blush slightly and saw her sister squeeze her mom's shoulder, reassuringly.

This was their first big family outing together and Toni and Raquel had worked hard convincing their mother that the only person self-conscious about this whole thing was her. Especially now that Toni was moving out to be closer to her auditions and their mom was moving in with Dolores. "*It would be mad rude not to invite her*," Raquel had said.

"You work at the Met!" John Temple said to her mother, pleased with himself for remembering.

"For now," she said, nonplussed. "I'm trying to make a career change. I'm hoping Raquel will be the one working at the Met someday."

Toni might have found Dolores boring and materialistic, but she had promised to support their mother while she finished her nursing degree full-time if she wanted, and Raquel and her sister both were pleased to see their mother being the one taken care of for once. To see that she wasn't being left alone by her daughters but left to begin a new life for herself.

"If she wants, I suspect Raquel could be running the Met one day," John Temple said, despite knowing that, for now at least, she had a different plan. Though he and Belinda Kim had eagerly volunteered to write her letters of recommendation for graduate school or to get her a job in a gallery, she had taken a chance on her own. After their piece about Anita de Monte was accepted by *Art in America*, the editor—impressed that this was based on findings of an undergraduate paper—asked what her plans were going forward. On a lark she said she'd love the chance to write for his magazine and, right there on the spot, he offered her an entry-level position. The pay was shit, but they promised to send her to all the art fairs.

"Like I told Belinda," Raquel said, "grad school will always be there if that ends up being the right path."

This wasn't just some rote thing that she said to placate her professors either. After year upon year of fear that the slightest misstep might derail her prospects for the future, or undo all of the work and commitment she had already put into thinking about her life, these last months taught her that nothing was yet set in stone. There were always second chances and unexpected opportunities, and if you were willing to stay open to them, new ways of seeing things.

* * *

"ALL RIGHT, THAT'S the last of it," Raquel said as she set down the shopping bags from the Ikea and Bed, Bath & Beyond run she'd just done with Julian. "How's the stereo coming?"

"Almost there," Marcus said from behind the TV table. He'd been determined to sync their stereo and speakers for as close as they could get to "surround sound" in their new place—which was half the size of their Providence spot and twice the rent. But, it was in Brooklyn. The day they got the keys, Raquel opened the windows to let some fresh air in and Marcus stopped her. "*Listen*," he'd said. The apartment was on the second floor of a side street in Clinton Hill and she could hear kids playing outside, a Mister Softee jingle, Lauryn Hill blasting from a car stereo, *and* a bolero coming from a window across the street. Noisy as fuck. "*We're finally home*," Marcus said, and smiled.

Between her loans and the rent, this would probably be a stretch—at least for now. But she wanted to give her mom and Dolores space, Marcus made for a good roommate, and it felt good to try to make it on her own.

Julian had moved to New York too; got a loft in Bushwick with some friends from RISD and had a grand plan of supplementing his studio assistant money by DJing parties there on the weekends. Raquel was skeptical of how successful this endeavor would be, but happy that he was relatively close. His friendship her senior year had surprised her. Evolved from trading mixtapes to catching movies together to things like today—driving them to Ikea and getting random shit for their new cribs. They were, she realized, more than friends. They'd kissed once—it had been lovely and nice and full of warm feelings—but Raquel kept it at that. She wanted to take it slow. Give them each some space to figure life out on their own as adults before diving into an existence together.

"Something came for you," Marcus said. "It's on the table. A messenger dropped it off."

"A messenger?" Raquel said, befuddled.

There, on their secondhand kitchen table sat a large flat package wrapped in brown paper, a thick creamy envelope taped to the outside with *R. Toro* written in a very precise cursive. Inside was a flat card with LFM engraved in navy ink at the top.

Raquel,

At Nicholas's request, please accept the enclosed as a gift. It holds very little value to me and, from what I understand, is of great importance to you. As you know, I have a very hard time refusing my son.

Sincerely,
Linda M. Fitzsimmons

Raquel's heart started fluttering in her chest, her pulse quickened. A hot flush came upon her and she wasn't sure if it was at the memory of Nick or his mother or the sense of fear she felt hearing from them after she had firmly placed them behind a wall called her past; a section of her mind she didn't like to visit very much.

"It's from Nick," she called out, heard her own voice wavering.

"What?" Marcus said, coming in from the living room.

She realized she was shaking. Shaking from anxiety of what *they* could possibly have that she would want. She had decided a year ago that the answer to that was nothing.

"Well, from his mother. Of course. I'm going to throw it—"

"Open it before you decide that."

"I don't want anything from them."

Marcus was reading the note.

"If you don't want to open it, I will," he said. "She's saying right here it isn't a thing to her—"

Raquel pushed him away; ripped off the brown paper, which revealed a gray linen box.

"Maybe it's his way of saying he's sorry," Marcus offered.

Raquel pulled the lid off the top and peeled back several layers of tissue and then let out a small gasp. There, wrapped in a clear photography sleeve, was Anita de Monte. It was an image Raquel had only seen once before—in an auction catalog—but she recognized it immediately. Anita de Monte. Naked and concealed in the earth but noticeable still by the mounds and mounds of wildflowers that grew from her breasts and eyes and pubis and legs. It was from her Iowa work; from her very first show in New York. When she'd come, raw and fresh-eyed and hungry for all of life that was before her. Charging through any door she could find, no matter if it was open to her or not. Anita de Monte, before she ever even knew Jack Martin. And Raquel felt, emanating from the box—from the image—the pure, wild energy of that woman. Felt it leap out as much as if Anita herself had been there.

She looked at the note and remembered what Nick had told Astrid that one time: that she was beautiful and deserved beautiful things. Raquel exhaled as she realized that, for the first time ever, she believed that for herself. And though by this point she'd been up close to many of Anita's works, she felt tears in her eyes as she realized that this one—this one now before her—would not go back into a vault or get shipped back to a lending institution, but would be here with her. In her shitty little Brooklyn walk-up and every place she moved to after that. That she could commune with its beauty and that ferocious, vital energy every day and remind herself that she was not the first to walk this path, nor would she be the last. Nor would either of them be forgotten.

Anita

NEW YORK CITY • SPRING 2000

If it wasn't for what happened later, everyone would have forgotten that night entirely. Not just because all of Tilly's parties are the same, but also because everyone had gotten so fucking old! Fourteen years seems like nothing, but especially when you are frozen in time. It was jarring to see how the wrinkles had ravaged faces, how bodies had gone to pot. Nobody more than Jack.

The Sun Ra had been replaced by Miles Davis. There were still not enough hors d'oeuvres. The young artists were fewer and farther between and the gallerists, who used to seem like renegades and pioneers, now looked like stockbrokers. Oh, it was a room full of rich fat cats. Nary a brown speck in sight. How quickly we lose traction.

And so the party was normal. Boring. And, as I always used to, I decided to make it a bit more lively. Because, why not? I was powerful again. Big and powerful. Raquel had helped me with that: little by little everything began to come back. My work, my name, my art! Oh, my babies! And also, my power. So I had run up, up, up to the ceiba and down into Tilly's apartment. Tilly never played fun music. When no one was looking, I changed the CD on the radio. It felt like a good night for "Graceland."

Oh, how la sueca gigante dropped her glass as soon as she heard it! Let out a little scream. Grabbed her purse and said, "*No, Jack!*

No!" Ran for the door. The whole party stopped, everyone stared. It was just Paul Simon. A classic now! Tilly yelled for someone to shut it off, but I kept turning it louder and louder. Who didn't love "Graceland"?

Jack. Jack did not like "Graceland" one bit. He started to move toward the little galley kitchen. Slowly. Very slowly. Not to be noticed, but because he could not be like me anymore—*Fast! Fast! Fast!*—before he could make it there, I was back! Flying, flying, flying through the apartment! My wingspan wider than ever.

Swooop!

Swooop!

Swooop!

The guests were all screaming and ducking for cover! People were rushing to the door!

But Jack could not rush. Jack could not run. Jack knew who the bat was coming for.

"Tilly!" he screamed, but Tilly was hiding under her piano. Tilly knew what was up.

Swooop!

Swooop!

Swooop!

Oh, yes! We're bouncing into Graceland!

Guests were squeezing into the freight elevator; Jack pushing his way out of the loft.

Swoooooop!

I hovered in front of his face. Smiled a little bit. He swatted me away and I battered his bloated, red-veined face with my powerful wings!

He ran toward the staircase, desperate to escape me.

I have a reason to believe you'll be received in Graceland.

Such a long flight of steel cast stairs. Just a touch. A shove with the tip of my wing. No more than a bully's push at a playground. That's all it would take. All it would take for him to have an "accident." Just like mine. And I swept up into the air, ready to nose-dive into him with all my might! So much might!

And then . . .

. . . I flew away.

I was tired of it, you see. Seven years in real life; twice that since I was dead: all of it the same. This same cycle of two people determined to make each other miserable. Two people drawn to each other because of magic and creation and art and who were pulled apart by so many things that were not that. I couldn't push him. Because once there was so much love there.

And because, well, since my work was back in the world, I guess I've just been a lot less pissed off.

After that, I was pretty much done with the haunting. How much vengeance could one person have? Don't get me wrong. There is nothing like being alive. Nothing like your lungs expanding in your chest to grasp air to scream your feelings out into the open. Nothing like blood pumping into your brain and churning out in the form of an idea! An inspiration! An action! Oh, to feel the hotness of passion flooding your groin; your legs wrap around the body of another. Even heartbreak! Even the pain of your heart shattering is something to be missed, because it comes with strength! Of picking yourself off the fucking floor because you can. So yes, what I wouldn't give to still be alive. To still need to breathe. In and out and out and in. But. I'm happier now. Now that I'm not forgotten. Now that I can fly again among the ceiba trees, see the other artists. Visit my sister, who is busier than ever, dealing with requests from my estate. I talk to my niece. I see Jomar, whose career has really blossomed. Sometimes I even visit Tilly, who still curses me out, but I swear these days she seems almost grateful for the company. And, of course, I take care of my Raquel. Life's never simple for women like us—women who won't just get with the program; women whose minds and mouths race faster than the world can keep up with. So I do what I can with the tiny tools in my toolbox to make it a little easier. And sometimes, when I am feeling particularly grateful and tender for her helping bring my babies back—energy!—well, sometimes I fly past her apartment in New York and bring her a little mouse.

ACKNOWLEDGMENTS

I start with my mother-sister-friend, Mayra Castillo, who is busy running the world and somehow makes time to read everything I write and who, above all, is a bestie, not a yestie, and was quick to tell me that the earliest draft of this book "was not right." And to Yelena Gitlin Nesbit, who continues to be my greatest fan and champion and friend and reader and whose enthusiasm and support give me so much artistic courage.

The journey to this book was a process. I'm overwhelmed with gratitude to have my amazing agent and friend Mollie Glick in my corner, as both a champion of my art and of me. Without the brilliant Megan Lynch, my editor, this work would not be what it is. Not only because of her tremendous guidance, but for providing me artistic space to also let the story discover itself. She is never afraid of weird, and her fearlessness makes me more fearless.

You are only as good as your team, and the orishas blessed me with a great one. Dana Spector, who consoled me through some of the darker parts of this writing process. Christina Chou, whose enthusiasm for this conceit convinced me to stick with it. André Des Rochers, who reminds me always to bet on me. Jamie Stockton, Melissa Breaux, and Jill McElroy—for their very early insights that helped get this ship on track. And, of course, Melissa Martínez-Raga—who is a dazzling and brilliant angel on earth who fiercely protects my time. Thank you for supporting the writing of this book with wonderful sensitivity (while also supporting the promotion of my first!). I am so fortunate to have you spending this stretch of your life with me.

Thank you to everyone at Flatiron Books—the best team to bring a book into the world with—I am grateful. Nadxieli Nieto, Kukuwa Ashun, Marlena Bittner, Claire McLaughlin, Katherine Turro, Nancy Trypuc, and all the wonderful humans who do the unseen work it takes to bring this book into light.

Love always to my fam: Sharon Ingram, Marcy Blum, Aja Baxter, Destin Coleman, De'Ara Balenger, and Indira Goris for keeping me sane and loved and cared for. Much love too to Alex Rosado, Kendra and Diallobe Johnson, Paola Ramos, Walt Brown, Yohance Bowden, Brandon and Iman Nelson, and Ian Niles.

I'm always grateful for my teachers, but in this particular case, extra gratitude for having had the chance to study, even briefly, with Kevin Brockmeier, who showed me that words can make other worlds. And Sam Chang, for her invaluable novel workshop—I still feel blessed for the divine timing of that experience. My time at Brown was defined by Professor Emeritus Maggie Bickford and the late Kermit Champa, who—in very different ways—gifted me with a love of art history and a sense of support that has stayed with me decades later. (Who says you don't use your major?!) At my beloved Edward R. Murrow, Scott Martin taught more than drama; he taught humanity. I use it every day.

I can imagine a lot of things in this world, except going to college anywhere but Brown—the exploratory place a curious young person can come of age—in the city of Providence, a home away from home for me. I am #evertrue. Just a handful of the people of whom I hold dear memories from this time: Celeste Perri, Heather Ortiz, Steven Colon, Lili Polo, Daphnée Saget Woodley, Catherine Maple-Brown, Carmen Vargas, Alegre Rodriguez, Jason Hairy Marsh, Malik Robinson, Phillip Contic, Mercedes Domenech, Karen McLaurin (for making the TWC home), Russell Malbrough, Dante Williams, Garfield Davidson, Arden Lewis, Lorna Gilbert, and everyone at 360 for memories that have outlasted my (very bad) free tattoo.

Thank you, Alfonso Gomez-Rejon, for being a part of this journey, not least for your corny text joke that triggered a memory, which led to a recollection, which sparked a crazy idea for a book. . . . Other artists and humans for whom I am grateful and inspired by: Teresita Fernández, Michaela RedCherries, Abigail Carney, Belinda Tang, Jeff Boyd, David McDevitt, Ife Nihinlola, Lizz Huerta, Mai Schwartz, Irene Solà, Jessica Pimentel, Ramon Rodriguez, Alynda Segarra, Suyin So, Elisabet Velasquez, Katie Lee, and Ryan Biegel. Research for this book took me to Rome and Cuba, where Sara Levi, Enzzo Hernández, Patricia García, José Ángel Nazabal, and Oscar Mesa made me feel at home. At Brown today: Christina Paxson for her vision, Sam Mencoff, Pamela Reeves, Carlos Lejnieks, Jill Furman, and all my colleagues there. Jeff Goldberg, Adrienne LaFrance, Honor Jones, and my colleagues at *The Atlantic*, thank you for the space to be curious and for making me a better writer and thinker. A giant shout-out to Jenny Dembrow and Ebonie Simpson and everyone at the Lower East Side Girls Club, most especially the girls. To those I've forgotten here, I thank you for your forgiveness.

There are so many spirits and ghosts running through this book. I'm grateful to them all for lending me their energy and grateful to God and all the orishas for blessing this process. And as always, for my grandparents, without whom I would not be here.

And to you, dear reader, for your time.

ABOUT THE AUTHOR

XOCHITL GONZALEZ is the *New York Times* bestselling author of *Olga Dies Dreaming*. Named a Best Book of 2022 by the *New York Times*, *Time*, *Kirkus Reviews*, the *Washington Post*, and NPR, *Olga Dies Dreaming* was the winner of the Brooklyn Public Library Book Prize in Fiction and the New York City Book Award. Gonzalez is a 2021 MFA graduate of the Iowa Writers' Workshop. Her nonfiction work has been published in *Elle Decor*, *Allure*, *Vogue*, *Real Simple*, and the *Cut*. As a staff writer for *The Atlantic* her work was a 2023 finalist for the Pulitzer Prize. A native Brooklynite and proud public school graduate, Gonzalez holds a BA from Brown University and lives in her hometown with her dog, Hectah Lavoe.